The Boy COLONEL

OTHER BOOKS *from* VISION FORUM

The Bible Lessons of John Quincy Adams for His Son

Summer of Suspense

Brothers At Arms: Treasure & Treachery in the Amazon

The Boy's Guide to the Historical Adventures of G.A. Henty

Coming In on a Wing and a Prayer

Destination: Moon

The Elsie Dinsmore Series

The Letters and Lessons of Teddy Roosevelt for His Sons

The Little Boy Down the Road

Little Faith

The New-England Primer

The Original Blue Back Speller

Peril on Providence Island

Pilipinto's Happiness

The Princess Adelina

The R.M. Ballantyne Christian Adventure Library

Sergeant York and the Great War

So Much More

Ten P's in a Pod

Thoughts for Young Men

Verses of Virtue

The Boy COLONEL

A SOLDIER WITHOUT A NAME

JOHN J. HORN

The Vision Forum, Inc.
4719 Blanco Rd., San Antonio, TX 78212
www.visionforum.com

ISBN   978-1-934554-76-0

Cover Design and Photography by Daniel Prislovsky
Typography by Justin Turley

Printed in the United States of America

To my father, who first read me tales of
high adventure.

Table of Contents

Preface

Dear Reader,

Historical fiction is, by definition, a mixing of history and fiction. It is the author's responsibility to faithfully combine the two, without misrepresenting the true facts of history. This has been my aim. The war described in the following chapters did not take place, so far as we know, but had it taken place, it would probably have been very similar in nature. The bravery portrayed has been equaled and surpassed many times in the true annals of war. Strange deeds are recounted, but stranger have occurred. With God, all things are possible. That you may enjoy the following story and profit from it is one of the greatest hopes of

The Author
John Horn
San Antonio, Texas

Chapter 1

"Fire at will!"

Spurts of flame flashed through the falling snow. Smoke clouded the pure white atmosphere, quickly changing the color to a hazy gray. A gust of wind momentarily cleared the fog and revealed a brilliant line of red uniforms outlined clearly against the Siberian landscape.

A narrow river of solid ice threaded its way through the center of the scene, its surface swept bare of snow by the swirling winds. Each bank was lined by a deep drift—the only barrier that the bare landscape presented against a maelstrom of bullets. Two lines of men faced each other, guns blazing. The farthest was a motley crowd, clothed in dirty blues and browns, with high fur caps on their heads. Within twenty yards lay their mortal enemies, arrayed in blue-gray pants and scarlet pelisses, many of which were dyed darker by splotches of blood.

The redcoats lay in a trench, which had been scraped into the snow behind the uneven drifts just hours before by the same hands that now frantically loaded and discharged their rifles. Wreathes of water vapor mingled with the billowing smoke as the hot rifle barrels melted embrasures in the drift.

A uniformed figure scurried a foot behind the soldiers' extended legs, hunched over to keep the mounded snow between his head and the enemy's line of sight. He was heading toward a knot of officers who crouched near the British line's center.

For a moment, the tip of his shako topped the drift. A spatter of Cossack bullets instantly sliced the air all around and he dived for cover, landing among the prone officers in a small avalanche of snow and ice shards.

"Edmund, you fool, are you trying to kill yourself?" demanded one of the prone figures.

"My apologies, Colonel." Edmund scraped a layer of snow from his face and grinned. He was young, probably about seventeen years old, but strong and well-built. His eyes sparkled. "It wouldn't make sense to end my own poor existence with so many Cossacks willing to relieve me of the duty."

The colonel smiled slightly. "You're a droll lad, Ed. I trust there's a reason for your rather reckless exposure?"

"Yes, sir." As Edmund finished dusting his upper body, a pair of epaulettes emerged, the single lace crown signifying his rank as lieutenant colonel. "A courier just brought orders to advance and drive the Russians from the other bank, sir."

"Advance? Very well. Are our flanks supported?"

"I don't think so, sir."

The colonel frowned.

"That makes no sense. Why didn't you bring the courier to me?"

"I tried to, sir, but a bullet got in the way."

The colonel's creases contracted further. They stood out on the otherwise smooth forehead—brought by many woes, not many years.

"Very well. If General Whitmore gave that order, he must have a plan."

The lieutenant colonel scratched his head. "Actually, it was an order from General Tremont, sir."

"Why is General Tremont giving orders?" the colonel asked sharply.

"The courier said that General Whitmore was just captured, which of course places General Tremont in command."

Captured? The colonel lay motionless. Whitmore was a friend. *If Tremont is in command*—he shook his head. A bullet screamed through the snowdrift a few inches above him and tore a button from the other boy's jacket.

"I'm afraid, Edmund, that the Cossacks heard you and are attempting to relieve you of your 'poor existence,' as you termed it."

"Very well then, you may write upon my tombstone that I died forgotten by kith and kin on a lonely steppe in Siberia, remembered only by my one dear friend in life."

The colonel grunted. "Order a charge. I don't agree with Tremont, but I can't disobey."

"But sir, they'll mow us down like ducks in a pen!"

"Not with the dummies. These Cossacks are new to the front. They can't be familiar with the 42nd's unpredictable methods."

The lieutenant colonel smiled. "Indeed, sir, dummies it is."

The bugle sounded a peculiar call, much like the charge, but with several key notes altered. Firing along the British line ceased. Each man rolled on his side, swathed his knapsack in red cloth, and fastened his shako to the top of the pack. Then they grasped their rifles and watched expectantly for the signal. The enemy fire had slackened. They too were waiting.

"Fire!" The colonel cried.

Each rifle belched forth its deadly contents in a volley of flame and smoke.

"Dummies!" the colonel cried, and each man tossed his knapsack into the air.

A withering Cossack volley tore through the dummies, spraying bits of red and brown fabric over the snow. "Forward!"

The true soldiers of Britain leaped up with a mighty roar and rushed against their unloaded enemies.

"It works every time." The lieutenant colonel drew his sword and placed himself beside his colonel. "Only a boy's ingenuity could have thought of that tactic!"

The colonel paused for a moment, one boot buried deep in the snow, the other resting upon the frozen river's treacherous surface.

"There is a reason they call me the 'Boy Colonel.'" He scanned the advancing line. The advance was slowing, the soldiers slipping and sliding on the ice. The Cossacks must not have time to reload. "A sure foot and a swift stride!" he shouted. "For God and country!"

A thousand throats echoed the battle-cry. The red line surged up and over the snow-bank and whirled into the Cossack ranks, steel to steel.

The colonel sent his second-in-command to the left flank and straddled the contested bank, his saber in his right hand and a pistol in his left. He scanned the chaos, ready to rally the men should the Cossack line prove too tough at any one point.

"Hooroo!" shouted a huge, red-haired soldier a few paces to the colonel's right.

"*Vive la republique!*" returned a short soldier by his side. They looked like giant and dwarf in comparison.

"Jack, yer fool," growled the giant, in a thick Irish brogue, "we're in a monarky, not a repooblic."

"*Peste!* Do you zhink zhat I, Jacques Lefebvre, do not know zhat? I did not hear zhat battle-cry shouted under zhe great Napoleon Bonaparte at Vaterloo to forget it upon joining zhe British army!"

A pair of Cossacks dashed toward them, their swords swirling over their heads. The colonel raised his pistol—too late. The pairs clashed, parried, and disengaged, the Cossacks thrown back a few paces by the recoil.

The Irishman eyed them calmly. "Ye've got tae understand, Jack, fightin's not aboot lookin' fer a nice place tae prick yer inimy, like ye Frinch are always tryin'. It's the downright cut as wins the day."

The Cossacks charged. The Irishman grasped his sword-hilt in both hands and brought it down with all his strength, crushing through his enemy's sword and skull.

"Like that one."

"Zhat is very vell for you to say, O'Malley," the Frenchman growled, dancing lightly around his opponent, "but I do not valk vihz my head in zhe clouds. I must go *up*!" He parried, feinted, and thrust up into the Cossack's stomach.

A throaty scream sounded close by the colonel's feet. He spun. A Cossack soldier thrust his blade upwards, aiming for the boy's exposed chest. The colonel struck at the sword and the momentum forced him forward and off the drift. A moment later he lay upon his dead opponent, half his sword buried in the Russian's torso. Gritting his teeth, he wrenched the sword from the wound, a spurt of blood following the cold steel.

A shadow fell on the dead man's face—it was more than the pallor of death. Something was blocking the sunlight. The colonel rolled onto his back, just in time to parry a Russian's downward thrust. Desperately, he threw up his left arm and fired his pistol at point-blank range into the Cossack's bending body. Hot blood gushed from a gaping wound, soaking his own arm and dyeing the snow crimson.

The dead man's bulk trapped him to the earth. He tried to wriggle out, but before he could do so a pair of unseen hands gripped the body and pitched it away. The Irishman looked down at his commander's gory body, his face twisted in consternation.

"Don't worry, O'Malley, it's not my blood." The colonel sprang to his feet. "Forward, the battle isn't over yet!"

Although only a few minutes had passed, the fighting had already receded from the bank and nearly half the enemy force directly engaged was dead on the snow, or fleeing in broken groups. The colonel gathered all of the soldiers still near the riverbank and led them toward the enemy's right.

"We must turn their flank," the boy said, half to himself, half to Jacques, who was running by his side. He tried to wipe the Cossack's blood off his arm. Death had been close today, but no closer than many times before. "If we can but bunch them into their own center, it will give Campbell's 30th a chance to cross the river, and then the day must be ours, excepting a miracle from God."

"It vould certainly be an unasked for miracle, if such vere to happen." Jacques grimaced.

"Indeed, and I do not ask for it. But look, Edmund is already upon them! The Russians flee!"

"*Ma foi*," Jacques exclaimed, "and zhere goes zhat impudent Irishman. He shall not take *all* zhe glory if *I* have somezhing to say about it!" The volatile Frenchman rushed off in pursuit of his comrade, outrunning even his colonel in his frantic haste.

The second English wave struck the Russians' left flank with overwhelming force, scattering the demoralized Cossacks like leaves on a windy day. The colonel ordered the recall to be sounded. The regular army could finish the bloody mopping-up. His job was done, and Britain's banners waved once more upon the field of victory as the early Siberian twilight obscured the last remnants of the fleeing troops.

Chapter 2

The next day, a caravan of wooden wagons rattled into the British camp. Smoke rose from hundreds of cooking fires and hovered over the broad expanse of white canvas tents. Tea-fragrance mingled with the smell of fresh snow, along with the less savory odors coming from the camp latrines.

One of the drivers pulled his team up next to the main supply depot and let a young man off. The passenger was wrapped in an overcoat and stamped the snow vigorously.

"Thanks for the ride!" he called.

The driver nodded and flicked his long nose. "Been a pleasure talking to ye. Dilworth's my name. P'raps we'll see each other around. Ye'd best be off before ye get volunteered to help unload these supplies."

The young man wandered off through the orderly confusion always present in a camp of war, threading his way through groups of chattering soldiers who huddled around their fires over plates of steaming food.

"Excuse me, friend," he said, accosting the first soldier who crossed his path, "can you direct me to the camp of His Royal Majesty's 42nd Regiment of Mounted Infantry?"

"The 42nd?" The soldier nodded to his left. "That way. Can't miss it."

Following the soldier's directions, the newcomer soon reached a section of the camp quite unique from its surroundings. In place of the usual triangular tents was row on row of snowy domes, each dome rising toward the center to about six feet. The young man paused.

"Igloos? That's odd."

A banner fluttered next to the largest igloo, the sun shining clearly on its waving folds. The fabric was embroidered with a red-coated soldier resting his weapon upon the saddle of a magnificent warhorse, with a large sun of red thread blazing in the background. The numbers "42" were boldly entwined with the luminary, while a golden crown floated breezily in the right-hand corner.

"I'm at the right place, at any rate." The young man rubbed his hands together.

"What are you doing here, young man?"

The newcomer spun on his heel to face his bearded questioner. "I'm looking for Mr. Pierce, correspondent for the *London Times*. Do you know him?"

The man grunted. "Thought you might be him. Do I know Pierce? Yes, rather well. I'm Pierce. Are you my replacement?"

"Yes, sir. My name is Alexander Somerset."

Pierce looked at him with cold eyes. "They're growing them younger these days. I thought they'd send someone established."

Somerset stiffened. "I believe that the *Times* has been satisfied with my work."

"So you would. Follow me." Pierce turned abruptly and led the other through the igloos.

As they walked, Somerset pulled a notebook from inside his overcoat and began jotting notes.

The older reporter frowned. "You'll have time enough for that later. I've been ready for your coming for weeks, and as a caravan's leaving this morning for the sea, I want to be on it. I've written down all the important information in a packet for you. Ask me what you think you need now."

Somerset stuffed the notebook back inside his coat. "Thank you, sir. I think the most obvious point to me at the moment is the cold." He chafed his hands. "How is it that war can be continued in these temperatures?"

"There's not much choice about the matter. If the Cossacks can fight, then so can our men. We do use some different techniques, though. If you take the time to look you'll see that no one uses metal scabbards—just a few leather straps to keep the naked blade from cutting. The steel will freeze to a metal scabbard."

Pierce paused next to a small igloo. "Step inside, won't you?"

Somerset scratched his head. "To tell you the truth, sir, I—well, I've never been in an igloo before." He looked sheepishly at the small entrance tunnel.

"Don't worry, they rarely collapse."

"Rarely, sir?" Somerset gulped.

"Yes. Will you go first, or do you want to follow?"

"By your leave, I think I'll follow."

The older reporter led the way. They crawled through the entrance tunnel, but it quickly opened into a large space, high enough to stand upright in. Although it seemed that the only heat came from a small candle on a desk in the center, the air was surprisingly warm.

"Not so bad, is it?" Pierce asked, taking his seat on a ledge that apparently served as a bed, and motioning Somerset toward a chair.

"It's actually rather cozy."

"Yes. It would be much cozier if those ventilation holes weren't there." The older reporter pointed to several small holes near the roof's summit, through which sunlight shone. "A bit too cozy. So, what's your experience in reporting?"

The young man sat down, the old chair creaking in protest. "Well, you might say I'm still at the beginning of my career, sir, although I have covered a few stories. My father was a reporter before me, and he also served as an editor at the *Times*, where I obtained my first real exposure to the world of news. I had just gotten back from a long story in Cornwall, at the tin mines."

"The tin mines? What were you doing there?" Pierce stroked his long gray beard with one hand, the other resting upon his knee.

"They wanted a story about the new improvements for the miners, and how they were living longer, and healthier. It took a few months, but I got some lively text. As soon as I got back to London, I was assigned to Siberia, to cover the war. Not quite what I was expecting, but the *Times* said that their correspondent, who would be you, I suppose, wanted a replacement."

"Yes. I've covered this war since the start—before you knew a pen-nib from a dictionary. Siberia is really a beautiful place, especially in summer, but the winter cold has finally gotten to my bones. Rheumatics."

"I'm sorry to hear that."

"Not nearly so sorry as I. You brought your kit?"

"Yes, sir. It's on one of the wagons from the supply convoy." Somerset cleared his throat. "Now, sir, do you think you could tell me a little about why we're here in Siberia, and the makeup of the army?"

Pierce laughed. "Why we're here? Not one man in a hundred could tell you that. It's a very convoluted situation, but essentially we're here in Siberia attempting to prevent the Russians from invading the Ottoman Empire, although why we're helping the Turks, I've no idea. More than that you've no need to know. It's your job to write what happens, the Londoners can write why it's happening."

"Very well, sir." Somerset made a note, and continued. "What condition is the army in?"

"Well equipped. Morale is decent, but it always gets better in summer. Theoretically, the army is composed of ten regiments. Practically, we rarely have more than five at one time."

"I'm sorry sir, but I have to ask. What is the purpose of these igloos?"

"Hah." The old reporter looked around fondly on the smoky snow blocks. The candle flared, revealing a stack of notebooks in the corner, tied together with string. "The 42nd have some interesting ideas. Igloos are one of the many unusual notions entertained by the colonel. They're much warmer than tents, because of the snow's insulation from the outside cold. At first I didn't take kindly to the change, but now that I'm used to it, it's not so bad." He took a pipe from his jacket pocket and packed it with tobacco.

Somerset's forehead wrinkled. "But, you're the correspondent for the entire army, not only the 42nd, correct?"

"That is true, but if there's anything newsworthy happening here, the 42nd are bound to be in the middle. I finally moved to their camp for more convenience, whenever I decide to accompany them on a raid."

"I've heard many rumors about this regiment over the years, but I've started too many myself to trust those written by others. What exactly *is* the 42nd?"

"What is it?" Pierce lighted his pipe at the candle. "The 42nd Regiment is one of the finest ever created. As mounted infantry they can fight however they want, wherever they want. It's a glorious sight to see them go into battle, banners waving and their horses' manes a-flying in the breeze. They're sent on the hardest missions, put into the toughest fights. The 42nd's real expertise is in assassination and raiding, and no regiment on earth is better in these two areas."

"You seem an enthusiastic convert."

"I am," Pierce said sharply. "You will be as well, the first time you see them in battle. But I can't describe it properly. You must see for yourself."

Somerset leaned back comfortably in his chair and crossed his arms. "Perhaps you could describe the colonel, instead?"

Pierce glanced up hastily. "Surely you know about the colonel?"

"I've heard rumors there also, but as I said, I never trust anything unless it is a verified fact. What I have heard are some of the most farfetched and unlikely lies ever created, and I believe I was selected specifically for this mission because I am not likely to believe the first dish of news I'm served."

"Then you will never trust the colonel, because there is very little about *him* that is verified in any way. He is one of the most farfetched men alive—if you can call him a man."

Somerset leaned forward. "What do you mean?"

"Colonel Nobody is not a man. He's a boy."

The young man sat silently staring at Pierce. His cynical green eyes narrowed. "Why are you trying to make fun of me?" he asked coldly. "Nobody is named 'nobody,' and boys are not allowed to be colonels in the British Army."

"Right and wrong. Nobody *is* named Nobody, because that's his name. True, boys are not normally allowed to hold commissions, but as I said, the 42nd is a different regiment altogether. There are special rules pertaining to the 42nd, and special allowances. There are no age limitations for its colonel or lieutenant colonel."

"But—but—that's preposterous!" Somerset spluttered. "What is so special about him that he should be the colonel?"

Pierce did not respond at first, but puffed quietly at his pipe. At last, he removed the stem from between his teeth. "I think the best way to answer your questions, and prepare you for your time here, is to tell you everything I know about Colonel Nobody and the 42nd." He raised his hand as Somerset was about to interrupt. "Sit down and be quiet. I talk to my own pace."

Somerset shrugged.

Pierce began. "There is very little known about Colonel Nobody, including his name. Whether he has another name, I don't know, and I'm not sure if anyone else does. His background is shrouded in mystery. At some time near the beginning of this war, he appeared with the 42nd. Mind you, I'm not saying that's when he came, I'm saying that's as soon as I know that he was here. The current colonel was named Hayes, and he was quite close to the boy, who was very young at that time. Some say that he was related to the child, and perhaps he was, but he said the boy was not his son.

"As to his name, no one ever knew it, so they just called him Nobody, and that became his name. He was trained intensively in everything pertaining to the army, and finally, when Colonel Hayes left the army, he had the boy placed in his position. The other regiments put up a fuss, but General Whitmore was in favor, so it stuck. He's done extremely well, and the other officers have finally accustomed to him. They view him as a sort of prodigy, but they respect his abilities, and his men adore him. And that's all I know of his story."

"What? But, isn't there anything else?"

"I'm sure there's plenty more, but I don't know it. There's a good reason that he keeps his identity in the dark, but what it is, I know no more than you."

"Mighty strange, isn't it?"

"Yes."

Somerset waited until Pierce had gathered his baggage, then accompanied him to the depot, both to see him off and to collect his own gear.

The older reporter seemed to soften somewhat as they stood together, waiting for the mules to be harnessed.

"Sorry to be sharp with you, young man. I'm a bit grouchy at having to leave this place." He stroked his beard. "There were many times, when I was out with the 42nd on patrols, that I didn't expect to return to camp alive. Now, at last, I leave it—probably never to return."

"I wish you a pleasant voyage, sir," Somerset said.

Pierce brushed his arm over his eyes. "Here now you listen, young man." He gripped Somerset's shoulder. "Writing a war is very different from writing a Cornwall tin mine. Here your true manhood is revealed, whether soldier or journalist. War brings out the best and the worst of human nature, and there's plenty of both in the British Army."

Somerset was stunned by the man's sudden vehemence. His shoulders ached beneath Pierce's vice-like grip.

"You've a duty, young man. There are two kinds of journalists. One's a field reporter. He goes out with the army, lives their hardships, their sufferings, *and* their victories, and then comes home and writes about it. That's me. The other kind is a poor weak cowardly creature, who lolls in camp while battles are fought, then talks to the stragglers and cowards who are always willing to praise themselves and tear down the men who really did the fighting."

Somerset writhed a little under the older reporter's fierce stare.

Pierce released his shoulders. "It's up to you to choose which kind you'll be. I've seen too many promising young men destroyed by the vices of camp. Don't be one of them." Without another word he climbed into the wagon and set off towards the Sea of Okhotsk.

Somerset trudged moodily back to the center of the 42nd's camp, where the largest igloo and the flag stood. He wondered what about this forsaken land could have so strong a grip on a hardened old reporter like Pierce.

"I suppose I should introduce myself to this mysterious colonel," he muttered.

A sentry snapped to attention at the door. "What business?"

"I'm a correspondent for the *London Times*, and I'd like to see your colonel."

The soldier frowned. "Impossible. The only *Times* man we have here is twice your age."

"Oh, I'm a new one, fresh from London." The soldier's rifle slowly lowered to a level with his chest.

"You have papers?"

"Well, yes, of course." He fumbled in his pocket and produced a stamped sheet.

The soldier read the paper slowly, mumbling the words to himself. "I hereby certify . . . Alexander Somerset . . . reporter . . . *Times* . . . Year of our Lord . . . 1836."

The sentry handed it back. "Pass." He stepped aside from the entrance tunnel.

The igloo's interior was spacious and well-lit by a small group of candles. Three or four tunnels led from the main apartment to more rooms deeper within. Two cots and a table constituted most of the furniture. Two boys sat at the table beside plates of half-eaten food, studying a detailed map, which lay in voluminous folds upon the rough wood. The farthest boy's uniform was stained and torn, and one of his companion's silver epaulettes was shorn from his shoulder, but both appeared to be unharmed.

"Name?" the colonel asked, glancing up from the map. His eyes were penetrating, of the same dark brown tint as his hair. His forehead was large and creased. High cheekbones and a well-shaped nose gave a handsome strength to his face, while his head's otherwise oval shape was sharpened by a firm chin jutting out beneath a small, decisive mouth.

Somerset introduced himself and explained his new position.

"A pleasure to make your acquaintance," the colonel said politely, though without great warmth. "I am Colonel Nobody, and this is Lieutenant Colonel Edmund Burke."

"Glad to meet you. It was my hope, young sirs, to ask a few questions of you, so that I can begin my first report."

"Such as?"

"Well, to begin, could you tell me somewhat about yourself?" Somerset poised a pen over his notebook and looked at Colonel Nobody.

"No."

Somerset blinked. "Excuse me, sir?"

"I said 'no.' You may write about what I do, in the context of this war, but you may not write about *me*."

"Oh, I don't mean personal information, just a few things such as the place of your birth, your age, simple things like that."

Colonel Nobody frowned. "Young man, you must learn something if you are to be with this army for long. When the colonel of the 42ⁿᵈ speaks, he has spoken. If I say 'no,' then I say 'no.' Is that understood?"

"Er, yes, yes, sir, definitely." Somerset backed hastily toward the entrance.

"Good. I am willing to answer generalized questions about the regiment, but I warn you, that if you attempt to learn about me personally, there will be consequences." The colonel returned to his map.

"Is that a threat, sir?"

"Hmm?" Nobody glanced up. "No, I never threaten. I warn. If my warning is unheeded, I act."

Somerset backed out of the igloo. He wiped his brow. "Rather touchy fellow. I'd bet five pounds that I can dig up some pretty interesting facts for the *Times* about him."

"What's that ye say, laddy?" boomed a voice in his ear.

Somerset spun round to see the neck of a gray greatcoat, through which peeked the crimson of the British uniform. Tilting his head, he found a jovial face looking down on him, with shocking red hair and a short beard of the same color.

"Oh. Good morning, sir." Somerset said.

"Ye must be new aboot here, laddy. I'm noo sir, jist a loowly private, that's all. Who might ye be?"

"Oh, just a news correspondent. Do you by any chance belong to the 42nd?"

"Indayd I do."

"Might I ask you a few questions about the 42nd?"

The Irishman tapped his chin thoughtfully. "I'm headed fer me mess, but if ye'd like I'll take ye along and ye can ask us as miny questions as ye want, whiles we eat."

Six men sat around a fire, quietly sipping steaming cups of tea, and watching a small Frenchman poking at a large pan of cooking porridge.

"O'Malley," the Frenchman called, "at last you are back. Vill you sit down and tell zhis Yankee zhat it is not *our* fault zhat poor Franklin vas killed yesterday?"

"Why sure an' ye're not blamin' *us* fer that, Dilworth?" The Irishman sat down on a vacant log and motioned Somerset to join him. "I don't want tae spake hard on any as are dead, but it's true that Franklin was no' as bright as could be hoped. The poor fellow popped his head up whin the dummies were thrown, and ye can guess at what 'appened then."

The man called Dilworth looked up, and Somerset recognized him as the talkative wagon driver. The soldier nodded casually at the reporter and removed the last of the fur wrappings covering his red pelisse.

"It's not that I blame you," Dilworth replied to O'Malley, "but that it somehow seems that I could've kept his head down, had I been here."

"P'raps so, p'raps not. At any rate, ye had ye're assignment up at the sea, so there's no use blamin' yerself or us."

Jacques ladled cupfuls of steaming porridge into the men's bowls. "Vhat are you here for, young man, eh? Perhaps you have heard of zhe amazing cooking of Jacques Lefebvre, and have come to test it?"

"Well, no, not exactly," Somerset said hastily, "I'm just a reporter, and I want to learn more about the 42nd."

"Oho, a reporter, I see." Jacques grinned. "Vell zhen, you have come to zhe right place. You zhe in the forms here before you zhe very heart of zhe glorious 42nd, vhich is zhe heart of zhe entire British army in Siberia!"

O'Malley chuckled. "As ye can see, Jack Frog here ain't one o' the more modest maymbers o' the army. Now, I should prob'ly introduce ye tae the others in our mess."

"No." Jacques smoothed his coat. "*I* vill. Introductions should be conducted according to zhe principles of civility and courtesy, by vun such as I, who am vell learned in such matters."

"Well learn'd in such maytters," O'Malley repeated indignantly. "That's nice fer ye tae say, when ye can't even speak the king's good English!"

Jacques choked on a mouthful of porridge. "Zhe king's good English? Vhat vould an Irishman know about it? You speak half barbarian and half savage, and entirely like a *boeuf*!"

"A boof? How dare ye call me a boof? What's a boof?"

"Come now you two," the Yankee said calmly, "stow the gab and let Jacques get to his introductions, or else I'll have to do 'em myself."

The Frenchman bowed. "I do not know what zhe vorld has come to vhen ve must look to *Americans* to show civility." He turned to Somerset. "My name is Jacques Lefebvre, a member of zhe glorious nation of France, and currently serving as a private in His English Majesty's 42nd Regiment."

"Alexander Somerset, reporter. A pleasure to make your acquaintance."

"Zhis," Jacques continued, pointing to the Irishman, "is Patrick O'Malley, Irish by birth, heart, and tongue."

"We've met."

"Here," Jacques said, pointing to the American, "is Richard Dilvorth, born at some time in zhe past on zhe barbaric continent of Nort America, in zhe country of nearly zhe same name."

"Massachusetts, to be more exact," the Yankee added.

"Zhe venerable ancient next to me," Jacques continued, "is William Stoning, zhe corporal *extraordinaire* of our humble rifle squad."

"Away with your venerable ancients," Stoning growled, but his blue eyes twinkled with good nature. "Glad to meet you, young fellow."

"Sitting beside our vhite-headed officer are zhe two apostles, of zhe same name and feature. Tvins." The tallest of the two stood up and jestingly pushed Jacques aside.

"Matthew Preston's the name, and my twin brother Mark there's, the same." He grasped the reporter's hand firmly, a pleasant smile on his square face.

"Thay're rhymers," O'Malley whispered, "think they're poets, or somethin'."

Jacques reclaimed the floor. "Last but not least, ve have good old Petr, a Russian vhiz a last name so barbaric zhat I vill not even *attempt* to pronounce it." Jacques finished with an exaggerated bow and flourish, while the bearded Russian nodded calmly at Somerset.

"Very nice to meet you men." The young reporter shifting uncomfortably on the tough log. "I assume you all belong to the same company?"

"You're looking at Squad One, Company One, in His Majesty's 42nd," the Yankee said. "There's generally eight to a squad, but as you probably heard, we lost a man in the battle yesterday."

"Please accept my condolences. Will you be getting a replacement?"

"Who knows? It's likely, but nothin's sure."

"I'm in favor of odd numbers, myself," Somerset said. "Seven is a powerful number. By the way, if I might ask, is there a reason that you are placed so close to the colonel's tent—or, I suppose I should say, igloo?" He pointed to the colonel's igloo, just a few paces away.

"Aye, there is," O'Malley said. "Ye see, we're sort o' a special group in the 42nd. Each one o' us has been handpicked tae fill a position in this here squad. We do the hardest and toughest work as crosses our path, and no extra charge, if I say so meself."

"So you're a special force *within* a special force?"

"Ye could say that, I suppose."

"Wonderful." Somerset scratched a note. "A unique body of men for a unique colonel—no offense meant, of course."

"Zhere now, careful vhat you say about our Colonel Nobody." Jacques twirled his spoon. "He is unique, yes, but he is also zhe best officer in zhe entire army, and a splendid strategizer."

"So you say. If you don't mind my asking, is he always so sharp when he's asked about his background?"

The soldiers instantly grew sober. As if by a uniting will they slowly turned their eyes to the old man, Stoning, who scrutinized the young reporter.

"Young man, I'll give you a friendly warning right now. Do not seek to learn about our colonel's history. Believe me, it is as honorable as any might wish, more so than some might hope. There are simply things which he does not want known about himself, and so he tells Nobody, literally and figuratively."

Somerset closed his notebook reluctantly. "I apologize for any offense I may have given. Simply put, I'm a news reporter, raised on finding out facts and delving into secrets."

"Find out all the plain facts you want, but don't be delving after secrets. Why, not even the lieutenant colonel knows much about the colonel before they met, and those two are closer than brothers. No, no, it's best not to ask too many questions in the 42nd."

As the veteran finished speaking, a chestnut mare dashed by, sliding to a halt in a flurry of snow before the colonel's igloo.

"Message for the colonel!" the rider shouted, leaping off his mount and entering the long black tunnel leading to the abode of the Boy Colonel.

Chapter 3

After dismissing Somerset and his personal questions, the two young officers settled back down to their study of the map.

"They most likely took General Whitmore towards their camp in the mountains, here." Colonel Nobody tapped a dark line on the map. "Perhaps to that fortress we've been hearing rumors about."

Edmund shook his head. "Perhaps. You never know with these Russians. They never follow accepted principles of strategy."

"On the other hand, neither do we." Nobody lifted a steaming cup to his lips. He choked upon the first mouthful. "That meddling Frenchman! How is it that he can make any article of food or drink possible except a cup of good English *tea*? This tastes like melted snow and peat moss."

"I think Jacques is trying to inculcate a desire for coffee in you, Noble." Edmund stroked the corner of his mouth.

"Yes, smile all you like. If he keeps making this mud under the name of tea, I'll have no choice *but* to succumb." He set the cup down and leaned once more over the map. "Back to more important matters. It's my opinion that the Russians will hold General Whitmore as a hostage for one of our high-rank prisoners. Do you agree?"

"Most likely. Unless we rescue him first, of course."

"Of course. Unfortunately, they'll be expecting an appearance by the 42nd. Still, I don't plan to disappoint them. I already have a few scouts out looking for ambuscades."

The muffled sound of galloping hooves came through the tunnel, and someone called out briskly—"message for the colonel!" A moment later an orderly's head popped from the tunnel, followed instantly by the rest of his body.

"Message from General Tremont, sir." The messenger saluted. "He'd like to see you in his quarters immediately."

"General Tremont? Very well, tell him I'll be there in a moment."

The sentry saluted and retreated through the tunnel.

Nobody stared after him, stroking his chin. "A very interesting development."

"What's that?" Edmund asked.

"Tremont is sparing no time in taking over command. It was only yesterday that General Whitmore was captured, and here Tremont is already referring to headquarters as *his* headquarters."

"I never liked Tremont."

"I can't say that I like him much myself." Nobody took his hat from the table. "Did you know that he wanted Colonel Hayes's position when he left?"

"He wanted to be colonel of the 42nd?"

"Indeed. Whitmore trusted me, and he knew the men trusted me, so I received the commission instead. I don't blame Tremont for not liking me. He's climbed the ranks more from deaths and discharges above him than by his own merit. Still, he's my superior officer, so I owe respect and obedience. Clear these dishes, Ed, I'll be back shortly."

"What about the new reporter?"

"Mmm? Oh, watch him. I don't want him prying into my history. Newspaper men have a knack at getting themselves into tight places. I'll leave it to you to ensure that those tight places aren't connected with me."

A sentry ushered Nobody through a narrow hallway into a comfortable room. A large fire crackled on the hearth, and the air smelt of wood smoke, leather, and cigars.

Didn't take long to comfy things. A plush sofa, several mahogany tables, and a massive four-poster bed were all new. General Whitmore never used any more furniture than barely sufficed his needs. The writing desk from which he was used to issue commands lay neglected in a dusty corner, outshone by an elegant heirloom.

A tall, thin door in the right wall near the foot of the bed opened, and a portly man in full dress uniform clattered into the room. Nobody smiled inwardly at the contrast between the door's straight outline and the general's rounded, paunchy form.

"Ah, Nobody," he said, in a high-pitched, nasally voice, "here at last. How do you like my new quarters?" He let himself sink into a plush chair behind the polished desk. "Of course, they are temporary, until General Whitmore is released. I had my man bring in an extra chair, not often what I do when *nobody* comes visiting." He laughed heartily at his own joke.

Nobody let him finish his laugh. "I hardly think you called me here to make puns about my name, or the lack thereof, sir."

The new commander-in-chief sobered. "No, I did not. Sit, please."

Nobody sat stiffly on the unpadded chair. The seat was low, so that Tremont, sitting on the other side of the desk, appeared taller in comparison. Nobody folded his hands in his lap and waited. General Tremont toyed with a pen, picking at its white feathered tip. His slanted eyes and large nose reminded Nobody of a hawk.

"I have been informed that the soldiers under your command are being housed in huts made of snow, commonly referred to as 'igloos.' Am I correct?"

"Yes, sir."

"What military precedent do you have in commanding such buildings used?"

"I don't know about military precedent, sir," Nobody said slowly, "but they are warmer than anything available except for wood huts, and we need all the wood we can find for fuel."

"I don't like them." Tremont glowered at Nobody. "I won't have them. You will have them removed and replaced by the regularly issued tent. Is that understood?"

"No, sir, I'm not quite sure that I do understand." Nobody shifted uneasily in the low chair.

"That's strange. I thought I made myself quite clear." Tremont tapped the table with his thumbs. "You would not be questioning my authority, now, would you?"

"No, sir, but I thought you may have forgotten that regular military regulations do not apply to the 42nd. Also, General Whitmore never had a problem with them, sir."

Tremont frowned. "Colonel Nobody, I have observed too much freedom in your regiment lately, and I intend to put an end to it. I am your superior, and I have issued an order. If it is not obeyed, you will be court-martialed. Am I understood *now*?"

Nobody bit his lip. "Yes, sir."

"Good. Now, to the next subject. According to my understanding, the 42nd is purported to be best when engaged in raids and assassinations."

"I hope more than purported, sir."

"Not my type of warfare, rather cowardly, indeed, to my mind, but nevertheless occasionally useful."

Useful. Yes, indeed.

Tremont waited for a response, but continued when none was forthcoming. "I have a raid for you. There's a regiment in Dvorarsk protecting an important bridge. I want you to take the 42nd and provide succor to them, as it is reported that the Russians have surrounded the town and bridge."

"Dvorarsk, sir? Very well, sir. Pardon me, sir, but you *do* know that Dvorarsk is at least fifty miles from here?"

Tremont dropped the pen and folded his arms. "What is your point?" he asked coldly.

"Well, sir, I can't help wondering what is so important about a bridge at that distance from camp."

The general's eyebrows narrowed. "Are you questioning my military judgment?"

"No, sir, not at all," Nobody said hastily.

"Good."

Nobody rubbed his fingers together. Something about this was very strange. "I suppose that you would have no problem telling me which regiment is at this bridge?"

"I have given you all the information necessary." The general rose. "That bridge must be held at all costs. You will start at daybreak tomorrow. Two days riding will be sufficient to reach Dvorarsk. Good day."

Nobody shut his mouth upon the rising flood of questions, regained his feet, and saluted stiffly. "Good day, sir."

He found Edmund dusting their military books, which stood proudly on a battered old shelf in one of the igloo's convenient nooks.

"Back already? What did he want?" Edmund asked.

"I'll give you a guess."

"Well then, I'd say he was congratulating you on your performance in the battle yesterday."

"Not exactly. We have a mission." Nobody grabbed a saddlebag and began stuffing it from two wooden chests.

"Splendid. Where to and with whom?"

"Dvorarsk. The whole regiment."

"I see. Who's in Dvorarsk?"

"Not who, what."

"Very well, what?"

"A bridge, apparently." Nobody strapped a brace of pistols to the bag.

"But, what's so important about a bridge in Dvorarsk?" Edmund scratched his head.

"The fact that there's a regiment guarding it, and that they're surrounded by Cossacks."

"A regiment? But I haven't heard of any regiments deployed at the moment. And why do they want a bridge that far away guarded, anyway?"

Nobody took a small knife from where it hung on the tent pole and sheathed it in his boot. "Your guess is as good as mine, and you now know as much about the situation as I do. Issue the necessary orders. We leave tomorrow morning at dawn."

Edmund shook his head. "Yes, sir, but I don't like it. I'm telling you, General Tremont is up to something, mark my words."

"Edmund, you're a born conspirator." Nobody slapped him on the shoulder. "If you'd been born in the times of the Romans there's a strong likelihood that you would have gotten your head chopped off by Nero, or one of those other chaps."

"Quite humorous." Edmund grabbed his own saddlebag. "Perhaps I'm not so keen on leaving our nice warm igloo and having to rescue some mysterious regiment on a rotting bridge in the middle of literally nowhere."

"Well then, I can relieve your feelings about the warm igloo. Looks like we're back to using tents."

"What?"

"Indeed. General Tremont is enjoying his newfound power."

Chapter 4

Nobody was awake and moving hours before the late Siberian dawn. He rubbed and saddled his own warhorse, a magnificent snow-colored stallion named White Fury. The whole regiment was mounted and in full regalia—coats spotless, buttons polished, shakos dusted. Every rifle had been scoured for leftover particles of grease and dirt. One or two of the more careless men had had to scrape dried blood from their swords, a remembrance of the battle two days earlier.

The moon gave an eerie soft glow which filtered through unseen clouds and lighted the column as it slowly wound out of camp into the morning's blackness. The snow blanket, though crisp and clean under the hooves of the colonel's great warhorse, was a trampled and sodden mess by the time the rear-guard came up.

As soon as they passed the last outpost, Nobody reformed the column into a broader formation more suited to the wide Siberian steppes than the narrow camp roads. Company One rode dead-center, with Two and Three on the flanks and the remaining units behind. Squad One stuck close to the colonel's heels.

"Aye, but it's been a stretch since we've had a night march," he heard O'Malley whisper to Jacques.

"Zhe longer zhe better in my opinion. At least ve vill not have any colonels besides our own to be suggesting, and commanding, and informing, and entirely mixing up our affairs. I vould sacrifice much sleep, gladly, if I knew zhat no one besides zhe 42nd, vihz our colonel at its head, vere taking the field."

"What are ye mumbling aboot?" O'Malley leaned his head to the Frenchman's level.

"I am vorried zhat vhatever officer ve are trying to relieve vill attempt to take command of *both* regiments, vonce we join zhem."

"Oh, come noow, ye're an eternal pessimist, that's what ye are. Isn't that right, laddy?" O'Malley turned to his right, where Somerset, the reporter, bestrode a new mount.

The young man muffled a yawn. "I really don't know what you're talking about," he said sleepily, "but if it has anything to do with the discomfort of early hours, I heartily agree."

"Horses, trot!" Nobody commanded.

Each man tapped his heels against his mount's sides, and the pace gradually quickened to a steady trot that could be maintained for hours at a time.

Edmund leaned close to Nobody. "I haven't found any information about a deployed regiment, either nearby or in Dvorarsk."

"Perhaps Tremont knows something we don't." Nobody cinched his sword-strap tighter.

"Maybe, but there's not much that the army knows about that the 42nd didn't find out first."

Shadows fanned out on each side of the column. These were skirmishers who would ride far in advance of the main body, guarding against ambushes and serving as the colonel's eyes and ears.

The men's knapsacks bulged with ten days' rations. In addition to these, several wagons lumbered behind the column with extra food and gunpowder. Nobody looked sourly at the unwieldy machines, thinking how much time they would cost him. *If only I knew what condition that regiment is in.*

They traveled as fast as possible across the barren Siberian steppe, not seeing a single human outside the ranks. They camped the first night on a rare hill, which was really just a rock outcropping twisted grotesquely like the architecture of some medieval cathedral.

It was late on Friday afternoon when Nobody first spotted wreathes of smoke on the horizon. They came from the cooking fires of Dvorarsk. The sun lay low on the horizon, dyeing the small hamlet red with its last rays.

"We should be seeing Cossack patrols soon." Nobody pulled on White Fury's reins. "Halt! Load weapons."

Cartridge-paper tore and ramrods scraped. Nobody jammed his rifle-butt into a strip of metal tied to the left stirrup. This held the gun steady while he poured a pre-measured powder charge down the barrel and rammed a greased bullet over top. It was another of the 42nd's peculiar inventions. Most of the men could reload at a trot.

Nobody issued the order to move out, and the column started again. They wound down through the unbroken blanket of snow into a cup-like valley, through which snaked a frozen river. A wooden bridge led into a tiny hamlet, composed of a dozen makeshift huts. A few withered stumps alone broke the vast smoothness of the surrounding hills.

"I don't see any campfires," Edmund whispered. "And there *are* fires in the village. I should think the natives would have fled as soon as fighting began."

"True." Nobody scanned the town. All was quiet. "In no manner could a regiment be crammed into those few huts, and besides, there are no signs of Cossacks." He rubbed his chin.

"I don't like it," Edmund said firmly. "It's too quiet."

A scout galloped toward them from the direction of the hamlet.

"What news?"

"No sign of Russians, sir," the scout said, reining his horse next to the colonel, "nor our men, neither. Everything's quiet as can be, sir."

Nobody frowned. It could be a trap, and yet, what kind of trap? "Very well, thank you," he said to the soldier, "fall into rank." He raised his voice, addressing the entire command. "42nd, ready rifles. First company, forward center. At the canter!"

He led them toward the hamlet. The bridge was scarcely wide enough for two horses. The planks clattered under the horses' hooves, but there was no movement from the huts. As the first company reached the opposite side they formed a semicircle, their rifles unslung and pointed at the huts. Nobody motioned Captain Peyton to his side.

"Surround the village immediately, harm none, but allow none to escape." Peyton dashed off with his company, letting the rest of the horsemen file across the bridge.

Nobody swung his leg over White Fury's rump and dropped wearily into the wet snow. He stretched his tight back muscles and kicked some feeling into his numb legs. Edmund joined him, and they stepped onto the bridge. Dark spots splotched many of the planks, and one board had entirely disintegrated.

"So this is our objective?" Edmund snorted. "A twenty-foot long rotting bridge leading across a frozen river to a dozen ill-made huts?"

"I don't understand," Nobody said slowly. "There is obviously no military use for this bridge, or this hamlet."

"I should say not. Why, there's not even a use for a bridge at all in winter! The Russians can simply march right across the ice, if they so desire."

"Very true. Remember, though, the bridge was not our objective, but the regiment defending it. Where are they?" He waved at the empty space, desolate save for his own soldiers and the tiny village.

"I'd say there are three possibilities." Edmund held up three fingers. "One, they already left, or two, the Russians won the battle and killed or captured the entire regiment."

"Impossible. There was no battle here. Look at the bridge. Not a single bullet mark or sword slash." Nobody ran his hands over the rough wood. There were a few ancient scars, probably from when the bridge was first built, but nothing to tell the tale of a recent battle.

"In that case," Edmund continued, "they must have already left, although for what reason I don't know, since they were under orders to hold this bridge. And, of course, there aren't any signs of Russians in the vicinity."

"We don't know that for certain. The scouts should report shortly. But you mentioned a third possibility, what is it?"

"I'm afraid you're not going to like it, Noble." Edmund folded his arms and stared at his friend.

"That never stopped you from voicing an opinion before."

The lieutenant colonel smiled. "True. Well, it's just this. The only other possibility is that this ghostly regiment never existed in the first place."

Nobody pondered these words silently, resting his elbows on the rail. "I'm not ready to accept that," he said at last. "It would mean foul play, and I don't wish to ascribe that to any English officer without firm proofs. Come, let's question some of the townspeople, and see what they have to say."

The British soldiers had gathered forty or fifty ill-kempt natives and huddled them together in the center of the village. They frowned at the redcoats from beneath shaggy eyelids and reindeer hoods.

Nobody pointed to a man in the front, who was dressed slightly better than the rest of the villagers. "Как тебя зовут?" he asked.

"Меня зовут Кирилл," the man replied, bowing profoundly.

Nobody enjoyed twisting his tongue into the outlandish figures necessary to Russian, his natural second language. He hadn't found a more fluent translator in the entire British army.

"Have you seen any English recently?" he continued, still in the Russian tongue.

"No, my worshipful lord, you are the first to visit my humble abode in many hunts." The man bowed once more.

"Are you certain that there have been *no* soldiers here to guard your bridge?"

"Yes my lord—" another bow "—I am certain. I do not know why any would have interest in our humble bridge."

"You have a point there, old fellow," Nobody muttered to himself. "But," he continued in Russian, "what of the Cossacks? Have you been visited by any?"

"Not since the last mating of the reindeer, my lord." He bowed twice for emphasis.

"Very well. We want nothing from you. We will camp close by tonight, but you need not fear, my soldiers will do you no harm."

The man expressed his gratefulness for this information by another bow, so low that a mass of snow stuck to his forehead and powdered his eyebrows.

Nobody issued orders to pitch camp on the opposite side of the river, taking care to ensure that their horses were well rubbed and each given a handful of provender from the wagons. Edmund joined him, looking extremely red in the face.

"Are you feeling normal, Ed?"

"I think I burst some internal organs." Edmund grinned. "You can't imagine how ridiculous that Russian head-man looked, bobbing up and down like a child's jack-in-the-box." He barely contained a chortle. "And there you were, gravely conversing with him just as if he were looking at you all along, instead of studying the snow for botanical specimens."

Nobody smiled gravely. If they were back in camp, he would no doubt see the humor—as it was, he never felt comfortable on a mission without a clear objective.

Somerset appeared at his side, holding the ever-present notebook flipped open in his left hand. "I had no idea that you spoke Russian, Colonel Nobody."

"No, I suppose you didn't." He stepped away to superintend the building of his temporary igloo. The reporter stuck by his side.

"Have you known Russian for very long?" he asked, as Nobody stopped next to Jacques and O'Malley.

"Yes, quite some time, Somerset."

O'Malley looked up from his work of slicing snow blocks and nodded at Somerset. "Aye, laddy, the colonel knows Rooshun like a native, no offence, o' course, an' he knows Frinch too, though why he should bother wi' that, I've noo idea."

"French is zhe language of civilization!" Jacques heaved a snow block onto the rapidly shaping dome. "Zhe colonel obviously realized zhe beauty and majesty of zhe French language, and so, he learned."

Nobody watched them calmly. He trusted their discretion. This was not the first inquisitive reporter to trail him. *You must be careful with reporters— one harmless phrase can become a world-startling article, if you set an eager blade with a sharp pencil on it.*

He helped O'Malley lift the capping snow block onto the dome. The finished igloo already looked cozy, with the temperature plummeting and the wind beginning to howl.

"Vhat is it zhat you vrite in zhat book?" Jacques asked Somerset. "Are you writing your articles upon zhe field, or simply making notes?"

"Just notes. There's no way that I could write my articles while the events happen—I just write enough to remind me of their existence, and then I pull the rest from memory."

"How do you do zhat?" Jacques asked

Somerset shrugged. "I just write down whatever strikes my fancy. For example, if I wanted to remember this conversation, I might write 'Jacques— notes or article.' Then, if I thought the event was of high importance, I might make a note as to weather, the time of day, or search for some poetic line about the sun's dying rays touching the horizon's edge." He raised his hand towards the horizon, and froze.

"What is it?" Nobody looked past his pointing arm.

A horseman had just crested the rise over which they had come and was now dashing towards them. Nobody unslung his rifle—there, in full pursuit of the solitary horseman, and silhouetted against the evening sky, was a band of horsemen in blue and gray.

The strange riders reined in their horses at sight of the English camp and fled to cover. The lone horseman slapped his steed furiously—it was one of Nobody's scouts. Foam dripped from his horse's mouth. Breathless, the man leaped from his horse and fell at Nobody's feet.

"Russians, sir," he gasped. "Thousands! They're all over."

Edmund grasped Nobody's arm. "Look!"

There, on the hill's summit and in all directions surrounding the village, emerged hundreds of shaggy horsemen.

Chapter 5

"That could be a problem." Edmund chafed his hands slowly.

"That would be an understatement, Ed. Quick! We must fortify our position." Nobody raised his voice. "42nd, every man to shovel and pick! I want walls of snow and as much of this frozen dirt as you can dig on both sides of the bridge!"

He dashed among the men, helping his captains to organize the working parties in the gathering gloom. A bearded man with a sharp, angular face confronted him.

"Sir, where do you want us snipers?"

These were the elite from Company Five, the best of a regiment already renowned for marksmen. They could change the battle's outcome.

"Take the village and loophole the walls. Petr!" The Russian from Squad One bounded to his side. "Go with the snipers, translate for them. Tell the natives that we're trying to protect them, and that they can stay in their homes, but we must have men with them. Any damage from the fight will be paid for." Petr saluted and raced away.

"Do you want the wall across the ice, sir?" Captain Peyton asked.

"Yes, and spread a layer of snow on the river's surface. I don't want chips flying at our faces every time a ball hits the ice. Overturn the wagons and incorporate them into the barricade."

The weary horses were herded together and packed as tight as possible in the circle's center, giving the men space to work behind the frail snow wall. A swath was scraped in front of the wall, forming a dry moat, but even the iron shovels couldn't tear the frozen Siberian topsoil from its icy embrace.

Nobody paused with Edmund on the bridge to survey the rising fortifications. "This will help in hand-to-hand fighting, but it's hardly an aid against bullets. Still, a soldier always feels more protected if he has something between him and the enemy, even if it is just a mound of snow."

Darkness soon cloaked the position and thick cloud cover blocked the moon's light. Visibility was nearly nonexistent. Men gradually dropped their picks and spades as the wall reached shoulder height, and squatted round their campfires.

"Perfect time for a surprise attack," Edmund whispered. He stood with Nobody by the perimeter wall.

"They may attack, but they will not find us surprised."

"Do you intend to wait here *until* they attack?"

Nobody stared over the wall at the black night beyond. Lights glimmered on the hill-crests, marking Russian bivouacs. Several shadowy forms crept from the English encampment and melted into the darkness. It would be a harsh night for the sentries.

"Edmund," Nobody said slowly, "I don't know. That's what we must decide. The Cossacks generally travel either in patrols of a few hundred, or as a small army of several thousand. According to our scouts' reports it must be the latter, meaning that we're outnumbered three or four to one."

"I've known worse odds. On the other hand, I've known much more defensible positions." Edmund wiped his sword with a dry cloth.

"Exactly. Tactically, our position is abysmal. They have the high ground, they can group and prepare for a charge unseen by us, and they should have the momentum to overrun our walls. We can kill a good number, but after that—" he was silent.

"So what are you thinking?

Nobody clenched his fists. He felt the great responsibility that rested on his shoulders. The lives of hundreds of Britain's finest soldiers depended on him. He knew what had to be done. "Edmund?"

"Yes, Noble?"

"You know that you are my best friend on earth?"

Edmund scratched his head. "Well, yes, actually, I've known that for years. Of course, I'm nearly your *only* friend on earth, so that's not saying very much."

Nobody scooped a handful of snow and balanced it in his palm. "Edmund, you see this bit of snow?"

"Yes."

"If you look at it here, suspended on my hand in the air, it's all alone. There's nothing of the same texture and character nearby." He stooped again, grabbing another handful. He ground both lumps into a single clump. "This is what happened when I met you. We became bosom friends, and the only ones of our type. There are no British officers like you and me in all of Siberia— maybe the world. I don't say this to boast, but it's true. We are peculiar."

"Very." Edmund smiled.

"As my friend, you are the dearest person to me on earth. That's why what I'm about to ask of you is so hard."

"It shouldn't be."

"What do you mean?" Nobody gently laid the snow on the wall and looked earnestly into his friend's face.

"I know what you're going to ask me. You want me to go through the Russian lines for help."

"Yes. How did you know?"

"It's the only option we have, and being such a conceited fellow as I am, I knew that I was the only man you would trust with the job."

"Man?"

"Well, man in training, at least. When do you want me to leave?"

"Now. You will have to ride as fast as you can, and I will attempt to hold our position until you return."

"How many men should I take?"

"How many do you want?"

"I say four at the maximum. Numbers aren't going to help me fight my way out, so the fewer the better for stealth."

"Very well." Nobody ordered a nearby sentry to find Squad One. "Edmund, you know that I would rather do this. I don't like sending my men into danger when I don't go with them. I would much rather take this mission upon myself, than put it upon your shoulders. But it's my duty to stay with the men. I've brought them here—it doesn't matter that I have been ordered to do so—I have brought them here, and it is my responsibility to get them out, not to go with you, even though your position is probably more dangerous. It's my duty to remain."

The familiar forms of Squad One emerged from the gloom, quickly forming a semicircle around Nobody and Edmund.

"Are all here?"

"Aye sir, that we are," the Irishman affirmed.

"Very well. Jacques?"

"Sir?"

"You are going with the lieutenant colonel to get help from headquarters. O'Malley, you go as well."

"Aye, sir."

"Now, I need two others."

Matthew, the eldest of the Preston twins, stepped forward. "I'll go, sir."

"No, Matthew. You're a good man, but I know that you and your brother don't like to be parted, and I want to send men of different expertise with the lieutenant colonel. You two are good soldiers, but you're too similar to send together."

"Very well, sir, I understand." The twin stepped back into line.

Dilworth cleared his throat. "Sir," he began, "if you're not against it, I'll speak my mind a little bit. You see, this is how I see things. If you want some different expertises, as you say, well, you see, sir, there's bucketfuls of different countries, and each country often has its own way of fighting. You already have France and Ireland accounted for, with Jacques and O'Malley, so how about sending along a representative from America? After all, we've had some good soldiers ourselves, as you English found out in 1812."

Nobody smiled. "I suppose you would consider yourself a good representative of American warfare?"

The Yankee smoothed his coat. "Well, sir, I don't mean to be boastful, but I'd say that there's probably not a better American in this entire regiment."

"Very likely, Dilworth, considering that there are *no* other Americans in this regiment." Nobody smiled. "Nevertheless, I think you're right. Very well, then. Edmund, you have some Scottish blood in you somewhere, don't you?"

"A little, I was told, through my mother, sir."

"Then you may represent the land of heath and moor. Jacques, take care of France's honor. I can trust, O'Malley, that you will do the same for Ireland. Dilworth, I expect you to make sure that the prowess of 1812 has not lessened at all in your bones. And you, Petr." He clapped the quiet Russian's shoulder. "Show these fellows that a good soldier doesn't need to be able to talk the ear off a mule."

Five of the best horses were hastily gathered and prepared for the journey. Nobody pulled a small map out of his saddlebag and wrapped it in leather.

"I would have recommended that you break through the lines away from Porsk, and circle back around, but I don't think it would work. The Russians are well used to warfare, and they will expect us to send for help. They will probably be looking for us to break out in the opposite direction—a very common ruse. Therefore, go straight at their line, and once you're through, ride like the wind."

Edmund leaped into the saddle, his restive horse prancing under the weight. Leaning down, he firmly grasped Nobody's hand. "Have no worries," he whispered in his friend's ear, "we'll be fine."

Nobody smiled painfully, an unwanted tear trembling in the corner of his eye. "God bless you, my friend."

Another moment, and all five were dashing toward the line of enemy campfires. The darkness engulfed their forms, and the quiet crunching of snow faded away in the distance.

"Are you all right, sir?" Major Macpherson asked.

"Yes, Macpherson, I'm fine." The officer moved on in his rounds, but Nobody continued to stare into the darkness. *Fine? Yes. If he dies—no. Who would I have left? God, be with them.*

***

A few rays of light broke through the dense cloud cover, momentarily gleaming on the messengers' rifles.

"Slow down." Edmund tightened his horse's rein. "We'll try to steal through as quietly as possible." He led toward a large gap between two fires. They advanced with heads bent low, partly because of the chilling wind, and partly to prevent their white faces from standing out in the darkness.

Snow crunched in the tarry blackness on their left. A horse snorted. Edmund fingered his trigger. Six or seven shadowy forms passed by, their riders quietly conversing in Russian. It was a patrol moving toward the English camp.

Edmund raised his hand and led forward. They were now on the same level with the campfires. Great bearded Cossacks sat round the fires, their fur caps silhouetted against the flames. A voice shouted a challenge into the clear night air.

"Друго," Petr replied, trotting his horse ahead of Edmund's.

"What is the password?"

"Down with Russia!" Petr charged his horse at the sentry. Before the startled Cossack could respond he was stretched in the snow by a blow from one of Petr's huge fists.

"Ride!" Edmund cried, all need for stealth now over. They dashed their heels deep into their horses' flanks and sprang forward into the light, bowling the bewildered Russians over like wickets in a cricket match.

Before the startled soldiers could gather their wits or their weapons, the English were through the line and racing towards their own camp, some fifty miles away.

Chapter 6

Five figures, bone-weary and covered with a powdery coat of snow, reeled into the English camp at Porsk. Edmund sent the four soldiers to secure fresh horses and made his own way to General Tremont's headquarters.

A line of sleek horses stood in front of the door, lazily letting a grizzled trooper rub moisture off their backs.

"Soldier, whose horses are these?" Edmund stifled a groan as he dismounted.

The trooper saluted. "General's havin' a meetin', sir." He eyed the lieutenant colonel's bedraggled mount. "Doubt you can go in."

"They'd better not keep me out." Edmund stepped toward the door.

The trooper stepped in front of it. "Sorry sir, but General Tremont's given orders for no interruptions."

"This is an emergency, soldier. Do you know who I am?"

"Why no, sir, can't say that I do."

"I am Lieutenant Colonel Burke, of the 42nd. Do you know who my commanding officer is?"

"Why in course, sir, it's Colonel Nobody. Who don't know who the 42ⁿᵈ's colonel is?" The soldier grinned.

"Yes, you're right, and I have Colonel Nobody's direct order to go through that door, no matter what orders there may be to the contrary."

The sentry wavered. "I'd be glad, sir, to let you in, but I'd get into awful trouble, sir." He scratched his grizzly beard.

"I'll explain. Let me in."

The veteran's face twisted with indecision, but still he made no movement to leave.

"Look, man," Edmund said angrily, "this is a matter of life and death. Let me in that door!"

The soldier took a deep breath and stepped out of the way. "Please sir, make sure I don't get into any trouble."

A low murmur of voices came from the last room in the rough hallway. Slight wreathes of smoke slipped under the door, carrying with them a distinct smell of Madeira. Edmund hurriedly smoothed his uniform and brushed snow from his epaulettes. The door swung open at his touch and there he stood, among the highest ranking British officers on the continent.

Conversation ceased. Half a dozen men sat round a long mahogany table, with General Tremont at the head. A glass decanter half-filled with Madeira rested on a silver platter beside a box of fragrant cigars. A large map of Siberia hung on the wall to the left, dotted with small red pins. All eyes were on the boy.

"I gave firm orders that this meeting should *not* be interrupted." General Tremont plucked a smoking cigar from his mouth.

Edmund removed his shako and clasped it under his right arm. "My apologies, sir, but I felt it necessary under the circumstances."

"*You* felt it necessary?" Tremont sneered. "It is true that I am only the general-in-chief temporarily, but since when does a drummer boy turned colonel's pet have the authority to disobey my orders?"

Edmund's face burned. The other officers stared at him with wide eyes, evidently waiting for a response.

"With all due respect, sir," Edmund said slowly, "my background has nothing to do with the reason for my appearance here. It is true that I was a drummer boy before being promoted to my current rank, but I strongly deny being the pet of any man."

"Why are you not with your regiment?" Tremont rose to his feet.

"I was. Colonel Nobody sent me to inform you that he reached the Dvorarsk bridge and found no English regiment there, and no information about one could be obtained from the natives. We were then surrounded by a force of several thousand Russians, who were undoubtedly informed by scouts of our arrival. The colonel asks that a relief force be sent at once."

"If you were surrounded by Russians, then how did you get out?"

"I rode through them, sir."

The officers murmured their approbation.

Tremont stepped from the table and approached Edmund. He clasped his hands behind his back, only emphasizing the expanded diameter of his waist.

"How is it that your *amazing* colonel let himself be trapped like a mouse nibbling at a bite of cheese?"

Edmund gritted his teeth. "Sir, I can assure you that no necessary precautions were overlooked. We were informed that a force of Russians already surrounded a regiment at Dvorarsk, therefore there was no reason to send scouts to any distance in search of enemies. If there had been an English force at Dvorarsk, we would not be so outnumbered, and could most likely fight our way out. As it is, we have very few options."

"I gladly offer my regiment for duty in a relief force," one of the officers said, rising and saluting.

"Thank you, Colonel Campbell, but I don't think that will be necessary." Tremont regarded Edmund icily. "You may inform your colonel that if he has allowed himself to be surrounded, it is then his duty, and his *alone*, to break out. I have important strategies to implement, and I have no time to be sending regiments gallivanting around the Siberian countryside."

Edmund stared in surprise. "Sir, you—you can't be denying help?"

"Can't I?"

"But sir," another officer protested, "he had no choice! At least send Campbell, if no one else."

Tremont turned angrily on the man. "Are you questioning my authority?" His high-pitched tones grew shrill with anger. "It is true that I but fill this place for General Whitmore, but if you dare to impugn my ability to command—"

The officer shrank back to his seat. "No, sir, not at all, simply suggesting."

"And I am saying 'no.'"

Edmund raised his head proudly, looking his superior officer in the eye. "Very well, sir, I believe I understand. I presume we have your permission to leave the bridge at Dvorarsk, in order to fight our way back?"

Tremont glanced quickly at his officers' faces. They were full of surprise and indignation. "Yes," he said at last, "you may leave the bridge."

Edmund saluted stiffly, turned on his heel, and left the room. As the door closed behind him, he clenched his sword-hilt. "I knew he was up to something," he muttered. "All that false humility about just filling in for General Whitmore. I'll be quite surprised if he actually *tries* to get the general exchanged."

The outer door opened and a rush of cold air cooled his heated head. He stepped into the snow.

The four soldiers from Squad One were astride four new horses, with an extra charger for Edmund.

"When doos the relief party ride, sir?" O'Malley asked, as Edmund jerked the fresh horse's head rope loose.

"It doesn't." Edmund thrust his left foot into the stirrup and swung his right over the horse's rump. "We go back alone."

"B-b-but, zhat's impossible!" Jacques stuttered. Dilworth and Petr pressed closer.

"Impossible, but true." Edmund donned his shako. "The general will not send help."

The Frenchman put his hand to his sword. "Vhat is he trying to do? Kill us all?"

"I don't know. Follow me. Colonel Nobody will have all the more need of our aid now!"

The door swung open and a jolly, red-faced officer ran out. "Burke, stop!" he shouted, puffing with the unusual exertion.

"What is it, Colonel Campbell? Has General Tremont changed his mind?"

"No, he has not changed his mind, but—"

"Then I have no time for more talk." Edmund turned his horse's head. "My colonel waits, and every moment counts. Forward!" He dug his heels into the horse's ribs and the small band rode off into the Siberian steppe, regardless of their weary bodies, thinking only of the fresh horses beneath them, and the danger of their comrades before them.

Chapter 7

After Edmund had left the camp at Dvorarsk, Nobody sat down by a campfire to watch the snapping sparks. He rested his chin in his hand, thinking about the position in which they were placed, and the friend who had just departed. *Quite possibly, I'll never see Edmund again.* The moon peeked through the thick clouds, shedding a soft pale light on the snow.

Bending nearer the ground, Nobody traced a large circle in the white powder, with a wavy line splitting its center. He scooped up the snow from the outside edges, making a little wall around the perimeter. "Here we are, and there they are." He made a much wider circle, which completely encompassed the first. "They won't attack from all sides at once. Even with their numbers, it would be too much ground to cover effectively."

He looked doubtfully at the miniature defenses. "I would expect four or five columns—probably four." He grabbed a handful of half-burnt splinters from the fire and stuck them into the ground, just outside the upper left wall. "I can expect the snipers to disorganize the attack from this section. If the Russians turn back soon enough, our men might also be able to enfilade one of the other columns." He pulled a pot from the fire and filled a metal cup with steaming black liquid. Cautiously, he put it to his lips.

"*Plah*!" he sputtered, spitting a mouthful into the fire. "Jacques!"

No one answered.

"Oh, of course, he's gone with Ed. What he's done to my tea rations, I have absolutely no idea. I do believe Ed's right—the Frenchman *is* trying to force coffee upon me."

His thoughts wandered to the friend now riding for help across the Siberian wilderness. How long had it been since Edmund had first come to camp to replace a dead drummer boy? Nobody leaned back and smiled, remembering the forlorn look, and the small uniform which hung limp on his skinny body. The boy was scared, uncertain, half-starved. He remembered the drum, nearly as big as the boy, which he tried to carry the first day. Somehow he managed to end up sprawled on his back, the drum resting firmly on his flabby stomach. It seemed like a decade ago.

He folded his arms, gazing up into the night sky. Edmund had persevered so diligently at his simple task that he attracted Nobody's attention—a rare feat for a drummer boy. He smiled as he thought of the many tests through which he had put the unsuspecting boy to determine whether he could properly command men. He could. Ah, those had been the days, when he was first appointed lieutenant colonel. So overwhelmed, and yet so eager to learn. And now. . . .

"Colonel?"

Nobody started. A man stepped into the circle of firelight.

"I'm sorry, sir, did I wake you?"

"Not at all, Somerset. Just thinking, that's all."

The reporter rubbed his hands over the fire. "Do you mind if I warm myself for a moment?"

"Make yourself at home." Nobody dragged the log a little closer to the fire. "Please, take a seat."

"Thank you, sir." He sat down and groaned. "Feels splendid. Not that I'm an old man, yet, but you're not exactly a grandfather either."

Nobody smiled. "No, nor a father, and no plans to become one in the near future. How is your writing coming? I would think that your present situation would be excellent fodder for an article."

"Indeed it is, sir. Although, I must confess, I'm rather concerned about having the opportunity to send it back to the *Times*."

"You're afraid of coming out of here alive?"

Somerset smiled nervously. "Well, yes, sir, that would be about right."

"We will not abandon you."

"Oh no, it's not that. It's just that, well—do you think we will be able to withstand their attack?"

Nobody looked sideways at the young man. Something akin to fear flickered in the reporter's eyes.

"Somerset, we will all do our best. Will our best be enough? We'll find out very soon." Nobody plucked one of the splinters from the snow and began whittling.

"Do you think the lieutenant colonel will make it through?"

"I can only pray."

Somerset looked up in surprise. "You pray?"

"Yes. I'm a Christian."

"Of course, so am I, but—you actually believe that God cares about things down here?"

"Indeed I do. How can you call yourself a Christian if you don't believe in God's sovereignty?"

Somerset blinked, and ran his tongue along his lips.

"Well, I just don't see how He lets so much bad happen down here. I suppose I shouldn't be surprised that you're religious—I've heard that you keep a pretty tight rein on the regiment. No swearing, hardly any spirits, no unpaid foraging. Is all that true?"

"It is. I would remove the entire ration of spirits, if it were not so imbedded in the soldiers' minds as a right. Of course, I don't see a direct command against alcohol itself, only against the results from too much consumption."

"Well, perhaps I can see you being a teetotaler, but tell me this, if you would, sir. How do you justify assassinating people, when murder is against the—oh, what commandment was it? Fifth, or sixth, or fifty-sixth, I don't remember."

Nobody tossed the stick away, rose, and crossed his arms. Somerset flipped open the ever-present notebook and waited.

"Before I answer," Nobody said, "I want to ask you two questions. First, are you actually interested in my answer, or are you asking for information for an article?"

"Yes, sir."

"Which?"

"Both, sir."

Nobody nodded. "I see. Very well, then, question two. Do you consider the act of killing a man in warfare as murder?"

"Why no, sir, not at all, do you?"

Nobody scowled. "If I did, do you still think I'd be a colonel in the army? Of course I don't. And that's why I have no problem with assassinations. Mind you, I'm speaking of military assassinations. I will not kill a civilian purposely, unless he is providing so much aid to the enemy that I can consider him a part of the military operation as well. I might kill a factory owner who is exclusively making firearms for the Russians. However, I probably wouldn't."

"So you assassinate, just not civilians?"

"Yes. I see no difference with soldiers whether I meet them on the battlefield, or track them down in their home town. They are still a declared enemy, and they have the right to kill me if I am discovered."

"Bloody work, isn't it?"

Nobody smiled bitterly. "Have you ever seen a man killed, Somerset?"

"No, sir, I haven't."

"Then you have no idea what bloody work is. The authors, especially you newspaper fellows, always try to make war sound so romantic. The glories of fighting for king and country, and defending your family. They're all good

56

things, glorious even, but when you get upon the battlefield—" he shook his head. "Those Russians whose campfires you see surrounding us, they have families too. It's when you look into the eyes of another human being and see the terror in them—and then jam a sword blade down his throat—that is the *real* face of war."

Somerset shuddered. "I'm not sure if I'd like that kind of war, sir."

Nobody looked sadly at the flickering Russian campfires. "It appears, my friend, that in a few hours you will be able to form an opinion for yourself."

Chapter 8

Nobody was out of his igloo long before light, his eyelids heavy from little sleep.

Light slowly dawned. The camp was quiet. Each man had his appointed post at the wall, or in the village, and all were watching the surrounding hills. Banners fluttered upon the hilltops, but there was no sign of the forces which they represented. One of the closely-packed horses whinnied shrilly and broke from his fellows to rush to Nobody's side.

"There now, old fellow, I'm still here." Nobody patted the stallion's neck.

Stoning and the Prestons stepped up. "Good morning, sir," Stoning said, "any orders?"

"No. Have you seen any sign of the enemy?"

"A few sentries on the hills now and then, sir, but that's all."

Nobody scanned the defenses. Every man had his rifle in hand and his sword by his side. A few had stuck sword-bayonets in the snow, to be attached when it came to hand-to-hand fighting, but most of the men preferred their sabers to the twenty-four inch blade that weighted the end of the barrel and made loading nearly impossible.

A gray banner fluttered in the breeze upon the closest hill.

"Preston," Nobody said quietly, gazing at the flag, "get me a sniper."

"Which Preston, sir?" Matthew stepped forward.

"Mmm? Oh, I'm sorry. You may go."

He soon returned with the captain of the snipers, the same bearded and angular individual who had requested orders for his men the previous day.

"You called, Colonel?" the man said gruffly, lowering a long rifle from his shoulder and saluting respectfully.

"Good morning, Daming, how are you?"

"As good as could be expected, sir."

"You see that flag?" Nobody pointed to the banner. It hung limply against its pole.

"I'd never have been a sniper, sir, if I didn't have eyes good enough to see that."

"Can you see that black speck on the right, a foot or so behind it?"

The soldier shaded his eyes. "Indeed I do, sir. It's moving around a little whenever a bit of a breeze comes by."

"Yes. I think it probable that it's the top of a Cossack's cap."

The sniper looked again. "It's possible, sir, but I couldn't say for certain."

"I want to find out. Can you put a bullet through it?"

Daming grinned through his shaggy beard. "If anyone can, I'm the man and Charlotte here is the gun to do it, sir."

He carefully examined the rifle's priming, stroking each part gently as if it were a human being. Methodically, he pulled a black cloth from his pouch and spread it out on the shoulder-level wall, as a barrier between the wet snow and his rifle's barrel.

There was a hush of expectancy as he aligned the barrel with his target, squinting along the dull metal with his right eye. He took a deep breath and stood motionless for a moment. *Crash!* The gun coughed out a cloud of smoke—a horrid cry rose in the still air. Nobody squinted through the smoke, barely making out a splash of red on the gray banner. Somewhere in the distance a bugle sounded—and with a mighty shout the heads and shoulders of thousands of Russian soldiers appeared over the crests of the surrounding hills.

"Wait for the command to fire!" Nobody shouted, as each man grasped his rifle instinctively and rose above the wall's summit. Just as he had expected, four distinct columns swept over the hills and charged, with discordant cries and brandished weapons.

"Ready! Present! *Fire!*" Each barrel belched forth its contents, sending a storm of hot lead into the charging Russians. Cries and screams testified to their accuracy, but not a Cossack slowed, except for those whose bodies had provided a resting place for the whizzing bullets.

"Prepare to load!" Nobody vaulted onto White Fury's back and raced from squad to squad. "Load!" Each man tore a paper cartridge open with his front teeth. "Prime!" The powder was poured into each pan. "'Bout!" Each man inserted a cartridge into the end of his rifle. "Rod! Home!" With a sound of scraping metal, each ramrod was pounded down the barrel, forcing the deadly lump of lead into the propelling gunpowder. "Ready! Present! Fire!" Another deadly volley. More empty saddles.

The Russians kept coming. Nobody hoarsely repeated the same orders, and the third volley crashed out. Piles of snow had drifted down the hills and collected at their base, momentarily slowing the Russians as their horses slogged through the thick powder. The deadly English rifles lowered for a fourth time—he thought he could see the closest column waver slightly. This was his chance.

"Fire and mount!" he shouted. As the fourth deafening volley pounded in his eardrums he slammed his heels into White Fury's side and tore into the acrid smoke. The wall loomed in his path. His horse gathered his powerful legs and sprang into the air, clearing the barrier in one bound. Close behind he heard a crash and a muffled exclamation. Matthew Preston's bony mount had not proved as agile.

His cap was off and his hair splayed wildly—his eyes dilated, but he gritted his teeth, fighting desperately to keep a cool head. He swung the long cavalry saber in a deadly arc, increasing in speed at each rotation. At his back rode the Preston brothers, screaming and brandishing their swords. Behind them poured a stream of the 42nd, tired of the long hours of tension, ready to release all in a wild fight for existence.

A tall Cossack officer in a brilliant blue and yellow uniform rode at the head of his men, encouraging them with shouts and cries. Seeing Nobody, he spurred his horse forward. Their mounts collided at full speed, throwing both riders into the soggy snow.

The Russian struck viciously at Nobody's head, but the boy parried it neatly and thrust back. The Russian glared at him with bloodshot eyes, his sword-arm shaking with anger or fear. Vaguely, Nobody felt the Prestons guarding his back. With a cry the Russian struck at his legs—the boy leaped back instinctively, the sword's edge slicing his leather boots. Before his opponent could recover himself Nobody struck downwards with all his force upon the Russian's head, cleaving through skull and brain.

Nobody looked round. The English and Russians were mixed together without order, their slashing swords on a level with his neck. Dodging round the head of a Cossack's horse he grasped the man's right boot and pushed up with all his might. The horseman gave a wild cry and tumbled out of his seat, which Nobody immediately occupied.

He found himself on the fringe of the fight, which was fast becoming a Russian rout. "Back!" Nobody cried, waving his sword in the opposite direction. "Back to camp! The Russians have broken in!"

He wheeled his horse and rode back through the gap in the wall. Two of the other Russians columns had broken through the wall and were engaged in a deadly hand-to-hand melee with the remaining Englishmen. "The 42nd!" Nobody screamed, dashing into the fray. "Huzzah for the 42nd!"

"What are you doing lad?" the eldest Preston shouted at Somerset, who stood bewilderedly in his path. He jerked back on the reins, and stopped just in time to avoid pulverizing the young man.

The reporter attempted to shrug. The hand in which he held his notebook shook violently.

"Come on, fool," Matthew growled, "it's time to drop the pen and grab the sword." He stooped low in his saddle, wrenched a blade from a corpse at his horse's feet, and threw it to Somerset. "Here's a sword."

"In case you're bored," his brother added.

"Now use it!"

"Or lose it!"

The poet-warriors dashed on to join the fierce melee at the wall.

Already demoralized by their losses, the Cossacks could not withstand Nobody's charge, backed as he was by the rest of the mounted British. With wild cries they broke and fled, rushing for the protection of the surrounding hills.

"Do not pursue!" Nobody ordered, rushing among his men. "They still outnumber us three to one! Back into camp!"

It was no easy task to stop the inflamed Britons, but Nobody charged among them, knocking down swords, and heading off horses. His officers joined him, and at last they calmed the angry men down and herded them back into camp.

There was no time to rejoice in their temporary victory. Men were instantly set repairing the many gaps in the wall, while others ran to the powder stores to take around fresh supplies. A fatigue detail was given the gruesome duty of burying the dead, many of whom wore red coats and English shakos.

Not a living Russian appeared on the surrounding hills. Bugle calls sounded as the afternoon progressed, but the notes were not retreating. They were reforming.

Somerset wandered to Nobody's side, still pasty with fright, and shaking every time he looked at the gravediggers. "D-do you think they'll attack again, sir?"

"They will either attack or starve us out. In either case it's quite probable that they'll win. I don't know why they attacked in daylight. Next time, I can assure you, it will be night." He turned away in disgust.

The regimental doctor stood knee-deep in bloody snow under the hospital tent, attending as fast as possible to each wounded man's needs. His wig perched crazily on one side. He called to Nobody and asked him to talk to one of the men.

A young soldier lay on his back, a gaping wound in his chest.

"He wants to see you, sir," the doctor said. He shook his head and moved to the next man.

Nobody knelt by the wounded man's side. "C-colonel—"

"I'm here."

The soldier's lips twitched. "Tell—Mother—brave." A paroxysm of pain gripped him and his head fell back.

That twisted face became his death-mask.

Nobody stood up. This was the face of war.

That day passed without alarm. The night was quiet. The Russians must have decided to starve them.

Darkness had already fallen the next day when a volley of musketry sounded on the other side of the hills.

"Prepare to receive the enemy!" Nobody caught up his rifle and hurried to the wall.

Hooves pounded the snow in the direction of the far-away English camp. Could it be?

"Don't shoot!" yelled an English voice.

"Edmund!"

"All right, it's me, don't put any holes in me."

Five horses broke through the snow wall and staggered into the firelight. They were safe.

"Edmund, you're back!" Nobody rushed to his side. "Oh, thank God!"

"Amen." Edmund could barely stand from exhaustion. "That was— exhiliarating," he mumbled.

"You fool! Why did you ride ahead of the relief force?"

The smile faded from the other boy's lips. "I didn't. There is no relief force."

All within earshot stopped abruptly. Edmund shook his head.

Nobody mechanically removed his hat and raked his fingers through his hair. "Tremont wouldn't send any?" he finally asked.

"None."

"Well then." Nobody loosened his saber. "Did he give a reason?"

"No real ones. He said that since you had gotten into this position, it was your responsibility to get back out."

"He said that *I* got us into this position?" Nobody laughed bitterly. "Oh yes, indeed. It's a new hobby of mine, prancing off every now and then to random towns to inquire after ghostly regiments. Quite enjoyable." He turned away.

Edmund staggered after his friend. "I did get permission from him to leave the bridge. I suppose that's something."

"Something?" Nobody kept walking. "Yes, it's something. It's also a little late. Of course, that's what Tremont hoped for. There's no doubt of it any longer. He's trying to either ruin or kill me."

Chapter 9

Steam rose in the cold morning air from the packed ranks of horsemen. The regimental flag fluttered in a strong breeze, making the embroidered soldier leap and dodge as if he were alive. The wall facing south had been leveled, and the remains of what had once been their tents lay smoldering in a huge fire. Thick clouds diffused the sunlight into a brilliant red glory, which covered the horizon in tints ten times more vibrant than any contrived on a painter's palette.

Nobody rode slowly along the front of his regiment, followed three paces behind by his lieutenant colonel. He passed each file silently, looking down the ranks at the expectant horsemen. At last, he reached the left flank, and turned.

"Men of the 42nd." He spoke clearly, so that all could hear, but not loudly. "Today we must fight. I won't disguise our position. Over those hills," he pointed towards the crests, silhouetted in the early light, "is an army of Russians. We have fought them once, and we were victorious. Now we must do it again."

As he spoke, he rode once more across the regiment's front, gradually quickening White Fury's pace. "We have been relieved of the duty of guarding this bridge. Therefore, we ride to the hill upon which we camped on our march here. It is defensible, and we should be able to hold out—for as long as our food lasts."

He was now trotting, rapidly nearing the right flank. Rising high in the stirrups he drew his sword and turned his face to his men. "No help comes from camp. We are left alone." His voice rose steadily higher, gaining power as he neared the end of the line. "It is up to the 42nd alone to win this day! Who is ready to follow me to victory?"

For a moment, no one spoke. The air hung heavy and silent. Then, by a common will, a mighty shout swelled from the crowded ranks. "We are!" each man screamed, raising his rifle towards the sky. "We will follow to the death!"

Nobody reached the end of the line. "Then forward!" he cried, wheeling his horse towards the hills. "Forward to death, and forward to life! Forward for king, for country, for home, for family! Forward, men, at the canter!"

As each rank stepped over the broken wall they opened formation, moving from a walk into a canter. Each warhorse felt the old call of battle in its bones and quickened its pace instinctively, following the trained veteran upon which Nobody sat. The wind whipped through their tails and manes.

"Deliver a running fire!" Nobody shouted. As they crested the hill the entire Russian army came into view, a grim panoply waiting for their attack.

With a mighty English "huzzah" the 42nd pressed onward, arranged in their most effective formation. Each company rode in the form of a "v," with the officers protected by both flanks. This meant that every soldier had a clear line of sight towards the enemy, and each leveled his rifle accordingly.

Nobody and Edmund spearheaded the column, with Squad One close behind as color guard.

"It's goin' tae be a bluidy day today," O'Malley whispered to Jacques.

"May zhe best man vin!"

"Aye, and may we be the best men!"

The Cossacks swooped like vultures, firing muskets and pistols indiscriminately, and uttering blood-curdling war cries. They met a sharp return from the 42nd as each rifle cracked and sent forth its leaden messenger of death. As quickly as each soldier emptied his weapon he jammed it into the metal strap next to his left stirrup and reloaded. It had taken long weeks of practice to learn, but the smooth snowy terrain made it easier.

Unable to reload likewise in the saddle, the Cossacks could only charge with the sword—a deadly move when faced by hundreds of rapidly firing rifles. They broke before the English advance, like an ocean wave against a solid rock, hovering just out of range with angry shouts. This, indeed, was a strange escort.

Thus the British traveled over the Siberian steppe, picking off the occasional reckless Cossack, and always gazing distrustfully at the larger hordes waiting to be unleashed. There would be no resting until the hill was gained.

"Why do we never gallop into battle?" Edmund asked quietly, pressing his horse to Nobody's side.

"I have my reasons, Ed."

"Can't I hear them? I *am* your best friend in the world, after all."

"That you are, and I will tell you one of them. It's very challenging to load while galloping."

Edmund laughed. "Certainly it is, but not much harder than while cantering. That can't be your only reason?"

"It's the only one I wish to give at this time." Nobody smiled sadly.

"Oh. Very well. I haven't said anything wrong, have I?"

"No, Ed, you've done nothing wrong. Let's change the subject. Have you seen the sky?"

"The sky?" Edmund shaded his eyes and looked at the horizon. "Yes, of course. Why?"

"It's red. Red as blood."

"Yes, I see that. What's your point?"

"Have you never heard the sailor's saying? 'Red sky at night, sailor's delight; red sky in morning, sailor take warning.'"

"No, I never have. Interesting way to predict the weather. How did you hear it, seeing that you're not a sailor?"

"I am a sailor. Or at least, I have been."

"What?" Edmund looked at his friend in great surprise. "I never knew that."

"There's much about me that you don't know, Ed." *I wish it didn't have to be so.*

It was late in the afternoon before the hill that was their goal loomed on the horizon, and their horses were showing unmistakable signs of weariness. Even White Fury was panting, and many of the lesser beasts stumbled at the least irregularity in the snow. The Russians sensed this, slowly tightening the circle around the 42nd like a huge python constricting round its prey.

"Why aren't they trying to take the hill before us?" Edmund called. Each moment brought the outcropping closer, but not a single Cossack tried to cut off their escape. If anything, they were edging away from it, farther towards the English rear.

"I don't know. I don't like it. It's obvious that we're heading there." *The Russians know how to fight. The only reason they wouldn't take that hill would be. . .*

A musket bellowed, and a bullet whizzed high over the 42nd. A smoke-puff rose from the boulder-strewn hillside.

. . . that they already have it! Nobody gazed in horror as hundreds of figures appeared, their muskets leveled. "Forward!" he cried, and at the same instant a withering volley blasted from the hill.

Not an Englishman fell. Nobody stared at his unbroken ranks in utter bewilderment. "That is impossible," he whispered, awestruck.

"No, not impossible!" Edmund's eyes blazed with renewed hope. "They're not shooting at us!"

"What?" Nobody stood in his stirrups and looked round. It was true. The troops on the hillside were not firing at the 42nd. They were firing at the Russians, who fled in the same state of bewilderment with which the English advanced.

"Why, sir, they're English!" Edmund exclaimed. "Look! They wear the king's uniform!"

The two forces met with cries of relief and thankfulness, shaking hands heartily and slapping each other on the back. Jacques, unsatisfied with these English signs of emotion, promptly rode up to the first soldier he met, hugged him, shook him, jabbered at him in French, and then skipped on to the next to repeat the process.

The commanding officer rode up to Nobody and Edmund, lifted his hat, and revealed the smiling Scottish features of Colonel Campbell.

"Campbell!" Nobody shook his hand heartily. "How did you come to be here?"

"To help you, of course."

"But—I thought—" Nobody pointed at Edmund. "Lieutenant Colonel Burke said that no force was to be sent?"

"He's right, none was to be."

"Then why are you here?"

Colonel Campbell smiled broadly. "The general wouldn't order any help to be sent, but on the other hand, he never said we couldn't go."

Nobody frowned. "From what Lieutenant Colonel Burke said, it seemed to me that he wouldn't give permission if asked."

"He probably wouldn't have, but I didn't ask." Campbell flicked a speck of snow off his shoulder. "I have the authority to command my men so long as I don't violate orders from my superior officers, and I did not."

"Rather the letter than the spirit of the law, I'd say."

"Perhaps, but it's a good thing for you that I did so. The Russians we found waiting here were preparing a warm reception for you, but it certainly wasn't meant to take the cold out of your bones."

"The hill was already occupied?"

"That it was. Of course, they were looking the other direction. I wish you could have seen the surprise on their faces. As it is, they are at this moment beginning to molder in the grave. I couldn't have offered you much hospitality with what we brought along, considering our hurried start, but the Cossacks were kind enough to provide some refreshments. Would you be so obliging as to join me in testing their quality?"

Chapter 10

Nobody and Edmund sat quietly by their table, poring over a map by candlelight. The dingy snow walls were not pretty, but they were familiar and homey—a blessed change after a week of tense warfare on the steppe.

"I will rescue him," Nobody said firmly, pushing the candle away so that the dripping wax would not mar the map. "Nothing is happening with these exchange negotiations. Tremont simply *will not* offer someone of equal rank."

A small fire burned in one of the igloo's side tunnels, its smoke escaping through an ingenious chimney. A kettle, placed among the ashes, began to show signs of inward life. The aroma of fresh tea filled the room.

"As soon as our spies report the exact location of General Whitmore we will begin. I only wish we had more Russian speakers in the regiment. It comes in handy when bribing guards."

"I don't think Tremont even *wants* the general free," Edmund said. "Why should he? All of his new found power would be up the chimney, and he'd be back to the old drudgery of second-in-command."

Nobody rested his chin in his hand. "That's certainly plausible. I won't go to great lengths to defend General Tremont's actions after what happened last week. I have strong doubts, Ed, whether we were supposed to return alive from Dvorarsk."

Edmund leaned comfortably back in his chair, resting it against the wall, and propping his boots on the table. "He's a slimy character, and that's all I can say. It really is too bad that you're the inferior and he the superior, not *vice versa*. You could do some amazing things as general-in-chief."

"I could." Nobody nodded slowly. "I believe that is what Tremont is afraid of. If anything, he is ambitious. He probably knows that, once I come of age, I can easily rise higher in the ranks. And, he probably knows that I am much more liked by the entire army than his worthy self. However, he probably does not know that I have no desire to advance higher. I am content as the colonel of the 42nd. I love my men, and my men love me. What more can I ask?"

"Not much, I suppose. Do we have to return to tents, still?"

"Hmm? Oh, no, we don't. Tremont reversed his order, probably under pressure from Colonel Campbell and other of my friends. There was no basis for his order, anyway."

The sentry challenged outside. Edmund leaned forward, bringing his chair back to its normal position.

"Please, sir." A voice rang through the tunnel. "It's an order from General Tremont to join him at dinner."

"Dinner?" Nobody grunted. "What splendid timing." He hurriedly brushed his uniform, smoothing out the many wrinkles. Edmund sprang to his side with a wet cloth and labored diligently at an old blood stain.

"There's something about Russian blood," Edmund said, scraping away, "it's so sticky."

Nobody wiped off his epaulettes and gave a quick shine to the gold buttons on his tunic. He pulled himself to attention and saluted. "Do I pass inspection?"

Edmund cocked his head and squinted approvingly. "You'll do fine for a colonel in the field. Just be cleaning it up a bit if you go before the king, eh?"

They both laughed. "If that's the only reason for a cleaning, Ed, I'm afraid these spots will be with me for quite some time. *Au revoir*, as Jacques would say."

He scrambled through the tunnel, regained his dignity on the other side, and brushed the fallen snow from his shoulders. Headquarters was near, and a brisk walk in the cold night air soon brought him to Tremont's door.

A crowd of jovial officers welcomed Nobody into Tremont's room of state. It looked just as Edmund had described.

"Come, Nobody, have a drink!" one of the officers called.

Nobody hung his sword belt on a rack by the wall, so that the naked blade wouldn't scratch the floor. "Thank you, Colonel Morris, but you know very well that I don't drink."

"What, don't drink?" cried a small man with a red nose. "Why, I think you would die rather soon with no drink!" He roared at his own joke and nearly spilled a glass of brandy.

"Good evening, Colonel Nobody." General Tremont advanced from a group at the far end of the table.

"Good evening, sir." Nobody saluted.

"We are having a pleasant little dinner party, to honor the memory of General Whitmore."

"I hope he's more than a memory, sir. I hope he's still very much flesh and blood, and soon to be back with us once more."

Tremont started slightly, but joined the others as they raised their glasses at this wish. He turned before Nobody could read anything else from his flushed countenance.

The food now entered, brought on steaming platters by a number of servants. Each officer took a seat, six to a side, with Tremont at their head. Nobody sat on the far end from Tremont, to his left, facing the map.

"Good cheer to ye gentlemen, one and all." Tremont raised his glass. It obviously wasn't his first. "God bless the king!"

Each man drained his glass of brandy and water patriotically, although the ratio of each liquid changed dramatically from man to man. Several colonels only took a few drops of the stimulating spirits for flavor, while the general and two or three of the older campaigners evidently scorned to sully the purity of the brandy by mixing it with a weaker beverage. Nobody was the only one present with a cup of pure water, but he was an accepted oddity.

All set to work on the food. Nobody had heard that officers in England often feigned indolence toward their food, but here in Siberia, they knew that the best way to keep body and soul cheerfully together was by proper application of food and fire. Conversation prospered. Tremont was surprisingly affable, but as this increased with the lengthening hours, Nobody ascribed it to the spirits.

The guests commented frequently on the quality of the food. The colonel of the 80th went so far as to compliment Tremont punctually after every ten bites. Thankfully, he took large mouthfuls.

"Here's to the army in Siberia!" Tremont cried at last, staggering to his feet.

"May the winters be short and the Russians few," added another. "Or, if need be, the Russians short and the winters few."

The assemblage broke into great merriment at this—the more sober officers politely laughing, and the most tipsy ones nearly rolling off their seats.

Tremont wiped the tears from his eyes and raised his glass again. "Here's another to brandy, the one consolation in this frozen wasteland." The cheers were somewhat checked by the 80th's colonel's attempt to drain his glass while masticating a large mouthful. The choking once over, the company settled back down to genial comradeship.

Nobody ate his fair portion, and responded to the toasts properly, but his mind wandered from the festivities. He scrutinized the map on the opposite wall, reconsidering the best routes to the most likely areas where General Whitmore might be held. *If he's at Pradsk, there's a splendid chance of getting him out. If they put him in that new mysterious mountain fortress, however, it will be a much tougher nut to crack.* He calculated the distance roughly between Pradsk and Porsk, assuming the map was to scale.

"Colonel Nobody!"

He stiffened. Tremont stood unsteadily supporting himself with his left hand on the table, a wineglass in his right.

"Here'z to Colonel *No*body, who zeems to get hiz neck in mozst zhe 'portant bizness 'round here, no matter hiz parentage."

Nobody's chair clattered on the floor. The 80th's colonel paused mid-bite.

"What am I to understand by that remark?" Nobody clenched his teeth.

"What I zaid, you fool, what you think I mean?" Tremont scowled at the boy.

"If I heard correctly, you are questioning the honor of my parentage."

"Zo what if I do?"

He swallowed. "My parents were honorable, and my heritage is honorable." His voice was level, but within his head a fire had begun to burn.

"Honor'ble?" Tremont snorted. "Yez, zo honor'ble that you won't even zay who they were." He waved a trembling hand for effect. "P'raps 'twas Mishter NoOne and Missus, too, eh? Or maybe there washn't no marriage, 't'all?"

One of the more tipsy officers chortled noisily at this sally, and the chewing colonel resumed mastication. The plates rattled. A glass bounced off the table and shattered. The chewer froze.

Nobody leaned over the table end, his clenched fist on the wooden surface. "General Tremont, I resent that as an insult."

Tremont blinked solemnly at him, like a newly awakened owl. "What you shay?"

"I said that I resent your inference as an insult. My sword, General Tremont, is under your command, but my honor and that of my parents is not, and I warn you that my sword will act in *their* defense first, not yours."

The general sobered remarkably at this statement. "Do you hear that?" he cried to the other officers. "Ish that boy threatening me?"

"I am not threatening you," Nobody answered, before any of the others could. "I never threaten. I warn. If my warning is unheeded, I act." He folded his arms and calmly faced his superior officer.

Tremont, for one very rare occasion, was at a loss for words. The major-general sitting to his right whispered something in his ear. Tremont shook his head violently, but the major-general insisted.

"Never." Tremont swore. "I will not."

"You must," his more sober friend urged. Again, the general shook his head.

"I'm sure we can settle this comfortably," the major-general said more loudly, looking at Nobody. He sounded the reverse of comfortable. "If, sir, you would kindly give us an account of your parentage, it will be quite easy to find who is in the right."

Nobody felt his cheeks burn. "I am sorry, sir, but I cannot provide that information."

"But why?" pressed the mediator. "If they *are* honorable, as you say, what is there to hide?"

"If I answered that question, sir, there *wouldn't* be anything, because it would have been revealed."

The officers looked at each other in perplexity. It was against army regulations for an officer to challenge his superior to a duel. Somehow, they must be reconciled peacefully.

The major-general coughed. "What if the general were to ascribe his remark to a momentary indiscretion produced by an over-application of brandy?"

"I shall do no such thing!" Tremont declared indignantly.

Nobody remained silent, watching the faces of the other officers. The chewing colonel had finished his mouthful and looked about to compliment Tremont once more, but thought better of it, and began the next round.

"Come now," Colonel Campbell said quietly to Nobody, "just forgive it this once. What of that Scripture about turning the other cheek, eh?"

"What of the Scripture about honoring your father and mother?"

Campbell rubbed his chin thoughtfully. An awkward silence prevailed. Nobody still stood stiffly at the foot of the table, while Tremont stood at the head and held his trembling body up with both hands. At last, the major-general took another stab at reconciliation.

"Come, sirs, let us forget this slight occurrence, and shake hands quietly."

"No!" Tremont growled.

Nobody shook his head firmly.

"Doesn't matter," Tremont said, raising himself from a sort of torpid anger. "Won't see him for a long time anyway."

Nobody frowned. "May I ask the meaning of your words?"

"Going to England," the general muttered.

"You are going to England, sir?"

"No, you are."

Nobody stared at him blankly.

"Perhaps I should explain." The major-general gently guided Tremont back into his seat. "General Tremont has decided to send you to court with dispatches about our progress here, to the king."

Nobody started violently. "The king? Me? But, sir, that can't be. I'm a fighting colonel, not a diplomat. I can't be of any use at court, and I can here." He drank some water and pressed the cold glass between his hot hands.

"I'm sorry, Colonel Nobody, but the general has made up his mind. You may take your lieutenant colonel with you, if desired, and also a few of your men as servants."

"But, sir, I'm planning a raid to rescue General Whitmore from the Russians. Surely General Tremont does not wish that to be interrupted?" For a moment, Nobody thought he could detect a slight smile on the lips of the half-sober general, but Tremont said nothing.

"The general has intimated his desires to me, and they must be carried out, Colonel. You will be given the dispatches tomorrow."

Nobody saluted mechanically. "Very well, sir. If that's the case, I'll be ready." He slowly buckled his sword belt and placed the battered shako on his head. *England! The king!*

Chapter 11

Nobody strode silently back to his igloo, brooding upon the startling orders he had just received. The sentry knew his colonel's form too well to challenge; he simply moved aside to let Nobody pass. He crawled through the tunnel quietly, thinking of Edmund's reaction to his news, when the sound of a voice stopped him abruptly.

Who could have visited me tonight? The only ones I would expect a visit from are still politely carousing around Tremont's table. He cautiously extended his head into the main room, searching for signs of unwanted company.

"I say now, that's true." Edmund sat sprawled in his chair, one leg over a chair arm, and another on the table. "But since that's true, here's another question. Why is it that we always canter, and never gallop? Now mind you, I'm not questioning Noble's authority—I'm just wondering, that's all."

Nobody searched the room with his eyes. A candle stood on the table, and the second chair leaned crookedly against the opposite wall. No one hid by the small bookcase. No pair of eyes glittered in the darkness of the other tunnels. No one was there, it seemed. The packed snow slowly melted under his hot hands and soaked into the knees of his trousers.

"You can sit there spluttering and fuming till doomsday for all I care," Edmund exclaimed. "Here I am, posing an honest question, and you won't give me an answer!"

He's talking to the candle? Well, well, Edmund is an odd fellow. Nobody smiled. *But there's no reason to interrupt; let's hear a little more, shall we?*

"Now I'll tell you why you won't talk, spluttering fool." Edmund wagged a finger at the candle. "It's because you're an inanimate creation, and as such you have no brain, and if you had a brain it would long ago have melted away with the rest of the wax you are so impolitely dripping on my table."

Edmund frowned at the stream of melted wax which led down the side of the candlestick and onto the table. "I being an animate creation of the Lord have the right to talk, *and* to speculate. Wonder, in other words. Now what I wonder is this—why do we canter into battle, when galloping gives more momentum and gets us there faster? We could canter along," Edmund imitated the bouncing motion from his seat, "a nice, easy canter, which isn't exactly slow, but it gives the Russians plenty of time to prepare. Or, we could gallop splendidly along," the imitation grew faster, "in the style of the knights of old, and smash into the Russians before they have time to collect their dim wits."

Edmund folded his arms. "It's my firm opinion, dear fuming fellow, that Noble has something up his sleeve far more profound than his little 'harder to load' excuse."

Nobody quietly crawled out of the tunnel and stood up. "Sorry to interrupt your conversation. Please, do go on. It would be extremely enlightening to receive the candle's answer, I'm sure."

Edmund jumped. "Oh be quiet, Noble. Can't a fellow have a private talk without you poking an ear into it?"

"Certainly, and it will be a very private talk when the other party is a candle. You know the saying, the best secret is kept when one of those involved is dead. Well, not only is a candle dead, but it never was alive in the first place, so you should have no worries."

Edmund playfully threw a saddlebag at his chief. Nobody dodged, and pulled a chair for himself at the table.

"I told Jacques to take the tea off after you left. I believe he's in one of the spare rooms, so I'll just hop out to order a new cup." Edmund rose, but Nobody motioned him to resume a seat.

"No, Ed, there's no need. I'd rather let Jacques get some training in England. I think it could produce a marked effect in his tea-making skills."

"England? What are you talking about? You'll be waiting an awfully long time for a cup of tea if it requires Jacques to go to England first."

"Not as long as you think."

"What do you mean?"

"Well, you see, I'm going to England."

Edmund laughed. "Is that so? Well, that's grand. I suppose you'll be seeing the king, too, and shaming all his courtiers by your sparkling uniform and cutting wit?" He smiled complacently.

Nobody was surprised. "I don't know anything about the uniform and wit, but the king, yes. How did you know?"

Edmund waved his hand. "Oh come now, that's very good. By the way, what did Tremont want you at his dinner party for? You're not usually invited to those sorts of things."

"And believe me, I'll not soon be seeking another invitation. But I just told you why, and somehow you seem to have already known."

Edmund leaned forward, resting all four chair legs on the floor. "What do you mean? I was just playing along with your joke about going to England."

"But it wasn't a joke."

"Wasn't a joke? You're trying to say that you're actually going to England!"

"No, I'm not *trying* to say, I've already said, *yes*, I'm going to England."

Edmund leaped to his feet. "Why on this white earth are *you* going to England?"

"You've already said in part."

"I have?"

"Yes. I'm taking dispatches to the king."

Edmund whistled. "That's a stunner. England. The king. What next? But why are *you* going?"

"I asked the same question." Nobody rose and began pacing.

"What did Tremont say?"

"Tremont? Oh, he didn't say anything. Too drunk. No, his mediator responded for him, somewhere along the lines of 'ask me no questions, and I'll tell you no lies,' but a much more polite version, of course."

Edmund heaved a deep breath. "Well, that *is* a shocker. England! So when do we go?"

"*We?*" Nobody turned to hide a smile. "Who said 'we?'"

"I did, of course, though I don't see how it matters. When do we go?"

"Why Edmund, I don't remember saying anything about 'we.' I do remember saying that *I* was going to London, and would be taking along a few trusty fellows as servants, but I don't see where that applies to you."

"But of course I'm going!" Edmund looked indignant. "You couldn't get along without me!"

"How's that?"

"You fool! Do you think I'd let you go to the king's court alone? You'd get into a scrape within the first ten minutes without me to watch your back and advise. And you say you're taking some of the men, and you're not taking me?" Edmund rose wrathfully. "Why if that's not the—"

"Of course you're going, Ed. I'd be lost without you."

Edmund laughed in relief, wiped the perspiration from his forehead, and resumed his seat.

"You don't take jokes very well, Ed. By the way, did you said that Jacques was in here somewhere?"

Edmund nodded.

"Jacques!" Nobody called.

"Here, sir." The Frenchman bustled out of a side tunnel. "Are you ready for your tea?"

"No tea for me, Jacques. How would you like to learn how to make a *real* cup of English tea, in England?"

The Frenchman scratched his small head. "I am sorry, sir, but I do not understand vhat you are saying."

"Well, it's like this. The lieutenant colonel and I are going to England, and we'd like you to come along."

Jacques looked doubtful. "I do not know, sir. I have always heard zhat zhey are barbarians zhere."

Edmund laughed heartily at this sally, but quieted down when he saw that Jacques was serious.

Nobody tried to subdue a smile. "Er, well, Jacques, you may consider this a missionary effort to—to establish civilization in the British Isles. What do you say?"

"May I ask vhy ve are going, sir?"

"Of course. I have to carry dispatches to the king, and no," he said quickly, as Jacques was about to speak, "you don't need to ask why *I* am being sent, because I don't know."

"I vas actually not going to ask you zhat, sir. I vas going to ask if zhat Irishman vas going vihz us?"

"If by 'that Irishman' you mean O'Malley, then yes. Is that a problem?"

"Not a problem, sir." Jacques shook his head ruefully. "It is only that I do not zhink ve vill be able to teach zhe natives civilization vhen ve have a barbarian vihz us."

"I 'eard that!" said a voice from one of the passages, and a shock of flaming red hair burst into the room.

"Why, O'Malley, what are you doing here?" Nobody asked in amusement.

"I was layin' oop a store o' firewood, sir, and couldn't help hearin' Jack Frog here impunin' me good name." The Irishman raised his head proudly, and banged it on one of the frozen slabs of snow. He quickly resumed a humbler posture.

Nobody laughed. "Don't worry, O'Malley, if it gets too bad you can file a suit for libel in the English court system. Will you come?"

"Indayd I will, sir, and gladly, wherever and whyever it playses yerself. I'm thinkin' there'd be no chance tae visit the ould country, now, would there?"

"I'm afraid not, O'Malley. The less time away from here the better."

"Aye, sir, I understand. I was jist thinkin' o' me ould grandmother, as still sends me letters every two months. Very well, sir, ye call me when I'm needed."

The two soldiers saluted and withdrew. Before their voices had faded in the distance, O'Malley was telling Jacques about the glories of Ireland, interrupted by passionate denials from Jacques.

"Oh those two." Edmund shook his head and laughed. "It's a wonder that they get along so well."

Nobody nodded, but said nothing. He was now wrapped deeply in thought, considering this latest move on the chess-board of life. Somehow, his plans to rescue General Whitmore must have come to the ears of Tremont. Truly this was a brilliant idea to get him out of the way for a time, under the pretense of doing him honor.

"Noble?"

"Mmm?"

"Are you excited about going to England?"

"Excited? I don't know. I've never been there before."

"Never been there?" Edmund was certainly excited. "I didn't know that. You have truly and honestly never been to England?"

"No, I have not, Edmund. As I said before, there is much that you don't know about me."

"Yes I know, but I always assumed you'd been to England. Have you ever been out of Siberia?"

"Yes, but I spent most of that time on the sea."

"So then this should be a splendid new experience for you."

"Yes, I suppose so," Nobody said thoughtfully. "It will certainly be a new experience. Whether it's splendid or not—we shall see. To tell you the truth, I have not the slightest idea of what to say to the king."

Chapter 12

The London docks were teeming with life. Wagons and carts came and went in a steady stream, leaving behind piles of wooden barrels and packing crates. Meat, salty enough to remind the men of the ocean upon which they sailed; biscuits, in which barrels the Adams and Eves of a hundred weevil colonies were just now exploring paradise; water, fresh at the moment, ready to undergo the proper amount of seasoning before becoming stale and sordid enough to suit maritime standards.

Porters steered round the stacked barrels and lines of grunting men, while bewildered civilians scurried at their shirttails, keeping at least one steady eye on the great trunks slung negligently over their shoulders. Wobbly-legged sailors swaggered amidst the confusion, laughing and chatting among each other in their mixed language of sea slang and profanity.

Numbers of ships lay alongside the wooden wharves, allowing the stream of provisions to climb their gangplanks and disappear below into the uncharted depths of their holds. A good many more, unable to find an open space at the wharf, lay anchored in the river. A fleet of small boats plied to and fro, some bearing passengers from arriving ships, some dropping them off for an outbound voyage. Rough blades and loose women mingled with lords and ladies. A host of bold vendors hawked their wares over the ships' bulwarks, giving sailors one last chance to spend any farthings leftover from the public house.

One of these boats, propelled towards the shore by two oarsmen, contained a little knot of men wearing the brilliant uniform of His Majesty's service, somewhat worse the wear from a long sea voyage.

Nobody scanned the scene solemnly. "Is it as busy as this every day?" he asked, looking to Edmund.

"Every day of the week. Believe me, there's many times I formed a part of that stream of humanity, looking for a chance job to fill my starving belly." Edmund rubbed his stomach at the thought.

"I would expect a city this large to have innumerable sources of work."

Nobody eyed the clustered buildings, which raised their heads high in the air as if trying to penetrate the thick clouds of smoke and fog and find some fresh air and unsullied sunlight.

"Oh, there's plenty of work," Edmund agreed, "and plenty of workers, too. London is England's sewer. If you lose your job, go to London. If you get into a scrape with the law, go to London. If your house burned down to the ground, go to London. If the moon dripped blood and drowned your family, go to London!"

Nobody smiled. "I presume that last occurrence was pulled from the realms of fancy?"

"Yes, but I've heard true stories in London nearly as improbable as a wounded moon."

Nobody leaned back against the rough wooden planks, shifting uncomfortably in search of a few more inches of leg space. He sat in the bow of the boat, at right angles with Edmund and Jacques. O'Malley sat on the other side of the oars, across from Somerset, the reporter, who was busily writing in the ever-present notebook. The Irishman tapped his knee.

"Helloo there, Pen-and-Paper. What's sae interestin' aboot yer notebook as to exclude yer fellow companions from yer frindly soci'ty?"

Somerset raised his head quickly. "I'm trying to complete a description of the voyage, and the picturesque aspect of the docks."

"Will the *Times* be a-readin' it?"

"Most likely, yes, although I am reserving some of the information for a book I'm writing."

"A book?" O'Malley snapped his finger contemptuously. "Niver read one. What's it aboot?"

"It's called 'Life With the Army: a True Story of the Siberian Wilderness,' written by Alexander Somerset, of course."

"Indayd. Are we in it?"

"Yes, you are. The colonel is a central character, which is why I came along with him to London, instead of staying in Siberia."

"But ain't it hard tae write aboot the war from London? There wouldn't hae been any need to sind a reporter out."

"I don't think the *Times* will mind. They want to know about the colonel. And the only newsworthy things that happened in Siberia seemed to involve Colonel Nobody. With him away, I doubt there will be anything to write about, besides snow and cold."

The rowers backed oars to escape colliding with another boat. The two wherry-men shouted a few derogatory epithets at the other vessel, and, their injured dignities restored, recommenced rowing.

"Why do you think," Nobody said to Somerset, "that your book would sell?"

"Why not?" Somerset shrugged. "People are interested in the war. Why wouldn't they want to get a first-hand perspective?"

"I'm not so sure that people *are* interested in the war."

Nobody removed the battered hat from his head and let the cool London air blow through his hair. He traced the creased leather with his finger. The plume had been shorn off long ago. *Decidedly annoying things, anyway,* he mused. *I suppose I must go in for a new uniform before seeing the king.*

"Not interested, sir?" Somerset said slowly, drawing him back to earth. "Why would the *Times* send a reporter out if there wasn't interest?"

"And why would the said *Times* be the only paper to send a reporter, and an inexperienced one, at that? I mean no offense, but you are not high in the ranks of journalists. I don't say you are a bad writer. I've never read your writing. Still, you are young, and must prove yourself, especially for such a notable paper as the *Times*."

Somerset winced a little, but seemed to take it in good spirit. "So you think the public doesn't care about the war in Siberia?"

"I do not. It is an isolated conflict, involving few of our regiments. The Russian and English governments make no mention of it in diplomacy. It's much like the 1500s, when Drake and his captains fought the Spaniards on the High Seas, not bothering to inquire whether the two countries had any formal hostilities. Most people have no idea what we're fighting about, and I don't blame them. I still am not quite sure, after several years of intensive study and involvement."

Another boat threatened their safe progress, causing a similar exchange of compliments between the rowers. Somerset continued.

"You don't mean to say that you don't know why you're fighting, sir?"

Nobody smiled slightly. "Well, I do have some idea. You see, somewhere in the hazy days of antiquity, someone's cousin's mother's nephew's uncle's great-grandson's daughter married another fellow of similar origin. This fellow somehow fell into bad grace with a relative of his wife, who happened to be in power. Their descendants continued to worry and bother about things, until, quite recently, one of the sides decided they liked the Ottoman empire."

Nobody readjusted his cloak. "I don't believe the Ottomans have weather like this. At any rate, the said cousin's mother's nephew's etc.'s descendant having evidenced this friendship with the Turks, the other side naturally took offense, and forthwith confronted the *first* side. After a complimentary exchange of insults, they took the only reasonable course, and declared war; a private agreement, you understand. And here we are."

Somerset blinked rapidly. "I'm sorry sir, but—what's the war about?"

Edmund laughed out loud, and Nobody smiled broadly. "Somerset, the more I study it, the more confused I become. My orders are to fight, and that's what I do. The important thing is that we win."

The wherry finally touched the dock. Nobody leaped out, tossed a few coins to the rowers, and nodded for Edmund to lead the way.

"Please, sir, just one question more?" Somerset asked.

Nobody sighed. "You *are* a reporter, aren't you? Very well, fire your last shot."

As Somerset opened his mouth, O'Malley, who had been looking in wonder at the surrounding confusion, tripped on a pile of rubbish and fell forward. He instinctively grasped the the young reporter's coat for support, and they both tumbled into a puddle of mud and filth.

Mud splashed in all directions, but most of it landed on the indignant Jacques.

"You *boeuf*!" he spluttered at O'Malley, frantically pulling out a clean handkerchief. "Vhy can you not look at zhe road? You are a clumsy, ill-mannered, barbarian *boeuf*!"

Edmund was holding his stomach in laughter. Nobody smiled and gave a hand to the grimy reporter. The Irishman jumped to his feet and glowered at Jacques.

"It's not *me* fault that they had to be puttin' rubbish in the road." He smeared the mud on his face with an equally soiled sleeve. "Now quit your jabberin' and tell me what a 'boof' is before I dunk *ye* in this puddle."

Jacques executed a neat pirouette and took refuge on the other side of Nobody. "It is not *my* fault zhat you do not know French. I may call you vhatever I vish." He placed his hands on his hips and looked defiantly at his tall friend.

O'Malley growled. "Colonel, ye know Frinch, I'm told. What lies is the Frog sayin' about me, a respictable Irishman?"

Nobody laughed merrily. "I'm sorry, O'Malley, but if Jacques doesn't care to enlighten you, it's not my place. Perhaps you should find a French tutor and try to learn the language again, so that you can understand each other better." He signaled two hansom cabs.

"A Frinch tutor?" The Irishman snorted. "Niver in a hoondred years again will ye find Patrick O'Malley degradin' his natural language and twistin' his tongue into *that* unnatural gibberish."

The cabs pulled up, and the two drivers jumped from their seats to open the doors.

"I pay for both," Nobody said. "Here's somewhat extra for any damage this mud may cause your cushions."

The drivers tipped their caps and invited them to enter. Edmund and the reporter took their places in the first, and Nobody prepared to follow. Jacques tapped his arm.

"Certainly, sir, you vill not force me to accompany *zhat*!" Jacques pointed at the Irishman.

"Get in, Jacques. That's an order. I want you two back on friendly terms by the time we reach our lodgings."

The Frenchman breezed past O'Malley, his nose lifted high in disdain. The doors closed as soon as the two parties were situated, and the cabs rattled off into London.

Nobody handed Somerset his handkerchief. "I'm sorry for your misfortune, though I must confess, it was rather amusing. What were you going to say before O'Malley invited you to a bath?"

"A bath indeed," the reporter grumbled. "I intended to ask why you are so well known in England, if they don't care about the war? Even in Cornwall, a place of much work and little else, I heard the miners discussing rumors about a strange colonel in Siberia."

Nobody waved his hand. "British curiosity. A tendency to stick one's nose into another's business. If they think they smell a mystery, they'll try to beat information out of any poor soul concerned in it. Once they find out the details it is no longer of interest; at the most, a nine days' wonder."

Chapter 13

The cabs pulled up at a small public house in a respectable neighborhood. Above the door hung a thick wooden sign, which was loftily inscribed "The Painter's Paradise." A rough palette was etched in the oak and daubed with bright colors. According to the cabby this was a quiet resort for aspiring artists and writers attempting to find a niche in the competitive London market.

The rooms were tidy. Nobody didn't need fancy apartments. He was used to army tents and igloos. He hoped to spend as little time as possible in London—there was no telling what damage the vindictive Tremont might be wreaking upon the 42nd in his absence.

Somerset cleaned up and left to report to the *London Times* office. Nobody and Edmund headed out for a new uniform. Edmund knew the streets of London as well as Nobody knew the length of his own sword, having lived, slept, and eaten on them for years. Here, too, he had learned how to command, and from the stories he told, London's street urchins were scarcely easier to control than England's soldiers.

Nobody assigned Jacques and O'Malley to purchase four scabbards, he being doubtful that the Londoners would appreciate the sight of naked blades.

The moment the two veterans left the inn's threshold they were captured by a stream of humanity and whisked past dozens of gaudy storefronts and soot-covered homes. O'Malley, bewildered by the hustle and bustle, astonished by the rainbows of colorful clothing, and sickened by the gutter-stench, stalked like a giant of old among the forms of his lesser mortals, while Jacques nimbly followed in his footsteps.

Occasionally he paused, attracted by some peculiar object displayed in the windows. Each time he did so Jacques was thrust unceremoniously into his back by the force of the traffic, reminding the Irishman of his surroundings and impelling him forward once more. At last, Jacques grasped his tunic and hauled him into the end of a small, dingy alley, quiet save for the snores of two besotted laborers.

"*Ma foi*! Zhis is a busy place," Jacques said, catching his breath.

"It's nothin' like back home in Antrim." O'Malley peeked down the crowded street. "I think there's more men on this one street than in all Antrim put togither!"

Jacques shrugged. "It is large—for zhe English. But to see a truly *great* city, you must travel to Pairee, zhe city of lights, zhe empress of zhe world!"

"Impriss of the world? I didn't know as they ran the press gangs in France."

Jacques maintained a stony silence until his comrade was finished laughing.

"Now," he said coldly, "shall ve get back to our duty? Ve must find a military shop."

They reentered the stream of humanity, and, by dint of numerous inquiries, obtained the location of a tailor's shop which also sold military accessories. The shop was small but well lit. Rolls of fabric lay in confusion on every available surface; chairs, tables, shelves, and window-ledges were all occupied by the tailor's stock.

In the center of the room stood a tall, proud-looking man, impeccably dressed. He rubbed his left eye-brow as Jacques and O'Malley entered, drawing attention to a glass ball that filled the eye-socket. The tailor, a gangly-legged skinny fellow, with a coat of pins for armor and a measuring tape for scarf, bustled round the room lifting rolls of fabric according to his patron's direction. He looked up in ill-disguised annoyance as the two soldiers stepped over his threshold.

"What do you want, can't you see that I'm busy?" he snapped, not pausing in his work.

"We're lookin' fer a couple scabbards," O'Malley replied. "Do ye have any in stock?"

"Yes, yes, in the corner. Pick what you want and put the money on the counter." The tailor thrust a handful of pins into his mouth, effectively closing the conversation.

The Irishman meandered over to a small rack, on which rested a number of swords and scabbards. Two plain sheaths sufficed for he and Jacques, and they selected two more decorated scabbards for the officers.

"Well, my men," said a deep, rich voice, "did some comrades play a trick and take your scabbards?"

The soldiers turned respectfully to the well-dressed man. "Nay, sir," O'Malley answered, "we haven't had scabbards fer some years noow. We're from Siberia, ye see, and we don't wear 'em there."

The man looked surprised. "Siberia? How fascinating. Then you must belong to the army presently engaged in battling the Russian Cossacks?"

"Zhat is true," Jacques said quickly, unwilling to leave the entire conversation to O'Malley. "Ve have been zhere for many years."

The rich man took a small box from his coat pocket, opened it, inhaled some snuff, sneezed, and shut the box. "What do you do in the great city of London?"

"We're with our colonel, sir, Colonel Nobody of the 42nd." The man started slightly as the name was pronounced, but said nothing. "He's come tae see the king, don't ye know, and has a report or somethin' o' the like for his Royal Majisty."

"How fascinating." The patron calmly flicked some stray bits of powder that had fallen from his wig onto his shoulders. O'Malley dropped the required payment on the counter, and the tailor paused for a moment to verify the quantity and quality. Satisfied, he resumed his labors. They tipped their hats to the rich patron, who nodded slightly in return, and then joined the busy bustle outside.

The two soldiers felt more comfortable walking the streets of London knowing that their uncovered swords were no longer objects of general interest and discussion. They made their way to a quieter street in which dozens of wooden stalls were set up, hawking beer, cheese, books, and a huge quantity of handkerchiefs. A group of street urchins lounged on a pile of refuse.

The Irishman bought two hunks of bread and cheese and sat down with Jacques on an overturned barrel.

"Ah," Jacques sighed, "zhis bread is not vorth two bites of a French loaf. England may have her advantages, but I am yet to find zhem."

"Ye know what, Jack? Ye're a conceited bigot, and that's the truth. If France had the market on everythin' that's good, there'd be thousands o' folks flockin' there every day, and ye'd have to go back to the gillotine jist to thin the numbers a bit."

"As if ve vant zhe riff-raff of Europe?"

One of the urchins gave a shrill whistle and pointed to the Frenchman. "Why lookee 'ere, Bill!" cried a small lad with white flesh and gaunt cheeks. "It's a Frenchy all decked out in 'is Majesty's slops!"

The others crowded round the barrel, grinning at Jacques's lofty look of disdain.

"P'raps 'e's a spy," suggested one lad.

"Or one o' Boney's chaps caught out o' work," added another.

The pale boy stuck his hands in his pockets, puffed out his chest, and sniffed at the disdainful soldiers. "Why don't you out with the story, eh? What's a Frog doin' in 'is Majesty's uniform?"

Jacques tasted his bread delicately, sparing no glance for the insolent urchin.

"Looks like 'e's a quiet chap," commented the boy, gravely scrutinizing the soldier's face. "I didn't know they made quiet Frenchers." He turned to his laughing friends and waved a hand majestically at the smallest of the band. "I'd bet a five p'nd if I had it that Scratcher can get 'im to talk. Whatdyee say, Scratch?"

The other boy scratched his dirty cheek thoughtfully, suggesting the origin of his name. "I'll do it, chief." His grin revealed two rows of dirty teeth. Without warning he stepped forward, snatched the Frenchman's shako from his head, and sprang out of reach.

Jacques leaped to his feet. "*Coquin*! Give me my hat at vonce!"

"He talks!" The leader laughed. "Here, Scratch, be a dear, the genn'lman wants 'is 'at."

The shako flew over the Frenchman's short head and landed in the pale boy's arms. "Good day." He bowed. "Don't worry, I'll keep your 'at safe and sound." Without another word he darted for an alley, his companions scattering likewise.

Jacques roared and dashed off in pursuit. "Arrah," O'Malley grumbled, stuffing the uneaten bread in his pocket. "And jist when I was injoyin' a bit o' rest!"

The lad evidently knew the tangled web of streets well, and he used this knowledge to his advantage, dodging through the dark alleys like a sprite. The furious Frenchman struggled with his sword as he ran and finally managed to pull it from the new scabbard, his natural reaction upon seeing a flying enemy.

"Arrah!" O'Malley repeated. "The fool! We're in Loondon, not Siberia. He'll be havin' us picked up and thrown into prison, fer sure!"

The boy scurried down an alley towards a small group of citizens. One man had a bucket of whitewash, which he daubed onto a dirty wall with a dirtier brush. Behind him sat an artist in threadbare clothing with a splattered palette in his hand, rapidly sketching the face of an obliging housewife, whose husband stood proudly watching her a few paces off.

Without breaking stride the urchin dodged between the whitewasher and the woman, but Jacques was not so agile. His short legs, still somewhat unsteady from the lengthy voyage, refused to convey their owner in any other route than that which led straight through the unwary whitewasher. O'Malley grimaced as the bucket flew through the air and splattered limey slops over the housewife's red face and portly figure.

Jacques plowed ahead, leaving O'Malley to bear the husband's rage.

"What are you doing!" The man raised his fists and blocked the Irishman's way. "Is that wild sword-waving *thing* your friend?"

"Er, well, ahem," O'Malley faltered, "you see, he's more, what ye could call, er, an associate."

"What does he think he is! He can't run around the streets of London knockin' down men and spilling buckets on innocent women!"

"Well, ye see, he's a Frinchman."

The angry man stopped abruptly. "A Frenchman? From France?"

"Aye, that's where most of thim come from."

The man nodded his head knowingly. "That explains it," he said, "but it doesn't explain this! Oh, my poor darling wife." He pointed towards the woman, who was frantically wiping gobs of whitewash from her red face and swearing with gusto. The young painter listened in horror, then turned his back and covertly added a few lines to the canvas. The face changed from a cherub to a gargoyle.

"And look at her beautiful complexion all marred by the whitewash!" groaned the man, wiping a stray tear from his eye.

O'Malley began to say that there wasn't much of a "beautiful complexion" to be marred, but he thought better of it, and instead offered a shilling as restitution.

Fearful that this delay had separated him from the Frenchman, O'Malley redoubled his speed, only to find Jacques prowling suspiciously round the next corner.

"Ye left me in a sorry mess," O'Malley growled indignantly, but Jacques waved him off.

"I saw him come round zhis corner, and I know he could not have made it down any of zhe ozher streets. He must be here somevhere."

"That's all very well, Jack Frog, but I've got a bit o' me mind to give ye before ye go off upsettin' any more whitewashers." He stepped in front of the Frenchman, effectually blocking forward movement. "Now ye listen tae me. We're in Loondon, noow, not Siberia. Ye can't be goin' round wi' ye're sword in yer hand. Put it back in yer new scabbard."

"But it is my habit to chase zhe fleeing enemy vihz a sword in my hand! It inspires fear and terror in zheir very marrow!"

"That lad ain't ye're inimy, not tae mintion that I doubt there's enough marrow in his bones to hold much fear. Now put the sword back." O'Malley shook his head wonderingly while Jacques reluctantly returned the blade to its scabbard. "An' ye say we *Irish* are barbarians? Paris must be an awful exciting place tae live in."

Jacques tossed his head. "My shako vas stolen, and I consider it my military duty to recover it or die!"

"Now look at me, Jack." O'Malley grasped his shoulders roughly. "My, but ye're short wi'out ye're shako." He smiled broadly, but Jacques stamped impatiently. "Now don't look behind ye, but I see the boy right now." Jacques froze. "Slowly turn as if ye're agreein' wi' me (no, that'd be deceptive, because ye nivir do agree wi' me), so jist turn quiet like, an' we'll jump the fellow."

They leaped at an overturned barrel, in whose depths O'Malley had seen a pair of flashing eyes. He did not notice that the eyes were yellow. The cat came out fighting, snarling demonically and scratching with all four paws. Jacques and O'Malley tumbled backwards into the street and the feline dashed over their prone bodies, leaving a deep scratch on the Irishman's cheek.

A fit of laughter greeted this mishap. The boy whom they were pursuing emerged from the shadow of a doorway, holding his sides in glee.

"Strike me dead if you aren't a pair of odd chaps." He slapped his leg. "Sure, I ain't the best fed boy you'll find on the streets, an' that's the truth, but I still wouldn't fit in a keg like that." He pointed disdainfully at the wooden cask.

Jacques struggled to regain his feet, but O'Malley calmly thrust him back down and stood up himself. "Come now, boy, ye've had yer fun. Now how aboot handin' over me frind's shako?"

"Here it is and welcome to it." The lad tossed it back. "I only took it for fun. I knew you'd chase."

Jacques sullenly replaced the hat on his head.

"That's a' right," O'Malley said, clapping his companion on the shoulder, "no grudges now." He turned to the boy. "Can ye tell us how tae get back to our inn, since ye've led us sich a merry chase this afternoon?"

"Aye, I could get you to most places in London, if you wanted to, or, what's more like, if I wanted to. Where do you come from?"

"They call it 'The Painter's Paradise,' but I don't know what the street name might be."

The boy cocked an eyebrow. "You paint?" he asked doubtfully.

"Faith, no, nothin' o' the sort. My colonel's taken up residince there fer a few days, as a nice quiet place. You know it?"

"Sure, I know it." Without further ceremony he walked away, followed by the two soldiers. "Where's your colonel from?"

"We're new in from Siberia."

"Siberia? Ain't that jolly."

"Aye, jolly cold."

"Humph. Don't hear much about the war out there. Ain't that where that Colonel Nobody chap is?"

"Aye, most times, but at the prisint he's in Loondon."

"London! Why, I had Mary read me the last paper, and there weren't any mentions of him in there. How did you know?"

O'Malley smiled. "Well, ye see, I came with him. He's me colonel."

"Your colonel!" the pale lad cried enthusiastically. "That's jolly splendid. He's an honor to our race!"

"He's an honor all right," the Irishman agreed, "but I'm not English, ye see, so I can't say as I share the honor."

The boy glanced disdainfully at the tall soldier. "As if I thought you was English." He snorted. "I mean he's an honor for us boys. You tall fellows, and even the short ones like your friend, look down their noses at us. Sure there's some bad fellows among us, but boys ain't that bad, generally, and I'm glad one decided to stand up and prove it!"

He stopped on a busy street, which the soldiers easily recognized as that on which the inn stood.

"There's your inn," he said. "Don't get lost on the way. You tell your colonel that if he ever wants some help in London, or wants to know about the goings on, just ask me, and I'll tell him if I know, and find him a boy who can, if I don't. There's not much that happens in London that can't be pieced together out of a handful of street boys, chimney sweeps, and the like."

O'Malley thanked the boy, and Jacques also threw in a few kind words. He was quick to anger, but also quick to cool. The lad waved a hand airily and disappeared down the narrow alley, leaving the soldiers to traverse the last short distance alone.

Chapter 14

Colonel Nobody was led to a magnificent room deep within the frowning brick walls of Saint James's Palace. His uniform was fresh and spotless, but he still felt plain and insignificant among the crowd of brilliant noblemen and applicants to the king's pleasure. He gained a little confidence by looking at the gilt-edged paintings on the walls—if someone took the trouble to paint battle scenes of men looking just like him, then he couldn't look too out of place.

A marble fireplace, which a servant whispered had been brought from Paris by the Duke of Wellington, was built into the right wall. An enormous chandelier hung suspended from the ceiling in ostentatious splendor, covered with a rich ormolu gilt. Nobody wondered how many igloos could have been lighted by that single candle-holder.

His attention was soon captured by the figure at the end of the carpeted room, where three steps led up to a footstool, which in turn led to a throne, and upon that throne sat the king. Not *a* king, *the* King, William IV, ruler and monarch of the British Empire. Above his head hung a canopy of crimson velvet, with sweeping curtains in the rear, upon which was embroidered the shield of the United Kingdom, held betwixt a horse and lion, and surmounted by a royal helmet.

A minister of state stood before his ruler, close enough to be heard easily by the royal ear, but keeping a respectful distance between the occupant of the dais and himself.

"Your Majesty," the minister was saying, "he is an officer from the Siberian front, with dispatches from General Whitmore."

William IV sat calmly on his throne, arrayed in rich garments of silk and a dark robe. He filled the seat well—his bulky stomach, meaty legs, and fat cheeks spoke for a life of well-fed complacency.

"What is the name of the officer who wishes to see me?" he asked majestically, glancing at the group waiting on the other end of the room. His eyes were somewhat dimmed by advancing age, but they still showed some of the fire and spark that once earned him the title 'Sailor King.' Many a jolly British tar had learned to love those same burning eyes, at a time when he had little expectation of receiving the throne.

The minister of state hesitated slightly. He gently touched his left eyebrow—a glass eye rolled in the socket. "He does not have a proper name, Your Majesty, but doubtless you have heard of the 'Boy Colonel,' often called 'Nobody?'"

"I have. Is it he?"

"It is, Your Majesty."

"Present him to me."

"Yes, Your Majesty."

The minister beckoned the boy to approach. Nobody felt deep gratitude in his heart to the tailor who had spent the previous day stitching, snipping, and fitting. A generous gift had furnished wings to the tailor's needle, but it would still have taken too long, had he not had some garments on hand that needed little alteration. He stepped forward gracefully, and bowed a little less so. There had not been much use for bowing and scraping in Siberia.

"Your Highness," announced the minister in a loud voice, "Colonel Nobody of His Royal Majesty's 42nd Regiment of Mounted Infantry."

Nobody bowed again, and stood with a rapidly beating heart, waiting his monarch's pleasure.

"I have been informed that you bear dispatches to me from General Whitmore, in Siberia?"

Nobody moistened his lips with his tongue. The room's splendor awed him. Buildings in Siberia were built for warmth and security, not show.

"Your Royal Majesty, it is my privilege to bear dispatches, but not from General Whitmore, for he has been captured by the Russians. General Tremont has taken his place, until negotiations can be concluded for his return."

The minister started slightly, shaking grains of white powder from the plentiful wig. The king nodded for him to go on. Pulling the bundle of dispatches from his breast pocket, Nobody offered them to William, who waved his hand at his minister.

"I will study them at my convenience," the king said, "but I wish to ask your own opinions concerning our war in Siberia."

"We have fought several battles, Your Majesty, and have been victorious, but it is the winter season, and not much has been done to carry your standards farther into Siberia. I believe that General Tremont is preparing plans for a spring campaign."

"Ah, yes, General Tremont. Are you satisfied with his direction of the war?"

Nobody hesitated. He didn't want to sound insubordinate to his commanding officer, but on the other hand, he had no intention of lying. "It is always a soldier's duty to obey his general's orders," he replied.

"That is true." The king looked grave. "I did not ask of your duty. Are you satisfied under his orders?"

Nobody shifted uncomfortably. "Your Majesty, it is true that I prefer the command of General Whitmore, and look forward earnestly to his release."

"Is there reason to believe the negotiations will be lengthy?"

"If we offered an officer of similar rank in the Russian army, as we now hold captive, Your Majesty, I do not think there would be any difficulties in effecting the exchange."

"Then your wish will soon be satisfied."

"I hope so, Your Majesty, but I am not assured."

"And why is this?" The king raised a scented handkerchief to his forehead, relieving the pale skin of a slight moisture.

"Your Majesty, General Tremont has not offered any prisoners of high rank in exchange for General Whitmore. A colonel is the highest rank he has presented, which, in my opinion, would be insulting to the dignity of General Whitmore."

The king frowned. "How now? A colonel. Tell me more of this General Tremont. I am not familiar with his career."

Nobody tightened his grip on his shako. Tremont was not a favorite subject. "He fought for a short time during the last war with Napoleon, but I am not aware of his occupation between that war and this. For several years he has served in Siberia, and was appointed during the autumn of last year to second-in-command. I am not aware of much more in his history, Your Majesty."

"What of his personality? Come, young man," the king said kindly, smiling slightly, "speak bluntly, as becomes an officer of my army. As you know, I am sometimes called the 'Sailor King,' and it is refreshing to hear an officer who is untainted by politics and petty disputes. It reminds me of my earlier days."

Nobody bowed his head in acknowledgment of the command. "As you have asked for my honest opinions, Your Majesty, I will answer you accordingly. As a man, General Tremont is known to be a loose-liver and profligate. As an officer, I have had no reason to admire his decisions, and some reason to suspect a jealousy towards myself, perhaps because I am on very good terms with General Whitmore. I was preparing an expedition to rescue the general from his captors, when I was ordered to bring these dispatches to you."

The king nodded gravely. "Why do you mention this?"

"I would not have, Your Majesty, were it not for your royal command to speak bluntly. However, it is my belief that General Tremont had been informed of my preparations, and as it is not normal for colonels to be selected as messengers, the suspicion did enter my mind that he did not want General Whitmore to be rescued at this time." Nobody slowly let out his breath, relieved at having finally made the plunge, but tensely waiting the king's reaction.

William smiled. "Colonel Nobody, you have certainly fulfilled my order to speak bluntly. I thank you, and will see that this matter is looked into."

Nobody, seeing that his interview was now over, made another bow, and backed away. As he was led through the halls to the palace entrance he was stopped by a well-dressed man who wore spectacles and appeared to be of continual short breath.

The man consulted a paper which he held in his right hand. "Do I have the honor to address Colonel Nobody, of His Royal Majesty's 42nd Mounted Infantry?" he panted.

"I am he."

"His Royal Majesty King William IV (God bless him) has extended to you an invitation to his royal ball, tomorrow evening at seven. He has furthermore particularly requested your presence," the man continued, again consulting his paper, "as he wishes to introduce you to one of His Royal Majesty's wards."

Nobody forced a smile to appear on his lips, and bowed. "Please convey my acceptance and thanks to His Majesty."

The chamberlain retired. Nobody exited the great wooden doors and left the palace grounds. A bitter wind blew, and he drew his new coat more closely round his shoulders until a hansom arrived.

"A ball!" he muttered. "Me? I want to get back to Siberia, not sit around London attending balls. The king's ward? Humph. Probably some young noble eating his heart out at court, and thinking of the glorious prospects the army is supposed to hold. A ball? Why, I don't even dance!"

Chapter 15

The stately passages of St. James's Palace glittered with myriads of lights, giving Nobody and Edmund an opportunity to examine the many paintings on the walls as they walked slowly behind a servant to the ballroom. They were greeted at the door by the lord chamberlain himself.

"Greetings, Colonel Nobody and Lieutenant Colonel Burke," he said, reading their names from a long sheet of paper. "You are early."

Nobody frowned. "Early? My utmost apologies, sir, but I am sure the clock struck seven just a few moments ago."

The lord chamberlain smiled. "That it did, that it did. I had forgotten, you are not from London. It has become fashionable of late to *be* late. Still, I expect all to be here before eight o'clock, that being the time set for His Majesty's entrance. Ah!" he exclaimed, catching sight of rustling dresses and top hats down the hall, "here are some more. You may leave your cloaks and hats in the room to my right."

The two officers bowed and did as requested, receiving tickets in return for their outer garments. They then entered the enormous ballroom, whose vast ceiling, polished floor, and distant walls all combined to give an agreeable sense of airy freedom.

"Not quite an igloo," Edmund commented.

"Let's look for a dark corner," Nobody said quietly. "And not too far from the refreshments, of course." He eyed the long low tables at the far end, piled high with massive plates of cut fowl and ham, jellies, trifle, and punch.

"A dark corner?" Edmund said in surprise. "Why?"

"So that we can see without being seen, of course."

"Who doesn't want to be seen? I, for one, intend to be dancing. Even an old ogre like you won't keep me from some well-earned leisure. By the by, I don't think we'll find any dark corners. That chandelier is much too massive to leave any shadows."

"Such is life," growled the Boy Colonel. "Eighteen hours of darkness in Siberia at the present moment, and here in London we can't get one shadow long enough to hide two boys!"

"One boy," Edmund observed dryly. "Remember, I've no wish to hide, and I don't know why you should either, especially since you're the one that everyone will be interested in."

"That's exactly the problem." Nobody crossed his arms on his chest, but immediately removing them for fear of wrinkling the starched fabric. "*I* must be the one talking to every jackanapes fop and peacocked lady who happens to be curious about the 'prodigy' from Siberia. I am not in the habit of attending circuses, let alone participating in them, no matter how well the audience is dressed."

"'What will be will be,'" quoted Edmund. "At any rate, I'd best show you a few tips on bowing. You shouldn't keel over at the middle as if a Cossack had just sliced your spine. As you bow, pull your left foot backwards, and bend a little bit on the right knee, like this." He demonstrated. "Now, you try it."

"Oh, this is jolly." Nobody imitated the action. "Not only do I feel like a fool but I look like one, too."

"That's not bad, let's try it again."

So he bowed again. And again. And again. He bent the fifth time, and began to straighten once more, when his lifting eyes encountered two smiling faces before him. He paused mid-bow, between the vertical and horizontal positions.

Two women, a mother and her maiden daughter, both arrayed in their finest, stood before him. The eldest of the pair smiled. "Are you having problems with your back, Colonel Nobody?"

"My back? Er, no my lady, not at all." He reddened and straightened the mentioned member.

"You are Colonel Nobody, are you not?"

"Er, yes, that is, yes my lady, I am he."

"Will you allow me to introduce my daughter?" Without waiting for reply, she continued. "Dear, this is the Colonel Nobody of whom Papa speaks so much, and this," she said, turning to the boy, "is my daughter Maria, future Viscountess of Hereford."

The 'future Viscountess,' a girl of sixteen or so, curtsied politely. She was of a dark complexion, with darker eyes that stared searchingly from beneath long black lashes. She was shorter than the boy, but the towering feathers in her elaborate headdress gave an appearance of added height. A wide and low neckline complete with drooping pleated shoulders and gigot sleeves made her look like a walking dome-tent. Nobody nodded nervously, but a furtive jab from his lieutenant colonel reminded him of his duty, and he bowed, at once forgetting all of Edmund's instruction.

A small group of gentlemen and ladies quickly gathered round the two boys. Nobody found that most had a very hazy idea of the war in Siberia, and knew really nothing about its cause. A few of the old noblemen, who apparently had once been soldiers, delighted in using their stock of military terms to impress the gathered company.

At last, several personages of high degree entered, attracting most of those crowded round the Boy Colonel. The 'future Viscountess,' however, remained near, with her mother, presumably a present Viscountess. She asked many questions, mostly pertaining to the customs of women in the British camp, to which Nobody responded vaguely. Indeed, there were very few English women at all in Siberia, and of those that did reside with their husbands in camp, Nobody knew little. As to the Siberian women, she showed no interest as soon as she learned that they were generally ugly, hard working, and plainly dressed.

Nobody was ill at ease among this glittering assemblage. The gentlemen's curly wigs contrasted strongly with his own closely cropped locks. He felt especially awkward when talking to the young ladies to whom he was introduced. Never before, could he remember, had he spoken to a woman under thirty years of age. Maria, in particular, had a disturbing way of looking at him out of the corners of her dark lashes which he could not interpret. *Show me a man's face and I'll tell you a surprising amount of information about him, but a woman? I can interpret horses better.*

It could not have been earlier than half past eight when the king finally entered, relieving Nobody of his unwanted popularity. *Just in time*, he thought. His thin patience was near the snapping point, and even the jolly Edmund had grown tired of the continual wall of dresses which surrounded them.

"You know you're in trouble when you're longing to talk to *anyone* without hoopskirts and fancy sleeves," Edmund whispered, as the king began his ceremonial walk round the room. "I'd even be thankful to talk to one of those dandies hanging about that belle!" He pointed to a beautiful young lady, around whom several powdered and perfumed fops stood gaily chatting.

"The lack of modesty amazes me," Nobody said.

"Aye. I'd like to see all the girls in this room packed up and dropped into Siberia for a night—I warrant they'd all be as wrapped up as a jealous sheik's wife by morning."

The two officers took their places at the end of the long line that led from the door to the rear of the room. The men stood to the left, the women to the right, and King William came down the center, holding the arm of his Royal Queen Adelaide. Behind them walked several attendants and a few noble young men and women.

"Remember," Edmund whispered, staring rigidly before him, "left foot back, right foot front."

Nobody felt the man to his left bow, and, after waiting a moment, he made the same obeisance. "Ah! It is our Colonel Nobody." Nobody felt the blood rush to his cheeks as he raised his head. The king was speaking to him!

"Your Majesty," he said reverently, and bowed again, not thinking of anything better to do.

"My Royal Consort," William said to Adelaide, "may I present the famous 'Boy Colonel' of Siberia."

Nobody bowed a third time. *This bowing business will be second nature if I stay here much longer.*

The queen smiled graciously, and whispered something in her husband's ear. "Indeed," he said pleasantly, "it had passed my mind." He motioned to one of the waiting forms behind the royal pair. A young lady stepped meekly forward.

"My dear," said the king, "this is Colonel Nobody, who fights in that Siberian war you asked me about the other day. Colonel Nobody," he continued, turning to the officer, "this is Lady Liana Halmond, Viscountess of Bayrshire, and ward of the king."

The girl curtseyed gracefully, her wide skirts gently sweeping the floor. Her dress was pretty but simple, of a deep green silk dotted by tiny blue flowers. No feathered plume adorned her jet black tresses, which fell in gathered profusion down her back, but a necklace of tiny pearls was clasped round her neck, and a red rose was pinned upon her bosom.

She was probably about seventeen, but looked much younger compared to the surrounding crowd of splendidly attired ladies with their puffed sleeves, low necklines, and stupendous hairpieces. There were plenty of prettier faces around, but the natural tint of her cheeks contrasted nicely with the rouge and powder of the older ladies.

As she rose from her curtsy these cheeks dimpled deeply, and her hazel eyes sparkled, but no teeth were visible through the rosy lips. It was a peculiar smile, full of mingled vivacity and reserve, gravity and grace.

"A pleasure to make your acquaintance," Nobody said politely. *Ward! Well, so this must be who the king wanted me to meet. Why would he want me to meet her?*

"Perhaps the colonel can answer your questions," King William said to the girl. "Talk to him for a time." He then waved a hand at the orchestra, having reached the end of the guests, and he and the queen led the way in a minuet. The lines of male and female dancers slowly advanced towards each other, waiting for the leading couple to pass, and then joined the procession.

Nobody fumbled with his fingers and glanced sideways at the young woman thus thrust upon his company. She also looked nervous, and he guessed that the red of her cheeks was not entirely due to healthful spirits.

Edmund left his side, advancing towards the opposite female, and nodding adieu to his superior.

The Boy Colonel coughed. "Please accept my utmost apologies, my lady, but I do not dance." The man to his left advanced upon seeing Nobody motionless, and the dance continued seamlessly.

The girl, who had been looking at the polished ballroom floor as the dance began, glanced up eagerly as Nobody stopped. "Really? That is—very surprising, because I also do not dance."

It was Nobody's turn to look surprised. "My lady, I *am* surprised. I had expected one so familiar with scenes of gaiety such as this to feel participation a second nature."

"Yes, sir, I've had ample time, which, of course, you must not have had in Siberia, but I do not dance from principle. Please, don't think that I am trying to be above anyone else, but my conscience does not allow me. I am a very devout Christian, and I think it unwise for unmarried people to dance, though I don't see it as a sin." She blushed. "The king calls me his 'little legalist.'"

Nobody crossed his arms, regardless of wrinkling, and laughed heartily. "That is exactly my reason, my lady, and I am glad that we share this in common."

"You are a Christian, then?" Her eyelashes raised expectantly.

"Whole-heartedly. And, I hope, much stronger in the faith than your normal 'religious' soldier."

"That's wonderful! So few at court are willing to talk through things of substance with me. The ladies say they don't understand it, and the men say that *I* am too young to understand." The minuet drew to a close, and the king and queen retired to a corner with half a dozen nobles, leaving the rest to enjoy livelier waltzes. Edmund joined the two young people, a cup of punch in hand.

"Ah, Edmund, here you are. My lady, may I introduce to you my friend, Lieutenant Colonel Edmund Burke, of His Royal Majesty's 42nd Mounted Infantry." She curtseyed.

"A pleasure to make your acquaintance," Edmund said. "I hope my colonel is not keeping you from dancing?"

"No." She colored again. "I don't dance."

Edmund raised his eyebrows, stared at them for a moment, and muttered something under his breath.

"I must say, Edmund, do you remember the Russian headman at Dvorarsk?"

"Quite well, why?"

"That's what you reminded me of just now, bobbing up and down along the line of ladies."

They both laughed, and Edmund made a threatening motion with his glass. "My lady," he said, "if you spend any time with my colonel you will soon learn that much lurks behind that awkward exterior of his."

"Awkward? Why do you say he is awkward?" Liana modestly folded her hands and waited the answer, while Nobody glared at his friend.

"Why, just take a look at him." Edmund cocked his head. "There's his left hand, hanging in mid air, because there's no sword hilt to rest upon." Nobody clasped both hands behind his back. "And then there's the pained expression on his face, as if he's facing a Russian interrogator, and is afraid of saying too much."

"That's quite enough," Nobody broke in. "I thought you came to England to keep me from saying fooleries, not *vice versa*."

The girl smiled at this exchange. "Perhaps, Lieutenant Colonel Burke, Colonel Nobody is made awkward by the present company." She glanced at his face.

He flushed. "To tell you the truth, my lady, I am not accustomed to talking with females. I have talked to women more tonight than in the rest of my entire life combined. They make me awkward, nervous, and unsure what to say."

She gazed at him with wide eyes. "Have you no sister? Have the officers no daughters?"

"My lady, most of the officers are unsuccessful in convincing their wives and families to join them in Siberia. It is not precisely the promised land for the military. As for the enlisted men, it's not common for officers to mix with their families."

A rustling of skirts behind his back announced the arrival of another of these dreaded females. "Colonel," called a girlish voice. It was Maria.

Nobody forced himself to turn and smile. "Good evening, my lady."

She glanced at the Lady Liana, and for a moment Nobody caught a glint of feeling in her eye, and a slight sneer on her lip. It passed, however, as soon as it came. "We are about to begin the next dance, and I am free." She batted her eyelids.

For a moment Nobody panicked, knowing that an invitation was expected according to etiquette. An idea flashed in his brain. He stepped aside smoothly and gently pushed Edmund forward.

"My lady, I am so glad that you are still free. This is my Lieutenant Colonel, Edmund Burke, who would be much honored with your company." Edmund opened his mouth to protest but a glance from Nobody snapped it shut.

The 'future Viscountess' also opened her mouth, but Nobody had Edmund by her side before she could object, and retired, bowing. "You must humor the lad," he called, as the musicians struck a few preparatory chords, "he is not accustomed to the waltz."

Liana laughed merrily as Edmund and Maria joined the rest of the couples and whirled off round the room. "You do know that she was not seeking an invitation from your friend, but yourself?"

"I presumed as much, but I had no desire to explain to her the reason I would not dance, and I thought it would be a splendid opportunity to give Edmund a taste of the inconveniences, as well as the pleasures, of dancing." They laughed together. "I suppose you are acquainted with most of the gentlemen of the court?"

"To some extent, yes, sir."

"Might I ask who that fop is?" He pointed to a fashionably dressed young man who was ambling towards them.

She glanced at him quickly. "It is Lord Bronner's eldest son," she murmured.

"Good even," said the young man languidly. "When I saw such admirable company communing together, I could not help but join myself to it." His face was red, and the skin looked stretched and unhealthy. "Well, young master," he continued, "King William has honored you greatly, and certainly given you a night to remember."

"My name is Colonel Nobody," the boy said coldly, "and I would appreciate its use."

The young man smiled. "Very well, Colonel *Nobody*, I would be glad to. I only thought that perhaps the name might be disagreeable to you, by reminding you of your unusual parentage." His lip curled slightly, and his nostrils flared.

Liana looked questioningly at her companion.

"Whom do I have the pleasure of addressing?" Nobody asked.

"Banastre Bronner, firstborn son of Lord Bronner." The young man bowed. Nobody did not.

"Lord Bronner," the boy said coldly, "I have perfectly honorable parentage, and it would not be well for any man to say otherwise." He touched his side pointedly, from which usually hung his sword.

"Of course," the young man said hastily, drawing back, "it was not my intention to insult you. I simply mentioned the common talk, I assure you."

"I have heard of this common talk," Nobody said steadily, "and it says much, even about nobility, and nobility's sons."

"What do you mean by that? Do you dare to insult me?"

"A gentleman never insults a man unwittingly."

The fop looked at Liana, then Nobody, then back to Liana. Liana had folded her hands quietly and was looking at the floor, while Nobody returned the young man's gaze boldly, and with interest.

"Lady Liana," Banastre said, "I must request that you no longer associate with this *Nobody*. He is not a fit companion for one of your intelligence."

"I think that is for the king to decide, and not you, Lord Bronner," she replied quietly. "His Majesty speaks highly of the colonel."

"Of course." Banastre smoothed his angry countenance. "I have no desire to challenge His Majesty's decision. It is but my desire that you experience no inconvenience at all in this world of trials that forced me to speak so." He bent forward slightly as he uttered these sentiments, and covered his heart with a scented hand.

"The dance begins, Lord Bronner, and I have no desire to keep you from it. No," she replied to his gesture, "you know that I do not dance myself."

"Then, you assuredly wouldn't wish to keep the colonel from enjoying the pleasures of the ballroom, would you?"

"The colonel," Nobody replied, "has yet to discover these 'pleasures of the ballroom,' and does not dance."

"Oh! Too high and mighty to join us, eh? Very well, have it your way." He bowed deferentially to the girl. "Good evening, Lady Liana. Good evening, Colonel Nobody." He stared icily at the boy for a moment before turning to seek another partner.

"To my unpracticed observation, Lady Liana, I should say that the young fop likes you, and that the sentiment is not returned."

Red suffused the girl's cheeks. "I see, Colonel Nobody, that you truly have *not* associated much with ladies. That would not be considered an appropriate sentiment to utter."

Nobody bit his lip. "I apologize if I have offended you. I'm afraid that my words came without thought."

"I understand, sir, and you meant well by it."

"I probably shouldn't say this, either, but it's been on my mind for some time, my lady, and I'd be glad to be relieved of the burden."

"Yes?"

He frowned and nodded at a nearby group of feathered girls. "Could I ask why those girls are staring at me?"

Liana started, then smiled. "As you have been very frank with me, sir, indeed, almost too frank, I will be frank in return. Those girls, I believe, have set their caps for you."

He stared blankly. "I did not know they wore caps, and if they did, how would they set them for me?"

Her dimples deepened. "Colonel Nobody, your inexperience is extremely amusing. That is a common expression for the more precise, though less gentile expression, of making you fall for them."

Nobody was quite unprepared for this intelligence. "What? But—I—ahem. Me? Why me? I have no courtly graces, no skill of flattery and compliments, and I've certainly made no advances. Why would anyone want me?"

Liana plucked her fan. "It may not be proper for me to say so, but because you have asked, I will. In their eyes, sir, you are mysterious, which lends a romantic charm, you are brave and strong, you have a splendid military career ahead, and you are also," she colored, "well, rather handsome."

"Me?" He frowned. "Nonsense. I'm an awkward tumbler compared to the gentlemen of the court. Now, I could see if they were interested in Edmund, who you see is coming to join us. He appears rather unhappy."

He was. "You coward!" he exclaimed, only half in jest, "how dare you shovel me off on that annoying girl in such a way!"

Nobody repressed a smile. "Come now, Ed, you know how much I abhor the fe—that is," he checked himself, "how little I like the majority of the female race, excluding present company, of course."

"That's very nice for you, but what about me? I had to spend an entire waltz with a girl who had no more desire of my company than I had of hers, and who knew that I thought that she thought that I thought that she thought very little of me." He paused for breath.

"That must have been a great deal of thinking. It must have been a novelty to you."

Liana laughed, and Edmund joined reluctantly. "At least," he countered, raising a knowing eyebrow, "you won't be enjoying your success for long."

"What do you mean, Ed?"

"I passed that group of girls." He nodding at the circle of feathered girls. "I heard one of them say something about getting introduced to you." Nobody spun round. Sure enough, several of the girls were approaching with their mothers in tow.

"Oh dear." Nobody turned quickly. "Oh dear. That's not good. That's really not good. Ed, you must do something!"

Edmund shook his head decidedly. "I don't think so. I've already taken one off your hands, there's absolutely no way that you'll stick me on five or six more. What could I do? Ask them all to a dance?"

"Oh dear," Nobody repeated, glancing about fearfully. "Very well, think, think. They don't know that I've seen them. Er, ahem, Lady Halmond, I hope you don't mind if we move somewhere else to continue our conversation?" She laughed and agreed. "Wonderful, er, Ed, form rearguard, and I'll take the van." He stepped off as inconspicuously as possible, disregarding Edmund's quiet laughter.

He planned to take refuge in the crowd at the refreshment tables, only to see a mother and daughter team coming from that direction. He stepped closer to the swirling skirts and coat tails of the dancers—*What? More? How many of these girls are there?* He turned round. *More.* Another direction. *Oh dear. More. I can't take it.*

"Ahem, Lady Halmond, please excuse me, but I must take a stroll in the hall."

"Are you that fearful of meeting a few girls?"

"I would rather meet ten Russians in battle than one of your London belles. I apologize for having taken so much of your time this evening." He made as if to retire, but she laid a hand gently on his arm.

"It is not proper etiquette to leave before the king, Colonel Nobody."

"Is it proper etiquette for them to be pursuing me? I don't see any other options."

She hesitated. "If you wish, I could take you from their sight until the king leaves."

"If you can do that, I'll be eternally grateful."

"Follow me." She led him speedily through the dancers, their forms momentarily hiding the girlish pursuers, and glided through a door in the wall into a small room, furnished with a few articles of furniture.

Nobody positioned Edmund by the door. "Ed, keep them away from this door. Tell me the moment the king has left, and we'll follow." Edmund walked away, and Nobody pulled the door shut with relief. He stood for a moment, fearing to see the knob turn, but it did not.

"You act more like an outlaw than a much-desired acquaintance."

Nobody turned to the girl, who sat on a sofa, her cheeks dimpled and a spark of light dancing in her eyes.

"I suppose I am a coward in these matters. I don't know what to say. I don't know how to flatter—we don't worry about that in Siberia. The only 'small talk,' as I believe it is called, that I know to engage in is about troop movements, casualties, inclement weather, and imbecile commissaries. It is easier to freeze me by putting me in front of a young lady than sending me on a raid with no fire and temperatures at thirty degrees below zero."

"And yet you said all that to a young lady."

"Mmm." Nobody scratched his chin. "So I did. I suppose it says something about human inconsistencies. I wonder why. Perhaps . . . but no, I shouldn't say."

"Say what?"

The Boy Colonel folded his arms upon his chest and studied the polished floor. "I don't know how to say it. Somehow it seems that you—well, it sounds very presumptuous after our very short conversation, but—if I were to have had a sister, it seems that she would have been somewhat like you."

He couldn't tell if she was amused or offended. Perhaps both. He didn't blame her.

"You never had a sister?" she asked.

"No. Please, ask me no more. I can't speak of such things. It is a danger both to me, and to those who ask the questions."

"May I ask about the war?"

"Certainly." He brightened. "The war is the only part of my life that I can talk about. Indeed, it is my life."

"I'm very curious, sir, so please don't think me presumptuous. Why are you fighting the Russians?"

"Mmm." He thought of the explanation he had given to Somerset. "It's rather complicated. Suffice it to say, I'm not entirely sure. It's the king's orders, and that's enough for me."

"Is it a just war?"

"What do you mean?"

"Is it defended by our Book of books and guiding star, the Bible?"

For a minute, Nobody did not respond. He leaned against the wall, contemplating the flowered paper that decorated the room. Liana waited patiently, her hands folded in her lap. "Well, I suppose so," he said at last. "Isn't it our duty to obey the king?"

"In all matters that do not violate God's law. But not in those that do. I don't know much about the war, Colonel, which is why I want to learn more. I can't judge whether it is just or not, but it would please me if you would think on it."

Nobody hesitated. "Yes, I will certainly think of it, both because you ask it, and because it is my duty before God. But what if it is not a just war?"

"I am certainly not an authority upon Scripture, sir, but it would seem to me that it would be your duty to leave, would it not?"

Nobody shuddered. "Leave the war? It's my life. My only friends are soldiers, my men love me, and I they. If I left the war—I don't know how I could." He straightened. "However, I will think more about its causes, and its righteousness." The door opened silently.

"The king's gone, Noble."

Nobody turned to the girl. "I thank you immensely, Lady Liana, for all that you have done tonight. It was a true honor to make your acquaintance, and I apologize for my awkward behavior."

She dimpled. "Thank you for being so frank, Colonel Nobody. If you had spent as long as I have in this court, you would know how refreshing it is." He bowed deeply. Edmund nodded approvingly, and they left the room.

Chapter 16

Somewhere in the depths of London's busyness lay a dim and dirty street, in which stood a dim and dirty public house, whose walls contained a number of dimwitted and dirty men. A rush light burned in one of the back rooms, but its flickering flame only intensified the shadows that played around a small group of well-dressed young men, who were sitting or slouching in various attitudes of indolence. Large numbers of empty mugs stood upon the table, explaining the flushed countenances and watery eyes of most of those present.

The scarred and wobbly table in the cramped room's center provided a convenient rest for four pairs of velvety elbows. The owners of the elbows were quite silent, their attention divided between the greasy cards in their hands and the frothy mugs on the table. Two others lounged nearby, glancing with amusement at the card players' frowning faces. Another young fellow occupied a rickety wooden chair near the rush light, his feet draped over the armrest. He held a book in his hand.

Wreathes of smoke steadily ascended from the assortment of cigars and pipes in the young men's mouths. The sooty condition of the walls attested to their frequent use.

"Trumped." One of the players, a short fellow with a tall hat and stiff collar, laid a card upon the table, allowed the others to see it momentarily, and then swept it up with the other three. His partner smiled. The opposing team did not.

A queen was led. The next in turn was a puffy-faced, long-nosed individual, dressed, according to the latest fashion, in well-studied negligence. He took the pipe from his mouth, refreshed himself with a swig from the waiting mug, and dropped a ten upon the table. The third man nonchalantly led an ace, much to the obvious chagrin of the fourth, who was thus forced to sacrifice his king with no effect. One card alone remained in each hand. Piles of golden guineas and pound notes lay at each man's elbow. The last trick was played—the long-nosed man and his partner were beat.

"Sorry Ban', better luck next time," laughed one of his opponents, dividing the currency between himself and his playing partner.

"Luck?" growled Banastre Bronner. "I make my own luck, and no thanks to others. I'm mortally tired of this never ending card-playing for such paltry sums."

The first speaker laughed. "If you call a-hundred pound odd a paltry sum, I'd be glad to relieve you of a *large* one."

"My dear fellows," said the reader complacently, his legs still draped over the armrest, "Ban' has a good point. We are gentlemen (at least so they say), but we act no different in our chance-taking than a group of everyday Tom-fools."

"What would you suggest?" Banastre downed the rest of his beer and waved his hand for more.

The reader yawned. "Aren't you engaged in any pursuits towards some much-desired goal?"

"All fun and no work," interposed one of the loungers. "But he's already there, so that's no good."

"Aha!" The reader gently removed a book mark from his pocket, placed it between the pages, and closed the volume. "What about that girl at court, the Lady Lin-something or other."

A slight tinge of red colored Banastre's cheek, but it was most likely the result of the beer.

"You mean pretty Lady Liana Halmond?"

"Yes, that's the name. Doesn't she have large estates in Lancashire?"

"They adjoin my future property."

"Future property, eh? What if your father disinherits you from some misguided impression that our company is, er, less beneficial than could be desired to your estimable self?" The young men laughed.

"I'm his eldest, so it's mine by right," Bronner said sullenly. "He thinks too much about the family honor to do something that drastic and scandalous. Besides, I intend to get some good estates through marriage."

"So it's true about the girl?"

The dissolute young man leaned back in his chair, sucked his pipe, and smiled knowingly.

"But they say she's a horrible legalist," the other continued, shuddering. "They say that she reads her Bible ever day, has all sorts of uncommon notions about life, and is generally unbearable! What would possess you to want her?"

"Good looks and money. Once I get her I'll be quite clear as to the way *I* want to live, and if she wants to read her dusty Bible stories she's more than welcome on the nights I don't want her. She's rich—at least her father was, and she's inheriting it all, so I'll be in rather flush circumstances myself. Perhaps I might even deign to remember my previous company at such a time, and have a few friends for a game of whist every now and then, eh?"

"Very well!" cried the reader, sitting up and rubbing his hands. "Let's be to business. What shall the bet be? Three hundred that you get her?"

"No, no," Banastre said in mock horror. "We must be more delicate than that! Besides, I'll need my old man's influence with the king to get me the girl, and I'll tell him about the bet to speed things up a bit. After all, we wouldn't want the illustrious name of Bronner to be mired by not paying debts of honor, would we?"

The young fools laughed immoderately at this sarcastic sally, well-knowing how many knew of their companion's excesses.

"Very well, then," the reader said, "let's work with estates. You say she'll bring the lands next to your own in Lancashire. I'll give four hundred that you don't get them, because the king won't take you. Any other fellows want to pitch in?" Various offers were made of additional amounts, soon totaling one thousand pounds.

"Come now," Banastre said, "what's a paltry one thousand guineas? Make it two thousand, and that will be something to scare my father with."

"Two thousand?" The young men gulped collectively. After some moments of hesitation a few bold spirits recklessly added some hundreds, and the calculating winner of the night's whist game made up the difference, remarking that he'd already won so much from Bronner over the months that he might as well give the lad a chance to make it back.

The bet was duly entered on the fly-leaf of the reader's book, where it stood out from the rest of the entries by its uncommon length. After a final mug of the landlord's beer the company broke up and retired to their more fashionable resorts. Banastre Bronner bid good evening and stepped into a waiting coach, after first removing all traces of dirt from his luxurious clothing. The dim and dirty street with the dim and dirty house was left, and they rattled into the aristocratic section, quiet as death, save for a few coaches returning like himself from late-night parties.

Bronner alighted in front of a massive brick building ornamented by supporting columns. A servant opened the back entrance for him, evidently accustomed to receive his master at unusual hours of the night.

"Any letters for me?" The young man paused in the gloom. The servant handed him a small envelope.

Banastre did not open the message until he had gained the privacy of his rooms. Here he stood amidst sofas, chairs, Oriental rugs, paintings, ancient curios, and other such articles that had pleased his fancy. The letter smelled of lavender, as if the womanly hand that had written the flowery words had also sprinkled drops of perfume upon the paper. With a smile, Banastre read it, and then threw it upon the massive four-posted bed.

"Your author will soon follow you," he said, smiling at the letter. "But duty first. I must seek out the old man and make my suit. Honor your father and mother, after all." He winked at himself in a mirror and departed. A light still burned in his father's study, where, according to habit, the older man sat reading the newspaper.

He looked up in surprise as his son entered the room. "To what unexpected occurrence do I owe the pleasure of this visit?" he asked.

Banastre leaned against the mantle, looking down his long nose at the elder man. "I have decided to marry."

"Have you?" The elder Bronner showed no surprise. "Whom do you desire to marry?"

"Lady Liana Halmond."

"Really?" The man rubbed his left eyebrow thoughtfully, the glass eye beneath glinting strangely in the well-lit room. "Why do you tell me?"

"Because you can help me. I have made a bet of some two thousand pounds that I will obtain the lands bordering ours in Bayrshire within the year."

"Two thousand pounds?" The minister of state jumped angrily to his feet and paced the room. "What possessed you to do such a foolish thing? Two thousand pounds! How many of my thousands have you already thrown away in vain follies about London? I would be a ruined man if your younger brother had followed your example, instead of being thrifty like his mother."

"So you've said. I've made the bet, and that's final. If I don't get the girl, I won't get the lands, and if I don't get the lands, that's two thousand pounds, and I'm sure that you would not want the illustrious name of Bronner to be sullied by an unpaid debt?" He smiled triumphantly.

The profligate's father paused in his steps and looked searchingly at his son's countenance. "Yes," he said slowly, "perhaps you are right. If I resolve this bet, will you promise to leave England, and work to reform your ways, before you bring any more scandal upon the family?"

"Reform my ways? Why, I'm as pure as the driven snow. Now I must be off, for I'm expecting company. Ta-ta."

"Yes," the old man muttered. 'Ta-ta,' is it? So he thinks that he can walk in here and dictate orders to me. Mmm. Perhaps—" he smiled, took a snuff-box from his pocket, sniffed, sneezed, and was satisfied. "Yes, my son, I will get you your estates, but not in the way you expect. How curious that my prodigal should be the eldest, not the youngest. Well, when your time of adversity comes, there will be no fatted calf awaiting you at *this* house."

Chapter 17

The sun rose late the next morning, but the minister of state would not wait for the great luminary's blessing. He silently traversed one of the many halls in St. James's Palace, followed closely by a young man of similar countenance. The youth was evidently a Bronner. His nose was prominent, according to Bronner fashion, but it did not have the appearance his brother's did of being perpetually screwed into a sneer.

They stopped before a door, which opened quickly after a slight rap. The minister of state entered reverently, but with an accustomed ease that showed much familiarity with royalty. His son's face showed mingled awe and excitement, not to mention a degree of apprehension. As they entered, the guard who had opened the door saluted rigidly and withdrew in response to a gesture from within.

The room was small and tastefully decorated, but not elegant. Oaken cabinets covered the sidewalls from floor to ceiling, while a sturdy desk of the same material stood near the back wall. Sheaves of paper covered this surface and barely left room for a large inkstand and several feather pens. Behind this litter sat an aged man in a plain waistcoat, with a wig resting neatly on his oval head and a tired expression in his bright eyes.

"Lord Bronner!" he said cheerfully, laying down his pen. "What brings you here at this early hour? I have barely begun reading the nation's wrongs, let alone addressing them."

"Your Majesty." The elder Bronner bowed. "May I present to you my youngest son, Thomas, of whom I have often spoken."

The king nodded graciously.

"Your noble father has mentioned your name on several occasions, and always as one who obeys and respects his will. Unlike your brother," he added, frowning. "I am glad to give consent to your service in the army, although I could wish that you had chosen the offered commission, as more befitting your father's legacy."

"I thank Your Majesty for your gracious words," the young man said reverentially, "and I appreciate the permission to enter the unit that presents the most opportunities, in my inexperienced opinion, to serve your interests in Siberia." The elder Bronner motioned his son to the corner, while he himself advanced closer to the king.

"It is evident that something is on your mind, Bronner. I have fond memories of that look from the days when we sailed together. It was always my misfortune that you were given active duty and the glory of losing an eye for the honor of the crown while I passed my time dreaming of battles and never fighting any."

"Yes, Your Majesty, I have very fond memories of those days."

"Yes. But what is it you would wish to relieve your mind of?"

"Your Majesty, I have been thinking of your ward, the Lady Liana. She is fast maturing into a lovely young maiden of marriageable age."

"The little legalist? Yes, yes, she is getting older, but it will be some time before she could be called an old maid. Why do you speak of her?"

"As Your Majesty knows, she was first made a ward of your Royal predecessor King George IV, as a young girl. King George made an agreement with the girl's father that she would be well-taken care of, and disposed of in marriage at the king's discretion. However, a somewhat unusual document was agreed upon, most likely because of the king's great friendship for the girl's father, which stipulated that, although the king could confer his ward upon whomsoever he thought fit, certain estates in Lancashire would be given back to his Royal Majesty if the girl gave her consent to the match."

"Yes, yes, I know. It was a wise provision, meant to make the royal head more, shall we say, compassionate, to the girl's wishes. What of it?"

"As Your Majesty knows, the Lady Liana has some rather unusual ideas, tending, as you have so ably stated, to a legalistic view of the Scriptures. I am afraid that none of the young courtiers I know of would live up to her standards."

"'Tis quite likely," the king agreed.

"I could not help but notice her lengthy conversation at the royal ball with Colonel Nobody. I have read several correspondents' articles about this mysterious boy, and he seems to hold many of the same beliefs as the girl."

"Colonel Nobody? Does he? I didn't ask about his beliefs, but I formed a good opinion of him from our interview."

"That is what I understood, Your Majesty, and the reason that I wish to propose that the two be united in marriage. I believe the girl would accept him, which would remove her from court, as I know that her presence has been irksome at times to Your Majesty, and Siberia is a long way off. On the other hand, the girl's estates, which happen to adjoin mine in Lancanshire, will come to the king because of the girl's acceptance of the match, and I would be glad to buy them, thus adding to the treasury."

The minister watched narrowly for the king's response. William pondered the idea, staring vacantly at the nearest sheaf of paper and tapping the table lightly with his forefinger. "Both are young for marriage."

"That is true, Your Majesty, for which reason I would recommend a betrothal, and not an actual marriage as of yet. The girl is somewhat young. I have no idea how old the boy is—no man knows. He may be extremely young, he may be quite old."

King William frowned. "But what of Colonel Nobody? You spoke of my ward's likely acceptance; what of his? Do you think that he will accept her?"

"He would be a fool not to. What young man in his right mind would fight against an extremely beautiful and wealthy young lady being bestowed upon him with really no effort required on his part? Besides, Your Majesty does not need to ask him. Inform him of the betrothal, by which means you ensure his compliance."

"Bronner," the king said, smiling, "you are a schemer. I am glad that you have decided to scheme for me, and not against me. As to this subject. We agree that the Boy Colonel would not be in his right mind to refuse our ward, but who knows whether he *is* in his right mind? Who knows anything about him? And, more importantly, who knows whether he is, by birth, a fit companion to our ward?"

This last impediment took the wind from Bronner's sails. "I had forgotten that, Your Majesty," he said ruefully. "That is an impediment." He rubbed his eyebrow thoughtfully. "Perhaps if Your Majesty commanded him to tell you the story of his birth? It is possible that he has noble blood in him."

King William mused upon this. "True, very true. Very well, I will! Summon him to my presence as soon as you depart."

Chapter 18

The "Painter's Paradise" was in a state of bustle very opposite to the picture of the Garden of Eden generally imagined. The innkeeper and his wife were regaling an admiring barroom crowd with an account of the last moments of the lodger who had only the day before had the insolence to die in one of the innkeeper's chambers. Various hypotheses were advanced about his past life, present calamity, and future state. A noisy argument was in process on the important subject of his last words, but everyone was agreed that one of them had been "rum."

Among the crowd of laughing onlookers slipped a small man, dressed in the livery of the king. He sniffed disdainfully, inquired where Colonel Nobody was staying, and slipped rapidly upstairs. The door opened to his knock and the whiskered face of an Irishman looked out inquiringly.

"From the king." The servant bowed and extended a letter. O'Malley took it and nodded pleasantly.

A high voice within the room growled. "If it is anohzer of zhese cursed barbarians vanting to know if ve knew zhe man who just died, vell zhen tell him he may go and die *himself* for all I care or vill say, and zhat *no* ve did not know him and zhat *no* ve did not vant to and zhat *no* ve have no money to give to him or anyvone else for zhat matter!" Exhausted, Jacques sank back into the chair from which he had risen.

"You should have taken Jacques with you to the ball," Edmund said, laughing, as Nobody took the letter from the Irishman's hand. "He would have taken care of any talking you didn't feel comfortable with. Of course, he might have added a little bit extra that would have made you more uncomfortable, but that's just an added benefit."

"It is an honor to be so complimented by your highness." The Frenchman bowed.

"Arrah there! Ye're bein' rather free wi' the officers, Jack Frog, and I'll remind ye that jist because we happen to be in Loondon town don't mean as they aren't still your superior—superior—ach, your all-round superiors is what I'm tryin' tae say."

Edmund coughed. "Then again, the Irish aren't always known for their taciturnity either."

Nobody was paying little attention to this banter, intent instead on the letter from the palace. He soon finished the short message, and folding his arms, gazed pensively at the opposite wall. At the table to his right sat Jacques, Somerset, and O'Malley. Edmund sat on a wide bench, leaning his back against the wall in indolent comfort. Both officers wore their undress uniforms, which were much more pleasant in the crowded quarters. O'Malley wore his full regimentals, but with the negligent air of one who obeys official customs but knows that his officers would not require the respectful and uncomfortable attire. Jacques was clothed likewise, but without the negligence. Somewhere in the dark and dirty city of London he had acquired a rose, whose gentle petals fondly graced a button-hole.

"What does His Majesty want with you now?" Edmund asked.

"Mmm?" Nobody started. "Oh, the letter." He glanced at the open paper in his hand. "Asking for the pleasure and etc. of my attendance in His Illustrious Majesty's etc. at the hour of one by the etc. for the purpose of not given. In other words, he wants to see me at one o'clock, and he doesn't say why."

"Perhaps he's holding another ball," Edmund suggested.

"A splendid reason to leave London quickly. Come, you shall accompany me to the ante-room."

"Accompany you? But I'm not in proper uniform!"

"Neither am I, so you have five minutes to shape-up." They retired to the adjoining bedroom, and returned in the allotted space of time fully starched, pressed, wrenched, bottled, capped, and otherwise incommoded by the full regimental uniform.

The three men stood to bid them farewell, and then settled back into their various pursuits. Somerset scratched vaguely at his notebook. O'Malley hummed an Irish ditty as he carved a bit of stick with a clasp-knife. Jacques examined the left elbow of his jacket, which he apparently considered was becoming too threadbare.

Pausing for a moment in his writing, Somerset looked up—and beheld Jacques and O'Malley staring at him. Jacques coughed and pretended to be examining the wall behind the reporter's head, while O'Malley returned quickly to his whittling.

"Is there something wrong with my face?" Somerset asked.

"Hmm?" Jacques shifted his gaze, apparently seeing the reporter for the first time. "Not zhat I can see, no."

The Irishman agreed.

"Then why were you staring at me?"

"Ah, oh, ahem." O'Malley looked at his comrade, who returned the compliment. O'Malley nodded his head. Jacques did likewise. Somerset cocked an eyebrow.

"Ye see, we were simply wonderin' if ye'd mind us engagin' in a little, recreation, ye might say."

"It is more practice," Jacques quickly clarified, "euh, keeping up our skills in, euh, varlike activities."

Somerset raised no objection, and the Frenchman disappeared into his bedroom, soon returning with an iron box. He inserted a key into the lock and rapidly emptied a stream of pewter soldier models onto the table. "Tactical readiness," he explained with a wave of his hand. "Zhe colonel used zhem back vhen he vas younger. Ve vant to, how do you say? Stay sharp."

Somerset was seized by a coughing spell.

The two friends eagerly arranged their battle lines and began warfare with courteous references to their respective armies as the "poor little Frinchmen" and the "unfortunate misguided English." Before Somerset had time to fill a leaf in his pocketbook the comments had intensified. Battle was now between "cowardly Frogs" and "bloodthirsty pigs."

"I'm not bothering you by my presence, am I?" Somerset asked.

"Ye'll not take me by a flanker!" O'Malley muttered.

Somerset scratched his chin. "Evidently not. Well, in that case I'll head down to the 'Jolly Bargemen' for the afternoon. You're welcome to stop by for dinner."

"Dinner?" Jacques stared vacantly at the reporter. "Ve vill be zhere. Irishman, your move."

Somerset nodded. "Very well, then. Don't get any blood on the walls."

He wandered about the streets for awhile and terminated in the "Jolly Bargemen," a small public house. A wizened old man with great horn-rimmed spectacles served him beer and he retired to a table in the corner, opened a newspaper, and perused the latest articles.

He smiled at one of the headlines. "*Latest news from Siberia! Just in from correspondent Alexander Somerset.*"

The public-house was sparsely occupied when the reporter entered, but it slowly filled as the afternoon progressed, and a large number of working-men were firmly established at the rough wooden tables by the time the sun began to descend. Conversation was loud and hearty amid the din of clattering forks and thumping mugs, punctuated by peals of coarse laughter from a noisy group of vagabonds in the opposite corner.

Two sailors swaggered through the doors just as the wizened owner ventured forth from behind his counter to light the greasy candles that served as centerpieces to his tables. Large gold hoops hung from their ears and swung with each swaggering step.

Seeing two vacant chairs at Somerset's table they "tacked to starbo'd," as one expressed the movement, and approached the reporter.

"Ahoy there, young'un," boomed the tallest, a man with long whiskers and a scar on his left cheek. "Requestin' permission t' 'eave anchor an' take up berth wi' ye for a turn o' the glass."

Somerset nodded pleasantly, and said he would be honored with their company. With this assurance each man grasped a chair's back firmly with both hands, as if afraid of its sliding away, and sat down. The landlord brought two frothing mugs of ale and replenished the reporter's cup.

The tall man leaned forward confidentially, his mug carefully guarded by two massive arms.

"We're jist back from Chiney," he explained. "Out on a spree arter takin' a poor messmate's chest to 'is old wooman. He's in Davy Jones's locker now, barrin' gettin' to Fiddler's Green, which I'd be a-doubtin', I would."

The other sailor, a small dark man with beady eyes, noticed Somerset's blank look and explained that his 'mate Jack' meant to say that one of the sailors on their ship had drowned in their last voyage. Somerset offered his condolences, which Jack accepted by heartily insisting that he pay for the young reporter's next mug. Somerset acquiesced, and the next round of drinks was brought. The conversation advanced "swimmingly," as Jack expressed it, not clarifying whether this state of affairs was due to the nautical yarns he was spinning for Somerset's benefit, or the amount of spirits all three were imbibing.

As the night advanced Jack loudly proposed a song, which was generally accepted by the company, and they set to singing with all their will. The choruses grew noisier and rowdier as the rum mounted to the singers' heads, and the sailors gradually reached the stage described as "two sheets to the wind." Somerset, having had a head start and being less used to spirits than the tars, was much closer to having three sheets to the wind, or, in landsman's terms, he was becoming stone drunk.

At last, Jack staggered to his feet. He gripped the table with both hands, as if facing a stiff head wind. "Ladeesh an' gennelmen," he said gravely, "or more impo'tantly gennelmen, since there'sh no ladeesh present, more's the pity, I propose a shong, in honor uv our benev'lent hosht. Let ush szing 'whiskey in tzee jar!'"

The company happily agreed, belting in drunken unison the much-loved ballad:

As I was goin' over the far famed Kerry mountains,
I met with Captain Farrell, and his money he was countin'.
I first produced me pistol and I then produced me rapier,
Saying: "Stand and deliver, for you are a bold deceiver!"
Musha rig um du ruma da, Whack for the daddy-o,

Crash!

The startled singers stopped abruptly and stared at Jack, who had just smashed his mug on the table and was glaring at Somerset. Somerset looked back in a state of pleasant imbecility.

"Ishn't dilly-o," the sailor growled. "Ish daddy-o."

Somerset shook his head jollily. "Dilly-o."

"Daddy-o!"

"Dilly-o!" Somerset grew angry in turn, and repeated it once more for good measure.

The tar slammed his fist on the table and shouted "daddy-o!" at the top of his lungs. The effort proved too much for his wobbly legs, and he collapsed, bringing the table with him. His companion blinked solemnly at his floored shipmate and promptly delivered a stunning blow in Somerset's direction. He misjudged the distance and missed Somerset's nose by an inch. The momentum propelled him forward, though, and both men tumbled to the floor in a heap of mugs and plates.

This served as a signal for a general engagement, and the public house erupted into a confused brawl of brawny bodies topped by muddled heads, most of which had no idea what the fight was about. Chairs, mugs, fists, and any other available objects were swung, thrown, and launched into the air, utterly regardless of their eventual landing-places. The wizened old innkeeper grabbed the leg of a broken chair and growled maledictions as he stood upon his counter and struck viciously at all within reach, evidently deciding that the fewer combatants left conscious, the less damage would be done to his property.

Somerset struggled out of the corner and made for the door, but Jack was too quick for him, and the two crashed together into the wall. Although young and impassioned by spirits, the reporter was no match for the powerful sailor. Their bodies locked together, the sailor's long pigtail slapping against his sweaty shirt as their heads waved back and forth. A stream of foreign curses came from the seaman's mouth, but Somerset had no breath for such words, even if he had known them. His ribs were being slowly crushed like a nut in a nutcracker. Gasping, he flung himself backwards, and both smashed through the door and rolled on the street into the path of a hansom cab.

Chapter 19

Upon leaving "The Painter's Paradise" Nobody and Edmund called for a cab so as to not spoil their uniforms in the London muck. Saint James's Palace loomed large as the bells struck the hour of one. The ante-room was sparsely inhabited. It must not be one of the king's official review days.

Edmund sat, but Nobody paced the floor with his arms crossed and stared at the floor. Time ticked by. Nobody scrutinized the portraits which hung pendant round the walls, wondering whether the stiff men and haughty ladies normally looked so morose, or if it was just a preferred pose for the painter.

Servants flitted in and out occasionally, sometimes calling one of the few waiting applicants for the king's favor, sometimes doing nothing but bustle and hustle about, as if proud of their positions and wishing to have someone to impress. The hours passed slowly, but no hustling servitor came in search of the two military boys sitting in an obscure corner of the ante-room.

"I say," Edmund whispered, "are you sure you got the date right?"

"Of course. Have patience. Royalty always takes more time than expected on anything that they take a mind to."

Edmund shook his head doubtfully, but Nobody was soon vindicated by a squat servant in a trim waistcoat, who requested the boy to accompany him to the king's chambers. King William was alone save for a few close friends and advisers, among whom Nobody recognized the glass-eyed man who had introduced him on his first visit to the palace. The formal procedures of bowing, greeting, complimenting, and so on were soon finished, and Nobody stood erect to await his Majesty's pleasure.

"Good afternoon, Colonel Nobody. I wish to present to you the son of our friend and adviser, Lord Bronner."

Nobody started, expecting to see the sneering fop from the ball. Instead, a younger man stepped forward. His face was fresh, but masculine. His prominent nose extenuated a smile, not a sneer.

"Colonel Nobody, this is Thomas Bronner. Thomas Bronner, this is Colonel Nobody."

The young man bowed, and Nobody nodded pleasantly.

"Young Thomas has heard much of your exploits in Siberia, Colonel Nobody, so much indeed that he has requested to be put under your orders. He has also desired, much against the usual wishes of applicants, to not be put into command as of yet. Therefore, we have arranged that he be enrolled as a volunteer and attached to that—what do you call it? Ah, yes, Squad One, I believe it is, of Company One."

"Squad One, Your Majesty? He must prove himself worthy indeed to serve among those soldiers."

"I have no doubt that he will."

"Assuredly I will, Your Majesty," young Bronner exclaimed. He bent on one knee. "May my bones freeze upon the wild steppes of Siberia if I do not."

That's a distinct possibility, Nobody thought, as the new volunteer returned to his father.

"So what do you think of London, Colonel Nobody?" the king asked.

"It's rather—well—it's much different than Siberia, Your Majesty."

"In a good way?"

"There are advantages and disadvantages, Your Majesty. There are many more people in London than are presently in most of Siberia, but this has made things very cramped and crowded, in my opinion."

"Would you like to live in London for the rest of your life?"

"No! That is," he corrected himself, coloring at his vehemence, "I would not prefer it, Your Majesty. I am a soldier, and I am happiest when facing the enemy. To be plainly honest, as it was requested of me in my last interview with Your Majesty, I would not be content in London, where the only enemy to fight is boredom."

The king smiled. "Have you lived all your life in Siberia, Colonel Nobody?"

"Largely, Your Majesty. I spent some months on the sea, and I have been to a few other countries, but most of my life has been with the army in Siberia."

"How long have you lived there?"

Nobody was silent. He bit his tongue until he thought blood would flow, but the king kept looking at him. Sweat beads popped out on the back of his neck, and on his legs.

"Your Majesty, with respect, it has been necessary that darkness be kept shrouded around the earlier years of my life, and I would ask that that obscurity be preserved."

King William folded his hands. "Colonel Nobody, I have respect for your feelings, but I also have a particular reason to wish to know the story surrounding your birth." He nodded to his advisers, who quickly departed. "I request, as your king, that you explain your origins."

Nobody felt the blood drain from his cheeks. He rubbed both palms slowly against the military pelisse, wiping off great beads of sweat. "This is Your Majesty's command?" he finally asked. His voice sounded hollow to his ears.

"It is."

The Boy Colonel drew himself up and forced his limbs to stop trembling. "Before I do so, Your Majesty, I must ask that you solemnly promise never to speak of what I am about to say to anyone in this world. It is worth my life, and likely the lives of others."

The king thought for a moment, glanced shrewdly at the boy, and nodded. "Go on."

The city bells chimed five o'clock when the king's advisers were recalled. Nobody stood in the same position in which they had left him, deathly pale, now, but composed. The king sat staring at him. His courtiers paused uncertainly. Motioning them forward, King William sat back in the tall-backed chair and breathed deeply, as if releasing some great burden from his lungs.

"Colonel Nobody has satisfied me that he is fit for the proposed match. My Lord Bronner, you will take care of drawing up the required papers."

A frown creased Nobody's forehead, and he looked questioningly at the king. "Your Majesty, may I ask what you mean?"

"What's that? Oh, bless me, I forgot all about telling him why. Ha, ha. Why, Colonel Nobody, you are going to marry our ward, Lady Liana Halmond."

The blood which had fled to his lower extremities returned just as quickly, and Nobody felt his cheeks flush red hot. He was stunned, confused, bewildered. "Your Highness," he gasped. "I—don't understand!"

"It is quite simple. The Lady Liana is my ward, and I have decided that you are to marry her. Of course, the actual marriage ceremony will not take place at this time, due to your youth, but the betrothal will take place tomorrow, and she will return with you to Siberia."

Nobody reeled backward. The picture of the girl flashed on his brain. *Me? Marry that girl?* "I—Your Majesty—you—I—why *me?*"

"Ah, Colonel Nobody, you should be flattered. My ward has developed a great liking for you." King William pressed his jeweled fingers together. "You do not have any objections, do you?"

Objections! How should I know? I've only talked with her once in my entire life!

"Colonel Nobody?"

"Your Highness, this is so sudden, I don't know what to think. I've only conversed with the lady once."

"Nonetheless, I assure you that the match is well suited. The betrothal will be at two o'clock tomorrow afternoon, here at the palace."

Nobody wet his lips. "Your Majesty, I'm not sure that I *should* marry her."

King William's forehead contracted into fat wrinkles. "Colonel Nobody, I have said that you are to marry. It is a wonderful match."

Nobody felt his pulse throbbing in his wrists. "Your Majesty—is she a Christian?"

King William laughed. "A Christian, Colonel? She's a perfect little legalist. Our only fear is that she is too Christian for you."

Nobody stared at the floor. *She seemed a very nice girl the other night, and the king verified her beliefs. This is the king's order—how could I disobey? Perhaps I could, but I don't think it would be justified. Lord, help me!*

"Very well, Your Majesty."

"Good. I can see that this has been somewhat of a shock, so you may leave now. Remember, the betrothal is at two o'clock."

Nobody bowed mechanically and backed out of the chamber. The carpeted floor spun before his eyes. Groping for a support, his trembling fingers touched a servant's shoulder, and he clasped the man to keep himself from falling. He shook his head when the servant offered to fetch a glass of water, and, pulling himself together, released his grasp.

Edmund stood up gladly as Nobody entered the ante-room, and stretched the kinks out of his back.

"Back at last! Come and let's be off to dinner, for I feel as if I could eat a horse with eight legs and—hello!" He paused abruptly and stared into Nobody's face. "What's happened? You look as if you'd seen a ghost!"

"I feel as if I'd seen a ghost." Nobody dropped into a chair.

"Why? What did the king say?" Edmund bent over him eagerly, helping to loosen his collar.

"I'm not quite sure how to say it, Edmund."

"That's not good. No! Don't say that the king removed you from the 42nd!"

"No, not at all, that's not it."

"Good." Edmund sighed. "That's a relief. So, what's in the air?"

"Love. I am going to be married."

Edmund stared at him blankly. "What?"

"I am going to be married."

Edmund blinked twice, narrowed his eyebrows, and laughed. "Splendid try, old chap! You almost had me believing you for a second. I say, you should have gone for the stage, you're a wonderful actor. How did you put on that white face?"

"I'm not acting. I may be dreaming, but I'm certainly not acting."

"Eh? You are joking, though, aren't you?"

"I'm not joking."

"You don't look like you're joking." Edmund gazed at his commander in consternation. "You mean to say that you're getting married!"

"Indeed I do, I think."

"But—but—that's impossible!" Edmund spluttered. "I didn't even know you were interested in anyone!"

"I wasn't."

"What? Well, but I didn't even know that you *knew* anyone."

"I didn't."

"Well then how can you say that you're getting married?" He raked his hands through his hair.

"That's what the king just told me. Lend an ear and I'll tell you all that I know, which is precious little, I assure you."

"Here's two ears, a mouth, and a nose, now tell me what's going on!"

"Very well. The king called me in, and informed me that I was to marry. At least, that I was to be betrothed, because we're both rather young. The betrothal takes place tomorrow."

"What do you mean 'we're both' young. Who's the other one?"

"Excuse me?"

"Who's the girl?" Edmund exploded. "Who are you marrying?"

"Lady Liana Halmond."

Edmund clasped his arms in silent wonder and rocked on his heels, slowly nodding at himself. "Lady Liana," he muttered. "Yes, I see, Lady Liana. Who would have thought? Why her?"

Nobody blushed. "It's rather strange to say, but according to the king, she—well, she—that is to say—oh botheration! She developed a liking for me."

"A liking for you? How dare she develop a liking for you without consulting me? And moreover, how dare she tell the king of her liking and have him arrange a marriage? The hussy!"

"It doesn't make sense." Nobody groaned and clasped his head in both hands. "I never would have thought her to be that kind of girl after talking with her at the ball. But how else could it have been done? That's basically what the king told me, minus the complaint of not consulting you."

"Noble, I tell you, this is a strange matter altogether. Why did you accept?"

"Accept? What are you talking about? I didn't accept, I was told I was getting married. I wasn't asked whether I wanted to, I was simply asked whether I had any objections on principle."

"Do you?"

"No, I don't think so, but then again how would I know? I've only seen her or talked to her once in all my life. And now I'm to marry her!"

Edmund raked his hair again. "You don't like anyone else better?"

"Anyone else? I don't know anyone else. The only other girl besides Liana that I have really talked to would be that Maria at the king's ball—"

"Don't mention the name!" Edmund interrupted hastily. "I couldn't stand that impudent girl. I do believe I'd strangle one or both of you if you dared to say you were going to marry *her*! No, I'd take the Lady Liana any month of the year compared to that designing female."

"It looks like you're getting your wish."

Nobody felt the cabby staring at his dazed expression, but he told the man the address and pushed inside before any questions could be asked. The cushions felt soft and comforting after the shock. He closed his eyes and rested his spinning head on one of them. *Things are changing more rapidly than I can process them. What could happen next?*

A violent jolt slammed him into the hansom's wall.

His head spinning, Nobody kicked the door open and jumped down. Two men lay wrestling in the muddy street, while a stream of light from a nearby public house showed a full-scale brawl within. Nobody squinted. There was something familiar about one of the men—Somerset! It was Somerset, with tousled hair and torn, muddy clothing, grunting and gasping in the arms of a brawny sailor.

"Somerset, you fool, what are you doing? Get up!"

"Can't," the reporter gasped. "Shailor—too—shtrong."

"Sailor, eh?" Nobody raised his voice. "All hands on deck!"

The sailor instinctively released his grappling hold and rose unsteadily to his feet.

"Aye, aye, cap'n," he said, reeling towards Nobody. "Hi, you're no cap'n!" His bleary eyes blinked like those of some great sea-owl. "How dares you?" He clenched his fist and swung.

Nobody calmly grasped the swinging arm and wrenched it downwards, effectually collapsing the tipsy sailor and laying him at the boy's boots.

"Wot's you doin' wi' me messmate?" A small, dark man staggered out of the public house and charged.

"Noo ye don't," growled another man, emerging from the shadows and pinioning the sailor in his arms. "If ye soo much as touch a hair on the head o' me colonel I'll grind ye intae cobblestones, an' if I don't, call me a Frinchman!"

"Zhat vould be the day." Jacques snorted. "Good evening, *mon* Colonel. Ve came for dinner vihz our friend Somerset, but it vould appear zhat he is already full, as are most of zhe pigs in zhat sty." He pointed disgustedly at the public-house.

"Good evening, Jacques, O'Malley, glad to see you. Perhaps you can help me with Somerset here."

O'Malley gave the sailor one last affectionate crush and set him down with a warning shake of the finger, before helping Jacques lift the bespattered reporter from the street.

"I'sh can help myshelf," Somerset slurred indignantly. "I'sh a man. I don't need help." He tried to take a step, wobbled, and fell back into O'Malley's arms.

"A man? Faith, but I'd hate tae see a beast."

"*Boeuf*," Jacques muttered.

Somerset's previous opponent had by this time gained his feet and was looking with his owlish eyes between his tingling mate and Nobody. "Wot's it doin'?" he demanded of his friend. "Ish wearin' a unifoorm, but air a boy an' no mishtake."

"Curshed drummer boy!" the dark man exclaimed. He charged past Jacques and O'Malley and clutched for Nobody's throat.

Something flashed in the boy's brain—he found his left hand clamped round the sailor's throat, crushing him against the inn's wall. In his right hand gleamed a long knife.

"Do—not—rouse—me." Slowly, very slowly, he let his muscles relax, releasing his grip on the terrified man. "I would *strongly* recommend that you pick your fights with those *not* on active duty in His Majesty's army. Thankfully for you I remembered in time that you're not a Russian—although perhaps you would have deserved it." He let the sailor slide down the wall until he came to rest in the gutter. "You fool! Do you think drummer boys wear epaulettes? No, be glad you're drunk, for if you had acted so in a sober mind I would have left a mark of remembrance upon your body."

Nobody turned back to Somerset. "Come on." He grasped the reporter's collar. "You're coming home with us."

"No!" Somerset tried to pull away. "I'sh wants ano'er drink before I'sh goes. Shirsty."

"Thirsty!" the Irishman growled. "He's alridy half-drownded himself wi' beer! Ain't there any place around these here parts as 'ould have a pail o' decint wather?"

Nobody held up his hand. "Let me try him first. Reporters live on news, so let's see if a tidbit doesn't sober him up a little."

Edmund smiled and signaled the cabby to take a turn round the block and come back in a few minutes. He folded his arms and leaned against the wall, while Nobody stepped face-to-face with the reporter. Somerset hung limply in the two privates' arms.

"Somerset, listen to me."

The reporter's head lolled on his shoulders, and he mumbled something about his thirst.

"Oh be quiet, will you? Now, listen. You're a reporter, right?"

Somerset nodded wearily.

"Good. Now, I thought you might want to hear a bit of news. Perhaps even the *London Times* might be interested in this news."

"Lon'on Timesh?"

"Yes, your employer. Stop rolling that muddled head of yours about and look me in the eyes! That's better. Now. I'm getting married tomorrow."

Somerset blinked rapidly as if a shining light had just been thrust before his eyes. "You jusht shay—gettin' married?"

"That's right."

"Oh," he groaned, letting his head sink low again, "I ish drunker than I thought."

"Fool! You heard me correctly. This is no alcohol-induced dream. I am getting married tomorrow, or at least betrothed, not quite married. The ceremony is at two o'clock tomorrow in the palace, and I'm sure that the *London Times* will be bursting to have a chance to see it. Will you be the correspondent?"

Somerset finally began to realize that this was reality. "What?" he said slowly, as the import of the news dawned on him, "yoush getting married? What? But I thought—that is—how—*who*?"

Edmund laughed. "That's the reporter again." They loaded a soberer Somerset into one of the hansoms and the lieutenant colonel took him home while Nobody and the two soldiers waited for another.

"Splendid idea aboot the weddin', sir," O'Malley whispered in Nobody's ear. "I can't think o' anythin' as would've been more startlin' tae him."

"It was true," Nobody replied in the same tone.

"What? But ye can't be serious!"

"Oh dear, yes."

159

Chapter 20

Nobody stood before the king. Next to the king was a gilded table, upon which lay the document that would bind him in the promise of marriage to the trembling girl by his side.

A circle of noblemen and noblewomen surrounded them, but Nobody looked past their amused faces to the little group far away by the wall. Jacques and O'Malley stood at attention, their eyes straight before them. Somerset wrote furiously in his notebook. Edmund stood next to Somerset, a smile on his face, but a tear in his eye. He caught Nobody's eye and grinned wider. A servant girl pressed modestly against the wall a few feet from him, her eyes bent solely on her mistress, the girl they called Liana.

The king ended his words of counsel. It was time to sign the covenant. Nobody gripped the pen. The six letters of his name were soon recorded. He handed the pen to the girl—their hands touched. She bent over the paper, and when she rose the act was complete, and they were betrothed to become man and wife.

They knelt to receive the king's blessing. Liana's cheeks were bright red, each dimple forming a bright valley. Her eyes sparkled.

Nobody tried to smile back, his own cheeks hot and his eyes twitching. He felt weary and careworn. *What have I done? Is this right, for me or for her? Can this sweet girl actually have been so forward as to arrange the marriage herself?*

King William lifted his hands from their heads and presented them to the gathered nobility. Nobody dutifully crooked his arm. Liana timidly slipped hers through, and thus they walked through the lines of well-wishers.

The last face in line stood out sharply from the aristocratic throng. The skin stretched up into a long nose, topped by a pair of hawkish eyes.

"My congratulations, Colonel," Banastre said. "You have gained a prize." An angry sneer replaced the smile. He leaned close. "See that you can keep her. She was not meant to be yours." Nobody gripped her arm and led her past him.

Liana's maid glided behind her mistress, and the soldiers formed rank and brought up the rear. A ship was sailing that very day, and the names of the party were on its passenger list. Thomas Bronner, the new recruit, joined them on the docks, and they were soon in a boat on the way to the *Daisy*, where their luggage was already stowed.

Nobody and Liana sat together in the bow. The wind cooled the boy's heated brow and played hide-and-seek through the girl's long hair. He pulled the cloak tighter around her slight frame.

She still held his hand. "I have never sailed before. I must trust you to help me if we meet any storms."

He tried to keep his hand from trembling. "It will be my pleasure to, Lady Liana."

"Lady?" She stiffened. "Colonel, I am your betrothed wife. Must you really use my title?"

"I suppose not." He forced himself to speak cheerily. "Very well, Liana, I will do all in my power to ensure your comfort on this voyage."

Slowly, she relaxed. Her cheeks dimpled. "And what should I call you?"

"People generally call me 'Nobody.'"

"But I am not 'people, generally.' I am in a much closer position. What is it that I've heard Lieutenant Colonel Burke call you?"

Nobody laughed. "Edmund, being a very loyal and biased fellow, calls me Noble, as a creative shortening of Nobody."

"Noble." She smiled. "I like it. May I call you 'Noble?'"

"If it pleases you."

Conversation flowed freely with the rest of the boat's passengers. Edmund and Liana's maid, Elyssa, sat behind the two betrothed, comparing notes about their respective superiors. Somerset had his little leather book out and was quizzing young Bronner on all things courtly. Jacques and O'Malley sat in the stern, gaily critiquing the surrounding shipping.

"There's our ship!" cried the Irishman, pointing to a schooner. "I can sae 'Daisy' written on her as clear as the mornin' sun. Aye but she's a beauty! Look at her masts, and her lines! Jack Frog, me friend, can ye tell me the last time ye saw such a beautiful ship? I can guarantee t'weren't in a Frencher's harbor."

"Bah," the Frenchman scoffed. "Vhat do you know about ships? Lines, you fool? You do not know vhat zhe lines of a ship are any more zhan you know zhe color of our great Napoleon Bonaparte's vaistcoat on zhe field of Vaterloo, vhich I do, vhen I vas among zhe grenadiers."

"A grenidier?" O'Malley choked. "Why, ye liar! Do ye think ye can get me tae believe as that the grenidiers were so hard up for men they started enlistin' dwarves? Even if ye had been old enough, which ye weren't, ye'd niver have been one. Bah, yourself."

"Vell," Jacques sniffed, "if I had been vihz them it is likely zhe day vould have ended differently. Perhaps Napoleon vould be zhe king of England at zhis very moment."

"Glad to see that ye'er humble."

Jacques waved a hand airily. "As humble as you. You pretend zhat you know ships. Bah. I see no lines. Her masts are zhin. Her sails are dirty. If something is not clean and orderly, it is not vorth vhile, and zhat deck is *not* clean or orderly."

O'Malley's retort was interrupted by their arrival at the *Daisy*. Nobody and Edmund climbed the rope ladder and helped hoist the two girls, after which the rest of the men climbed on board.

The schooner was packed tight with stores for the army, but the sailors had managed to knock together three small cabins on deck for the use of the party. The girls and their luggage were deposited in one, Nobody and Edmund claimed the second, and the other four were left to shift for themselves in the third. Hammocks were the only available bedding, but only Bronner and the girls were unused to them, the other five having had ample time to grow accustomed on the long voyage to London.

"The sooner I get used to roughing it the better," Bronner said cheerily, stowing away his trunk.

O'Malley laughed and shook his head. "There's many a time ye'll think back to this here hammock as luxury's lap, me young friend, whin all ye've got is a blanket between ye and the snow, and all that's above is a frozen sky droppin' frozen bits o' itself upon ye."

The sunset was magnificent as the party stood leaning upon the bulwarks that night. The sky filled with a kindling glory of red, orange, and every shade between.

"'Red sky at night, sailor's delight,'" Nobody quoted.

"You said that before," Edmund replied. "Is there any truth to the proverb?"

"Seems to be. It's biblical, you know."

"Biblical? How's that?"

"It's in the gospels somewhere. Same idea, though not rhyming or about sailors."

"Hmph."

They relapsed into silence, even the volatile Frenchman awed by the majesty of the night. Liana placed her hand in Nobody's and timidly laid her head on his shoulder.

"What will they call me when I am your wife, Noble?"

"What do you mean?"

"Is Nobody your first and last name? Will I be Mrs. Nobody, or Mrs.—Nothing?"

"What do you think of Lady Liana, wife of Nobody?"

She threw her head back and laughed merrily. "Why, Noble, if I went around saying that, people would think that I was brazenly looking for a husband, proclaiming to the world that I was unmarried."

Nobody stiffened. "Of course, that—that wouldn't be good." He stood up abruptly, and released her hand. "It is getting late, and time for you and your maid to seek your pillows."

"Very well, if you insist."

"Good night."

"Good night?" She hesitated. "Is—is that all?"

He swallowed against the lump in his throat. "Good night, my dear." A quick dimpled flash and she was gone.

Nobody leaned against the bulwark again, holding his aching head in both hands. The sea breeze blew against his heated brow, but it did not refresh him. The sun slowly sank, but it did not disturb him. The company broke up, making for their beds, but it did not move him. At last, a strong arm grasped him round the shoulders, and Edmund stood by his side.

"Why are you so sorrowful?" he asked. "This is almost your wedding day—a major step in that direction, for sure. Why?"

He clenched his fists. "Ed!" He tried to muffle the passion in his voice, but couldn't. "Ed! I don't feel right. I don't love her. She seems such a timid little thing, but she—she! arranged a marriage between us! How unwomanly? How unseemly? Even taking that into consideration, I respect her. She's sweet, calm, good-natured, well-informed, and more—but I don't love her!"

"Why not?"

"How should I know? I've never been in love before. Is there some mental cord that I can pull and suddenly be in love? If I had grown up with a father and mother I might have learned these things, but I didn't!"

He stopped and gazed into the waves. "How discontented we humans are. The boys of England read about me, who was raised in the camp with no loving parents to guide my ways, and they envy me. I hear of their happy homes with parents and brothers and sisters, and I am tempted to envy as well. *You* know what life is without parents. Certainly, old Colonel Hayes was very loving to me, and raised me like his own son, but he never spoke of such matters. Perhaps you knew, perhaps you didn't, but he himself had a real family once, and a bolt of lightning set his house on fire, and burned every one of them to death, except him, because he was out that night. No, he never talked of the softer side of life with me after that."

Edmund gasped. "I didn't know. Is that why he became so—interested— in Greek fire?"

"Yes, that is why. It grew upon him, until eventually he left the 42nd to find materials he needed for his experiments. That's when I took over. But Edmund, what must I do? I feel like a hypocrite talking to this girl who is promised to be my wife, and not loving her."

"I don't see why you shouldn't love her."

Nobody raked his hand through his sweaty hair. "Ed, why do you think she wanted to marry me? She could have gotten a much better match elsewhere, and I'm sure there would have been plenty of interest available if she were open to courting. Why should she choose me?"

Edmund clapped his shoulder. "Noble, old fellow, can't you see? She loves you. Believe me, I spent many years on the streets of London. It's not a very good school, but the one thing it does teach is how to read countenances, to understand what men, and, more importantly right now, what *women* think."

Nobody said nothing, so he continued. "She also holds many of your same beliefs, from what I'm told, and I don't know of any courtier who does the same. What could be a more perfect match as far as the way you understand the Bible and want to live your life?"

"Where in the Bible does the young woman initiate a marriage?" Nobody asked bitterly.

"Ahem, well, now that you mention it, the book of Ruth."

"Oh bosh! You know very well that she did that because the marriage was supposed to happen by law, because he was a kinsman, not just because she met him one day and decided she liked him."

Edmund squeezed his shoulder. "All I know is this, Noble—women can't stand rejection. If you really don't love her, don't let her see it. I'm not saying to lie and say you do, but don't act so stilted and unnatural as you have today. Be at least as friendly as you are to me, who, although your closest friend on earth, am not anything near as close as your wife will be." He led Nobody away from the bulwark. "Let's be off to our hammocks. It's been a long day and I'm thoroughly tired."

Chapter 21

The next day broke fair and fresh, and with the last vestiges of night fled the final glimpse of England's coast. Plumes of smoke wafted heavenward from the galley, and breakfast was soon announced to the drowsy passengers, who bundled into their clothes and piled out of doors in time to see a table placed on the quarterdeck. The wind was calm enough to warrant this measure, but Nobody knew that if it picked up at all, they would have to eat standing. A portly man in stained slops followed by two sailors approached the table, bearing the morning's repast. Evidently the captain had impressed upon his cook's mind the importance of their guests, and a meal of meat had been prepared for their consumption, which was quite out of the ordinary for breakfast at sea.

Nobody gallantly handed his betrothed to a seat, while Edmund did the same for Elyssa, who had been included as a normal passenger among the group much against her will. She colored at this attention and sat with her eyes upon her plate, but Nobody cheerily told her that anyone close to his intended wife must be treated with due respect, no matter what the cold world thought about in regards to supposed social scale. Edmund threw out one of his witticisms for general remark, and the company was soon laughing and joking together as the cook and his attendants uncovered the food.

The captain and first mate joined them. Nobody surprised the sailors with a short prayer, and they began. Before he had a chance to lift his fork to his mouth a spluttering sound emanated from the opposite end of the table, and Jacques broke into a fit of violent coughing. The Irishman struck him heartily on the back, hoping, most likely, to dislodge the impediment to his digestion, but nearly dislodging the entire digestive system altogether. When the Frenchman had finally recovered, he gasped out a request to the captain to be allowed to aid the cook during the voyage in his culinary endeavors. He particularly stressed the word *endeavors*. The captain laughed, and said he had no objection, and the volatile fellow was forthwith installed technically as cook's assistant, but in reality the driving force in the galley.

The breakfast, although not quite as bad as Jacques's reaction might have suggested, did have some distinct failings, such as a tendency of the meat towards leather, and a surprising amount of weevils in the biscuits for so short a time at sea. Finishing his meager repast, Nobody signed Bronner to follow, and led him between the main and fore masts. Edmund saw to it that a few chairs were placed for the girls, and that they had books to interest them, before he himself jumped into the rigging and climbed to a comfortable perch on the first cross-tree.

Nobody nodded at his betrothed's book. "Interesting story, Liana?"

She dimpled and turned a trifle red. "Yes, quite. It's a romance. I suppose I really needn't read them now that I'm in a romance myself, but—" she stopped. "Yes, it's quite interesting."

"Never read a romance myself. War isn't very romantic." He turned abruptly to the new volunteer. "Do you think there's much romance in war, Bronner?"

"Why, yes, sir, I do."

"Think again." Nobody drew himself up, his back to the foremast, his face towards the nervous young man. "You've come to fight with the 42nd, therefore you're going to learn *how* we fight, and I am going to train you." He nodded up at Edmund. A sword and scabbard dropped from the rigging.

Nobody tossed it to Thomas and drew his own sword. "You will learn the rifle, but you must also learn the sword. Because we use the rifle, we do not use bayonets. They make firing nearly impossible, and lend to the damage of the weapon. Therefore we use the sword. Have you taken lessons?"

"Oh yes, sir! I'm quite proficient with the rapier."

"This is no rapier work. This is a cross between the broadsword and the saber, tending more towards the broadsword. We don't worry ourselves much about thrusting. Certainly, if your opponent leaves a spot unguarded you should take advantage, but generally melees in Siberia involve hacking and cutting. Not very scientific, you might think, but there's still plenty to learn. Draw!"

Thomas slowly drew the long blade from its scabbard.

Nobody twirled his blade. "I've no doubt you've learned to fight like a gentleman. That's fine. War is a very ungentlemanly business. I don't say that we fight like blackguards, but there are certain rules that must be forgone. For example, you hold your sword now, waiting for me to say *en guarde*." Bronner nodded. "Well, I will never say *en guarde*, because that is not done in Siberia. You see a Russian, the Russian sees you, and your swords meet as soon as is practicable. Of course, even if you said *en guarde* the Cossack couldn't understand you, but it doesn't matter. War is not like a duel. War is war. Are you ready?"

"For what, sir?"

"To begin, of course. I must see how you fight."

"Ready, sir." The young volunteer lowered his blade, and began shifting round in a circular pattern.

"Remember, Bronner," Nobody said quickly, "I am testing your abilities right now, not showing you how I would do it."

"What if I wound you, sir?"

Edmund snorted from somewhere in the rigging.

Nobody smiled. "Don't be afraid on that score."

Lunge, parry, lunge, parry, sweep, parry. Bronner's breath came in gasps as he continued to circle the colonel, dashing in with blows that were always blocked, but never returned. Nobody waited quietly for each attack, a half-smile on his face. At last, Bronner dropped the edge of his sword and wiped a sleeve across his dripping brow.

"I must have a short break, sir."

"Very well. I know how you fight now. We will begin the lesson as soon as you have recovered your breath."

"Begin?"

"Certainly. I told you previously that I was just testing your skills."

"Oh, right, yes, sir." Bronner did not sound encouraged.

"It is best," Nobody said, "now that I know how you fight, that you see an example of how *we* fight before engaging yourself. Edmund!"

The lieutenant colonel promptly climbed hand-under-hand from the rigging and drew his sword. "Sir?"

"Are you ready?"

"Hurrah!"

The fight ensued. Bronner stared dumbly at the flashing blades all around him, the air a perfect flurry of glistening metal. Liana gave a little cry and covered her eyes. Even the sailors paused in their work and gazed wide-eyed.

"This," Nobody called from the middle of the battle, "is real fighting. Not what you read about in the novels Edmund so avidly devours."

The two had practiced so much that each knew exactly what the other's response would be. They moved back and forth across the narrow deck with perfect footwork, occasionally creating variety by placing a mast between them. It felt good to be cutting and slashing after the weary restraint of London. Edmund looked like he was enjoying himself thoroughly, occasionally dashing into the rigging or somersaulting away from his commander's swift strokes. Nobody decided to keep his dignity intact without risking it by bouncing around the deck like an India rubber ball.

At last they desisted and Nobody turned to Thomas Bronner. The volunteer licked his lips.

"Don't worry," Edmund said cheerfully, "he's not going to kill you. If he wanted you dead you already would be."

"Come now, Bronner. Shall we begin?"

There was no question as to who controlled the fight. Nobody led the young volunteer wherever he wished, pushing him back, luring him in, sidestepping, tapping, parrying, delivering blows that he thought of as child's play, but left Bronner gasping from the effort of parrying. All the while he maintained the part of teacher in a confiding, conversational style.

"In a melee we use everything to our advantage. The wind, the sun, the snow, or, in this case, the deck. We use our bodies, our opponents' bodies, our friends' bodies; in short, everything and everyone. Always keep a good lookout for those nearby, if perchance they need a friendly blow to even the odds. Of course, they will do the same for you. Also remember that the goal is not necessarily to cut a Russian down—it is to win. You can use your body for that purpose."

Nobody thrust his pupil's sword aside and dashed in, catching him by the throat and thrusting him against the mast. "Like that." He let him go, and the game continued.

The next weeks passed similarly. Some days the sun shone brightly, and some days great wind-gusts whipped the waves into a white fury, but every day Nobody fought his new soldier up and down the decks of the *Daisy*. There was much to learn, but Thomas had a ready mind and a quick hand. Occasionally, Nobody would have Edmund step in, so as to demonstrate the best techniques against multiple enemies, but most often the lieutenant colonel entertained the girls, sometimes reading to them, sometimes conversing. Thus the voyage passed, and by the time they reached the Sea of Okhost, Bronner was ready to take his place among Squad One, Company One, of the 42nd Mounted Infantry.

Chapter 22

A heavy blanket of snow deadened the wagons' wheels, but the wooden planks connecting to the springs creaked and groaned all along the convoy. It was still early morning. The convoy had started long before dark as an extra measure of protection against roving Cossack bands. Colonel Nobody thanked God as they bounced into the English camp at Porsk. He wasn't concerned for himself, but a running battle during Liana's first week in Siberia would not have been the best introduction.

"Here we are, my dear," Nobody said cheerfully, jumping down and helping his betrothed to alight. "Home sweet home, such as it is."

Edmund did the same for Elyssa, while O'Malley, in a moment of levity, reached a hand up towards Jacques. The Frenchman knocked O'Malley's cap over his eyes and jumped down indignantly.

"*Boeuf.*"

Nobody intervened before they could begin arguing, and they set off amiably for the 42nd's encampment.

Passing soldiers saluted him cheerfully, and a small knot of officers made as if to greet him, until they saw the girl by his side and stopped short.

Nobody stepped up to them. "Hello Colonel Campbell, Colonel Hastings, Colonel Blackwater, splendid to see you! I have the honor to introduce to you my betrothed wife, Lady Liana Halmond." The officers gaped at him in astonishment. "Horrid thing about the cold," Nobody remarked to Liana. "Every now and then it actually freezes the words in your throat. Good day, gentlemen!"

The same dingy igloos were standing, row in row, in the 42nd's camp. A small group of men stood gathered near the center of camp, among whom Nobody recognized several members of Squad One. As soon as they saw their long-absent commanding officer, they rushed at him.

"Oh, sir, I'm glad to see you!" Matthew Preston said, his stiff salute belied by the gladness in his eyes.

"You, sir, and the others too," Mark added.

"Good to see you as well, men." Nobody returned their salutes. "What are you fellows doing? There's mischief in your eyes, Prestons."

Old Corporal Stoning winked. "The Apostles are preparing a little surprise for Petr and the Yankee, sir. Would you like to watch?"

"Certainly, Stoning, I'm glad I arrived in time." They moved towards Squad One's igloo while the Prestons glided off on their mission. "How are you, Stoning?" Nobody asked the old man.

"A touch of rheumatics now and then, sir, but nothing uncommon for a man my age."

"Glad to hear it. This girl, Stoning, is my betrothed wife, Lady Liana Halmond, from England."

"An honor to meet you, miss." The old veteran bared his frosty locks. "Begging your forgiveness, but it goes against the grain to be calling you 'my lady' when you've still got such a bloom of youth on your cheek, and you're marryin' my own colonel, who I've always thought of a little in my heart of hearts as a sort of godson."

"And so you should, from what Noble has told me." Liana smiled warmly.

The two Preston brothers approached Squad One's igloo cautiously. Matthew held a blanket in his arms. Mark gave a boost to his slightly elder sibling, and they soon clambered up the slippery walls. Smoke steadily ascended from the protruding chimney, but the blanket soon blocked its sooty path. As soon as the coarse fabric was firmly secured, the culprits leaped from the roof, their fall deadened by the snow, and dashed to a large pile of snowballs. Jacques and O'Malley quickly joined when they saw the intended fun.

In a few minutes a muffled sound came from the igloo, and two heads burst through the doorway. A plume of black smoke followed them into the cold air. As soon as the targets came into view a flurry of snowballs met them, eliciting bellows of fury. The Yankee promptly charged at the first man in sight, but his vision was so blocked by the incoming balls that he did not see who his proposed antagonist was until he dangled from O'Malley's extended arm.

"O'Malley! Why you fool of an Irishman, what are you doing here?" Dilworth gasped for fresh air and looked vacantly around until he saw the colonel and his party, and light dawned in his thick Yankee skull.

Nobody spent the remainder of the day in a flurry of activity. He reported to headquarters and delivered the latest orders from the War Ministry, receiving a cold nod from Tremont which was no more than he expected or desired. Colonel Campbell's wife was delighted to receive Liana and her maid, and he felt confident that no harm would befall her in that good lady's company. Once these pressing engagements were complete, he called for Major Macpherson to see him in his igloo.

"How have things gone in my absence, Major?"

"Bad, sir, very bad. I don't know what General Tremont is up to. We haven't sent out anything, even a raid, since you left for England, sir. Discipline in the regular troops is worse than I've ever seen it."

Nobody rapped his desk thoughtfully. "What about General Whitmore? Anything in process to rescue or exchange?"

"Not a bit that I've heard of, sir. But what I've said isn't the worst. General Tremont actually tried to transfer some of our men to another regiment!"

"What?"

"Yes, sir, that's what I said when I heard. As I was left in command, sir, I felt it my duty to keep the 42nd together, so I appealed on the grounds of our special privileges, that only the colonel of the 42nd could break up the regiment. General Tremont still wasn't satisfied, but the other officers agreed with me, and it's been left like that. I don't understand what is going on, sir."

Nobody rested his chin in his hands, gazing pensively at the standing officer. Macpherson seemed ill-at-ease. He kept rubbing his hands on his tunic.

"Macpherson, has General Tremont been trying to malign me behind my back?"

The major swallowed. "Well, in a manner of speaking, yes, sir."

"I was afraid of that. Oh well. If he will not play the gentleman, I must. It's not easy to get respect from men so much older than I. Thank you for standing for the 42nd, Major Macpherson."

"Yes, sir!" A salute, bout-face, and he was gone.

Nobody leaned back in his chair, holding his callused hands before his face. *You have shed so much blood, fought so hard in the king's service. And now this? A jealous general takes a disliking to me, and he tries to take it out on my men? Behind my back? No. Tremont, your day will come. Perhaps not at these rough hands, but at God's, for certain.*

He devoted the next weeks to reestablishing discipline, inspiring the men to harder training, and—Liana? The very thought tore at his heart-strings. If he was to marry her, and it certainly seemed that was the case, it was important to know her very well. And yet—he also did not want to show the confiding girl that he did not love her. He must avoid this at all costs.

Nobody finally settled into a pattern of visiting the Campbells' tent three times a week, and spending an hour or two conversing with the girl. She evidently wanted to spend more time with him, but she was too timid or too respectful to ask.

The blooming month of May came quickly, and with it a long-awaited thaw. The refreshing sound of trickling water once again filled the interminable steppes, and mountain streams emptied their crystal drops into deep pools still covered each night by layers of paper-thin ice. Winter was not finished. It still had a few blizzards under its frozen sleeve, but a rejuvenated spring was rapidly gaining ground. With the pleasant weather came fresh bands of Cossacks who hung daringly round the camp's outskirts, skirmishing occasionally with the pickets.

Near the middle of the month one of the 42nd's fast-moving patrols brought in news about a Russian base camp within easy striking distance. Nobody quickly summoned his force and quietly left camp as soon as darkness fell, trusting to swoop down upon them before morning broke.

The raid was successful. A small force of sleepy Cossacks was scattered into the dawn, their stores burned, and their horses captured. There were no signs of the enemy on the return trip, but as they rode over the last hill before camp, Nobody reined in White Fury and gazed wide-eyed at the plain. Great plumes of smoke rose from the camp, and single horsemen dashed to and fro. Something was dreadfully wrong.

Chapter 23

"An attack!" Nobody exclaimed. "Liana!" He dug his spurs into White Fury's flanks and dashed toward the confusion, leaving his men to follow as fast as they could. "What has happened?" he called to the first soldier he met.

The man saluted. "The dirty Cossacks attacked last night, sir, burned a portion of the camp, but we beat 'em off without too bad casualties."

"Was the 30th attacked?"

"I don't rightly know, sir. There's been a ruckus by Colonel Campbell's tent, so I'm supposin' he probably was."

Nobody dashed forward, leaping his horse over piles of rubbish and half-burned tent canvas. He drew up beside the colonel's tent, which was charred and sooty, but still standing.

"Colonel Nobody, thank God you're here!" Colonel Campbell rose from a camp stool. His right arm was in a sling.

"Campbell, what's happened? Where's Liana?" He jumped from the saddle and made as if to enter the tent.

"She's not in there."

"Then where is she?" He grasped the older man's shoulders. "Where is my betrothed wife?"

"We weren't expecting the raid. They just came from nowhere, and were among us before we could do anything. They put the torch to everything they could, and killed everyone they came across."

"No!" Nobody shrank back a pace. "Dead?"

"No, not dead, only captured." Campbell sat back down, his wrinkled face aged by the violent night. "Whether they took her for ransom, or exchange, or something else, I don't know."

"I don't care what they took her for, I *will* get her back!" Nobody sprang into his saddle. "I don't blame you, Campbell. It wasn't your fault. Our pickets must not have been alert because of the loose discipline that General—" he stopped, gritted his teeth, and sped towards the 42nd's halted column.

"I go to follow the Russians!" he shouted to his men. "Who will come with me?"

"Huzzah!" rose the answering cry, and the men turned their weary steeds with new energy to follow their beloved leader.

"Wait!" Edmund grabbed Nobody's reins. "This could be a long chase. We need food."

"You're right. Each mess send one man to collect what rations he may at the double! The rest of you, switch saddles onto the Cossack horses. They're fresher and hardier." He rode impatiently among the men as these rapid transitions were accomplished, encouraging them, even lending a hand where needed. He found Somerset by his side.

"Colonel," the reporter began, rubbing his hands nervously together, "perhaps, er, that is to say, maybe I should—ahem. Maybe if it's just the same to you I could—well—"

"What, Somerset?"

"Well, sir, I thought that perhaps it would be better if I stayed here at camp."

"You don't want to come? There should be plenty of news to bring back, I should think, if we come back."

"That's the thing, sir." He laughed nervously. "I'd rather keep my skin whole."

"Stay if you wish. You're a reporter, you may go where you like."

"Thank you, sir. I hope you don't think I'm cowardly at all, do you?"

"I think what I please."

"Oh. Right, sir, thank you." He retired shamefacedly, without a single word of farewell from any of the soldiery.

"I thought there was more than that in him," Edmund whispered to Nobody. "He didn't do too badly in that affair at Dvorarsk, especially for being so new."

Nobody shook his head. "Bravery is not judged by how hard a man fights when he knows there's no way out. It's when a man is shown a desperate situation, and has the option to leave, and doesn't—that's a brave man."

"Speaking of brave men and not-brave men, here comes General Tremont."

The general waddled angrily towards Nobody, shaking his fat finger after the long-departed Russians. "Go after them at once!" he commanded shrilly. "The confounded Cossacks stole my best horse! Burn every village they passed through—that will teach them a lesson."

Nobody saluted mechanically, barely paying attention to his words. The food was brought, the horses exchanged, and they were off across the plain, following the path of trampled grass. Not a man looked back as they passed over the first hill's crest. It was death or victory, and they knew it.

Chapter 24

Nobody hoped to catch up with the raiders the next day, but the sunshine hours passed without a figure on the horizon. Dead horses, cast-away knapsacks, broken wine bottles, these became common sights, but not a single living Cossack. The fresh young blades of grass were trampled into a sodden mess by the weight and force of the horses' hooves, and as long as the thaw lasted, the English could use these signs to track the enemy. If it snowed—banish the thought.

The raid had taken place Monday night, and the 42nd had set off in pursuit mid-morning on Tuesday. Late on Wednesday afternoon they reached a small native settlement on the banks of a stream. Herds of caribou wandered in the distance, attended by most of the male population. As the 42nd rode into the dirty hamlet of make-shift huts and tents, the women of the place slowly emerged with scowling faces and swarms of children hiding behind their skirts. Nobody promptly dismounted and went up to the one that looked the most promising candidate for information. She was small, somewhat younger than the rest, and carried an infant in her dirty arms.

"Greetings, good woman," Nobody said in Russian, "may I ask you a few questions?" The native was so astonished to find an English officer speaking fluent Russian that she forgot to answer, and the question had to be repeated before she gave her assent. "Have any Cossack soldiers passed through your village?"

"Yes, my lord," she replied, forming the Russian words slowly with her native tongue. "Many soldier this morning. No stop to steal. We happy."

"No time to steal," Nobody muttered. "Did they have a woman with them?"

She raised her eyebrows. "Woman? Me not know. Me son see closer. Want ask him?"

"Please."

A young boy soon emerged from behind her skirts and shyly bowed to the English officer. "Me see one woman. Bright clothes. Horse close to big Cossack horse. Hands tied."

"Hands tied, is it? Very well, thank you good woman for your information."

Edmund tapped him on the shoulder and led him aside. "Noble, what about the village?"

"The village?" Nobody looked around. "What do you mean, Ed?"

"Tremont said to burn all the villages that the Cossacks passed through. Do we burn it?"

Nobody stared blankly at the frightened natives. He had forgotten Tremont's last words in the heat of the chase. Burn the village? *What do I do? These natives had nothing to do with the Cossacks—I can't wantonly burn down their homes. But orders are orders—no, God's orders are higher than Tremont's, and it would be wrong to needlessly destroy civilian property.*

"Edmund, I can't burn down their homes. It's not right."

"I agree that it's not right, Noble, but Tremont ordered—" Edmund stopped and bit his finger.

"Tremont's not higher than God, no matter what he thinks. Move out."

He dropped several Russian coins into the woman's palm and remounted. "They have somewhere around five hours start of us," he said loudly, addressing the men. "By the route they have taken I think they intend to join the army stationed in the vicinity of Troak. It's likely that's where they came from—a raiding party sent to test our defenses. We must stop them before they reach that army. We'll camp at dusk."

Each day took them farther from their base and lessened the amount of food in their knapsacks. They were slowly gaining on the Russians, but could they catch up before the Russians reached their army? That was the all-consuming question. They moved as fast as their horses could, and when the tired beasts were ready to drop from exhaustion, their equally tired riders would feed them and let them rest for a few night-hours.

Each night Nobody sat piled in blankets by the campfire, straining to see the printing in his Bible by the flames. He was tired enough to sleep, but his overloaded brain couldn't rest until he had solved the burning question first raised by Liana, and presented again by Tremont's order. *What is a just war?* He flipped through the Chronicles, the accounts of the Kings, Joshua and Samuel—there were wars that God supernaturally commanded and wars against invaders—nothing like what they were doing in Siberia. Edmund remonstrated with him, telling him that his face was growing haggard, and that dark sacs were bulging under his eyes. He said nothing, but kept reading.

It was Saturday morning, and they still hadn't caught sight of the Russians. Nobody crawled out of his two-man tent into a blasting wind. Wild fowl filled the air with joyous cries as they returned to their summer hunting grounds. The horses whinnied happily as their masters approached, eager to receive a meager feed of oats before the day's work began. Here and there a pot clanged, but most of the men ate their rations cold to save time. Jacques presented his smiling face with two cups of steaming coffee—it was ten times better than his attempts at tea.

Edmund dunked his head in a bucket of half-frozen water. "I feel it in my bones! We'll catch them today for certain."

"The only thing you feel in your bones is the cold," Nobody said dryly, lifting the saddle onto his horse's back. "Whoa, boy, easy there, old fellow."

"Come on you old grumbler, can't you see this beautiful day?"

"I can, and I thank God for it."

"Well then why can't you rejoice in it as well?"

"Ed, I don't feel well. Last night—but no, I'll tell you as we ride."

As soon as the last man was in the saddle they set out, riding rapidly towards the north. They were in a range of hills, each crest rising higher than the previous—a dangerous place for ambushes. Scouts were sent ahead to give warning if any suspicious signs appeared. They were barely out of earshot, and fully within reach of Nobody's anxious eye, when they stopped abruptly upon a crest, turned, and galloped back.

"Rifles at the ready!" Nobody shouted. Each man unslung his rifle at command and moved into battle formation.

"Sir, sir, it's the Russian camp!" one of the leading scouts shouted, pointing back at the valley. "Smoke still rises from the fires. They can't have been gone long."

"Forward!" the colonel shouted, and over hill and valley they raced, the fresh earth flying beneath the pounding hooves. Nobody did not stop to study the signs of encampment. The telltale fires alone were enough to give him wings. The highest hill in the range loomed before them, the sun shining brightly on its jagged summit.

The last few feet of earth vanished under White Fury's hooves and man and beast stood on the crest, looking down upon a wide plain. Upon that plain rode a scattered body of horsemen making towards some object in the distance. Nobody opened his mouth for a shout of triumph—but what was that? That long line of gray in the distance, slowly advancing to meet the fleeing Russians. It could not be—it was. The Russians had reached their army at last.

The 42nd raced up the slope in their colonel's path like a red inundation blotching out the vibrant green grass. Not a word broke the silence as each man breasted the crest and saw the unfolding scene below. Nobody sat like a statute, his head bowed upon his horse's neck. He gently stroked the stallion's mane. White Fury whinnied and reached his long snout round to touch his master's hand with his nose. Nobody raised his head.

"There they are," he said simply. He patted the warhorse's rump, and horse and rider moved forward slowly, followed by the grim troopers. The Russian forces had combined, and were now moving back across the plain toward the 42nd.

Nobody turned his horse and faced the men who called him colonel.

"Men of the 42nd. This is my last charge with you." His voice was low and deep with passion. "We have fought on many fields together, and shed much blood together. Many friends have we seen struck down by the Russian. But this is my last charge."

He slowly removed his shako and wiped the sweaty locks from his forehead. A mist formed in his eyes.

"You know that I am a Christian. I have made that very clear. And you know that I follow the Lord's commandments. Well, I've been studying those commandments, and I have come to one conclusion. First, my allegiance is to God, and to His law. Second, to my family, to those I am bound to protect. And third, and only third, to my king."

The men murmured.

Nobody held up his hand. "The Bible also says that there are certain rules for warfare. No, they're not laid down like the ten commandments in one place where you can go and say 'do this, and don't do that.' No, you must find them, and I've spent time and I've found them. Men, we are not in a just war. Therefore, it is my duty, as a follower *first* of God, and then the king, to leave this army."

The men gasped, but Nobody raised his hand again.

"My men, I don't want to do this! I have been with the 42nd for all of my life, I don't want to leave you now. All I know is war, and this army. I don't want to leave, but I must, because I must obey my God. When we return to camp I will resign my commission. But—" he threw down his hat and drew his sword. "This last charge I consider *not* for King William, but for the King of kings, because it is according to *His* law that I must protect my family. There, among those Russians, is my betrothed wife, a captive. It is my duty to rescue her before harm can befall her—but this is my duty, not yours. I do not ask you to risk your lives for me or mine. I will not command you to risk your lives as if this were for King William. I go. Those who wish to follow may. Those who do not I do not blame."

Edmund grabbed his arm, but Nobody shook his head.

"No, Edmund, this is right. Edmund, do you understand, this is not what I want! I was born for war, I have lived my life in war, and I will very likely die in war. But," his voice lifted in the clear air, passion swelling his tones, "I do not intend it to be *this* war! I go." Without another word he quietly removed Edmund's hand and turned his horse.

The sorrow-stricken men gazed at him with tears spilling from their eyes and coursing down their weather-beaten cheeks. Veterans of a score of battlefields covered their faces and wept. But the colonel's passionate words did not only elicit sorrow. With fire flashing from his blue eyes the tall Irishman stood in his stirrups.

"If ye're goin', sir, then so am I, an' I say that anyone as doesn't is a coward an' deserves tae die! Who will go wi' the colonel?"

The regiment raised their swords. With one voice, they answered. "I!"

Nobody turned. "Very well, men. If you choose thus this day, you must know that we go, in all likelihoods, to our deaths. I have said that this is my last charge because I will depart from the army, but most likely it is my last because I will not live to see the ending of this day. Now, forward, the 42nd will ride— at the gallop!"

"The gallop!" screamed five-hundred throats at once, and the earth shook beneath the pounding of their hooves.

"The gallop, Noble!" Edmund cried. "Now I understand why we always cantered!"

"Yes, my friend." Nobody drew his sword. "I knew that this day would come at last, though when and where I had no idea. The enemy knows that the 42nd does not gallop, and when they see us doing just that—they'll know that it's victory or death. If they do not break from fear, we are lost. Men! This day is ours, and whether it is for death or glory, it is for the right! Shout, and when you shout—yell like Furies!"

"For the right! For the right! For the right!" The men raised the battle cry to heaven. Jacques and O'Malley, Petr and Dilworth, the Preston brothers and Stoning, Bronner and all the others who so loved their colonel—upward they shouted and onward they spurred.

Side by side Nobody and Edmund galloped onward, their swords raised to the sky. Tree and bush, bright sky and sodden earth—all vanished before the impetuous charge. The Russians paused abruptly as this vision of death opened before them, personified by the most feared British unit in Russia. They could see clearly the Boy Colonel at the head of his troops, his hat lost under the churning hooves, a sword in one hand and a pistol in the other, the rifle strapped to his back bouncing at each stride.

"Они галопом!" they cried. "Они галопом! They gallop! They gallop!" The officers pressed forward, cursing their men's fears and ordering them to fire, but the terror-stricken Cossacks would have none of it. Many devoutly believed that the 42nd's colonel was a devil. All knew what the 42nd was, and the way it fought—and all knew that they never galloped into battle. Slowly, at first, they edged backwards, dodging the blows from their infuriated officers, but as more retreated, others followed suit, and when the 42nd uttered one final scream of fury they turned and fled, loosed like waters rushing through a dyke.

"The Lord be praised!" Nobody shouted. "He has given us the day!"

"Amen." Edmund slashed the air with a vengeance, pressing his horse faster on the flying Cossacks' heels. "Now for the mopping up. O'Malley! Why haven't you drawn your sword?"

"I'm tryin' tae, sir, it won't be a-budgin' for anythin'." The Irishman was struggling with his hilt, trying to pull it out of the metal scabbard.

"Vhy, you Irish fool, you have kept your sword in your scabbard and zhey have frozen togezher!"

"Why so it is." O'Malley's face grew red. "I wasn't expectin' that bit o' frost last night."

"*Boeuf!*"

"Oh come now Jack, ye needn't be gloatin' over it. Where's ye're own sword?"

Jacques tossed his head. "Vhere do you zhink it vould be but here in my—scabbard." He desperately wrenched at the hilt, but it was frozen just as solidly as the Irishman's.

"Hypocritic Frog," O'Mally growled. "I suppose we'll have tae go back to the days o' cloobs." Without more ado he whipped out a knife and sliced his sword-belt, grasped the weapon in his huge hand, scabbard and all, and went for the closest Russian.

"Irish barbarians," Jacques muttered, unbuckling his own belt with some trouble because of the galloping horse beneath him, and firmly holding the scabbard by its middle. "Leave it to zhe French to show skill." He flung it javelin style at a furious Cossack officer, neatly caught the falling man's unsheathed sword, and calmly joined the fight with an edged weapon.

Nobody dashed recklessly among the fleeing Russians looking for Liana, but naught save bearded Russians and dirty uniforms met his eye. Edmund rode just behind him, guarding the desperate boy from blows. Somewhere in the distance came a muffled scream—that was no deep-throated Cossack! Nobody struck his heels into the horse's flank, plowing through the terrified enemy soldiers in search of the fair form that had uttered that cry for help. What was that! A tall Cossack pressed through the panicked crowd, something draped over his saddle-pommel. Liana!

A red mist floated before his eyes—all he could see was the back of that Cossack. Instinctively, his hand gripped the pistol like a vice. He could feel the fighting fury overcoming his willpower. Desperately, he leveled the pistol and squeezed the trigger.

The Cossack dropped to the earth like a sack of flour with Nobody's bullet in his brain, while the boy grasped the insensible girl gently in his arms. Her face was white, and her hair fell in disorder over his arms. In a moment the fury drained from his body and he sat motionless on his horse, cradling her head in his rough hands.

His triumphant troops quickly overtook their colonel and passed onward, but he called them back. The Russians, though routed, still vastly outnumbered the jubilant band, and now that their object was attained their best course lay in a speedy return. With much thanksgiving and rejoicing the loyal men obeyed, though a few bold spirits cast longing eyes at the distant masses still rushing pell-mell from the scene of their ignoble rout.

Chapter 25

General Tremont faced Nobody angrily. His tunic was only half-buttoned, and the awkward slant of his disordered wig made the boy think of a half-sheered sheep with its fleece just falling off. Nobody sat stiffly in the low wooden chair, grasping a leather satchel in his hands.

"I suppose you've come here to gloat," General Tremont snapped, jumping nervously from his chair and pacing the room. "Not that I didn't expect you'd come."

"I don't understand you, sir. What would I have to gloat about?" The boy frowned, wondering what new scheme Tremont was concocting.

"Bosh. Don't try to play an innocent with me, boy. You know very well that I have been relieved from my command—'transferred,' they called it, to a rotten commissioner's duties. Oh yes, you needn't look so surprised. The accursed dispatches just came, and I probably have you to thank for the new 'respect of my accomplishments,' as His Majesty so *graciously* puts it." He sneered, and spat into the low burning fire.

Nobody blinked. "I assure you, General, I had no idea of any such matters."

"No? As if I believe that. I have received positive instructions to negotiate an exchange for General Whitmore. I know you were wonderfully friendly with him. You probably maligned me in front of the king and his whole court, didn't you, just to get him back?"

"I did not malign you, sir."

"Did you speak badly of me?" Tremont swept the table clear with one angry motion of his hand and glowered down at the boy.

Nobody returned his gaze calmly. "The king asked me to give my opinion of matters in Siberia, and I did so."

Tremont slammed his fist upon the table. "Did you speak badly of me?" he shouted shrilly.

"I spoke the truth, sir. If there was any bad in it, it was not my fault, but that of he who created the bad."

The angry general sat down and laid his fists upon the table. "Colonel Nobody, I am well aware that General Whitmore maintained a dislike for me. Did he at any time ask for your opinion of me?"

"He did."

"Did you give it to him?"

"I did."

"What was it?"

"I'm not sure that you would like to hear it, sir."

Tremont struck the table again, this time reinforcing the blow with an oath. "Tell me every word you said, boy!"

Nobody smiled coldly. "If you so desire. Remember that it was your idea, not mine. General Whitmore asked me first my opinion of you as a general. I said that you were unfeeling to your inferiors, fawning with your superiors, and generally disliked by the men." Tremont rose to his feet but the boy held up his hand. "General Tremont, I am not finished. You asked for everything, and that is what I will give. He next asked me for my opinion of you as a man. I said that you were loose-living, profane, arrogant, and blackguardly. I could not accuse you of cowardice, having never seen you close enough to the front line to know whether you would turn tail and run."

Tremont gasped, his face white with fury. "And you said that behind my back? Who's the blackguard, I ask?"

"I do not say anything about a man that I will not say to his face," Nobody said quietly, "as is obvious by what I just said."

"Why did you come here, Colonel Nobody?"

"To resign my commission." Nobody took a sealed paper from the leather satchel at his side and dropped it on the table.

The furious general gasped again, this time in disbelief. "To what?"

"To resign my commission. I have come to the belief that we are not fighting in a just war, and therefore I consider it my duty to leave. I do not expect you to understand—indeed, it would surprise me if you did. However, if you would be so kind as to accept the resignation, we can part and go our separate ways."

"You want to leave the army?"

"No. It is my duty, not my inclination."

"Hmm, very interesting." Tremont clasped his hands behind his back and paced the floor. "So, you want to resign." He paused abruptly and glared at the boy. "Colonel Nobody, it has been reported to me that you ignored my orders to burn the villages through which the Russians had passed. Is that so?"

Nobody hesitated for a moment at this unexpected turn, but responded in the affirmative.

The veins on Tremont's forehead bulged. "You are saying that you distinctly and purposely refused to obey my orders?"

"If you care to put it in that way, sir, yes, but only because—"

"Silence! You can't reason your way out of this one, or call on General Whitmore to back you. No, Colonel Nobody, I do not accept your resignation. I hereby discharge you dishonorably from the Army of His Royal Majesty King William IV for contempt of orders."

Nobody stiffened.

"It is my last act as general, Colonel Nobody, and a satisfactory one, I assure you. I know very well how ambitious you are, and how much you have wanted to rise."

"So ambitious that I would resign my commission?" Nobody laughed bitterly.

"I don't know what's behind that act, but nonetheless you are dishonorably discharged from the king's service. Get out of my sight."

Nobody saluted. "Very well, sir. I should have expected something like this from you. My quarters will be at the disposal of my successor tomorrow, as will the igloos of those men who choose to leave."

"What men who choose to leave? Officers may resign their commissions, but men cannot leave simply because they so choose."

"In the 42nd they can." Nobody removed another paper from the satchel. "Every man signs this before entering my—my former regiment. They are the regimental papers, quite different as you know from most because of the unique formation and purpose of the 42nd." Nobody tapped the paper. "Here, you see, is stipulated that at any time the colonel of the 42nd changes, for any reason, whether it be death, promotion, resignation, or discharge, all soldiers of the 42nd have the right to leave the regiment, whether to transfer to another corps, or to leave the army altogether."

The general snatched the paper from his hand and read the stipulation. It was true. Because the 42nd was similar in organization to an extremely organized guerrilla force, it was deemed wise to include this in their papers, because the soldiers would be likely to form attachments to their colonel. Tremont crumpled the paper in his hand and cast it furiously into the fire.

"Then go, and good riddance!" he hissed. "We will meet again. Beware."

"You are no longer my commanding officer, I am no longer a soldier. You have given me a dishonorable discharge that I cannot contest, though I have done nothing to merit it. I do not threaten, but I warn you that if at any future time you interfere in my life—it is *you* that must beware!"

The birds sung brightly in the clear air, but they did not cheer Nobody's injured soul.

Dishonorable discharge. Contempt of orders. Folly and nonsense, but nonetheless on my record. Tremont had better thank whatever demon he worships that I do not believe in revenge, or else he would be a dead man before the week was out.

The news had already spread that he intended to resign his commission, and it was with sorrowful looks that many a soldier saluted as the boy passed. Nobody's belongings were already packed in trunks and loaded onto an oxcart, where they awaited their master before the convoy set out for the coast.

Among the regiments gathered in the parade ground was the 42nd. Silent and still, the men waited in a hollow square for their commanding officer to give his last address. They opened ranks to let him pass, and closed about him.

"Men of the 42nd. My men, you have been, but are no longer. My friends you still are, and nothing can change that. I leave this bloody land today. My ship sails for the Pacific Ocean, where I hope to find an island and become a simple trader. You have honored and respected me. You have served me well. I thank you. Your future careers are now in your hands. You may continue in the 42nd, transfer to another regiment, or leave the army. I know that many do not have large means, and that if you were to leave it would cause hardships. I also know that you will not serve under most colonels. I ask no man to come with me, but if any man desires to do so, I will provide him employment in my future station. You are fighters! Think well about your choice before you act— the 42nd may remain a noble regiment no matter who its commander is."

"A noble regiment," Edmund whispered bitterly, "but not the same without Noble at its head."

The ranks stirred. Matthew Preston stepped forward and saluted gravely. "Colonel Nobody, I request the privilege to speak."

"Permission granted."

"Colonel, I have been asked by the men of Squad One, Company One, to express our feelings for you. I am sure that I speak for many other men as well in the unworthy verses I and my brother have penned."

He took a paper from his pouch and unfolded it.

"To our colonel, to our colonel, to the 42nd's colonel,
It is you that we have followed into bloody frays of death,
'Tis for you that many soldiers have expended their last breath.

To our colonel, to our colonel, to the 42nd's colonel,
Fame and glory have been added to our everlasting name,
White and hoary we may grow and yet we'll ne'er forget the same.

To our colonel, to our colonel, to the 42nd's colonel,
We will follow where you lead us, though it be the ocean floor,
Throughout life we will attend you, whether rich or whether poor,
To our colonel, With our colonel, For the 42nd's colonel!"

As the men echoed the last line, Nobody covered his face. The 42nd had long been his only family, father, mother, brother and sister. To leave now—the agony!

Edmund must have understood his feelings, for he ordered the men to form into two bodies. Those who would stay in the 42nd must stand in front of their commander, those that would leave, behind him. Not a soldier wished to join a different regiment. A hundred weather-beaten faces gathered behind their colonel, and with one voice they proclaimed their desire to follow him. The papers of discharge were signed, their kits gathered, and the heart and soul of the 42nd mounted his warhorse one last time.

"Farewell!" Nobody cried. "Farewell to snow and ice, farewell to bush and tree, farewell to man and boy. Your faces are etched in my heart. Wherever a soldier of the 42nd may find himself, let him ask for his old colonel and I will brave fire and storm to give you aid. Farewell!"

Chapter 26

White clouds floated airily over the Sea of Okhotsk, their vapory mists hardly dulling the sun's intense rays. Gulls screamed noisily from their perches on the masts of the large schooner which lazily meandered through the gentle waves, the sails hardly filled by the light wind. The sailors' busy actions belied the calm aspect of the weather. Ropes needed coiling, decks needed scrubbing, and a pile of old sails waited for rehabilitation by the sailors' needles.

The *Robinson Crusoe*, as she was called, awaited her companion, a sister-ship of same build which was just leaving harbor. She had originally been named the *Friday*, as the captain told Nobody, but the superstitious seamen objected so strongly to this literary touch that she was rechristened the *Illusory*. Both ships were deep-hulled and wide at the beam, providing more space for cargo and passengers. They were not fast ships, but sea-worthy, and well-proved already upon the ocean.

Nobody, Edmund, and the members of what was previously called Squad One sat inside one of the *Robinson Crusoe*'s staterooms, discussing their future plans. Somerset also sat with them in his official role of reporter, having decided that the *Times* would still be interested with the colonel's post-military career. His presence was accepted, but not requested. Nobody had scarce talked to him since the day he turned from danger.

Nobody bent over the table outlining his plan of action. He wanted to find a small Pacific island with a good harbor and some natural resources. He had engaged both ships and their cargo space and loaded them with suitable goods for trading, making sure to reserve enough space for the men of the 42nd, most of whom were aboard the *Illusory*.

He tapped the general area on the map where he hoped to find a suitable island. "By setting up a trading station, we can provide a convenient stopping point for mariners. I hope to purchase several ships for our own uses, which can be manned by the 42nd. These I propose to send to various questionable areas where native pirates are thought to roam, and therefore the lucrative trade possibilities are not developed. With a stout crew of 42nd men, a decent armament, and plenty of rifles, I daresay our ships could beat off any native riggers they come across. What do you say?"

Edmund raised his hand. "It sounds like a good plan, Noble, but won't it take a mint of money to do?"

"It will not be inexpensive, but I have sufficient resources."

"Resources? From a colonel's pay? I don't say anything against King William (God bless him), but he's not known for overloading his officers with money."

"It's quite possible that I have other means, Edmund. Enough. Friends! I hope, with God's aid, to provide employment to all of you for so long as you may wish it. Somerset, you will abide by the terms of our contract?"

"Certainly, sir. I'll obey your orders, and wait for your approval on articles I send back to the *Times*."

"You will. I'm still not entirely sure why I've let you come. I suppose it's for old Pierce's sake, the man you replaced. He was the only news reporter I really liked. Follow my provisions, and you can stay. Violate them, and you will have a passage booked for you to London. Now, men, that's all. Hurrah for the tropics!"

Thus began a voyage symbolic of much more than a simple sea-journey. Nobody left behind his life, his authority, his family; all that he knew and loved except for the few loyal men now gathered round. But there was one other—Liana. As the men filed out of his cabin, his mind wandered to the floor of the London ballroom that fateful night. Images of the trusting young form who knelt by his side before the king crowded his mind. His fingers still tingled from that first time he touched her soft hands. He pushed his chair back and wearily rested both legs on the table. He remembered the hot fire that burned in his brain when he saw the tall Cossack carrying away his betrothed. That day was the first he ever succumbed to the fighting fury.

Why is that scene still painted vividly in my mind? Why does my heart quicken every time I think of her insensible body, so frail and defenseless, lying in my arms as the Russians fled past. Is this love? No, it can't be. I don't feel that I'm in love. I respect her, I honor her, and I would gladly lay down my life for her. Is that love? A scene rose before his eyes—there he stood before the king, pale and shaken as he was informed of his new partner in life.

'Our ward has developed a great liking for you.' The words rang in his ears, the hot blood pounding in his cheeks. Every time he thought of the girl, and whether he loved her or no, this dark phantom rose, blotting out the shining face and dimpled cheeks.

Come, Nobody, you leave the army and you become a melancholy sap. Out of it, man, life doesn't stop while you engage in these fantasies. A gentle rap upon the cabin door interrupted his thoughts, and he looked up to see the girlish figure just ensconced in his mind's eye glide into the room.

Her dimpled cheeks glowed. "I have come to command your attendance at my table. Elyssa and I managed to bake a few rolls before you so ungallantly dragged us from dear Mrs. Campbell, and as your penance you must come this very moment and partake of our tea." She held the door open with an encouraging smile.

"I could think of many harder penances, Liana." Nobody rose from his seat. "I would be even more encouraged of my favorable reception if you showed a few of your teeth in that smile."

The dimples deepened. "I cannot help my natural tendencies. It will be a fine time for my lips to smile as well as my cheeks when you tell me who you are."

Nobody sobered. "No, Liana, do not wish it," he said earnestly. "Better a hundred times that your smiling eyes and cheeks suffice than that you be burdened with such a dangerous secret."

His vehemence evidently disturbed her, but she made no comment and led the way to her tiny cabin, where they found Edmund assisting the young maid in setting out the service. Nobody liked the meek girl, whose golden locks and blue eyes contrasted so strongly with Liana's darker beauty. Although nominally a maid she was as close as a sister to the older girl. The boys seated the girls first and then took their own places round the small table, from whose surface rose the calming aroma of English tea. Nobody sat across from his betrothed, Edmund and Elyssa sitting likewise, and the meal began.

Liana played the hostess quite prettily, gravely residing over the teapot and encouraging the boys to partake heartily of the bread, for which there was no second encouragement needed.

"I had no idea Nobody was marrying a bakeress," Edmund joked, laying a thick coat of butter upon his third roll.

"I had no idea he was marrying anyone at all," Liana said merrily. "I assure you, I never thought that the awkward, blunt, odd young man I met at the king's ball would ever become my husband."

Nor did I, Nobody thought. "I hope this voyage is as uneventful as our last. Speaking from personal experience, most events on the sea are neither pleasant nor profitable. A clear path and a brisk wind are all I ask."

"Have you sailed much, sir?" the little servant girl asked timidly.

"A good bit for my short life, Elyssa, but naught compared to a true sailor. You don't make much headway with your bread, I see. I'm afraid the vessel's roll doesn't agree with your stomach?"

"I do not think I should ever be a sailor, sir." She looked at his cup. "You do not attend much to your tea, either, sir. Do you also feel the swells?"

Liana glanced at him inquiringly. Nobody reddened. "You see, I always thought that Jacques was horrible at making tea, but I realized while in England that it does not agree with my palate."

"Why Noble, you're not a proper Englishman if you don't like tea!" Edmund clicked his tongue. "So much for patriotism and 'king and country.' Mercenary fellow, selling yourself to African coffee instead of hearty British tea!"

"Very well, Edmund," Nobody said composedly, "then I suppose I'm mercenary. Would you be so kind as to pass another roll?"

"How do you intend to occupy yourself this voyage, Dear?" Liana asked. "I was speaking with your funny little Frenchman the other day, and he said that Thomas Bronner was well-taught, and played a man's part in the battle. Do you intend to continue training him now?"

"Probably a bit, but not as hard as aboard the *Daisy*. He acquitted himself well, and is quite on the way to proving an honor to Squad—but I forget. There is no Squad One." He frowned. "I will probably attend to one or two of my war books—perhaps Caesar's *Commentaries about the Gallic War*, or maybe that old Chinese Sun Tzu's *Art of War*, so helpfully translated into French."

"Believe me, Lady Liana," Edmund interposed, "you are going to have a very unique husband. Only fellow I ever met who learned a language just to read one book."

"French?"

"No." Nobody laughed. "Latin. I learned French because it's so common and useful a language, and in part, I confess, because I wanted to know what Jacques was saying. You probably didn't know, but O'Malley tried to learn at the same time as myself, and I suspect for the latter reason, but he gave up in disgust after the first lesson, saying that his tongue was put into his head for hard honest speaking, not jabbering."

They laughed, easily picturing the tall Irishman's contempt and Jacques's response. Liana and Elyssa began to clean the plates and cups in a bucket of fresh rainwater, laughingly refusing the boys' offers of help.

"Come, Edmund, let's see how the *Robinson Crusoe* makes way. She's shaped so much like a tub that I doubt they can get more than six knots from her, even with a stiff breeze."

Active sailors bustled about on deck, coiling ropes, securing chicken cages, and laughing and joking with each other. The two boys found a quiet spot near the quarterdeck and leaned against the bulwark, breathing great breaths of the invigorating air.

"So," Edmund said. "Do you love her?"

Nobody folded his arms and gazed down at the churning green water. "No, I don't think so."

"Then you're a fool! You're the oddest fellow I ever met! Here you have a sweet, lovely, sensible, meek, principled, intelligent young lady dropped, as it were, into your lap, without an ounce of work required from you."

"That's the thing. I didn't have to work for her and I don't feel that I deserve her. She's all those things and many more, but what am I? A cross, awkward, rough young fellow who would sooner handle a rifle than a lady's hand, and is more familiar with blood than tears. What kind of a husband could I be? Yes, yes," he said impatiently as Edmund opened his mouth, "I know what you're about to say. A *loving* husband, is it not? Yes indeed, and I would gladly be. I respect her, she has a splendid personality, a really fun, but also deep girl. And yet! Every time I think that I love her I see rise before my eyes an awful phantom. How would *you* like it if a girl decided she wanted to marry *you*, and that was that!"

"I wouldn't take it very kindly, but on the other hand she's a splendid girl in other respects. She'll make a splendid wife."

"Yes, a splendid wife, but for what a husband! You would be better than I, Edmund. You know the right things to say, the polite courtesies to show, you enjoy the same novels, you can make her laugh, or cry, or both. What can I do?"

Edmund clapped his friend on the shoulder. "No, no, my dear fellow, I wouldn't dream of it. You ride yourself down too hard. It's true that you're not exactly a polished diplomat, but you're strong, capable, wise, much-loved, and skillful, much more than I can say for myself. No, no, my dear fellow, you're quite fit for her, with the one exception, of course, that a man should love his wife."

"Indeed. What would you have me say? I could put on my most tear-wrenching face and ooze about how she is 'beautiful, my darling, the love of my life, my adoration, my shining star, my—'"

Edmund coughed.

Nobody spun round. A wisp of a green traveling cloak disappeared into the girls' cabin.

Nobody gasped. "How much do you think she heard?"

Edmund scratched his head. "I only just saw her come out—probably that bit about beauty, adoration, your shining star, and what not."

Nobody groaned and dropped his head into his hands. "Now what? If she's heard that, she thinks that I meant it, and not that I was saying what I *couldn't* in good conscience say! Oh, Edmund! I can't go to her and say 'oh, by the way, Dear, disregard what I was just saying to Edmund out there, I really don't love you one bit.'"

"I wouldn't recommend it."

"So here I am, practically sailing under false colors, with a betrothed wife I don't love and who thinks I adore her! Oh, why couldn't I have been born as some simple peasant lad, never needing to fight, never needing to rise in the ranks or attract attention?" The miserable boy slumped against the bulwark.

Edmund folded his arms. "Here's a case of human nature for you. Do you know how many boys would give all they have, five times over, just to be in your boots for one day? And here you are bemoaning yourself, and wishing you could be in their place."

"I know it's selfish, Ed, and that's what I'm saying. I don't deserve Liana, she's far too good for me."

"And yet the only reason you present for not loving her is that she was forward in arranging your marriage, and therefore *not* good in that respect. What a convoluted, confused, odd fellow you are!"

"Ed, you're not helping me!" Nobody took a deep breath. "Please, go back into the cabin and tell the girls that I can't come right now, and that I must have a conversation with the men, which is true, I will, and then amuse yourself however you normally do with your books, or discussions, or whatever it is that you know so well and I can't fathom. Go!"

The next weeks passed calmly for all aboard the sister-ships, in outward appearances, at least, but one heart aboard the *Robinson Crusoe* weighed heavily with a multitude of emotions. Each day that Nobody spent with his betrothed wife strengthened his respect for her, and each day increased his amazement that this sweet girl could have been so forward. His face grew a shade paler, notwithstanding the increasing power of the sun as they approached the line of the equator, and his brow often remained furrowed in thought, but he did his best to conceal his ill spirits. Edmund alone was his confidant, and many a weary hour did they pass together discussing the subject.

It was a bright sunny day, with clear skies and a pleasant breeze, when the captain of the *Robinson Crusoe* informed his passengers that they would cross the Equator that very day. This caused a stir among the soldiers, most of whom had never approached the most famous imaginary line in the world. This information must also have instilled an interest about nautical matters in Jacques and O'Malley, for they cornered one of the sailors, within earshot of Nobody and Liana, and began plying him with questions.

The seaman, a crafty, weather-beaten old fellow with one ear and a limp happily obliged

"You see, shipmates, I've been on the ocean nigh on thirty years, but you might think it'd be closer to forty after clappin' eyes to this old hulk. You want to know how to tell the difference between a good ship an' a bad? Why it's as easy as fallin' overboard. Can't you see the difference 'tween two folks on land? Aye. So's it's the same with ships."

"But how exactly *do* you tell?" Jacques pressed.

"Like I said, it's as easy as fallin' overboard." He paused to spit a dark stream of tobacco juice over the bulwark. "Now I'll gi' you a true picter of a ship as it ought to be, and no mistake. I can just see her now, the queen o' all ships, plowin' the brine wi' her taffrail, a squall on her beam, an' loose sheets all about."

The two veterans leaned closer, listening with baited breath to the seaman's 'picter.'

"Aye, shipmates, that's a perfect ship for you, wi' sails reefed to the top, an' a triple-ration o' grog, for good luck. It's then you'll see the captain's daughter walkin' on deck."

"The captin's dauchter?" O'Malley exclaimed. "He's got a dauchter?"

"Aye, an' a pretty one, too, but she's most always locked up in his cabin, she is."

"Zhat is odd. Vhat is she like?" Jacques glanced at the captain's small cabin.

The sailor crossed his long arms and gazed meditatively at the sails. "Oh, she's a witty one, almost cuttin', you might say. Well-seasoned, too. I'd say she'd fit you just fine, but the gunner's daughter would be a bit young."

"Zhe Gunner's daughter? Zhere is anozher voman aboard as vell?"

"Aye, but like I said, you'd be rather *old* for her. Ain't that right, master?" he asked, turning to Nobody and giving him a sly wink.

"Yes indeed," the boy returned, pretending to scrutinize the forms of his faithful followers, "rather old. Have you two been enjoying Bill's representation of a perfect sailing scene?"

"Aye, sir," O'Malley cried with enthusiasm, "it must be splendid tae be a sailin' man!"

Nobody grunted. "Do you two understand—ahem, that is, do you two know the meanings of the terms Bill has been using?"

The two landsmen coughed, and sheepishly admitted that they weren't quite sure, but Jacques added that "it sounded more beautiful zhan I ever could have zhought sailing could be."

"Indeed. What do you think, Bill, should I give them a little landsman's translation?"

The sailor nodded his head gravely.

"Very well." Nobody turned to the two soldiers, his face breaking into a large grin. "You should probably know, my dear fellows, that the picture just painted in words by your friend, Bill, shows a ship diving stern-first into the ocean with a blasting wind on her side, loose ropes hanging all about, sails so tied up that they can do nothing, and a crew of drunken sailors."

Jacques and O'Malley stared blankly at the grinning sailor. "It's a lie?" the Irishman shouted fiercely, glowering at Bill.

"No, more of a joke, you might say," the sailor said, backing away nervously. "Rather funny, don't you think?"

"Not a bit. What was the part aboot the dauchters all aboot, then?"

Nobody tried to keep his composure. "You see, O'Malley, the 'captain's daughter' is another way of referring to the cat-of-nine-tails, and the 'gunner's daugher' is a lighter instrument normally used on midshipmen or ship's boys. Which, of course, is why you would be too old for her."

The soldiers grinned sheepishly and joined in a half-hearted laugh before retiring from the scene of their embarrassment. At this moment the captain strode by, commenting, as he passed, that they were about to cross the Equator. Soldiers and sailors crowded the deck, staring with interest at the water all around, and giving a cheer as the captain announced that they had come, roughly, to 0° Latitude.

"Ahoy ship!" cried a strange voice, and an even stranger figure scrambled over the bulwarks amidships and confronted the laughing sailors. It was dressed grotesquely in gaudy sheets, down which streamed brine. A rough-hewn wooden crown tilted cockily on its head, below which hung a wide strip of black fabric with three holes cut for eyes and mouth. A bronzed hand reached out of puffy sleeves and grasped a large pitchfork, which also dripped with brine.

Two similarly dressed figures, minus the crown and pitchfork, followed this oddity and the whole group gravely made their way towards the stern, where most of the 42nd were gathered. Nobody frowned as they approached, but he folded his arms and resigned himself to what was coming.

"Neptune calling," the man announced in gruff accents. "Court of sea established. Nymphs, bring the first man." The supposed sea-god's attendants stepped forward and clapped two hands onto poor Jacques. "Frenchman," the interrogator growled, "have you crossed our ocean before?"

"Unhand me! I do not know vhat you mean! I have crossed zhe ocean before, but it is no more *yours* than it is mine."

"Have you crossed the Equator," the man demanded roughly, shaking his pitchfork.

"No."

"Let the baptismal begin." The two attendants dragged Jacques towards a barrel of water, but O'Malley jumped forward and thrust his huge body in the way.

"What's this?" he demanded. "Who do ye fellows think ye are?"

"O'Malley, it's best not to interfere." Nobody waved him away. "It's an ancient sea tradition that all who cross the Equator must be suitably welcomed by the line's veterans."

"Oh." The Irishman scratched his head. "But *I* haven't been o'er the line, sir!"

"I know."

Jacques, meanwhile, had been roughly set upon by the "Nymphs," along with help from several of the crew. First they dunked him in the barrel of water, then they dried his face, produced a blunt razor, and painstakingly shaved his curling whiskers. The indignant Frenchman once finished, they continued down the line, welcoming sailor and soldier alike with jokes and leering grins.

"They wouldn't dare do it to me—would they?" Edmund whispered.

"Have you crossed the line?"

"Well, no."

"In that case, prepare yourself, because here comes Neptune."

The pretender crowed. "Here's a gentleman o' the land come aboard!" He stepped up to Nobody. "Has this gentleman ever crossed the middle line o' our dominions?"

"Yes."

"Wot? You've crossed the Equator before?"

"Yes indeed, and I am quite familiar with the doings of Neptune, though I must offer my condolences for your leg."

"My leg?" Neptune frowned.

"Yes. You must have banged it against some coral reef, I suspect, judging by your limp. Oh, also, you must have some very talkative Nymphs down there to have talked off your divine ear." Bill laughed and removed his mask.

"You're a smart one, an' if you've crossed before then I've naught to do with you, more's the pity. Ah!" He shifted his eyes behind the annoyed colonel. "Here's one who hasn't, or I'm a Dutchman." He leered at Liana and beckoned his attendants to his side. "Here's a pretty little thing, and we must show her the hospitality o' the sea, eh mates—that is, Nymphs?"

The men laughed coarsely as the frightened girl instinctively shrank against her betrothed. The sailor tipped his crown back and studied the girl critically. "I say, boys, we can't shave this one. P'raps we should be more creative, eh? I think I've just the thing." He stepped closer. "Here, my girl, give us a kiss for good luck."

In an instant Nobody's keen sword lay upon the man's outstretched wrist.

"Lay a hand upon her and you lose it!" Nobody cried.

Edmund also drew his sword and put his body before Elyssa. "You'll get the same here," he said fiercely as the Nymphs recoiled before his flashing blade.

Bill pushed the blade away with a scarred hand. "Come now, guv'ner, you wouldn't do that, now, would you? I'm just welcoming these two girls past the Equator, that's all, and askin' pr'aps for a closer acquaintanceship wi' their beauty. Now I know you wouldn't dare hurt me, *sir*." He sneered.

"Sailor," Nobody said steadily, "I have killed more men in my life than there are crew aboard this ship. I do not desire to add to the list, but if necessary—I will not hold back."

The sailor retreated a step, his complacent smile turning to an angry frown. "This ain't fair, capting," he called to the *Robinson Crusoe's* captain. "It's long been our privilege to welcome seaman and passenger alike, an' I say it's ours now wi' these girls. It's bad enough luck to have women aboard at all."

The sailors gave angry grunts of assent and slowly moved towards the four young people.

The captain stood on the quarter-deck, fiddling with his cap. "Perhaps, Colonel Nobody, if my men's idea of proper baptism were slightly modified—"

"Not a chance. The man who lays a hand upon either of these two ladies will lose both the hand and the head, I solemnly promise you."

By now a crowd of angry seamen were gathered in a dense mass, keeping just out of sword-reach from the boys.

"Let me paint you a picture, Captain," Nobody cried. "On board your ship are two ladies. Also on your ship are two men, or boys, I don't care what terms you use, who will lay down their lives before a hair on these ladies' heads shall be touched. Here before us is your crew; a rapscallion lot, I daresay. At the moment the odds seem rather against us, but odds change rapidly in love and war. 42nd—to me!"

The angry sailors divided like the waves of the Red Sea as twenty men—nineteen, actually, without counting the reporter who stood vacillating near the main mast—dashed to their commander's side and formed into two ranks, leveling their rifles at the retreating miscreants. The habit of many years could not be broken in one month, and each man still carried his rifle strapped to his back, with a sword clinking at his side, though never dreaming it would be needed for such a cause.

"Now," the Boy Colonel continued, "you see a different picture. Here are twenty-one men fresh from the killing fields of Siberia, and there is your unarmed crew. Is my point clear?"

The captain nodded nervously, but Nobody was not finished. He glanced significantly at the Irishman, who nodded to Jacques, and the two dashed forward, seized 'Neptune' by the throat, and hurled him over the ship's side.

Not a man of the crew moved. Each stared at the line of long muzzles facing them. Nobody quietly sheathed his sword. "I believe that the proper term would be 'man overboard.' You might want to throw the fellow a rope."

The tars sullenly rescued their sodden mate and the crowd dispersed, but it was clear by the glowering looks that they would not forget the insult.

Chapter 27

"Land ho!"

Bare feet pounded upon the rough planks as sleepy sailors tumbled out of their hammocks and rushed on deck.

"Where away?" shouted the captain.

"Two points to the starboard bow, sir." The lookout pointed to a low black mass on the horizon.

"It's certainly an island," the captain confirmed, removing the spyglass from his eye. "Coral reef on this side, coconuts and palms all over the place. Helmsman! Steer two points to port. Prepare to take in sail!" Seamen sprang into the rigging as the *Robinson Crusoe* yawed, and a signal flag was hoisted on a halyard to request the *Illusory* to do likewise.

Although it was midday, the sun was covered by clouds, forming strange shadows on the approaching island. A stiff breeze blew among the trees and ruffled the face of the water, impelling both ships forward at a brisk pace. They doubled a long low spit of ground fringed by white foam from the coral reef and found a small harbor conveniently protected from the wind. A number of huts stood upon the shore. Lime and wild vanilla scented the air.

The captain scrutinized the village through his spyglass. "There's definitely a European taste about that village. I see a few canoes—no, not war canoes.

I fancy there's a woman coming out of one of the huts—yes, I'm sure of it, and she's rigged out in full style—can't be a native, they're not known for overdressing."

"What's that?" Nobody squinted at a mist rising from the interior of the island.

"Looks like smoke, sir."

"I'd like to take a boat ashore, Captain. The harbor is good, but I must see what the native disposition is."

"It looks rather strange to me." The captain shook his whiskered head. "Normally you'd have a crowd of canoes here by now selling fruit and trinkets, and what not. I don't see a soul stirring besides that European woman. I don't like it."

"Do you think there's danger?"

"Can't say for certain."

"Well, I will take my soldiers with me, and they should give a good account of any native war party."

Liana stood at his side. "Please take me with you, Noble," she whispered.

"My dear, don't you see that it's much safer to stay on board?"

"With these sailors?" She glanced fearfully at the tars as they laughed and joked about the island's prospective hospitality.

"Very well, Dear, we will all go. O'Malley, muster the men, we go ashore at once. And," he added behind his hand, "make sure our most valuable baggage is aboard. I don't want it missing when we return."

The humid air drenched the oarsmen as they pulled at the rough oars, forcing the heavily loaded boat through the choppy waves. Beads of sweat trickled down the seamen's bare backs and sparkled in the sunlight. No sound as yet came from the village, and no eager inhabitants crowded to the beach to welcome them. The deserted shore, the waving treetops, and the darkened sun combined to give a cheerless aspect to the scene, unaided by Jacques's mutterings about cannibals and cooking pots.

With a harsh grating sound the boat's keel struck the sand and a following wave pushed it forward upon the beach. Nobody and Edmund aided the girls to disembark while the soldiers and sailors quickly dragged the boat out of the waves' reach. They adjusted their weapons and moved cautiously towards the silent village, which was comprised of twenty or thirty huts scattered along a trodden path.

As the party approached, a man ran out of the nearest hut, and, uttering a cry of delight, rushed towards them. He wore a strange mixture of clothing, consisting of a straw hat, a red neckerchief tied loosely about the throat, a morning coat that hung to his knees, and a pair of ragged trousers hardly any longer, giving the ludicrous impression of a bare-legged native in fashionable attire. His face, however, was kindly and intelligent, lean, with a long nose and bright blue eyes. The speed at which he ran pointed to a healthy constitution, but Nobody judged him to be at least forty years old by the tinges of gray in his dark beard and hair.

"Please, sir, you must help us!" the man cried, seizing Nobody's hand. "They're going to bury him alive!"

"I beg your pardon, sir, but could you first explain who you are, who 'they' are, and who 'he' is?"

"What? Oh yes, of course." The man untied his neckerchief and dabbed at the sweat on his bald forehead. A touch of asthma, added to the exertion and his nervous mental state, prevented him from speaking for several moments, during which Nobody noticed several scared faces peeping from the huts at him. "Excuse me, sir," the strange man continued, "but this day has been very trying to me. I am the missionary to this island, you see, and I have been here for about a year, and the natives have shown great interest but they are still far from converted. A hermit lives on this island, a European, I believe, but I have only seen him from a distance, and the natives suspect him to be a witchdoctor. Well, one of the tribal leaders grew sick the other day, so they dragged this hermit down in order to heal him, but of course he wouldn't because he isn't a witchdoctor, and because of this they are going to bury him alive!" He gasped for breath.

"Very providential timing, I must say. Where are they?"

"I will guide you myself."

The missionary ran like a madman along the thin path that wound through dense forests of strange and exotic trees, totally unfamiliar to Nobody. Edmund, who was more studied about these matters, emitted frequent ejaculations of pleasure at the rare species. The gloomy atmosphere was intensified under the waving treetops. Shouts were heard in the distance, along with the slow regular beat of a drum.

"They have not done it yet!" the missionary exclaimed.

"Noble," Liana gasped, "I can't run this fast." Nobody silently pressed the panting girl's hand and left her and Elyssa to follow with an escort of four soldiers while he pressed on towards the scene of the intended crime.

At last they broke out of the dense trees into a wide grassy glade upon whose sward sat several circles of grave natives. In their center stood four powerful men, brown-bodied and heavily tattooed. Each man had a hand on a long bundle that groaned and grunted—it was a white man, bound hand and foot, laying next to a shallow grave. The tallest of the four natives had one hand raised towards the sky and was chanting in a wavering, high-pitched voice.

"Stop!" the missionary cried, dashing through the sitting onlookers and grasping the native's shoulder. "No good, I say, no good. Other white man say so too."

The native looked angrily at the excited man, and more suspiciously at the rifles strapped to the 42nd's backs. "Where they come from?" he demanded.

"English ship, come to island. Say no kill man, not witchdoctor."

The dingy native scratched his head with a dirty hand. "See fires with own eyes. Bad man, must die. Witchdoctor must be bury alive." Angry grunts from the audience agreed.

"What fires is the man talking about?" Nobody whispered.

The missionary rubbed his hands nervously. "The hermit is a bit odd, certainly, but not harmful. There is continual smoke over his house, while a contraption somehow drips fire, or something that looks just like it. I don't blame the natives for not understanding it, but I do not doubt it is some used-up scientist come to study an old theory."

"He's harmless, you say?"

"Wouldn't hurt a fly. I've only seen him face-to-face twice, but I've observed him from a distance many times."

"Very well." Nobody turned to the chief, who had been waiting the outcome of this discussion with much impatience. "Chief," he said, pointing a finger at the man's broad chest, "you lead warriors. I am a chief too, and I lead warriors." He pointed to his own men, who stood in a group, uneasily fingering their sword-belts. Nobody did not draw the chief's attention to the loaded rifles strapped to their backs, but he knew the warrior would see and take note. "That man is no witchdoctor. I have much trade on my ship. You give the man to me, and I will send for the trade, and give you a kettle, twenty buttons, and four mirror glasses."

The chief glanced reluctantly at his intended victim, but cupidity, combined with fear of the soldiers' rifles, overcame vengeance. After all, no doubt he reasoned, if the little white man was a witchdoctor, couldn't he come out of the grave and haunt him? A kettle, twenty buttons, and four mirrors sounded much better. With a broad smile the swarthy native delivered the 'witchdoctor' to the missionary's care and accompanied them to the village, gravely followed by most of his tribe. They were powerful specimens of tribal ancestry, broad-chested and long-legged, their brown bodies delicately stained with blue, yellow, and red pigments. Some of the men had adopted English leggings, while others retained a simple strip of cloth about the waist. The women wore short grass dresses, and, probably because of the missionary's influence, European blouses with cut-off sleeves.

Nobody sent the ship's boat for a package of trade goods and joined the missionary in his hut to examine the long bundle. The long bundle turned out to be a tall, wrinkled old man with white hair and a flowing beard. Scared blue eyes protruded from his sunken eye sockets, and the air whistled with each breath through his nostrils.

"Come now, my dear man," the missionary was saying, "you're safe, no harm will be done to you. Come, take a drop of water." The hermit drained a gourd within moments and devoured a piece of bread.

"My fires! My fires!" The old man struggled to stand. "They will die." He spoke in a strong English accent which corresponded with the dirty trousers, frilled shirt, and waistcoat he wore.

Nobody quietly pressed him back down on the palm matting. "My dear sir, you are not well yet." He turned to the missionary. "Might I ask you, sir, to leave us alone for a few moments?"

"Are you sure it's safe?"

"Quite, don't worry about me. I should like to ask him a few questions, that's all." As soon as the man of God left them alone, Nobody turned eagerly to the old man, and the hand that he laid upon the hermit's shoulder trembled. "What do you mean by 'your fires?'" he asked gently.

"My fires, my fires, I must get back to them. They cannot die. Please, help me." He struggled to get up again.

"I will, I will, just tell me; where are your fires?"

"At my hut. I was allowing oxygen into the liquid when the natives took me."

"Liquid?" Nobody frowned. "I thought you said you had *fires*."

"Yes, yes," the old man said impatiently, "my liquid fire."

"Liquid fire?" *Is the man mad?* "My dear sir, there is no such thing as liquid fire."

A fire of his own burned in the old man's eyes as he leaned closer. "Ah, yes, yes, there was once, don't you know, there was once."

"Why, you must mean—Greek fire?"

"Yes, yes, I have almost found it, I have almost found it."

"Found it! But—" Nobody started and gazed into the old man's eyes. "Colonel—Colonel Hayes?" he whispered tremulously.

"Who said that?" The hermit glanced hurriedly round the room. "Who called me that?"

"I did."

The old man looked at the boy with mingled astonishment and fear in his cloudy eyes. "I have not heard that name for—for a long time," he said at last.

"Oh Colonel Hayes!" the boy cried. "Do you not know who I am?"

The old man stared. "Your face—is it—could it—Nobody?"

"Yes, yes, it is I, Uncle! Oh, Uncle, you don't know how I have longed to see you again, to press your warm kindly hand in mine." Tears fell from both men as Nobody grasped the withered hand of his long-lost uncle and colonel and pressed it to his forehead.

The old man grinned childishly. "You have come, you have come at last. I have dreamed of this day. It never seemed so real. It must be."

"Feel my hand, Uncle, it's strong. Feel my tears, they are wet and salty. Feel the hair you so often tussled in my younger days. They are real, and I am real!"

"My boy, my dear boy, my sister's son."

"No, Uncle, please don't speak of that. I am still Nobody—none know my story save you and Stoning." *And the king.*

"Ah, my dear men. But why have you come? I see log walls, palm roof; not Siberia. How did you come here?"

Nobody pulled a chair to the man's side and sat down, bending over the wasted form with almost womanly tenderness. He gently smoothed the long white hair upon Colonel Hayes's forehead and wiped away tears and sweat with his own handkerchief.

"Colonel Hayes, I am no longer the colonel of the 42nd. I have left the army, but it was my own choice. No, no," he cautioned as the old man was about to speak, "I will explain later, you must rest now. Nearly a hundred of the men came with me, and among them are Squad One, and many faces that will be familiar to you."

"Squad One?" The old man relished the words in his mouth, repeating them over and over to himself. "Squad One, Squad One, here, at last. Dear old Stoning, is his beard as white as mine?"

"Yes, sir, just as white."

"Ah, dear fellow. He knew your secret. Petr?"

"Yes, Uncle, Petr is here, and Jacques, and O'Malley."

A smile lit the pale countenance. "Do they still banter? As of old?"

"It gets worse every year, sir. I think the stronger the friendship grows the more they try to hide it." He grew sober. "Milton died soon after you left, and Hammer some months later. I filled their places with two brothers, twins, actually, named Preston, and they've turned out to be splendid fellows. Dearingson also met a Cossack bullet, and instead we have a Yankee named

Dilworth, American as can be but worth his weight in salt. Poor Franklin died a few months ago. We have a young fellow as replacement, appointed direct by the king at his own request. I have seen the king."

"The king?" With an effort the old man sat up again, this time propped in his nephew's strong arms. "You have seen the king? Why?"

"I will tell you, Uncle, but you must be stronger first, and I have other news to share as well."

"Other news?" the old man croaked. "What?"

Nobody blushed. "Well, you see, Uncle, I've actually become betrothed to a—" he paused as the door flung open and the missionary rushed in, once more out of breath.

"Your ship is leaving," he gasped, pointing out the open door.

"Leaving? What on earth do you mean?"

"It has put up sail and is leaving the harbor, and your men don't appear very happy."

"Excuse me, Colonel Hayes, I must go; I will return as soon as possible." He sprinted for the beach, followed distantly by the panting missionary. Sure enough, the *Robinson Crusoe* was making her way out of the harbor under full sail, disregarding a rapid series of signals running up and down the *Illusory*'s halyards.

"The black knaves are leavin' us, sir!" cried the enraged O'Malley, gesturing violently at the departing ship. "Shall we swim oot and board 'er?"

"No, O'Malley, that would be a very bad idea. Did they show any signal before putting out sail?"

"Nay, sir, nary a one. We thought we could see some sort o' consultation, you might say, an' I know fer sure I saw one or two of the blackguards wavin' his arms, but I don't know what it all means."

Edmund strode angrily across the fine white sand, his fine manly face afire with indignation. "I'm afraid they've gotten back at you, Noble. Undoubtedly that rascal Bill is behind this, though how much I have no idea. Do you think Captain Miller went along with the plan peacefully?"

"I don't know. Perhaps so, but more likely the crew threatened him if he would not. Where is Somerset?"

"The reporter? Oh, he's over in the village sketching the houses. Shall I bring him?"

"Yes. Jacques, put down that rifle! What do you think you're doing?"

The Frenchman turned inquisitively. "Vhy Colonel, I vhas going to try to pick off one of zhe miscreants vihz my rifle. Zhe range is far, but I zhink I could do it."

"No, shed no blood. If we ever meet up with the *Robinson Crusoe* again we will demand full restitution of our goods. Here comes a boat from the *Illusory*, tell them to disembark all our soldiers and their families, as well as the trade goods. It appears that we'll be pitching camp here, as long as the natives don't give any trouble. O'Malley, did the most valuable cargo and personal possessions come ashore?" The Irishman nodded. "Good. Show me the pile. Ah, Somerset, here you are."

Edmund had returned with the young reporter, who stood nervously awaiting the boy's pleasure. "Somerset, you were not so bold aboard ship as the rest of us, I noted, but for this I say nothing. Your bravery is a matter between you and God so long as you are not one of my soldiers. What I want to know is if any of the crew spoke to you of a plan to sail away from us, in essence robbing us of her cargo?"

"No, sir, none. One or two of the seamen were inclined to take me into their confidence, I believe, but I made clear that I would have none of it, so they desisted."

"Hmph. Sometimes, my young—excuse me, I forgot, you're older than me. Sometimes, Somerset, it is better to know the enemy's plans. As Solomon said, 'there is a time for everything,' but oh well, what's lost is lost. Carry on."

Nobody rapidly paced the wet beach, sending messengers hither and thither to prepare for the disembarking soldiers, discussing plans with the missionary for a convenient site to build their new homes and storehouses, and allaying the natives' fears that the Englishmen had come to take over their island. The native chief, who called himself Tambao, was quite willing to allow the new arrivals permission to settle on the island after a large gift of trade goods, and the forest soon resounded with ringing axes and the shouts of men as they cut and shaped wood for their homes.

It could not have been less than an hour before he found time to return to the missionary's home and look in upon his old commander, but when he entered the hut he found no occupant. Colonel Hayes was gone.

Chapter 28

Brightly plumaged birds flew noisily round an overgrown path, crying shrilly at Nobody, Edmund, and their native guide, as they stood hacking at the thick growth. A bead of sweat dripped into Nobody's eye and stung as he slashed through a wet trailer with his razor-sharp machete. The native was a tall, silent fellow, with a palm tree tattooed onto his broad chest and serpentine figures winding round his bare ankles. The boy admired the skill with which he followed the ancient path, sometimes so overgrown as to render it almost indistinguishable from the surrounding foliage.

Even in its best days the track could not have been well defined. It wound among vast patches of taro plants and the strangling creepers of banyan trees whose parent stems must have first raised their heads through the rich green earth centuries before. Nobody paused at a magnificent specimen of one of these and sat down on a root, wiping his streaming face with a pocket-handkerchief.

"This is a little more arduous than I expected," he said to Edmund, who also took a seat. "It's much wetter up here than down by the village. It must take a powerful amount of rain to keep these plants and trees growing at such a rate, though I daresay there's a number of streams here as well."

While the two boys rested and surveyed the scenery, their silent guide scaled a nearby coconut tree, few of which grew in such dense areas, and brought down three small green nuts. Three quick cuts with his machete soon divested them of the top husk, revealing a filmy liquid contained in a dense ring of white, jellylike fibers. The native stolidly handed a nut to each boy, and putting the remaining one to his thick lips, drained the contents.

Nobody shrugged. "Why not? Here's to good health and sailing ships." They tapped the nuts against each other and poured a draft of delicious liquid down their parched throats.

"Splendid!" Edmund cried. "It's almost like lemonade!"

"Quite good," Nobody agreed. "Well, shall we continue?"

They trudged onwards through the dripping rainforest, winding their way towards the mountain summit which they saw looming high above through patches in the dense canopy. It was on the very bottom of this mountain that the hermit's hut was reported to lay. As they came closer to their objective, Nobody tapped the native on his shoulder and pointed to the sky. "Volcano?"

The native scrutinized the ribbon of smoke winding through the treetops and shook his head. "No. Hut."

"Aha. Well, carry on. I say, Edmund, I hope the old man is here. I can't imagine where else he would have gone yesterday, but he certainly couldn't have taken the path we came by. No doubt there are others around." The bleating of a sheep interrupted him. "Hello, what's this? Why, it's a perfect little farmyard!"

The path terminated at a rude fence, against which leaned a short ladder. Here the native stopped and motioned that he would go no farther. "Very well, my silent friend," Edmund said cheerily, "you've fulfilled your commission and that's good enough for us. Wait here till we come back, will you?"

A number of tame sheep wandered about the little enclosure, munching upon the luxuriant grass while several lambs frisked and played about their mothers' heels. A cow lowed somewhere in the distance, most likely from the low lean-to next to the hermit's hut. This hut was of curious construction, thatched with palm leaves and walled with short wooden logs tied to stakes by natural creepers. Its back stood directly against the mountainside, and a thin smoke-wisp curled from the chimney. A dull metallic clang sounded deep inside the walls.

"Looks like he's home," Edmund said, reaching for the latch.

"Indeed. Let's hope 'he' is the one we're looking for."

Edmund pushed the door open and a sulfurous smell filled the air, so very like gunpowder that Edmund started violently, as if he thought that a gun had been fired. Nobody pushed past his friend and entered the hut.

"Colonel Hayes?" he called, blinking in the gloom. A fire burnt, not upon the hearth, but in a metal basin on the table, and the hunched figure of the old hermit was peering into its depths and muttering to itself like some weird witchdoctor preparing an incantation. Nobody called again, but the old man made no motion. Something flashed close beside the boy and he jumped back against the wall, his pistol in his hand. It flashed again—it was like a drop of water, only not water, but liquid fire that dripped slowly out of a long tube hung upon the wall.

Edmund followed close on his friend's heels. "Dear me, it would be hard to get a fire insurance policy for this place."

The Boy Colonel stepped up to the hermit and placed a hand upon his hunched shoulder. The old man started wildly.

"Don't take me!" he screamed. "I'll do anything but don't take me! I must finish this experiment!"

"I don't want to take you anywhere, Colonel Hayes." Nobody held the old man in his grasp lest he should accidentally burn himself. At this name the hermit's manner calmed, and he sunk into a chair. Edmund stared at the old man wide-eyed. "Yes," Nobody said quietly, "it is old Colonel Hayes. I didn't tell you before because I wanted to first see how he was."

"But—Colonel Hayes—here! In this fiery den!"

"Yes." Nobody looked at the charred walls and stinking pots of earth and powder. "Strange, isn't it? I told you that a bolt of lightning burnt his house down, and it was after that tragedy that he became so interested in Greek fire. He still appeared normal before the men, but I who knew him so well was certain that something was wrong. The search for Greek fire grew in him until it became an obsession. He collected every scrap of writing that he could— indeed, here a few of the old books."

Nobody paused before a small bookcase. "He has added to his collection. The obsession grew so strong that he at last decided to leave the 42nd altogether and journey in search of some elusive ingredient he believed he could find in the South Seas. Of course, the men had the option to join him and many would have, Stoning, in particular, but he wouldn't let them, and he told Stoning to stay and watch after me. Perhaps you were unaware, but Stoning and he grew up together in the same town as childhood friends. His sister was the colonel's wife."

"Stoning was a true friend." The old man's sepulchral voice startled Nobody. "A true friend," the old man continued. "Wouldn't let him come. No, my job alone. To find Greek fire. And I am almost there!" With this last sentence a gleam of life returned to his eye, and he rose once more to look at the fire.

"Do you remember young Edmund Burke?" Nobody asked, gently directing the old man's attention to his friend.

"Edmund Burke? Edmund Burke? Yes, indeed. Good boy, cheerful."

"This is he."

"Is it?" The hermit scrutinized the boy's appearance. "Yes, indeed. A little older. All of us older. Why are you here?"

Nobody lightly pressed him into a chair and drew another for his own use. As briefly as possible he explained why he had left Siberia, and why he was now at the island, particularly stressing the point that he planned to stay there for at least several years. The information made a slight impression on the old man, but the idea of his fire could never be quite driven out, and he frequently interrupted the narrative to drop fuel into the metal basin.

"Married, are you?" he asked as the story was drawn to a conclusion.

"No, sir—betrothed. Promised to marry."

"Oh. Hope she's a nice girl. Would like to come down and see her, but I must not leave my work right now. Horribly interrupted by those natives, put me back a few weeks at least."

"What do you eat here, Colonel Hayes?"

"Eh, what's that? Eat? Food. Little garden outside. Tend it while experiments in process. Milk cow. Meat."

"I may come to visit you again?"

"Yes, yes, come. Glad to talk to someone. Will show you my latest discovery. I believe it has put me on the right track to finding the exact proportion of nitrate." The hermit became engrossed again in his fire, and the visitors sorrowfully withdrew, drawing the latch and rejoining their guide, who still waited at the fringe of the forest.

"It's a sad case," Edmund remarked. They picked up their machetes and plunged into the trees.

"Aye. It nearly breaks my heart to see our old colonel brought so low. He was always eccentric, certainly—the 42nd never would have been formed without a unique head. He was never anything like this, though. Still, I could see intimations of a coming change before he left us, and I would have accompanied him myself, but he forbade me, and left the command of the regiment in my hands. That was when I earned Tremont as an enemy."

"Did you notice how easily he talked about anything pertaining to fire, and how disjointed and confused the rest of his words were?"

"Yes." Nobody swung savagely at a sapling, the force of the blow severing its young head and sending it deep into the jungle. "It's part of the monomania. Obsession with one subject to the exclusion of all others. I'm surprised he continued to devote time to preparing food. I suppose he must have decided that he couldn't discover Greek fire by starving to death."

"Do you think he'll actually rediscover it, Noble?"

"I don't see how he could, Ed. Scientists have tried for a dozen centuries without success."

Chapter 29

Three weeks of steady work brought great changes in the landscape of Rahattan Island. An entirely new village had sprung into being, directly across the harbor from the older collection of huts where the missionary lived with his native congregation and a few white families.

The new rows of neatly-placed huts housed the former members of the 42nd and their belongings, along with the trade goods brought by the *Illusory*. Storehouses were under construction close to the water's edge, but they would have to wait unfilled until the stores stolen by the *Robinson Crusoe* could be replaced.

A slight eminence gave the new settlement a splendid view of the deep blue waves that constantly beat upon the sandy shore. An endless crashing came from the distance where the ocean and the coral reef met in eternal battle. However, instead of interrupting the peaceful serenity of the island harbor, these distant heralds of conflict only increased Nobody's feeling of security and isolation, as he sat with a small party of friends under the shade of a coconut grove.

It was a peaceful, shady spot, and a favorite shelter from the midday sun. Nobody and Liana sat together upon a bench, gazing silently over the huts below at the harbor, which looked like a bright diamond skillfully encased by a fringe of white sand. Behind them loomed the mountain which Mr.

Brougham, the missionary, called "Hermit's Mountain," but which the natives termed the "Hill of Strange Fire" in their own language. Its forested slopes extended to the very edge of the coast, creating sheer cliffs that would smash to pieces the remnants of any poor vessel that struck on the coral reef.

A lush valley separated this mountain from another, slightly smaller neighbor, whose foothills extended so far across the island as to nearly cut it in two. Not a breath of air stirred the drooping leaves above the small group's heads as they waited silently for Jacques and O'Malley, who were preparing a mixture of coconut water a few steps away in Nobody's new house.

The Boy Colonel's home was a small, three-room affair, a shack according to European standards, but a palace in the eyes of the natives. The first room served as a combined parlor, sitting room, dining room, and study. An open passage led into his bedroom and another entrance way opened into the kitchen, from which originated the tantalizing aroma of roast pig and greens that betrayed the Frenchman's culinary preparations.

The missionary and his wife, with whom Nobody had placed Liana and her maid, were conversing with Edmund about the normal rate of visits to the island and the likelihood of profitable trade.

"We're on the regular track of trading vessels," the missionary said. "It is rare that two months go by without having a visit. I have no doubt that they will make this a regular stop once news spreads of your trading station. That will be good news for you, Lady Halmond, for I heard you tell my wife that most of your dresses sailed away with the *Robinson Crusoe*."

"That is so, Mr. Brougham. My dear Noble told me only to bring my most valuable belongings, on the chance that the sailors would rifle our boxes while we were gone. I didn't think they would have a use for my dresses, so I brought only the one I wore, and another that was in my baggage."

Nobody raised an eyebrow. "You never told me that, Liana."

"You never asked." She dimpled. "Boys are not known to interest themselves overmuch in feminine apparel."

"Well no, I suppose not. To tell you the truth, I don't believe I ever thought about the clothes you wore before." He scrutinized the light afternoon dress which extended from her neck to the tips of her dainty shoes. "Yes, I see that it's getting a little dingy from overuse. I'm certain we brought some fabrics among those bales of trading goods. Remind me to send you our tailor, and he'll rig something up. Ed, what's our tailor's name?"

"Our tailor?" Edmund removed a blade of grass from his teeth and looked vacantly at the rows of huts. "Oh, you must mean Brown, the regimental tailor. Yes, I daresay he could do something for Liana."

"Splendid. Any other complaints, my dear?"

"Nothing that I can think of, Noble. Elyssa and I are doing marvelously, aren't we, Elyssa?"

"Yes, my lady, it's a beautiful place."

"Beautiful people, too," Edmund said, glancing at the shy maiden.

"The natives?" Nobody laughed. "Do you really think so?"

"Well, no." Edmund turned red. "I meant to say, er, ah, wonderful climate, isn't it?"

Nobody nodded gravely. "Yes, it's a good climate." Edmund shifted uncomfortably beneath his friend's searching glance until he was relieved by the entrance of the two soldiers carrying mugs of cold coconut water.

"To Rahattan Island!" Edmund proposed, grasping a mug. "May we live in prosperity and good fellowship, and soon see many sails in her harbor." The toast was drunk with good cheer and many exclamations of delight from the girls at the drink's tangy sweetness.

One alone of the small party left his mug untouched. "Look!" Nobody cried, pointing to sea. "Edmund's hopes are already fulfilled. A sail!"

There, indeed, was a schooner's jib slowly rounding the spit of land that formed the harbor's left shore, followed by the drooping main and mizzen sails. "Heigh-ho!" O'Malley exclaimed, baring his arms to the elbows. "There's work ahead fer us this day! Hurrah fer trade an' the Sooth Seas!"

A boatful of wobbly-legged sailors grounded upon the beach and their leader cheerfully introduced himself as 'Captain Mathers,' of the *Miriam*. A nest of unkempt hair peeked from beneath the crushed brim of his wide-awake and blended neatly with a pair of bushy eyebrows.

"Welcome to Rahattan Island." Nobody shook hands with the shaggy officer. "I am Colonel Nobody, recently discharged from the 42nd, and owner of this trading station."

"Colonel Nobody!" the captain exclaimed. "Why, how do you do? I'd heerd some rumors that you'd left Siberia, but I can't say as I expected you to turn up in the South Sea Islands. A trading station, you say? Splendid! You have any copra?"

"Yes indeed." Nobody beckoned him to follow. "I've set the natives to work harvesting coconuts and collecting the kernel. I will happily sell you all I have so far for the market price."

"Splendid." The bushy captain rubbed his hands in anticipation. "I'd only expected to refill vittles and water here. Nearly full of sandalwood, we are, but I warrant we'll find some spare cargo space. So you've set up trade here? That'll work out nicely for my new route, takes me right by here, it does. Where'd you get all the men?" He pointed to the gangs of soldiers carrying crates of copra to the shore.

"Soldiers from the 42nd. They came with me when I left. I hope to get a ship or two and train them in navigation."

"Not a bad idea. Looks like a snug berth you've got here."

"Yes, it's certainly quite a change from an igloo in Siberia. Would you like to join us for supper? I have a wonderful French cook, and I'm sure it would be a pleasant change from salt beef and hardtack."

His main room was occupied by a wobbly table, the ungainly product of O'Malley's ingenuity. The exotic planks were scarce visible beneath a profusion of platters, plates, pots, and bowls, containing the results of the Frenchman's labors. Four rough-hewn chairs stood ready for their occupants.

"It looks marvelous, as always," Nobody complimented Jacques. "You must have had O'Malley's help to make such a feast as this."

"Zhe Irishman? Do you zhink I vould let a *boeuf* roam in my kitchen?" Jacques snorted. "Bah. I have him constructing a chimney zhat does not smoke every time zhe vind turns. Young Bronner has been helping me, and he has done vell, for an Englishman."

"That's high praise, Jacques. Do treat him well, will you? I daresay that helping a Frenchman in a South Sea kitchen was not quite what he expected when he joined Squad One. Carry on."

Jacques bowed. "Yes, sir. Vould you like me to borrow an extra chair?"

"No, don't worry about it, just bring in the bench from my bedroom and remove one of these chairs. That's right, set it on the left. Captain Mathers, if you would take the foot of the table, I will take the head, and we can converse most easily. Liana, Dear, sit on my right. Ed, squeeze onto that bench with Elyssa. Splendid."

After a short prayer the hungry Englishmen dug into the piles of fresh breadfruit and pork, while Liana filled their mugs from an enormous pitcher of coconut water.

"I must say, Colonel, I was not expecting a greeting like this," the captain declared through a mouthful of taro. "How long have you been here?"

"Nearly three weeks. Ed, pass the rolls, please. Long enough to establish ourselves, short enough to still relish this fresh pork."

The sailor smacked his lips. "Do you expect to pick up a decent trade here?"

"Yes indeed. I intend to keep large amounts of necessaries such as linen, sailcloth, spars, barrels, etc., to supply sailing ships. This, with any normal trade articles we may pick up and copra, should supply our wants. As I said before, I plan to purchase a sailing vessel and train some of my former soldiers in the mysteries of navigation."

The captain nodded. "Good plan. Couldn't think of a better myself, only I couldn't stand being on shore so much. No, give me a stout ship under foot and a clear sky overhead and I'm a happy man." The seaman glanced at Liana. "I didn't know, Colonel, that you had a sister."

"I don't have a sister," Nobody said in surprise. "Ah, excuse me, you must mean Liana. Pardon my lack of manners, I should have introduced you." He smiled gravely. "Captain Mathers, this is Lady Liana Halmond, my betrothed wife. Liana, this is Captain Mathers of the schooner *Miriam*."

"Pleased to meet you, my lady." The captain knuckled his forehead. "I hadn't heard of the colonel's taking a wi—that is, a betro—er, what do you call it?"

"I'm pleased to meet you as well, Captain," Liana said quickly. "I hope the coconut water agrees with you?"

"Oh, yes, jolly well." He took a swig. "Not quite rum-and-water, but a jolly good taste, all the same."

"I'm not surprised you didn't hear of our betrothal," Nobody remarked. "Do you read the *Times*?"

"Not for some time, sir, the only papers I see nowadays are a few nautical gazettes."

"That explains it. The *Times* was the only one that had any good information on it, though I'm sure several other papers made a note of it as well. For some reason the people of London have an interest in my adventures, you see, and so I have a young reporter attached to me. Speaking of Somerset, I'm sure he'd like to send a batch of articles home with you. Do you know where he is, Ed?"

"Out on some naturalistic trip, I believe," Edmund replied. "I heard he was collecting sketches for his reports."

"Are the natives friendly in these parts?" the captain asked.

"Decently." Nobody leaned back in his chair, his simple wants easily satisfied. "Mr. Brougham, the missionary to this island, says that there is a small, semi-hostile tribe across the mountains, but they haven't bothered this side of the island for several years. Our natives are quite friendly, and Mr. Brougham already has a growing congregation. Indeed, the whole tribe is half-Christianized, you might say, which has its benefits for trade, although it can create some rather ludicrous situations."

"In what manner?" asked the seaman.

Nobody laughed. "Well, you see, according to Mr. Brougham, when he first came the whole tribe were thieves and liars. He's been working on the lying part for several years, and he's progressed so well that I daresay there are less lies told in a week on this island than in a day aboard your ship, no offense, of course."

"In course."

"Well, he's begun work on their thieving habits as well, but greed is a hard master to shake off, and we currently have a respectable tribe of honest thieves. They'd steal the shirt off your back if they thought you wouldn't notice, but all you have to do is ask for it and they'll give it straight away because they won't tell a lie."

The sailor laughed. "I say, that must be a jolly lot."

"Indeed. Poor Jacques, our cook, spends most of his time perched in the kitchen on a high wooden stool, jealously guarding our foodstuffs. He's much better than a dog in that respect." Nobody coughed. "Don't tell him I said that last bit."

Chapter 30

Summer, autumn, and winter passed swiftly for the inhabitants of Rahattan Island. Pleasant winds filled the harbor with numerous sailing ships, eager to replenish their supplies and buy fresh copra. Trade prospered, and Nobody expected his first ship to arrive any day after its maiden voyage. The *42nd's Venture*, as he called it, was manned by a complement of 42nd men into which a sprinkling of true sailors had been mixed to teach them the ropes.

It was with great joy and a small degree of pride that Nobody stepped onto his verandah one fine morning and viewed the expansive scene before his eyes. The marital status of each in the huts below was easy to tell. If there was a prosperous garden round the hut, and a few budding fruit trees next to the doorstep, it was a family dwelling. If not, the occupant was most likely single. Several of the soldiers had brought their wives with them from Siberia, and these had managed to raise three or four daughters to compliment the number provided by the missionary's settlement. In addition to these, several of the men took wives from among the converted native girls, and Mr. Brougham became expert in performing the marriage ceremony.

Nobody found thoughts of marriage pleasant until they wandered back into the one constant channel of his mind—his own marriage. Liana had grown from a blooming girl of seventeen to a blooming woman of eighteen, more beautiful than ever and well able to manage a household, thanks to Mrs. Brougham's tutelage.

The traits of character developed during girlhood had blossomed, and a more sweet, gentle, kind, joyful, and steady girl would have been hard to find. She certainly did not exist on Rahattan Island. And yet—the old phantom was still there to rise before his eyes and darken the brilliant sea and lush greenery. There he stood once more in the king's presence; there, once more, he heard the king's order and those fateful words—"*Our ward has developed a great liking for you.*"

With a groan Nobody clomped into his house and buried his aching head in a bucket of water. He looked at himself in the mirror. His face was deeply tanned by the tropical sun, and creased by care. *Still*, he mused, *I wouldn't call it an ugly face. Not exactly handsome, but I don't think it's ugly. Not that it matters.* He settled into a comfortable chair next to his desk and selected a volume of Caesar's *Commentaries* for a quiet day of reading.

"Good morning, Noble!" Edmund greeted him cheerily as he stepped unannounced through the doorway.

"Back from fishing already?" Nobody kept his place with a finger. Edmund looked flushed and hot, as if he had been running a race.

"Aye. We had a splendid catch. Jacques hooked one big fellow that would have sent him for a dive if O'Malley hadn't caught his coattails." Edmund plopped into the chair on the other side of the desk and leisurely propped his feet upon the wooden surface. "I sent a basket of them to the Broughams."

"Good idea." Nobody resumed his book.

The clock in the corner, an old reminder of their igloo, ticked away the minutes, but neither boy spoke. Nobody was soon far away among the Roman legions, beating back hordes of screaming barbarians.

"Noble?"

"Mmm?"

"Can I ask you a question."

"Mmm."

"Even though you're not married yet, you would be considered Liana's male head, correct?"

Nobody raised his head sharply. The mists of antiquity were gone in a moment as he set down the dusty book.

"Yes. Why?"

Edmund nervously hacked at a piece of bark. "Oh, I was just thinking that since you were her authority, you would also be over her—property?"

"Yes, I suppose so," Nobody agreed. "What's your point?"

"Oh, well, it just struck me that since you're over her property, you would also be over her—her servants, correct?"

"Edmund, I did not sign up for a lecture in sophistry. Please, get to the point."

The knife moved furiously, and Edmund's cheeks reddened. "You see, Noble, what I'm trying to say is that—as Liana's head—oh very well, I'll say it. Elyssa has no male relatives alive, so you would be the closest authority, because she is Liana's maid, and you're Liana's betrothed husband. Right?"

Nobody grinned. "So, the day has come at last." He folded his long arms and leaned back in the chair. Edmund looked away. "Yes, that would be about right. I presume that question has a motive?"

"Well yes, of course, but I'm afraid you have no idea what it is."

"Ha. That's a good joke. As if I didn't have two eyes in my head. Why, man, do you think I'm an idiot? I know what you're feeling right now, though I've never felt it myself." He paused involuntarily, and wiped a hand over his forehead. "If I'm not mistaken, you have come to ask me for permission to court Elyssa. Am I correct?"

Edmund gulped and nodded. "How did you know?"

"As I said, my dear fellow, I'm *not* an idiot, and I know you too well to not know what you are thinking. You're much too open of a fellow (which by the way, I like), to be able to hide something so weighty from me."

"What do you say?" Edmund clasped his hands and nervously chewed at his fingernails. Nobody squinted at the short nails—it didn't look like this was the first time Edmund had gone to them for comfort.

"Well, Ed," he began, "I have had much time to think of this matter, although this is the first time you have broached it to me. Before giving you my opinion I must ask; have you spoken of this desire in any way, or through any gesture, to Liana's maid?"

"Certainly not!" Edmund cried stoutly. "No gentleman would do such a thing!"

"No need to get testy, Ed. I've found it always best to declare the rules of engagement before entering battle, and that applies to conversation as well. Now that we have that preliminary aside, I will give you my opinion. You, Ed, are my best friend under the sun. We have fought side-by-side for years, felt the same feelings, frozen in the same snowstorms, and shared the same roofs, whether under the snowy igloo, the cramped ship-cabin, or the current palm leaves above us."

Edmund leaped to his feet and paced the room with quick, short strides, holding his hands behind his back like a sea-captain on his quarter deck. "I'm just a little worked up, don't mind me."

"Very well. As I said, we are extremely close friends. I would never be so close to someone unless I had the highest opinion of them in *all* respects. As you probably know—" here he paused, his brow contracting into a frown. "In strict confidence, Ed, that is why I am so hesitant to marry Liana—but enough of that, this is your business I want to discuss. Rest assured, I have the highest possible opinion of you. I have known Elyssa for a much shorter time, but I also have a great respect for her. I have asked Liana much about her history and character, and she seems in all respects to be fitted for you. Mark, I said *all* respects. These being my feelings, I consider the match to be a very good one, but although I must give consent to the girl's choice, she has not yet chosen. A time of courtship will be a very positive thing for both parties to get to know each other, and for you to seek to win her heart."

Edmund wrung his friend's hand. "Noble, you're the most splendid friend a man ever had."

"I rather doubt that. Love does warp a man's brain. There is still one thing required, though."

"What is that?" the boy cried breathlessly.

"A formal request."

Edmund snapped to attention. "Colonel Nobody, permission requested to court Elyssa Bradley, current lady-in-waiting to Lady Liana Halmond,

Viscountess, with the express intention of eventual marriage if accepted as a suitor."

"Permission granted, Lieutenant Colonel Burke."

Edmund saluted in the stiff military fashion, his eyes straight before him. Nobody rose from his chair and returned the gesture in the same form. For a moment they gazed gravely at each other until, with a hearty laugh, Nobody grasped his friend's hand. "Come, Edmund, no Tremont is needed to issue *this* mission. To the missionary's house!"

The sun never shone more brightly, nor had the birds ever sung more sweetly, according to Edmund, as they clattered across the busy docks and hurried around the harbor's shore to the native settlement. A horde of laughing brown-skinned children set up a shout of "Nobood and Emoond" as the two boys approached, clustering round them with bright smiles and eager faces.

"Good children," Nobody said, patting the heads of the closest. "No presents today, I'll bring some next time." The cheerful brown bodies resumed their light-hearted frolicking without demur, and the two friends quietly entered the missionary's hut.

Fresh air and sunlight streamed together through a pair of open windows, lighting a scene of domestic harmony. Mr. Brougham sat writing at his book-covered desk, preparing notes for his next sermon. At his side sat his wife, a large-hearted, big-minded woman, with a body to match. A piece of knitting rested in her lap, and the click-clack of needles made a pleasant sound in the small room. Liana and her maid sat somewhat apart, their heads bent together in confidence over a piece of embroidery.

"Welcome, Mr. Nobody," said the missionary's wife. "We hadn't expected a visit from you today."

"No ma'am, it came up rather unexpectedly. Do you mind if I have a few private words with Liana?"

"Not at all," Mr. Brougham agreed. "Why don't you two take a walk?"

"Thank you sir, we will."

Liana pushed her work into Elyssa's lap and rose. Nobody offered her his arm, and they set forth.

"Is something on your mind, Noble?" the girl asked, pressing closer to his side.

"Liana, how am I supposed to walk if your skirts are tripping me?"

The girl shrank away. "I am sorry for offending you, Noble."

"Oh bother it," Nobody growled, angry at himself for being so cross. "It's no offense. Come, you can walk as close as you like." He wrapped his long fingers about hers and tucked away the tender arm. "Things have been changing drastically for me today, Liana."

She looked at him curiously. "Has something gone wrong in the business?"

"No, no, the business is fine. It's Ed. I'm sure you've noticed some rising interest in his manner towards Elyssa?"

"Yes," she agreed, slowly, "I have."

"He's asked permission to court your maid, and I agreed. Do you have any objections?"

"Why, no, but—Elyssa? What does she think?"

"I have as much of an idea upon that subject as a native boy does on the king of England's clothes. That's one of the reasons I've come today, in order to ask you to broach the matter to her, and ascertain whether or not she is interested. If she is, then splendid, the courtship begins. If not—no harm done. No lasting harm, that is, for I'm sure that I'd have a grumpy, down-in-the-mouth fellow about my house for many months thereafter."

Liana laughed lightly and sat down in the sandy soil underneath a palm's lofty fronds. Jacques and O'Malley stood at the water's edge, evidently arguing about a yellow crab who crouched defiantly in the sand and menaced them with its pair of pincer-like claws. The Frenchman was on his hands and knees and was reenacting the crab's shuffling pace, illustrating some point of nature to his friend, who stood stiffly with arms akimbo and shook his head gravely at his companion's antics.

Liana pushed a strand of hair away from her glistening eyes and drew a deep breath of the salty air. "Noble," she asked timidly, looking into the watery distance, "if there were to be a wedding between dear Elyssa and Edmund, do you think there might be—another wedding at the same time?"

Nobody gazed out to sea as well. Gulls cawed from their perches, greedily searching for mankind's crumbs. Sunlight glinted on the silvery scales of a jumping fish. He wished he could jump on that fish and fly away from his troubles forever.

"I don't know. Perhaps. It will depend."

"It's not that I do not trust you," she explained hastily, with a tighter grasp on his arm, "it's just that I love you so, and am so ready to be your wife."

"Yes, yes, of course." He coughed, aware that this sort of speech was not the common style among lovers.

She smiled. "Do you love me?"

Nobody stiffened. "I—Liana, how could you ask such a thing?" he dodged. "I'm no courtier, and I can't turn out pretty sentences, but if I could, I would."

"I don't want you any different." She laid her head upon his shoulder. "It is such a beautiful day."

"Yes, indeed." He coughed awkwardly. "Why look, a ship just rounded the spit and is lowering its anchor." He grasped eagerly at any change to the subject. "I do believe it's an entirely new one. Well-cut. I should say it could keep a steady nine knots in fair weather."

"Isn't their flag a little different?" Liana asked.

"Yes, you're right. I can't quite make it out from this distance but it looks to me like—yes it is! It's the Union Jack, but not of the common style. It's not a navy ship, that's for sure. It must be a commissioner of some sort for the king. Well, well, I'd recommend putting on your best dress, for I expect company tonight."

With a merry good-bye she skipped off to do his bidding. He dug his hands savagely into the sand. Now she thought for sure that he loved her.

A boat lowered from the ship's side and six rowers descended the ladder, followed by another figure in a cockaded hat. *I wonder what they want here*, he mused. *Probably just a victualing stop. If it's a commissioner, I should welcome him formally.* He called the two soldiers to his side and gave them orders to receive the boat and send its commander to Nobody's house.

Nobody positioned Edmund on his verandah as welcoming committee and doorkeeper. He himself requisitioned a pitcher of coconut water from the kitchen and set two glasses on his table. The corner clock solemnly ticked away the time, first ten minutes, and then twenty, but no sounds broke the stillness outside save for the screeching of birds and the scratching of drooping coconuts upon the thatched roof. Nobody rose impatiently as the clock struck half past one. *I'm probably making a fool of myself. Either he's not a commissioner, or he's just looking for food and water and doesn't care about meeting the station owner.* His hand was upon the knob when footsteps crunched outside.

The heavy steps halted abruptly. "Lieutenant Colonel Burke!" exclaimed a nasal voice.

Edmund gasped. A chair thudded on the compact earth.

"General Tremont!"

Nobody clenched the doorknob. *Tremont?* He pressed his eye to a knothole and looked out. Edmund's back blocked his view, but there was no mistaking the sneering tones of the former general.

"Lieutenant Colonel Burke," he repeated, "or perhaps I should say *former* lieutenant colonel. What are you doing here?"

"I live here."

"You don't say. Well now, isn't that interesting. Why, I do think you've grown a little. Three or four more years and you'll be on your way toward manhood."

Edmund clasped his hands behind his back. His fingers twitched. "If that is the case then we do not share the same perspective on manhood."

"No, no, perhaps not, my boy. Well, well, I'm glad to see that you no longer carry a sword. It always concerned me, seeing such a sharp blade by your side, lest you should accidentally cut yourself."

"How compassionate. I must say, you've grown quite a bit yourself."

"Grown?" The general growled. Nobody imagined his sneering face. "What do you mean?"

"I meant from side to side."

Tremont stamped his foot. "I did not come here to be insulted by you, *boy*. I came to talk to the owner of this trading station, for whom I presume you occupy the post of doorkeeper. I certainly hope he is more polite than his servants, although I suppose I should not blame you after having been so much in company with that boorish *Nobody*. I never thought you would leave his apron-strings, but I suppose even *you* could not bear his unsupportable snobbishness any longer."

Nobody resumed his seat and picked up a glass.

Edmund coughed. "I'm not so sure of that."

The door swung open and Tremont entered. He stopped with one foot over the threshold. Nobody nodded.

"Good afternoon, General Tremont. Please come in."

The older man jerked himself together and entered, throwing his cockaded hat upon a chair. "Colonel Nobody." He nodded slowly. "Well, well, well, I should have known you were here after seeing *that*." He sneered at Edmund, who returned the grimace with an exaggerated bow and retired.

Tremont cautiously seated himself, at the same time scrutinizing the room with his slanted, hawk-like eyes.

Nobody pushed a glass of coconut water toward him. "Welcome to Rahattan. I certainly never expected to see you here. May I be so bold as to ask your business?"

Tremont lifted the glass to his lips, swished a mouthful of the tepid liquid, swallowed, grimaced, and pushed the glass away. "I had forgotten that you don't drink brandy."

"Again, may I ask your business?"

"Pirates," Tremont snapped. "The queen has heard that there are problems with pirates in these waters, but the Navy ships are all occupied elsewhere. I have a strong crew aboard, and a versatile ship, which can easily be disguised as a trader in distress. We expect to attract and destroy any pirates. I have a young lord along as well, who has command of the fighting contingent."

"Why does the queen take such interest with pirates?"

"Because they're hurting our trade."

"Of course, I understand that. I asked why the *queen* took such interest, instead of the king."

"What? Haven't you heard?"

"Heard what?"

"King William is dead!"

Nobody nodded slowly as he digested this startling intelligence. "I see. And so—"

"And so, Queen Victoria (God bless her) is now ruler of the Empire, and has decided to inaugurate her reign by placating the merchant sector and sending a ship of pirate-hunters, with myself as her commissioned commander, and my young friend as leader of the fighting-men."

"How very romantic." Nobody tapped the table. "A young friend, you say? I was not aware that you had friends."

"I have few." Tremont downed another mouthful of coconut water. "I like the young fellow. He's like me, and he's rich."

"Dear me," Nobody muttered. "A wealthy blackguard."

"What's that?"

"Oh, nothing. Please continue."

"I don't have more to say."

"Very well. What did you say was the name of this young lord?"

"I didn't."

Nobody frowned. "Look, General Tremont, neither of us likes the other, we both know, and I'm quite content to continue that way. However, if you're going to be around here for a time, we might as well be civil. What is his name?"

"Civility is a choice." Tremont rose. "If you want to make it then I cannot stop you. Don't expect me to do the same."

Nobody rested his chin on his fists. "Very well, so be it. After all, I don't particularly care what his name is."

"What?" Tremont exclaimed, his hand on the door. "Are we still talking about the fool? Why, who cares whether you know his name? You can't have known him, anyway. He's not your type. Name's Bronner—Lord Banastre Bronner."

Chapter 31

Nobody stared at the wall. Lord Banastre Bronner—the young fop who had warned him on his betrothal day that Liana was not meant to be his. "See that you can keep her," were his words.

Very well. I will keep her, whether I love her or not. You, my fine feather, had best not interpose your sneering countenance between us.

Edmund bounded into the room. He grasped the chair in which Tremont had sat and threw it into the corner. Tremont's glass of coconut water was on the table. Edmund growled and hurled it through the doorway.

"That's what I think of him!"

"Rather hasty, don't you think, Ed?"

"Hasty? Humbug. I only wish Tremont had still been sitting in that chair." He pulled a new seat for himself and collapsed, propping one foot upon the table. "Did you hear who else is with Tremont?"

"You mean Lord Bronner?"

"Of course that's who I mean. The arrogant, profligate, good-for-nothing brother of the hearty, likeable, energetic fellow who helps Jacques prepare your meals."

Nobody had forgotten that Thomas Bronner was the lord's brother. "Yes, I don't suppose either will be delighted to see the other."

"Delighted? I'd be delighted to *kick* the other, and I may do it, too, if he brings his sneering face around here!"

"He will have to bring it here, Ed. No matter how much, or how little, I like him, it is my duty to extend hospitality, as owner of this trading station."

"That's all very well and good, but what about Liana?"

"Believe me, that was my first thought." Nobody walked to the window and looked out upon the beautiful scene, now darkened to his eyes by the anchored schooner in the middle of the harbor. "According to courtesy, we must invite them to supper. I expect that Tremont will refuse—I don't know about Lord Bronner. I don't think the dictates of courtesy would require a second invitation."

"Tonight?"

"Yes. I should like to get it over as soon as possible."

"You don't require my attendance, or Elyssa's, do you?"

Nobody smiled. "No, I suppose not. After all, it wouldn't be very polite if you were to throw him out of the window."

"And," Edmund pressed, "can I talk with Elyssa?"

"Oh, Elyssa, that's right. This new matter had nearly driven the courtship from my mind. Yes, yes, you may go to the missionary's hut and talk with her, as long as one of the family is by. Find Jacques while you're on your way, and tell him that I need a good dinner prepared, and that I would like young Bronner to be waiting in the kitchen. You never know, he might come in handy. Also, inform Liana of the situation and of my reasons for inviting the fop, and ask her to come up to play the part of hostess. With such a pair of villains around I will always feel more comfortable with her by my side."

Edmund saluted and retired.

About five minutes passed before a knock came on the door. *Liana.*

"Hello, Dear," Nobody said, throwing open the door, "you came qui—oh." He paused abruptly as Jacques's inquisitive eyes met his. "Well hello, Jacques, er—come in."

"Zhank you, sir. Sir, did I just hear—"

"No, you didn't hear. Never believe your ears. Is young Bronner with you?"

"Oui, Colonel, ve are bohz ready."

"Good. Have you heard the news, Bronner?"

"Yes, sir, Jacques was just telling me that General Tremont will be here for a few months." Thomas tossed his head. "Don't worry, sir, he won't dare to play any tricks *here*. You aren't under his command, and we 42nd men won't take kindly to any insults."

"Thank you, Bronner, I appreciate the sentiments, but that's not the news I was referring to."

Thomas looked quizzical. "Then no, sir, I don't believe I have heard."

"Your brother is with Tremont."

If an igloo full of Cossacks had fallen from the sky, Nobody doubted that the young fellow would have looked more surprised. "Sir?" he asked blankly.

"Yes, I was rather surprised myself. I'm not sure why he's along, but somehow he was given the enviable position of pirate-hunter in these areas."

"I think—I'd like a cup of water." Jacques rushed to the kitchen and returned with a glass, which Bronner quickly emptied. "I'm sorry sir," he said weakly. "I wasn't expecting this. We're—not exactly on the best terms. Is he coming here tonight?"

"Yes, he is. I may call you in, so that he knows you're here. I may not. It depends on circumstances, but please be on hand."

"Yes, sir."

Another knock came on the door. While Jacques bustled into the kitchen, Nobody opened the door cautiously, half expecting O'Malley to be there. No, it was Liana this time. She had a green shawl half draped round her head. She looked pale.

"Is it true? Is that—is Lord Bronner really here?"

"I'm afraid so. Do you understand why I must invite him to supper?"

"Yes. I trust you, Noble."

"Indeed. Horrid conventionalities. I'd rather dunk him in the harbor than invite him to dinner, but such is life."

"Do you think—will he make trouble?"

"I don't know."

When Bronner did come, he was dressed as for a ball. His lip curled in the same perpetual sneer, and his red skin was noticeably puffier. He smelled of brandy and garlic.

"Well, well, times have changed since our last meeting." He coolly removed his coat and hung it upon the rack. "Why Liana, you're ten times prettier than last time I saw you!"

"I must request that your remarks be addressed to the Lady Halmond," Nobody said stiffly.

"Ah, my apologies." The lord took a seat. "So, it is the Lady Halmond, is it? I suppose that means that you're not married yet—unless the colonel has taken your name to himself, in lack of a better of his own."

"The colonel," Nobody said, "finds his name quite sufficient."

An awkward silence ensued.

"Would you like some coconut water?" Liana asked at last.

"Certainly! Pond water would taste like the sweetest nectar if poured by your fair hands."

Nobody calmly removed the pitcher from her hands and poured the drink himself. "How was your voyage?" he asked. He meant to keep the conversation away from Liana.

"Atrocious. Can't stand the water. Only thing I could keep down was brandy."

"Indeed? I apologize at our lack of brandy, but as you know, we don't drink spirits here."

"Ah, do not worry." Lord Bronner produced a black bottle from his pocket. "I always take care to ensure the proper amount of refreshments."

A drunken Lord Bronner? A sober Lord Bronner is bad enough, but a drunken one? Perhaps I should have left Liana with the missionary.

258

Lord Bronner raised the bottle. "To the lady!" he cried. Jacques entered at this moment, balancing a load of dishes in his hands.

"I hope you find these native delicacies to your liking," Nobody remarked coldly.

"Mmm." The lord poked cautiously at a pile of taro. "Brandy and roast beef are more in my line."

"I'm sorry to hear it," Nobody said politely, thinking that he was very much the reverse of sorry. "The brandy you have provided; as for the beef, you must talk to my cook."

"Indeed, so I must. You've a lovely dress on, my lady. Such a gorgeous red sash, and such *elegant* blue satin." He took another drink. "You know," he continued, leaning forward, "I've seen a great many young ladies in my time, and some rare ones at that, but none with such a beauteous tint of red in her cheek. Ah! It deepens!"

Nobody rose from his seat. "Lord Bronner, I request that your conversation be directed completely towards *myself*, this evening."

"Come now, my boy, you mustn't be jealous of me. After all, I am your elder, and am entitled to some of the—you might say, the joys of life." He suppressed a hiccup with another application of the black bottle.

"Perhaps you don't understand, Lord Bronner. It is quite possible that you will spend some amount of time on this island, and I think that it is extremely important that you know my mind. This lady is my betrothed wife; any words which you may care to address to her may be offered through me. You are a nobleman, and you think that as one you can do as you like. Perhaps that's so in England, but we're not in England. We're on Rahattan Island. I will resent and demand justification for any insult offered, and I assure you, the sympathies of the residents of this island will *not* be in your favor."

"You threaten me!"

"Not at all. I warn. After warning, I act. You are warned."

It was now Lord Bronner's turn to rise from his seat in wrath. "Foolish boy, I've had enough of this nonsense. What price do you want for the girl?"

"Price?" Nobody balled his fists. "What are you asking, Lord Bronner?"

"How much do you want for her?"

"Lord Bronner, I am not certain that I understand you, but if you are saying what I think you are saying, you had best depart while you can."

"Oh come now." He took a silk purse from his pocket and dropped it upon the table. "There's plenty in there to satisfy you. Silly boy, did you actually think I would let you marry her? Why, you don't even want her. I can see it in your eyes, you don't love her. I do. You take the money, I'll take the girl, and everyone's happy, you see? Tut-tut, there's no need to act so angry. We're in the South Seas, no one will punish you. The natives do this sort of thing every day."

Nobody wrenched his sword from the wall.

"Scum!" he hissed. "Leave this house at once!" He swept the table aside, unmindful of the cascading dishes, and confronted the astonished lord with the blade's keen edge.

"There now young fellow, calm down!" Bronner edged against the wall, the bottle still in his hand. "I don't understand you. It's obvious that you don't love her, so why should you be in such a passion to keep her?"

Liana grasped Nobody's arm and tried to pull him away. "Please don't make a scene, Noble, I pray you, just tell him that you do love me, and we can be at peace once more. There is no need for violence," she pressed, as he remained silent, "only tell him the truth."

"The truth?" Nobody said bitterly, lowering his sword. "What is the truth?"

"Why, that you love me!"

Nobody made no answer.

"Noble!" Liana grasped his free hand in both hers. "Why will you not say it?"

"Because—because it would not be true."

Her arms fell. She shrank back from him. Her deep eyes met his, brimming with tears of horror and hurt. "You—you do not love me?" she faltered.

"Liana!" He sprang to her side. "I respect you more than anyone else in the world, and I will protect you with my life but—I cannot say that I love you!"

She broke from his arms with a sob and sank into a chair, her face in her hands.

"You!" Nobody wheeled on the bewildered lord. "This is all *your* doing! Get out of my house this moment or you will pay for this!"

"No." Bronner hiccupped. "Only a boor like yourself would leave a lady in such a distraught condition, and as you can only make things worse, I must take it upon myself to offer consolation to her." He moved as if to come to her side.

"If you do not leave my presence this instant—" Nobody gulped, trying to keep his voice calm. "Then you will force me to do something I may regret."

"I will take that as a threat!" Bronner drew his own sword and lunged. The kitchen door burst open and Jacques sprang into the room, but Nobody did not wait. He struck down with all his strength and the lord's sword fell shattered upon the planks. He grasped Bronner's neck and dashed him through the door. The lord landed in a shower of wooden splinters, torn lace, and broken glass from the brandy bottle—a moment later increased by a shower of rejected sovereigns from the scented purse. Battered and bleeding, he crawled away, calling back imprecations and vowing vengeance.

Trembling, Nobody turned to his betrothed wife. She stood with her shawl round her shoulders, a picture of offended dignity. "Liana—"

"I am the Lady Halmond, Viscountess of Bayrshire, and I request that my proper rank be used if you see fit to address me." A tear streaked down her face, but she brushed it impatiently aside and continued hurriedly, as if afraid of being unable to finish her words. "I am your betrothed wife, Colonel Nobody, and as such I must marry you, if you wish it, but I cannot see why you still would, or ever did ask for me, if you do not love me. I request permission to return to Mr. Brougham's home now."

A mist rose between her bloodless face and his. His temples echoed each heartbeat. Her eyes, once the bright passageway to her inward thoughts and emotions, were hard.

"I! I ask for you!" Nobody clasped his head. "What can you mean?"

"I do not understand you, Colonel Nobody, but I do not wish to converse with you longer. Will you let me go?"

"Go."

She went.

Thomas and Jacques stood with gaping mouths.

"Go!" he said hoarsely. "Go and send Edmund to me. My life has been short—I feel it will never be long—but I could almost wish it had never been, if I am chosen to blight the hopes of one so fair and pure. Leave me. I must have Edmund by my side."

Chapter 32

Nobody stared into his hands.

The room darkened slowly.

Crockery crunched under Edmund's boots as he found and lit a candle.

The anger was gone, replaced by dull apathy. Edmund must have realized it, because he simply waited for Nobody to speak.

He must have been there for hours when Nobody finally raised his head from the table. It felt like days.

"You know what happened?"

"Yes."

"She knows I do not love her?"

"Yes."

"Edmund, what do I do?" For the first time, he met his friend's gaze.

"It is a hard thing to do, Noble, a very hard thing, to tell a girl—your betrothed wife—that her affections are unwanted and unreturned."

"What else *could* I do?" Nobody leaped from his seat and paced through the smashed crockery. "I couldn't lie. I never before said that I loved her—I never even asked her to marry me. It was she who arranged it, not I!"

Edmund shook his head wearily. "Noble, forget all that for a moment, and watch me." He touched the base of the candle with his finger, and a piece of hot wax adhered to his skin. He rubbed the morsel into a tiny ball and held it towards Nobody in his palm. "This wax attached to my finger, even though I didn't pull it off. It was soft and pliable, and I rubbed it into a ball; it conformed to my motions. You see?"

"Yes."

Edmund tilted his hand and the tiny ball rolled off and dropped to the floor. "That wax was a girl's heart. It attached to a man's, perhaps of its own doing, I don't know, and I don't understand, but it was pure and soft, and it attached. The man accepted it, and it grew even more attached, until one day—this day—it realized that the man did not want it, and it dropped like this bit of wax upon the floor, and it is now lonely, desolate, and blighted."

"Do you think I wanted things this way?" Nobody cried. "Do you think it was my *purpose* to break her heart? Never! I would rather that I had found a lonely grave in Siberia, as I should have done more than once if your sword had not interposed, than have given Liana such pain. How can I help if I do not love her? I respect her, I honor her, I will defend her—why is it that I cannot love her?"

Nobody sank back into his chair. The candle spluttered.

"Love," Edmund said. "It's a powerful word, often misused. What do you think it means?"

Nobody paused. "It means—well—I don't know, exactly. It seems some sort of feeling, or desire, or—I don't know. I don't understand it."

Edmund slowly folded his arms and leaned closer to Nobody, his face serious, his eyes grave. "Noble, I'm not as old as you—well, maybe I am, I don't know if you're ten or twenty—but I know much less than you in most areas. Still, I have had some experiences that you have not. I saw much when in the streets of London, though I never felt anything personally, and now, as you know, I love a girl, and so I know something of what love is. Will you hear me talk?"

266

"Talk 'til the roosters crow." Nobody sighed. "I wish it could do some good."

"Perhaps it may."

"Then talk, Ed, I'm listening." He rested his chin on his chest.

"You don't know what love is?"

"No."

"Well, I think I do, or at least I think I understand some things about it. I think there are two elements to love. They always say in books that people fall in love, as if it were a pool of water, but I don't think that's how it works. Yes, love is a feeling, but it's more than a feeling; it's a decision. You say you honor and respect her. You think she is qualified biblically to be your wife?"

"If I did not I would not have accepted her hand."

"Very good. That is the first and most important step. The second is, do you think you could live together? Do you think your personalities would be similar enough?"

"I think so. Our upbringing has been different in most ways, and yet similar."

"Very good again. The third step is normally, 'will she accept you?' This isn't necessary since you're already betrothed."

Nobody slowly raised his head. "What are you trying to say, Ed?"

"That there's no reason on earth not to love her, and that you're deluding yourself by thinking that there is some magical feeling, and that suddenly you're giddy in the stomach and you find yourself head over heels in love! It's a decision, Noble, and *then* a feeling."

The candle sputtered in a draft and died. Darkness engulfed the room. Only the ticking of the clock and Nobody's labored breathing filled the silence. Minutes passed, but neither boy moved. Nobody's thoughts whirled faster than he could process. His brain felt like a blizzard.

"Edmund."

Edmund jerked at the sudden sound.

"Edmund!"

"Yes, Noble?"

"You're right." With a convulsive energy Nobody dropped to his knees by his friend's side and clasped his hands, hot tears streaking his cheeks. "You are right, and I have made the decision! Edmund, when I first saw that look of pain and sorrow in her face I felt a pang I have never felt before. Edmund, you are right. I have not only made the decision, but I feel the emotion as well— Edmund, I love Liana with all my heart and soul, next only to God!"

"Praise the Lord!" Edmund returned his clasp. "I knew you would come around. It's about time. All is right once more!"

"No," Nobody replied. "All is not right." He squeezed Edmund's shoulders and released him. "I love her, but all is *not* right. I have just told her that I don't love her. I have just rebuffed her affections, and betrayed her trust, as she must think. I can't go to her tomorrow and tell her that I actually do love her, and that we can now return to our life of happiness."

"You're right," Edmund agreed. "Much ill has been done today. You cannot simply *say* that you love her, now, you must *show* that you love her."

"Show? How do I show it?" Nobody fumbled in a drawer and produced a fresh candle. Edmund struck a spark, and together they lit it and placed it upon the table. Nobody hastily wiped the tears from his eyes and settled into his old place at the table, eagerly beseeching his friend for advice and guidance.

"Come now," Edmund said merrily, "this is a pleasant change, you asking me for advice, instead of me offering it unasked. Well, for once, you're up to your own devices. I don't know how to show that you love her. After all, she's *your* betrothed wife, not mine."

"But—but, what can I do? You must help me, Ed—can't you think of something?"

"It's your problem, not mine, Noble. I've got you in love, now you'd better think of a way to show it."

"But how do I start?" Nobody pressed.

"Well, here's an idea. Why don't you have Jacques make a splendid dinner tomorrow, and spruce the place up yourself. Show some care, get flowers, and candles, and what not. Arrange things nicely."

"But I'm not artistic!" Nobody yanked at his hair.

Edmund burst into a fit of laughter. "Artistic? Noble, you're the oddest fellow I ever met. Artistic? Who cares? You can make it look nice, can't you? Try flowers and candles for a start, and have Jacques do the cooking—I know you can't cook, whether you're artistic or not."

Nobody rubbed his hands nervously. "Candles, flowers, right. Jacques cooking, right. But, but—what if I get the wrong color flowers?"

"The wrong color! Noble, they're *flowers*! They don't come in wrong colors. You—oh dear, you really aren't artistic, are you? Well, do what you can, and hope she appreciates it. You won't win her back in a day, but keep after the prize, and don't lay off."

"I won't Ed, and—thank you."

"Quite all right, old chap, quite all right. I assure you, it was largely selfish—you have no idea how boring you are when you're bothered about something."

"You must have had a boring year, then, Ed."

"I should say so! And a horrible six months before that, too! Why, if I hadn't finally gotten some sense into that thick head of yours before much longer, I would have done something drastic—you'd better win her heart back soon, or I still might."

Chapter 33

Nobody was up before dawn, and the sun's rays had scarcely kissed the horizon before he was far inside the forest searching for the hidden glades that contained the choicest flowers. A few drowsy birds twittered notes of welcome to the unusual visitor, but the rest of the animal world lay snug in their warm dens, either resting from the night's labors, or catching a few last winks before the morning hunt began. If any human eye had been lurking among the clustered palms and banyans, Nobody thought, it certainly would have been surprised to see a tall English boy, with a rifle strapped to his back and a sword hanging from his belt, dashing through the forest with an overflowing basket of flowers on his arm.

He moved hastily—this was no pleasure excursion. He wanted to finish gathering the flowers before Jacques began intensive work on the ordered feast, so that he could supervise the work and ensure that all was done just right. Why exactly he thought that the Frenchman's practiced skills would fail on this particular day, he couldn't explain, but there was always that distant possibility.

His course had taken him towards Hermit's Mountain, though not by the usual road he took when visiting the old colonel. That path, at first so difficult and overgrown, was now kept up regularly by much use, trodden down by O'Malley's ponderous tread, Jacques's mincing step, and the rest of Squad One, among whom only the secret of the hermit's true identity was known. Glancing upwards, Nobody easily distinguished the eternal thread of smoke from the gray rocks behind, an ever-present reminder of the old man's consuming passion.

A muffled footstep disturbed the boy's muse, and he turned hastily, expecting to see a native. Instead, he found himself a few feet away from the hermit himself, who crouched in the dirt, so engrossed by the rich earth that he had not yet noticed Nobody's presence.

"Good morning, Colonel Hayes," Nobody said softly, approaching the old man's side.

"Hey, what's that?" The hermit sprang up and lifted a shovel over his head. "Oh, it's you my boy. God bless you. You startled me."

"I'm sorry, Uncle. I hope I didn't disturb your work?"

"Hmm? Oh, no, no, not at all. I think I've found it!"

"Found what?"

Colonel Hayes carefully thrust the shovel into the earth and lifted a quantity of the dirt towards his nephew. "It's a mineral! I think it's what I need to keep the pressures under hand so that they won't explode in the siphon!"

"Oh. I'm—I'm glad to hear it, Uncle. Does it put you closer to making the fire?"

"Closer!" The hermit dumped the dirt with trembling hands into a leather bag, which he carefully sealed and tucked under his stained waistcoat. "My boy, closer. I may find it in my lifetime!" He shouldered the shovel and set off towards the mountain, but Nobody gently relieved him of the burden and walked with him, at the same time taking good care not to crush his flowers.

"How much longer do you think it will take, Uncle?"

"Mmm? Take? I do not know. I do not think of time. Too often disappointed. Perhaps—a chance—small, but a chance—but no, I don't think so."

"What don't you think?"

The hermit paused and glanced suspiciously at the trees. He whispered. "It might be very soon, if this mineral be what I need. But no," he continued in a louder voice, resuming his stride, "never as I hope. You come visit me, my boy?"

"I would love to, Uncle, but—could it be another day? I have some things in hand today that can't be delayed."

"Things, eh? Something with flowers?" The old man laughed, and tapped the boy's shoulder knowingly. "Not what I used to be, I know—perhaps a loose lock, we used to say in the army, but I know young men don't normally go flower picking."

Nobody reddened.

"Mmm." Colonel Hayes grunted. "I thought you said—already betrothed. Strange world. Maybe changed since I left it. Very well, boy, go back home, do what you will with flowers. Do not forget to visit me soon. Life is lonely, even for a shriveled man like me. A strange life—my closest friend is fire—and my worst enemy."

He lapsed into a murmuring muse. Nobody left sadly, thinking of the creator and former leader of the 42nd, now brought to such a state and consumed, as it were, by the same element that had consumed his wife and children so many years before.

Nobody descended the hill to find his house in confusion. Jacques's crew of helpers were scurrying between the kitchen and the storehouses by the wharf, carrying such a number of baskets, barrels, kegs, sides of meat, bottles of oils, and boxes of spices, that he feared the earnest Frenchman had mistaken the number of guests. He picked his way through a confused pile of furniture and foodstuffs to the crowded kitchen, where Jacques and O'Malley were engaged in a furious discussion.

"Ye can't have a proper feast withoot it, I say!"

Nobody thrust his head through the door and found O'Malley jammed into a corner by Jacques, who was making hostile passes at him with a long-handled frying pan. The kitchen was a small room, mostly filled by a sturdy table, upon which rested a slab of beef covered in cloves, greens, and other vegetables. The fireplace was in the right-hand wall, and two plump chickens slowly rotated over the fire on a single spit. A gentle trade wind blew through the open door, reducing the smoke and mingling the tangy scents of fresh coconuts with the more substantial aroma of roasting chicken.

"You say!" the Frenchman exclaimed, threatening the huge Irishman with his culinary implement. "Who are you? A butcher of men, a *boeuf*, an Irishman. Vhat am I? A cook, a chef, a preparer of exquisite dishes and zhe most *magnifique* sauces zhis side of Pairee!"

"What seems to be the problem?" Nobody inquired. He stepped between them and diplomatically relieved Jacques of his frying pan.

"Zhe problem?" Jacques gulped for breath to relay his woes, but O'Malley cut him short.

"The prooblim, Colonel, is that this crazy Frog doon't knoow the first ingredient fer any feast, an' he won't listen, neither." O'Malley shook his shaggy red hair indignantly, and, folding his arms, looked pityingly down upon the furious Frenchman.

"Vill you tell him, sir," Jacques cried, "zhat *I* am zhe cook, and not *he*! I do not care vhat zhose barbarian Irish eat vhen zhey have feasts—I do not vant to know, if it is as bad as the Scots' revolting *haggis*—and I vill make zhis meal right!" He snapped his finger in defiance of the Irishman's suggestion and, smelling the unpleasant odor of burning chicken, rushed to his fowls' rescue.

Nobody slapped the Irishman on the shoulder and leaned closer. "What is it that you think Jacques is missing?"

"Why, sure an' I thought ye'd know, Colonel. It's murphies, an' a feast can't be complete wi'oot 'em."

"Murphies?"

"Aye, sir."

"What are murphies?"

"Zhat is just vhat *I* have been trying to ask," Jacques interjected.

The Irishman sniffed contemptuously at Jacques's lack of culinary knowledge and smiled knowingly at Nobody. "Why, sir, don't ye knoow? They're taters!"

"Taters? Oh, I see. Potatoes."

O'Malley smiled broadly. "Of course, sir, an' isn't that what I've ben sayin' fer the past five minutes? I haven't digged bushels of 'em wi' me grandmoother not to know what I'm talkin' aboot. If Jack had on'y known the king's prooper Inglish, he would've understood me in a priming's flash."

"Zhe king's proper Engleesh?" Jacques turned red. "Vhat do *you* know of zhe king's proper Engleesh? Nohzing, you fool of an Irishman!"

"Oh, so ye'll be insultin' of meself an' me language, will ye? Well at least I'm man enough not tae take advantige o' ye're small statur and poond ye fer it!"

Nobody interposed before Jacques could begin an frontal assault, and proposed that the Irishman remove himself to the wharf, where he could superintend whatever work was in progress. O'Malley grumbled a bit, but he cooled down quickly, and left with a good grace—until his fiery head shot back through the door and he angrily demanded what the Frenchman meant by calling him a *boeuf*.

Nobody replied by shoving him through the door and seeing him safely down the path.

The day sped quickly, as days always do when there is much to be done, and the dinner-hour arrived. Footsteps sounded upon the path, and Nobody made one last frantic check around his chamber before opening the door. The table was drawn into the center of the room and covered with a spotless cloth, which O'Malley had foraged from a bale of goods. A pair of burnished silver candlesticks shed a gentle glow upon the steaming mounds of beef and chicken, and a scarcely less appetizing array of breads, fruits, vegetables, and, of course, potatoes. Each silver knife and fork had been scoured until it reflected like a mirror, and the delicate glasses of coconut water invited the thirsty to partake. Festoons of flowers filled the room with dashes of brilliant reds, oranges, and yellows, handsomely contrasted by the dapper blues and pure whites. Everything was in order. *Splendid! Oh dear, I hope she sees that I made an effort for tonight.*

She evidently did see, for she hesitated momentarily upon the threshold as the unexpected scene came into view. A sky-blue dinner dress with matching shawl covered her slight form and hung low enough to sweep the plank floor. They greeted each other awkwardly, the girl keeping her eyes upon the floor, but before anything more could be said, Edmund was in the room, and his bright cheerfulness helped to put them, if not at ease, at least into a less uncomfortable situation. Elyssa also appeared joyful, and readily joined in the conversation. Nobody wondered if this unaccustomed departure from her normal timidity was due to Edmund's courting, or whether he had instructed the girl before coming to dinner.

Jacques and Thomas Bronner bustled between the kitchen and the table with loads of dishes precariously balanced on their eager hands. Nobody moved towards Elyssa as if to lead her to a seat, but Edmund saw his intention and rapidly seated the maid himself, at the same time slyly nodding his friend towards his betrothed. The Boy Colonel approached Liana with fiery cheeks, and offered her his arm. The girl touched it slightly, but remained expressionless.

The topic of weather was soon exhausted, followed by an awkward silence.

Edmund finally spoke. "So, Noble, have you seen the hermit lately?"

"I actually saw him early this morning when I was near his mountain. He was out digging up some minerals."

"What were you doing near his mountain this morning?"

"Oh, I was—" he paused uncomfortably, and shot a fierce glance at his interrogator. "I was walking."

"Ah, indeed. I had enough walking in Siberia to last me a lifetime."

"And I had enough of your private complaints about walking in Siberia to last *me* a lifetime."

Edmund laughed. "Why Noble, I do declare you're getting jolly in your old age! But why were you out walking so early?"

Nobody grasped his glass, restrained himself from throwing it at his friend's head, and took a sip instead. "I was picking flowers," he muttered.

Liana glanced up from her plate. "Then—you picked them yourself?" she asked.

"Yes, actually, I did. I thought they would brighten the room." His heart leaped. *First time she spoke to me this evening, and it was about flowers! Perhaps Edmund was right.*

Another awkward silence ensued. Thomas replenished their glasses from a flagon of coconut water and Jacques darted around the table with a tray of meat. Edmund cleared his throat nervously.

"I don't know if you heard, Noble, but a ship, the *Falcon*, just came into port, and her captain told me that he passed the *42ⁿᵈ's Venture* a few days ago. They should be here anytime today or tomorrow."

"Indeed?" Nobody grasped eagerly at this thread of conversation. "Well huzzah for old Corporal Stoning! I knew he'd handle her well. I wonder if the Prestons are still composing verses."

"Probably. As Mark would have said, they'll 'not stop 'til they're in their hearses.'"

Nobody smiled. "Did I ever tell you about the time that Stoning told them to stop rhyming?"

"No, I don't think so." Edmund leaned back comfortably and popped a handful of candied pineapple chunks into his mouth. "Go for it."

"Well, it was some years ago, and we'd been in the field for a month and a half. Tempers were running a little high—you can imagine Jacques and O'Malley. Stoning was trying to keep Squad One in line, and restrain Dearingson from getting himself killed."

"Poor Dearingson, he always *was* in the thick of the fight. It took three bullets and a burly Cossack's saber before he went down."

"Yes, well, he wasn't dead yet, and Stoning was trying to keep it that way. Our twin Apostles were happily rhyming themselves as always, and Dearingson was getting rather perturbed. Stoning finally took them aside.

"'Privates Preston,'" he said, "'you'd better knock off with your rhyming before Dearingson deserts to the enemy just for the chance of a potshot at you.'"

"'Corporal,'" Matthew said, "'we respect your opinions and honor your cheek.'"

"'But,'" Mark added, "'we ain't your minions, and that's how we speak.'"

"Needless to say, they've been rhyming ever since."

Jacques and his assistant profited by the laughter to clear the table and move it against the wall, at the same time setting the chairs around the fireplace.

"Shall we adjourn to more comfortable seating, ladies?" Nobody glanced cautiously at Liana. She nodded coldly. Her eyes were clear, but they did not sparkle. He swallowed. He knew that he was the reason for her grief. There was hardly a trace of the dimples that played in her full cheeks only two days before.

Edmund made no motion towards the chairs. "Actually, Noble," he said, "I've some business to attend to outside. Don't wait for me."

"Business?" Nobody was surprised. "If it's so urgent, why didn't you finish it before dinner?"

"Er, splendid question, I'll answer it later." Edmund smiled weakly at his puzzled friend and backed through the door.

Nobody shrugged. "Well, then, I suppose we must entertain ourselves." He stepped to the fire and pulled three of the chairs into a semicircle.

Without warning, Edmund's head popped through the door.

"Oh, Elyssa," he called, "could I have your help for a few minutes?" As she curtsied to Nobody, the boy realized Edmund's plan. Edmund returned his glare with a complacent smile.

So, friend Edmund has executed his wily plan and has given us several minutes of solitary conversation—exactly what I didn't want! What do I say? He turned to Liana. The girl's stiff figure and rigid face gave no encouragement.

He crossed his arms and leaned upon the mantel. She would not meet his gaze—the fireplace, the blackened hearth stone, the sturdy planks, the bare walls—her eyes roved from one to the other, and back again. At last, he steeled his nerves.

"Lady Halmond, I can take this no longer. I must speak. I apologize to you with my whole heart for last night's happenings, and I am heartily sorry for it all."

"I am not." She maintained her gaze upon the floor.

"You are not? Why not?" He could take no more. "Liana!" he cried, dropping to his knees and grasping her cold hands. "Don't you see? I've changed since yesterday. I have finally resolved the matter in my mind—I love you!"

She swallowed, and shook her head. "You say you are sorry for last night. I am not. I have learned a new lesson. Humanity is fickle and deceptive—do not trust a man you have seen but once. I should have known that it was my money you wanted—not me."

"Your money? But—Liana!" *It was she that arranged the marriage! She accuses me!*

"I have expressed my wish to be called by my title—Lady Halmond. I hope you will honor that request, Colonel Nobody. You obviously feel a sense of remorse for your actions toward myself, and wish to make me believe, and perhaps yourself also, that you do love me. It is folly. You spoke the truth last night. I don't understand your motives, however, I am your betrothed wife, and as such must in time become your actual wife. I will act as a wife should—I am still a Christian, and will not be bitter—but you must not expect love from me, when you do not give it yourself. May I go?"

"Liana—Lady Halmond! It *is* true, I love you! Oh, how can I prove it to you?"

"You say you love me," she repeated coldly. "I do not believe it. You would prove it? Then do not make me marry you."

Chapter 34

The *42nd's Venture* glided into harbor at two bells in the afternoon watch. The Union Jack waved proudly from her mainmast, followed a few inches lower by the *42nd's* flag. A crowd of soldiers assembled on the dock and welcomed their comrades with cheers, while others rolled up their sleeves and prepared to unload the long-expected cargo. As soon as the gangplank fell, Nobody and Edmund dashed aboard to greet old Corporal Stoning. They found him superintending the slings that were lifting the barrels and bales onto deck from the hold.

"Welcome back, Stoning!" Nobody grasped the old soldier's hand. "How was the voyage?"

"As well as can be expected, sir." Stoning looked old and tired, but he had for many years. "Weather was rough round the Cape—lost a sailor overboard in a storm. Cargo good—better prices than expected." They walked away from the bustle at the hatch towards the quarterdeck.

"How did our men do as sailors?"

Stoning laughed. "I'm glad we had a good complement of real sailors along in the beginning. Our men were more used to reining horses than reefing sails—but we managed, and they learned fast."

"How did Squad One do?"

"Oh, they did well, sir, but it didn't seem right without Jacques and O'Malley along to keep everybody in good spirits and argue themselves hoarse."

"Don't worry," Edmund interjected. "They're still going at it harder than ever ashore. What I want to know is if the salt air put an end to the Apostles' rhyming."

"Not in the least," Stoning said. "They're even worse—added a boatload of nautical terms to their vocabulary. Good fellows, though, and I can't ask for better men in a pinch."

"Petr and the Yankee?"

The Yankee himself appeared at this moment, and answered for himself and Petr that they enjoyed the trip immensely. "Voyage would have been perfect, sir," he added, "if only you had let Jacques come as cook. I'll be just fine if I never see another bowl of salted pork so long as I live, and that goes for Petr too, I daresay."

The phlegmatic Russian nodded his agreement.

"Hello sir," rang a cheery voice, and Nobody turned to find Somerset offering his hand.

"Ah, it's you." They shook hands. "Did you get anything interesting for the *Times*?"

"Quite a bit, sir, and I wrote a few short stories besides. I hope there's a ship leaving soon, so that I can send my notes along." He patted his salt-stained notebook with the air of a satisfied man, and scanned the harbor. "What's that ship doing with so many guns, sir?"

Nobody followed his pointing finger. "That's a pirate-hunter, actually, commanded by our old friend Tremont."

The reporter started.

"Strange world, isn't it?" Nobody turned to Squad One. "See that you don't run afoul of any of its crew. As far as I can tell, they're the scum of Europe's collected ports. A large number of Spanish and Italians, too, who are always quick with the knife, and aren't pleased with the lack of strong drink and sociality they expect in these island trading-posts. Stoning, see that the cargo gets completely unloaded. I want her hull scraped before next voyage."

An active week passed. Nobody spent every second of his unoccupied time planning and executing ways to show his love for Liana. Fresh bouquets of flowers lay upon the missionary's doorstep each day. Delicacies from Jacques's kitchen had a strange way of appearing upon the missionary's table each night, with Nobody's compliments. Liana found a mysterious blue dress draped over her dressing table, doubtless unconnected with Elyssa's innocent interest in her measurements, or the tailor's recent activity. Never, however, did Nobody accompany one of these demonstrations of emotion. Upon the morning of the *42nd's Venuture's* arrival he had sent a message, through Edmund and Elyssa, to the effect that she would not be inconvenienced with his presence until she wished again to see him. Each evening he quizzed Edmund after his visit to Elyssa, and each evening the same reply was returned. Liana had not mentioned his name.

It was with great excitement, therefore, that one night he received an invitation from Liana to lunch at the missionary's.

He presented himself next day in full uniform, and with a fresh-picked bouquet in hand. As always, a crowd of eager children crowded around their beloved 'Nobood,' and shouted with glee at the trinkets he managed to produce, after a great show of perplexity, from his numerous pockets.

The missionary's door was thrown wide, displaying the inner room in a very sudsy condition. It was evidently washing-day. Mrs. Brougham and several native helpers had just returned from an expedition to the river, and the area surrounding the missionary's doorstep looked like a second-hand garment shop. He ducked beneath a pair of Mr. Brougham's flapping trousers and nearly flattened Miss Hacket, the island's self-appointed laundress, a tall, bony spinster of thirtyish, who had a way of jerking her long arms when she talked as if perpetually beating dirt out of a soiled garment.

"Excuse me, Miss Hacket, I didn't notice you there. Is Lady Halmond inside?"

"Of course, why shouldn't she be?" The spinster jerked an arm toward the open door.

"Why, there's no reason that she shouldn't be. I was simply inquiring."

"Quite right, quite right. Go on inside, and please don't mind the suds. Mrs. Brougham didn't realize how bad off we were for clothes, till Mr. Brougham asked for a clean pair of trousers an' none was left."

Mrs. Brougham came out at this moment and added her apologies for the state of the house, which Nobody brushed aside as unnecessary.

"I haven't seen Lady Halmond all morning," Mrs. Brougham said. "It surprises me, Mr. Nobody, for I thought sure that she would help with the washing this morning, as always. Perhaps she slept late. She did seem agitated last night, and was up past her normal hour."

Nobody glanced at the closed door which led to the girl's room. "Does she often sleep this late?"

"No, not at all." Mrs. Brougham shook her head wonderingly. "She must be sleeping heavily, too, for I've called twice since we returned from washing, and so has Elyssa, and no answer."

A vague fear instantly sprang into Nobody's heart. "Has anyone been here this morning?" he asked sharply.

"Why, no, Mr. Nobody—not that I know of, at least, for we've all been gone washing, and my husband is visiting some of the sick natives."

"None of your domestics were here?"

"No, sir. As I said, we were all washing by the river."

Nobody stepped to the girl's door and rapped twice with his knuckles. No answer. "Lady Halmond!" he called, pressing his ear against the rough wood. No sound from within. "Lady Halmond, are you in there? Lady Halmond? Liana!" No answer. He pushed upon the wood, but it did not yield.

"It's latched from the inside," Mrs. Brougham explained.

Nobody thrust a hand through his neatly-combed hair, splaying it in all directions. "Mrs. Brougham, I greatly fear that something is wrong here. Have I your permission to break down this door?"

"Break down the door?" The missionary's wife gasped and covered her mouth with her hands. "What do you fear?"

"I don't know, but perhaps—" he didn't waste another moment, but leaped back from the door, braced his body, and lunged. The wood fastening upon which the latch caught tore from the frame and the door flew open. He scanned the room frantically. The blankets on the bed were rumpled, and half on the floor. His gift, the blue dress, hung over the chair-back. Her leather bag was gone. He dashed to the writing-desk and caught up a note, hastily scrawled upon with ink:

> We were not meant to marry—I go to another. Do not follow.
> Lady Halmond, Viscountess of Bayrshire

He reeled. He hardly felt Mrs. Brougham snatch the note from his hand. He hardly heard Mrs. Brougham's cries, or the native servants' screams. The air felt close and oppressive, and there seemed to be a faint smell of wine to his scattered senses—he moved to the open window.

She has gone. She has gone. For another? Do not follow? And why not? She is mine to protect! If the other is who I think, then it can be but for her everlasting good that I stop her from this mad course! But how could she flee? A ship.

Without a word to the distraught missionary's wife he grabbed the crumpled note and raced for the shore, not heeding the wondering looks of the soldiers or the yielding sand that spurted beneath his heavy boots. There, sure enough, were the dwindling sails of a brig, just departed that morning.

"Arrah, Colonel, is there a prooblem?" O'Malley stepped to the boy's side. "Pardon me if I'm bein' at all presumptuous, sir, but I couldn't help but notice ye chargin' doon the dock like the old days, on'y wi'out ye're trusty horse."

"O'Malley," Nobody commanded tersely, "I must catch up with that ship. Get a boat under sail immediately, and load a carronade for a shot across her bow. Step lively, man, it's life or death! Or, what's the same, honor or dishonor." He dashed into his house and slung his old battle-sword from the wall. "Down with your book and on with your sword!" he ordered Edmund.

"What the—Noble, are you mad? What's wrong?"

"All's wrong, Edmund." He buckled the sword belt and planted his shako firmly upon his head. "Follow me, and bring your sword. I mean no violence to her, but I can't help but think that someone else is involved—you know who I mean."

"I'm not sure what you're talking about, but if you mean Bronner or Tremont, hurrah! for there's nothing I'd like better than a chance to cross swords with the fiends!"

They pounded down the well-worn path and sprang into the waiting boat, followed by a dozen nearby soldiers and Somerset. O'Malley hauled the sail into place single-handedly, and the stiff breeze quickly caught the canvas and stretched it tight before the mast.

"Oars out!" Nobody called. Each of the six oars was instantly double-banked, and the light boat shot from the jetty in pursuit of her quarry. "What ship is that?" Nobody looked at Edmund.

"Er, splendid question. Matthew, what ship is that?"

"I'm Mark, sir." The soldier saluted respectfully, and nodded towards his twin.

"Matthew," Edmund growled, "what ship is that?"

Matthew jerked a small, leather-bound nautical ledger from his pocket. "It's—the *Miriam*, sir, schooner, English, bound for London with a miscellaneous cargo of copra, spices, sandalwood—"

"Matthew! That's quite enough, thank you."

Nobody slid the spyglass open and pressed it to his eye. The schooner's sails were stretched taut against the sheets by the wind. Nobody swept the deck with his glass. Two sailors were tying down a chicken coop by the main mast. Others were coiling loose ropes, their baggy trousers flapping in the breeze. No sign of Liana.

"Fire across her bow."

O'Malley tugged at the carronade's lanyard—a spark ignited the gunpowder and the cannon crashed, hurling the twelve-pound iron ball far in advance of the *Miriam*'s bow. The wind quickly whisked the smoke from their eyes, showing a crowd of sailors in the schooner's rigging, reefing the sails.

Nobody cinched his sword-belt tighter. *What will she do when I come aboard? If she really is running away from me, will she come back?* "Back oars!" *I can't believe that she would do this! I know Tremont must be behind it. Will she come home with me?* "Edmund, follow me."

A rope ladder fell from the ship's side. Nobody grasped the rough hemp and clambered up, bracing himself for each swell that banged him against the dripping planks. A splinter caught the knuckle of his right forefinger and ripped the skin. Nobody gritted his teeth for a final heave—someone caught his hand and pulled him over the bulwark, where Edmund joined him a moment later.

The captain stepped forward and shook his hand. "Welcome aboard, Colonel Nobody. I hope you've a good reason to tack me about in such good weather."

Noble glanced round the deck—nothing but a crowd of morose sailors. There was something very familiar about the captain's crushed hat—"Ah, Captain Mathers, I didn't realize it was you. Please forgive me, but I must ask to see your passenger list."

The captain tugged at his shaggy hair. "I'm sorry, Colonel, but we doan't have any. Too much trouble and quarrellin'."

What? No passengers? Nobody looked searchingly at the *Miriam*'s captain. Mathers had proved trustworthy in his dealings. There was no reason to doubt him, but this was not a time for hesitating civilities. "Are you perfectly sure you have none, Captain?"

"Quite, Colonel. Who might ye be looking for?"

"A girl—well—a young lady, I suppose, beautiful, with black hair and hazel eyes."

The captain crossed his arms. "You'd be talking about Lady Halmond, I suppose?" Nobody nodded shortly.

"Sorry, sir, but I make 'no passengers' a policy, most especially no women. They're a heap more trouble than they're worth, in my opinion, leastways aboard ship."

A dash of spray leaped over the bulwark and coated the three men. Nobody felt his hand stinging, and found the blood trickling from the injured knuckle. He pulled a handkerchief from his breast pocket and bound the finger to protect it from the salt air.

"Is there any way that she could have been smuggled on board, Captain, perhaps with help from one of the sailors?"

"Anything's possible, sir, but I doan't see as how it could be." He called his first mate from the crowd of sailors, and put the question to him.

The first mate, a young man with a large head and weak knees, replied in the negative. Nobody excused himself for a moment and turned to Edmund, who had remained quietly in the background.

"Did any other ships sail this morning or last night?"

"Probably, sir."

"Do you know definitely if any did?"

"No, sir."

He turned back to the captain. "I'm sorry, Captain Mathers, but I must request that you return to port for a day or two so that your ship can be searched. I will pay any money the delay may cost you."

"I ain't goin' back!" yelled a voice from the crowd of sailors. "Bad wine an' no women."

"Silence!" Captain Mathers roared. "What scurvy bilge rat dared to answer the colonel!" The sailors shifted discontentedly, but no one answered. "My apologies for the ill manners, sir," he said, turning to Nobody, "an' I'll be glad to come back for anything you may want. Heaven knows you've put more than a few pounds in my pocket with this here trading station." He glared at his men. "I'll keelhaul the next dog of you as says a word!"

The *Miriam* was anchored next to the dock and boarded by a full complement of soldiers. Nobody led the search, accompanied by Captain Mathers and his first mate. They descended into the depths of the hold and rooted around among the bales of copra and spices, but no Liana. The galley, the fo'c'sle, the captain's cabin—no Liana. Every bulkhead was sounded, every imaginable and unimaginable hiding place was searched—no Liana.

"I'm very sorry, Colonel," Captain Mathers said, as they emerged from the hold into the sultry tropical air. "I doan't see that she could be here anywhere. Perhaps she's hidden on the island somewhere?"

Nobody sat down on a gun carriage and wiped his dripping brow. *No need to ask myself if I love her now! I'd give my life gladly to see her safe from harm— but that's my duty for any woman. What's the difference? Perhaps—*A touch upon his shoulder dissolved his reverie.

"Noble, he's talking to you." Nobody turned his head to follow Edmund's pointing finger, and found that the *Miriam* was anchored close beside Tremont's pirate-hunter, *The Hound*. Tremont's ship was careened on the beach to scrape barnacles from her hull. Tremont and Bronner stood nearby supervising the work, and Tremont's hands were cupped round his mouth to form a speaking-trumpet.

"Good afternoon, *Nobody*," he called. "Have you lost something of importance?"

Nobody started fiercely at the hated tones. Bronner stepped forward, doffed his cap, and bowed. As he rose, their eyes locked—and for a moment the aristocratic mask of indifference peeled from his face and the arrogance, the hate, the triumph, shone through. A red mist swirled before Nobody's eyes, and he reached for his sword. Pain instantly coursed through his right arm, and the mist evaporated.

He looked at his sword arm and found Edmund digging his fingernails into the skin. "Think before you speak!" his friend hissed, jerking his head at the two conspirators.

With a mighty effort, Nobody crushed down the rising passion and molded his face into a polite mask. "Nothing that I can't find again!" he called. "Please excuse me, I have some business to attend to."

He paced the white sand, unmindful of the breaking waves which foamed over his boots. Edmund dutifully trudged a step or two behind. Small knots of his men gathered under coconut trees, and he knew that the stalwart fellows were talking about him. He felt smothered by a blanket of despair.

"Do you really think she left me, Edmund?"

Edmund stepped quickly to his friend's side. "I'm glad you finally asked, Noble. I can't accept that Lady Liana ran away. She might have wanted *you* to go away, but she's too principled to run away herself, especially if it were with a scoundrel like Bronner."

"You saw what Liana wrote, Ed."

Edmund scratched his head. "Actually, I didn't see it personally, but it doesn't matter. Do *you* think she's run away?"

"I can't believe it, but what else can I believe? I've behaved like a fool and worse to her, and now it serves me right that she's gone."

"Did she say that she went on a ship?"

"N-no, I don't think so."

"Then perhaps—I don't say for certain, only perhaps—she might still be on the island. I talked with the dock-watch while you were digging around in the *Miriam's* hold, and they had seen no women or girls go aboard any ship either last night or this morning."

"On the island!" Nobody turned his head to gaze over the village at Hermit's Mountain, towering above the dense jungle, with its thin column of black smoke rising toward the sky. "It's a large island, Ed."

"True, but we have a large workforce. Every man of the 42nd will drop his occupation at a moment's notice and rush into the jungle, if you desire it."

"I'm afraid they wouldn't do much good in the jungle, even if they got there, Ed."

"No, probably not, which is why you should send the converted natives there instead. They all know you, and their children love you. If you wanted, there could be five natives on every path and track on this side of the mountains before nightfall."

Nobody felt Edmund's cheerful spirit gradually dispelling the despair. Perhaps there was still hope.

"Furthermore," Edmund continued, "we can set our men to rake both villages and the beach area. That covers the island, and, if she's here, we're bound, with the help of God, to find her."

The blanket of despair was gone. "Edmund, my friend, I can't tell you how thankful I am to have you with me. You've given me hope! Go straight to Mr. Brougham and get the natives in the jungle immediately. I'll give orders to O'Malley and Jacques to organize the search force here on the beach."

Edmund grinned. "That's the Noble I know. Yes, sir!"

"Meet me on the dock as soon as you've delivered your message. I have a few ideas of my own."

Chapter 35

"Nothing!"

Nobody collapsed into a chair and kicked his boots into the bedroom.

"All day, and not a sign! No tracks in the jungle, nothing strange on the beach. Everything searched, double searched, triple searched. Nothing!"

Edmund quietly stirred the coals in the fireplace, and, lifting one, lit the lamp on the table. Nobody wearily removed his battered hat and pillowed his aching head on his arm. The kitchen door opened, and Jacques set a plate of cold chicken and pineapple before him.

"I'm sorry, Noble." Edmund rested his chin in his hands and gazed sorrowfully at his friend. "I said it was only a chance."

"Life is but one irony after another." Nobody closed his eyes. "It was not long ago that I sat here with you wondering whether I even wanted Liana, and almost wishing that I had never met her. And now she's gone—and my heart is torn in two."

Neither spoke for a time, and neither needed to. Nobody didn't need Edmund to voice his compassion—he felt it by the pressure of his friend's hand on his shoulder. The clock ticked, the fire crackled. Jacques locked his cabinets and left for the night.

At last, Edmund broke the silence. "May I see the note, Noble?"

Nobody pulled the paper from his breast pocket. Edmund looked at it, frowned, looked at it again, and frowned again.

"Are you sure this is it?" he asked, holding the paper for his friend to read.

"Yes, of course. Wait, no," he said slowly, "it looks like—oh. That's a set of prices from the laundress for washing." He dug listlessly among his pockets and found the right note.

"'We were not meant to marry,'" Edmund read slowly. "'I go to another. Do not follow. Lady Halmond, Viscountess of Bayrshire.'" He laid it on the table before him and stared at the words. "Do not follow—do not follow—do not—humph. Noble, do you have any other notes from her?"

"Mmm?" Nobody grunted. "I suppose so. Why?"

"May I see one?"

Nobody scanned his friend's face. *What's he thinking?* He found an old letter from Liana in a chest and handed it to Edmund.

"What is it, Ed?"

Edmund waved his hand for silence. "They don't match!" he exclaimed. "The hand-writing—it's different!"

Nobody snatched the note from his hand. Edmund jumped to his feet and pointed eagerly at the writing. "They don't look a bit alike! They're both womanly handwriting, and that's all!"

"But—" Nobody shook his head. "They must be the same. She was agitated when she wrote this last note, perhaps that's why."

"I tell you," Edmund said excitedly, "they're not the same, and *this* is why!" He thrust the laundress's paper in front of Nobody's eyes. "Look! The f's in both have long staffs, and the m's in both are bunched together like an 'n'. And look at the rest! It's the same!"

Nobody grasped the back of the chair to steady himself. "But then—if the laundress wrote that note—"

"Then Liana didn't run away, and she's being held captive!"

"Thank God! Oh, Edmund, thank God and thank you!" He threw his arms around Edmund in a passion of tears.

Edmund grunted. "Come, Noble this is no time for blubbering. We still have to find her."

Nobody nodded, and choked back the tears. *She did not leave me! Oh, thank God, she did not leave me! There's still hope that she may love me!* He thrust his feet into the discarded boots and crushed his hat onto his head. "If someone is holding Liana captive, Ed, they are about to become very, very sorry."

"I'm with you. Come on, old boy, let's go find that laundress!"

The streets were deserted. Most of the houses were dark and silent, but here and there a lamp shown in some late sleeper's window. A dog howled at the two boys as they passed one of these houses, but was quickly silenced by a sleepy broom-wielding housewife.

The laundress lived alone in a small hut on the outskirts of the village. No light shone through the single-paned window. Nobody tapped softly on the door. There was a rustling sound inside, as of someone turning over in a bed, but no answer. He knocked again, this time louder. The rustling noise resumed, and soft footsteps approached the door.

"Wh-who's there?" asked a timid voice.

"Colonel Nobody."

"Wh-what is it?"

"I need to talk to you."

"Now?"

"Now."

Someone fumbled with the latch, and the door creaked open far enough to let the thin laundress pass through and close it behind. She was an eerie picture in the moonlight, with a white nightgown hanging to her ankles, a shawl round her shoulders, and a bobbing nightcap on her head. Stringy brown hair peeked under the cap.

"Wh-who is that?" she asked, jerking an arm at Edmund.

"Edmund Burke, my personal friend. Miss Hacket, I will be brief. Where is my wife?"

She started violently. "Y-you're wife, sir? I-I didn't know you had a wife."

Nobody crossed his arms and watched her sternly. "Miss Hacket, laundress; where is Lady Halmond, my betrothed wife?"

"Well—I—that is, why—how should I know?" She backed against her door.

"Because you wrote this." Nobody calmly placed the forged note in her trembling hand. "You needn't waste breath denying it. Where is my betrothed wife?"

The spinster recoiled from the paper as from a serpent and fell to her knees, her hands clasped. "Please, sir, I didn't want to do it, sir, they made me do it. I didn't want to, I tell you, but they made me do it."

"*Who* made you do it?"

"Oh sir, I can't tell you sir, indeed I can't! They said they'd kill me if I said anything, and I don't want to die so young, sir, indeed I don't!"

Edmund snorted in the background, and said that there was no fear of her dying young, because it was already too late. Nobody motioned him to be silent.

"Miss Hacket, let me make myself clear. You will tell me where my betrothed wife is, and you will do so *now*. Do you understand?"

"Oh sir," she groaned, still on her knees, "I'd so like to, honest I would, but I don't want to die, sir, not so young."

"Miss Hacket, I have over one hundred men on this island who will obey any order I give. If—I do not say if, *when* you tell me where my wife is, you will be fully protected from her abductors."

"But, sir—"

"No 'buts,' Miss Hacket! Where is she?"

The laundress wrung her hands and whispered, as if the men she feared might be listening around the corner. "I don't know where she is, sir. There were three sailors as come to me, and threatened me, and told me they'd kill me if I didn't tell them when the lady would be alone, and write the horrid note."

"Where did the sailors come from?" he asked impatiently.

"I don't know, sir, indeed I don't. They came upon me when I was washing alone. The one who spoke to me sounded foreign, sir, an' he had great hoops of earrings in his ears, and the other two kept saying words, but they weren't English."

"Probably some scoundrels from *The Hound*." Nobody growled. "And to think that they have my Liana! Do you think they took her on board ship?"

"I don't know, sir, indeed I don't. They smelled awfully of wine, an' the one that talked to me had a red stain on his shirt, but I don't think it was blood, sir."

"Are you saying that they were drunk?"

"No, sir, I don't think so, sir, but they smelled awfully of wine."

"Very well. I'm sorry that all this happened, Miss Hacket, and I will make sure that you are protected. Do not tell a soul what you have told me. If I find her, they will not know that it was you who talked, and you should be safe. Good night."

She fled inside, and they continued their silent way towards the dock.

"If they smelled of wine, sir, shouldn't we check the inn?" Edmund asked.

"They searched the inn today, and I myself assisted. I don't see that she could be there."

"Perhaps not, sir, but we've already looked everywhere. Where else could she be?"

Nobody stopped short. "Ed, where else is there a large quantity of wine on this island besides the inn?"

Edmund scratched his chin. "Well, I suppose the only other place would be the storehouse."

"Exactly! The wine storehouse, separated from the others and nearly hidden in a grove!"

"But they also checked that today, Noble."

"Then we'll check again. Follow me, Ed."

The storehouse was only a few hundred yards up the coast from the dock. A grove of creaking coconut palms shaded but did not completely hide it from the outside. The waving fronds blocked all but a few slivers of moonlight, leaving a dark, gloomy passage to the door.

"We should have brought a lamp," Edmund whispered.

"And pistols," Nobody added. "Draw your sword."

There was a slight rasping of metal as they drew their blades, but all remained still inside.

"I will go first," Nobody whispered. "Follow at my heels, and be very, very, quiet."

He unhooked the latch and pushed. The door scraped over the rough plank floor. A dusty smell of wine and spices permeated the air. As his eyes adjusted to the gloom, Nobody saw a dim wall of kegs before him, mirrored by both sides of the room and the space on either side of the door. He groped to the right, passing between the wall of kegs and the true outside wall. The second half of the room was no different than the first—every wall was covered with barrels and kegs.

"Anything?" Edmund whispered from the doorway.

"Nothing. Kegs in the middle, kegs on the walls."

"Any loose boards on the floor?"

Nobody tramped up and down each side of the keg partition. "Nothing. It's strange, though, Ed—it seems that there is less floor space in this back portion than the front."

Edmund joined him. "I wonder—" he froze. "Noble, look out!"

The wall of kegs they faced was falling. Nobody dropped to his knees and covered his head as the barrels crashed down. An iron hoop gouged his right shoulder. Wine spattered over the walls and sloshed about his knees. His sword was trapped by the weight of the load. He heaved upwards and surfaced from beneath the fallen kegs like a swimmer emerging from the waves.

Someone grabbed his throat and pressed him down again. Fighting desperately, Nobody wrenched himself to the right, trying to keep his unknown opponent from crushing him down.

"Edmund!" he gasped.

"Noble! What—"

Something dark leaped over Nobody's head and crushed the other boy to the floor. "Keel 'eem Giuseppe!" hissed Nobody's assailant, tightening his grip on the boy's throat.

Nobody's chest heaved for air—the passages were blocked. *Skill, not strength! Skill!* He fought the rising panic in his breast and let the straining muscles relax, making his body limp. For an instant, his opponent eased his grip, giving just enough time to swing a left-hander through the darkness at the man's head. *Crunch.* Blood spurted from the big man's nostrils and he let go to claw at his wounded nose.

Nobody drove his head forward and crashed into the sailor's stomach. The man groaned and collapsed. A dark shape took his place and a massive fist struck Nobody on the chest. Fire shot through his bones and he in turn fell to the floor. *Three of them!*

His new assailant grabbed a small keg and dashed it at the boy's head, just missing the skull. Nobody gathered his legs and leaped backwards, landing upon Edmund's attacker. Something sharp struck him in the side. He clasped his arms round the man's head and rolled, releasing Edmund from a headlock.

"Edmund, grab the dirk from my belt!"

The third sailor roared and leaped onto Nobody's back, crushing him into the man below. Something crashed. The third sailor rolled lifeless from his back. A hand grasped the dirk in Nobody's belt, and a moment later the man beneath him was gasping in his death agony.

The dirk clattered upon a keg, and Edmund knelt by his side.

"Noble, are you wounded?"

"Just—bruised, I think," he managed to gasp.

"Thank God. I finished that fellow on top of you with a wine keg—a new weapon to add to my list. Wasn't there another fellow around?"

"Die!" screamed a voice, and Nobody's first opponent bounded towards them. Edmund leaped forward and met the sailor halfway, plunging the dirk into his unprotected chest.

"Well, he's not around anymore." Nobody struggled to his feet. "Help me forward." Edmund hooked an arm round his shoulders and led him through the litter of broken wine kegs to the end from whence they had fallen. "Liana!" Nobody cried, dropping to his knees by the girl's prostrate form. "Edmund, the knife."

He sliced the ropes that bound her limbs and pulled a sodden handkerchief from her mouth.

"Colonel Nobody, is it really you?"

"Yes my dear. Thank God that I have found you again!"

He couldn't see her face in the darkness, but he brushed the wet hair from her eyes and helped her up.

"Thank you, Colonel Nobody. I'm sorry to have been so much trouble to you." She staggered as the circulation returned to her wrists and ankles. "That beastly sailor told me the trick they played on you. I thought you might not—" she paused. "Thank you for coming."

"Oh Liana, you don't know what I've been through."

"It's my guess that she's had a bit rougher time than you," Edmund remarked dryly. "I'm glad to see you safe, Lady Liana. Now let's get out of here."

Chapter 36

"I hear you had quite an interesting adventure last night. Are you experiencing any pain from your injuries?"

Nobody looked across his table at General Tremont, thinking that the older man looked pleased at the prospect of his being in pain.

"Nothing I can't bear, General Tremont, thank you."

"Mmm. I—er, I must offer my congratulations at the rescue of Lady Halmond." He attempted to smile, but the result was a ghastly grin.

"Thank you. Did you know that the men were from your crew?"

"Why, yes, I did hear something to that effect. Of course, you don't hold me liable for their actions."

"I don't?"

Tremont frowned. "Of course not! I was in no way connected to them, other than being their captain."

"So you say." Nobody shifted uncomfortably in his seat, trying to ease the pressure on his bandaged right side where the sailor had sliced him. "General Tremont, I'm a busy man. I presume you had a reason for coming here today, so I'd be obliged if you would state it now."

The former general slowly produced a sealed packet from his coat and set it on the table. It was stamped with the seal of England.

"I was ordered by the queen (God bless Her), to give you this packet if I found you during my voyage."

Nobody stared at it. "Then why, may I ask, did you not do so when you first landed?"

"It slipped my mind." Tremont remained expressionless.

Of course he didn't forget it. He had a reason for holding it back. No wonder Bronner came along, if part of this old rascal's commission was to find me. He sliced the wax with his fingernail and unfolded a long legal document.

"Do you know what this is?" he asked, looking over the sheet at Tremont.

"I do have that pleasure, yes."

He looked back at the paper. *Her Royal Majesty . . . Queen Victoria . . . Commission as colonel of the 42nd Regiment*—he stopped. "General Tremont," he demanded, "do my eyes deceive me, or is this a commission as colonel of Her Royal Majesty's 42nd Regiment of Mounted Infantry?"

Tremont rubbed his hands. "Yes, it is, for warfare in Spain. Her Royal Majesty wishes for your services. Apparently, she didn't agree with my reasons for discharging you."

A commission! To be a colonel once more, over the same dear men, in a just war! But—no. There must be a catch. Why is that fellow grinning at me?

"Now, *Nobody*, I must fulfill the other, less joyous reason for my visit." He rose to his feet and assumed a stiff pose. "Nobody, surnamed Nobody, it is my duty to inform you that you are arrested in the name of Her Royal Majesty Queen Victoria for piracy on the high seas, to be taken to England for trial."

Nobody sat dumbfounded. "Piracy? What are you talking about?"

"The cocks must all come home to roost some day, *Nobody*." Tremont chuckled. "It looks like this is your day. You were witnessed firing upon the schooner *Miriam*, unlawfully boarding her, and taking bodily possession of her. Bring in the witnesses!"

The door opened, and the *Miriam*'s weak-kneed first mate walked in, followed closely by a one-eared sailor in slops.

"Mr. Trumble," Tremont said shrilly, "did I state the case clearly, and are you prepared to swear so in open court?"

"Yes, quite so, General Tremont, quite so," the young man replied nervously.

Nobody laughed. "This is sheer folly, I assure you." Tremont continued to smile. "Why, call for Captain Mathers, and he will set all aright."

"I regret to inform you," Tremont replied, still smiling, "that Captain Mathers met with an accident this morning, and drowned."

The whole wicked plan flashed before his eyes. The signal gun, boarding the *Miriam*, redirecting her course—no court afloat or on land would rule it piracy, but it had just enough truth to allow Tremont to use his commission and arrest him. Captain Mathers had been made away with, no doubt, and this weak first mate was evidently controlled by someone else—probably the sailor behind him. Nobody scrutinized the one-eared man. *Bill. From the* Robinson Crusoe. *Neptune, who I threatened to decapitate, and had thrown overboard for a swim. Now it all makes sense.*

"Now," Tremont continued, "between you and me, I would really wish to show you some mercy. In fact, I might go so far as to show lenience for your crime, in light of extenuating circumstances."

"What do you want?"

"Oh, well, that's not a very nice way to put it. Let's consider it a business proposition, shall we?" Tremont rubbed his hands faster, and smiled wider. "It may so happen that there is a certain person, shall we say, connected with you, for whom you do not care very much. It may also be that I know a certain person who cares very much for that other certain person. Do you see where I'm leading?"

"Cut to the chase, Tremont. What do you want?"

"Well, if the first certain person—"

"You mean Lady Halmond, I suppose?"

"Yes, actually. Well, if that person were given to the second certain person—

"Lord Banastre Bronner."

"Yes, exactly. You really do catch on. As I was saying, if the first were given to the second, then I might be so kind as to overlook your—er—water-related activities, and allow you to go to Spain and take your old commission again. Are we agreed?"

With a rising indignation too powerful to resist, Nobody slowly lifted himself to his feet, regardless of the bruises and bandages, and confronted Tremont.

"General Tremont, I want to make one or two things very clear to you, once and forever. Firstly, the Lady Liana Halmond is my betrothed wife, and she is *also* the nearest and dearest thing to me on earth. Secondly, I will kill the man who tries to take her from me. Thirdly, I have in no way acted unlawfully, and had full permission of the murdered Captain Mathers, as you know, to do what I did. Fourthly, get out."

Tremont smoothed his coat nervously. "I don't think you quite understand, Nobody. Either you go to Spain and give up Liana, or you go into the hold of my ship in chains, and Liana goes in the same ship."

"If I go to England in your hold, the Lady Liana does *not* go with me."

"Ah," Tremont said smoothly, "but I didn't give you an option. Pirates don't get options. The Lady Liana *will* go with us, to ensure that no harm comes to her person."

"Scoundrel!" Nobody hissed. "Get out of my home this instant, or I will treat you the same way I treated Bronner."

Tremont retreated to the door. "You don't have a choice, *boy*. Go to Spain or England, either way Liana comes with us. Make the best of it that you can! You have one day to choose, at the end of which time I will have you arrested by force, if necessary."

He might have said more, but it would have been to a closed door.

Nobody leaned against the inside panels, cold sweat dripping down his forehead. The kitchen door opened, and Liana came out.

Chapter 37

"You heard?" Nobody asked.

Liana nodded.

"I want you to stay inside today, and I'll set a guard of 42nd men, on the chance that Bronner has anything else planned. Please, don't go outside."

"Noble—" she hesitated. "Colonel Nobody, what do you intend to do?"

The boy buckled his sword-belt and donned his hat. "I'm not sure, Lady Halmond, but I give you my word of honor that I will die before I see you in *his* hands. I must talk with Edmund. Stay inside."

As he had expected, Edmund was horrified and indignant when he heard the ultimatum.

"I say we board *The Hound* and scuttle her with all hands on board!"

"That's not exactly a legal undertaking, Edmund—besides, I have a plan."

Edmund brightened. "Does it involve giving a volley to those ruffians?"

"Only if they try to stop us. Listen closely. We must secretly provision the *42nd's Venture* and be ready to sail with the tide at dawn. That means that nearly everything on the island must be left as it is, but at least we'll escape Tremont's clutches. We can sail to England and plead our case before the queen, and of course, once the facts are declared, we'll be declared free as feathers. Understood?"

"Yes and no." Edmund glanced from their position on the dock to the *42ⁿᵈ's Venture*. "If we try to provision her, Tremont will know what we're up to and arrest you immediately."

"Yes, I know." Nobody wracked his brain for ideas. "Is there any way to conceal the activity?"

Edmund shook his head. "We're anchored right next to *The Hound*. They're busy reloading her, but they still have eyes, and if they see streams of men carrying provisions into our ship it's all over."

Nobody scanned the beach. "Is there any way we could create a diversion?"

"Such as?"

"I don't know, Ed, I'm asking you."

"Fires work well, but I don't know what you would burn."

"We need to have some plausible excuse for loading stores into the *42ⁿᵈ's Venture*."

"Hmm." Edmund snapped his fingers. "That's it!" He pointed to the storehouses. "Have our men ready, then light one on fire and send the men scrambling to get the provisions out of the storehouses and into the ship for protection."

"Brilliant!" Nobody cried. "I knew I could trust you, Ed! Get to work immediately."

Within half-an-hour every man of the 42ⁿᵈ was lounging on the beach, or the village, ready to sprint towards the storehouses at the first sign of smoke. A crew of picked men casually walked aboard the *42ⁿᵈ's Venture* and dropped below decks to prepare for the cargo.

A steady breeze, perfect. We'll light the building closest to Tremont. The smoke will cause more confusion and less time for him to bother about us. He strolled along the beach between the storehouses and the village. *Thank God, the doors face inland.* He paused at the last in the line. Sailors aboard *The Hound* laughed and chatted as they reloaded her with the beached stores, but the building hid them from view. Another moment and he was inside.

Boxes of copra and a few barrels of thick coconut oil filled the room. Nobody pulled a lantern from under his coat and set it on a barrel. He pulled a hatchet out next and smashed the barrel heads open, pushed them to the center of the room, and dropped the end of a fuse into one. Carefully, he opened the lantern shutter and applied the free end of the match to the flame. The flame caught and instantly began creeping up the fuse towards the exposed contents of the barrel.

He blew out the lantern and stuffed it back under his coat along with the hatchet.

He stealthily opened the door. No sailors in sight. He rejoined Edmund in the village.

"All's ready, Ed. Get men on the stores the second you see smoke, and do your best to let the flames catch the next storehouse. The bigger the blaze the better. I'll be at the native village bidding farewell to the Broughams and bringing Liana's baggage over. If anything goes wrong, try to avoid violence."

When he reached the native village, a crowd of natives was gathered on the beach watching the conflagration across the harbor. The missionary and his wife greeted him anxiously, asking if he needed help.

"No, Mr. Brougham, thank you. My men have it under control."

He looked back at the flames. *How odd that a pillar of smoke first brought me to this island, and now a pillar of smoke sends me away.*

Chapter 38

A touch on the arm jolted Nobody out of his sleep. He sat up and blinked at the gloom. *Why am I on the kitchen floor?*

"Zhe clock has struck four o'clock, sir."

Nobody blinked at the Frenchman. *Four o'clock? Oh.* It all came rushing back. *My last day in this snug house, on this grand old island.* He picked himself off the kitchen floor and stumbled about, groping for his uniform. With practiced fingers, he buckled the worn leather sword-belt round his waist, slung his trusty rifle over his back, and stuffed two pistols in his sash.

"Turn out, you elongated bedbug." He kicked Edmund awake and stepped into the main room.

"I haf prepared a small breakfast for you, sir." Jacques set four plates of cold meat upon the table. "Zhe ladies are avake and dressing. I am sorry zhat zhe coffee is cold, but you ordered zhat no fires vere to be lit."

"Yes, of course, there's always a price to pay. Where's O'Malley?"

"I set zhe *boeuf* on guard outside."

"The rest of Squad One?"

"Zhey are bunked togezher near zhe dock."

"You passed the word to rendezvous at four-thirty?"

"Yes, sir, as ordered."

"Good work. What's the wind?"

"Zhere is a steady land breeze, sir. It feels zhat it vill hold."

"Let's hope it holds long enough to get us on our way to England."

Jacques pulled back Nobody's chair. "I talked to zhe reporter, Somerset, yesterday, and he asked vhat vas going on. I told him zhat it vas a secret, but zhat ve vould not be here in zhe morning. He looked very, ah, how you say, *agitated*?"

"Most likely. I don't need any cowards aboard."

Liana and her maid came out of the bedroom, dressed in muted traveling cloaks. They ate hastily and bid a fond farewell to the snug cottage that had seen much mirth and much sadness in its short life. Nobody tucked Liana's satchel under his arm while Edmund took charge of Elyssa's baggage.

As they maneuvered down the path, Edmund struck his forehead. "Oh, Noble, I entirely forgot! Colonel Hay—I mean, the hermit, showed up by my side yesterday while we were fighting the fire."

"The hermit! I nearly visited him yesterday, but I was afraid it might make Tremont suspicious. What did he want?"

"Well, to tell you the truth, he wanted you. I was watching the men empty the storehouses when he tapped me on the shoulder and asked, in a strange voice, for you. I told him that you weren't available. He told me to tell you to come to him as soon as possible in the mountain. I said that you probably couldn't, but he said you must. Then he left, and I forgot all about him, I'm afraid."

"I wish you had told me, Ed. It's too late now."

The dock loomed into view, and with it a shadowy group of soldiers with rifles slung over their shoulders and swords hanging from their belts.

"Squad One reporting for duty, sir." Dilworth saluted.

"Where are the others?"

"We're all here, sir, except for Corporal Stoning, who's on board, and Jacques and O'Malley, who you brought. "

"No, not Squad One, I can see you. The others. The rest of the 42nd. Where are they?" A pink glow on the horizon was gradually dispelling the darkness, but it revealed no other forms on the lonely dock.

Dilworth shook his head. "To tell you the truth, sir, we've been wondering the same thing. I was thinking that maybe you'd given us different orders than the rest of the troops."

"No, not at all. They're supposed to be here." Nobody dropped the bag. "Something's wrong. Edmund, follow me, the rest of you stay here."

Nobody rushed into the silent village. Roosters were crowing, and a dog or two mournfully welcomed the sun, but there was no movement in the dark houses. His heart hammered his chest.

Knock—knock—knock. He pounded at a house door.

"I'm coming, I'm coming, confound you," growled a voice inside. "Who's making such a racket out there?"

"Colonel Nobody."

"Oh, sir, I'm sorry." The door opened and revealed a bearded triangular face. "Corporal Daming, sir, at your service."

"Daming, what's going on! Why aren't you on the dock? Where are the rest of the men?"

The sharpshooter stepped out and eased the door shut. "I'm—I'm sorry, sir, I truly am. We all are. We all wanted to go with you, but—"

"But what? Daming, what's happened?"

"General Tremont, sir." Daming spat and wiped the name from his mouth. "He must've gotten word somehow that you intended to leave, an' he sent round last night to all of us old 42nd men. He said that if we aid you in escaping we'll be violating the law and be counted outlaws, and be hunted down by the Crown's troops."

Nobody felt his chest deflate. "I see."

"It's—it's not that we don't love you, sir, or want to be with you," Daming explained hurriedly, "but we can't go against the queen (God bless her). I might do it myself, sir, in remembrance of the old days, but I've got a wife and a child, and I can't leave them to go hungry, sir. You understand, sir, don't you?"

Nobody nodded wearily. "Yes, Daming, I understand."

"Please don't think hard of us, sir, please! We'd follow you anywhere in a fight, or a voyage, or anything like that, but we're British subjects, sir, and we can't go against the queen!"

"Yes, Daming, I understand," Nobody repeated. "You're right. I shouldn't have asked you to come. This is my fight, not yours, I can't expect *you* to suffer for it. I'm sorry."

"No, sir, *I'm* sorry."

Nobody patted the distraught man on the shoulder, and forced himself to smile. "You've made the wisest decision, Daming. You're right. Tell the men that, and tell them that I don't blame them, and I don't reproach them. They've made the wisest decision. Tell them that I think they're some of the best men in the world, and tell them—well, tell them good-bye."

Daming dashed a hand across his eyes and nodded fiercely. "I will sir, I will."

"Good-bye, Daming. And God bless you."

The sharpshooter raised his trembling hand and saluted. Nobody returned it.

The group on the dock was anxiously watching the rising sun.

Stoning had just come from the ship. "What is it, sir? What's taking so long?"

Nobody looked round slowly at the waiting men's faces. "I've learned something today, Stoning." He touched the old man's shoulder. "I never should have asked anyone to accompany me on this flight. This is my fight, and mine alone. I have no right to involve anyone else. Stay here, and live prosperously, or join the army again, or go somewhere else, it's your choice now. I'm sorry."

Eight blank faces stared back. Edmund stepped forward.

"Tremont has declared that any who aid Colonel Nobody is a traitor and an outlaw to the Crown," Edmund explained.

"An' who's Giniral Tremont tae say a thing like that?" O'Malley asked angrily.

"The holder of the queen's commission."

"Soo the others won't come, will they? Then thay're traitors, says I. Traitors!"

"No, they're not," Nobody said sharply. "They've made a wise decision. Thank you for obeying me, but I don't ask you to do so anymore. Good-bye." He lifted Liana's baggage and took her hand.

"Goot-bye? Vhy, vhat do you mean, sir? Ve are not leaving!"

"I told you, Jacques, I can't ask you to go with me. This is my fight, and mine alone. Good-bye."

"Goot-bye, nohzing! Who cares if you ask or not? Ve are Squad One! Ve vill never leave you!"

"That's right, Noble." Edmund grasped his friend's shoulder. "I've been with you too long to leave you now. Like the Bible says, 'your people will be my people, your God my God,' and so on. You're stuck with me forever!"

"You don't understand. I mean to die before I give up Liana, and those with me will meet the same fate."

"There are worse resting places than a grave."

"But—"

Stoning coughed. "Sir, he's right. I've reached a ripe old age for a soldier, and I'm fully prepared to meet my Maker. I fought for Colonel Hayes all my life, and when he left, I fought for you. I'm one of the two men in the world who know who you really are. I'm not leaving you now."

It was Nobody's turn to dash a hand across his eyes. "Jacques?" he asked.

The short Frenchman drew himself to his full stature. "Sir, I would not dare to dishonor zhe glory of France by being a traitor."

"O'Malley?"

"If it were fer nothin' else, sir, I'd 'ave to go along to take care of that half-pint of a Frog. There's noo tellin' what trouble he'll get 'imself into."

Nobody smiled sadly. "Petr?"

"Sir." The Russian doffed his cap. "I will follow. If you go, who will I speak Russian with?"

"Хороший человек. Good man. Dilworth?"

"Well, sir, if we're talking about the honor of countries, I might just add that America's got quite as much honor as any other, and I'd be proud to represent it with you."

"My Apostles?"

Matthew cleared his throat. "Colonel Nobody, when I read that poem in Siberia and said that we'd follow where you led, though it were the ocean floor, we meant it. And I'd further add that we'll follow you to an early grave—"

"Being strong, and being brave," Mark ended.

Nobody brushed away a tear and turned to young Bronner. "It's one thing for these men to pledge themselves to me, Thomas, but it's a very different thing for you. It's probable, almost certain, that we'll come to blows, and your brother will be on the opposing side."

"No brother of mine! I disown him. He's a scoundrel and a knave, a disgrace to our family and a disgrace to humanity. I'm with you, Colonel Nobody, to the death."

Nobody searched his face. Every line showed loyalty and determination. He looked at the rest of his men. The same. He raked a hand through his hair. *Is it right to lead them to their deaths?*

Somewhere aboard *The Hound* a man shouted, and sailors appeared on deck with drawn cutlasses.

"Very well men, if you insist upon throwing your lives away, thank you, and follow me!"

Ten men and two girls could not sail the schooner away from Tremont's bloodhounds. His only option was the jungle.

Chapter 39

The village was still silent save for a few sleepy headed women, who shrank back in fright as the armed party glided past their homes.

"Jacques and O'Malley, take the front," Nobody commanded tersely. "Petr and Dilworth, form rearguard." He tossed Liana's bag to the Prestons and took her hand in his, Edmund following suit and dumping Elyssa's luggage on young Bronner.

Nobody wasn't afraid that the sailors would catch up—sailors were not known for their running skills. It was not the fear of being caught, then, that felt like a sack of bricks on his chest, but the fear of having nowhere else to run. The island was large, but not so large that he could hope to remain hidden. Tremont had a large crew, and doubtless he could threaten or bribe some of the merchant sailors, if needed, to join in the search.

The jungle gloom woke him from his whirling thoughts. Jacques and O'Malley had paused just within the edge of the trees on the path to the hermit's hut, waiting for his direction. Liana leaned heavily upon his shoulder, gasping for breath, each cheek blotched red by the exertion. Edmund stumbled to his side, half-carrying Elyssa.

"We must give the girls a moment to rest," Nobody said, slinging the rifle off his back. "Let's show those scoundrels behind us what 42nd shooting looks like."

The steep hill had destroyed all semblance of order among the pursuing sailors, who struggled toward the waiting soldiers like a crowd of schoolboys playing hare and hounds. Nobody dropped to the earth and rested his rifle on a rotten tree stump.

"Wait for my signal to fire." He felt his breathing become calmer each second. *Two hundred yards. One hundred and fifty. One hundred.* "Now!"

He squeezed the trigger and a bald sailor collapsed, grasping at his chest. Nine more shots cracked. Startled, the sailors turned tail and fled for cover. He counted the bodies quickly—ten men lay dead or dying on the grassy slope. He expected nothing less.

Nobody took Liana's hand and raised her from the ground. "Are you ready, Dear?" She nodded, and for an instant he thought he saw her hot cheek dimple. The last time he had seen her smile was before that dreadful night when she asked if he loved her.

I wanted a way to show her that I loved her. This may be the way, but I hope she realizes it before I'm dead.

He knew there was something wrong at the hermit's hut before they turned the corner. There was no smoke. The old man was bent over a barrel with his back to the path, banging on a strip of metal. Five or six sheep were picking at the overgrazed grass. The milk cow blinked lazily at the strangers and gave a low moo.

"Good afternoon, Colonel Hayes," Nobody called, forcing himself to sound cheerful. "Have you let your fires burn out?"

The hermit spun round when he heard the boy's voice and gave a low cry of welcome. "My dear boy," he said, brushing past Liana and grasping his arm, "I knew you would come. Didn't ask for anyone else. I can show only you. And Stoning."

"Wait, Uncle, I must explain why we're here."

Liana gasped. "Uncle? You never told me that the hermit was your uncle!"

"Yes, I'm sorry, Liana, it was one of the things I did not think it advisable to tell you about myself."

"Colonel Nobody," she said softly, "you have told me *nothing* about yourself. I don't know who you are. I don't even know your name. You asked me to be your wife, and I told you everything. You told me nothing in return."

"I asked you!" Nobody exclaimed. "What do you mean? *You* arranged the match, not I!"

She gasped. "I?"

The men shifted awkwardly and pretended to examine their rifles. Young Bronner stepped forward, his hands fidgeting with his cap.

"Excuse me, Colonel Nobody, I'm tremendously sorry to poke my head in your business, but I think I might be able to help."

Nobody frowned. "In what way, Thomas?"

"Well sir, I haven't said anything before, because I wasn't sure that it was my place, but I think I should now. According to my understanding, you think that the lady arranged the match. Is that correct?"

"It is."

Liana groaned and covered her face with her hands.

"Well sir, I was there when the match was arranged, and it was none of her doing, I promise! My father didn't want my brother to marry her, and the king wanted the lands that would revert to him if she married with a willing heart, and so they arranged it among themselves. I—I hope you're not angry with me, if I've spoken out of place."

Nobody reeled. *She didn't arrange it! She wasn't a forward hussy, as I've thought these many months! But then she must have thought—*"Liana!"

She raised her sad eyes to his, and in that instant he saw her soul, as it were, open before him, bleeding, rejected, wanting love, and yet frightened to ask. Her childhood, frowned upon by her guardian for her pure beliefs, and separated from childhood companions for the same reason, so suddenly broken by what she thought was a proposal of marriage, bliss for a season, and then the pained realization that she was not loved, the feeling of betrayal and rejection only deepened. His mind was made up. He *would not* ask a girl to follow him to the death without sharing his deepest secret with her—the secret of his identity.

"Edmund, place scouts and prepare to guard this area. Our pursuers will be very slow and cautious after our last meeting, and should not be here for some time. Uncle, please excuse me a moment. Liana, follow me."

He led her into the dark hut and sat her down on a chair. Kneeling by her side, and clasping her cold hands in his, he began.

"Liana, it's not right that I should keep secrets from my betrothed wife. I have not told you who I am because I wanted to protect you, as well as myself, but I know that I can trust you, and I can keep quiet no longer."

She pushed his hands away. "Colonel Nobody, I do not ask for your secrets. You have told me that you do not love me, and that is enough. I know now that you never asked for me, that I was pushed upon you, and seemed—" she sobbed "—and seemed to be a very different person than you first thought. I am sorry, and so are you."

"No, Liana, I'm not sorry. Don't you understand? Haven't you seen anything that I've tried to do? Liana, listen!" He sucked a breath of air. "Many years ago there was a Russian Czar named Paul the First. He had three sons; Alexander, Constantin, and Nicholas. When he was assassinated, Alexander came into power as the eldest son, and ruled for many years."

She opened her mouth, but he stopped her.

"While upon a trip to Tagnarog he died, followed a few months later by his wife. His younger brother, Constantin, was next in line to the throne, but he had secretly abdicated from this position, and so Nicholas became czar. A group of revolutionaries, called Decembrists, used this to start a revolt, saying that Nicholas had usurped authority, because Constantin had not publicly abdicated. They were soon crushed, and Nicholas was recognized as ruler. He is still czar today."

He took her hands and gently pressed them together.

"That is what the history books say, Liana, but that is not what happened. Alexander did *not* die in Tagnarog. He was secretly kidnapped by the Decembrists and his burial was faked. They knew that Constantin had abdicated, but they also knew that they could use Nicholas's assumption of power as an excuse to revolt, which is what they did. Alexander was kept in close confinement, and his wife died only a few short months after his supposed death. There was an Englishwoman also in his place of confinement, why, I don't know, but they fell in love, and were married. They had a son—and then the revolt was crushed, and Alexander's captors let him go free, so that Nicholas would be forced to step down. Alexander and his English wife left their baby behind, to be brought later, and traveled to Moscow. They were never heard of again." He paused.

"Why do you tell me this, Noble?"

"Because *I* am that baby." He released her hand and stood erect. "I am that boy who was never named, who was sent to his uncle, the English wife's brother, to be brought up in the English army. *I* am the son of Alexander, Czar of Russia, and I am the rightful ruler of Russia."

Liana shrank back in the chair, her eyes blank with astonishment, her lips parted with fear. "You," she gasped, "the ruler of Russia?"

"Rightfully, yes. But thankfully, rights are not always recognized. I do not want the throne of Russia—I would not take it if it were offered me. That said, if Nicholas knew that a man was alive who could, at least by right, if not might, displace him from the throne, my life would not be worth the burnt-out ashes on that hearth. There would be a regiment of assassins more skilled than any in the 42nd upon my trail, and both I and those who knew my secret would be butchered. Now do you see why I am called 'Nobody?'"

She nodded sadly. "Yes, Noble, and I also see why you could never love me, or have me as a wife."

"What?" Nobody dropped to his knees and seized her hands. "Liana, what do you mean?"

"You are royalty," she answered slowly. "You could never wed one so lowly as I."

"So lowly as—Liana, you're higher in my thoughts than any empress in the world could be, and more beautiful in my eyes than any woman I have seen or ever will see. My birth is a secret from the world, and none but you and two others know it. The old hermit outside, my poor uncle, is one—he would burn to death in his own Greek fire, if he ever makes it, before he says a word. Stoning is the other, the last living member of the Squad One that existed when I came to the 42nd as a babe, and who helped raise me to what I am now. He will never speak. And you will never betray my secret, I know."

"I will never—"

"I am not finished, Liana. It appears that we both thought poorly of each other, neither knowing what the other thought. You are my betrothed wife, but I have never asked you to be so, and so I ask you now, from my knees—will you be my wife? I can promise nothing but hardship, and an early widowhood if Tremont has his way, but my heart will be yours as pure and true as the mountain snow, no matter what befalls."

"You really mean it, Noble?" Tears dripped down her cheeks and wetted his upturned face.

"I do, Liana. I love you."

For the first time in his life Nobody saw the red lips part and two pearly rows of teeth gleam forth. She fell on his shoulder and wept forth her love.

He stroked her glossy hair with one hand and touched his sword hilt with the other. *God grant that this pure girl be protected from harm, though it takes my life. I am willing to die.*

Chapter 40

Edmund stared inquisitively at Liana's tear-streaked face, but Nobody shook his head, so he let it be and turned to more pressing details. Jacques had just run in and reported a body of the enemy approaching cautiously, with flankers watching for ambushes. Two other less known paths dumped into Colonel Hayes's farmyard, necessitating a guard on each. The Prestons were assigned to these. Petr, Dilworth, and Thomas Bronner were posted on the main path at twenty yard intervals. The rest were held in reserve.

Colonel Hayes grabbed Nobody's arm and pulled him to the barrel over which he had been bent. His hands trembled. "Nobody, my boy, you've made me wait too long, too long. Come. Look!" He pointed to the barrel. "At last! At last! I have made it!"

A pair of hand bellows was fastened to the top of the barrel, or keg, and one of the boards was pierced by a strange tube capped by a metal head with a slow match stuck into one of its grooves.

"What do you mean, Uncle? What is it?"

Colonel Hayes hugged himself with joy. "Greek fire! I have made Greek fire!"

Nobody stared at the barrel. *He did it?*

"Uncle, that's—wonderful. Congratulations."

"Oh thank you my boy, thank you!" The old man was literally jumping with joy, his haggard face brighter than Nobody had ever seen. "I have accomplished what the ancients could never replicate! I found the one illusive mineral that when combined with the right amount of nitrate, sulphur, and quicklime—" he waved his hand expressively.

Shots cracked on the main path.

"Our men are being pushed in!" Edmund grasped his rifle. "Orders, sir?"

Nobody glanced quickly at the situation. *Ten men and two girls plus one hermit, in an open clearing, equals a massacre—never found that equation in those dusty old mathematics books. Either we stand and fight or run. Stand and we die, but we take a good number of them first. Run—to where?*

"Uncle, we must escape. Is there anywhere on the island where we could successfully hide?"

"Eh, what's that?" Colonel Hayes turned from his barrel. "Oh. You want to escape. I see, I see. Idea. Small coaster in bay. Used it to search for minerals, one, two times. Run to bay, board. Stoning and I hold enemy with fire."

"Uncle, we can't leave you here!"

"Do not worry. We will not be lonely. Or cold." He grinned and pointed to an overgrown path in the rear of his hut. "Follow. Go quickly. I know a shorter way, but you would lose path without me. Stoning and I will follow on that. Go!"

The three soldiers on the main path burst into the clearing at top speed, followed by shouts and shots. Seconds later, the Prestons appeared from their posts.

"Outposts driven in, sir!" Dilworth cried.

"Fall back along this path. Uncle, God bless you! Don't wait too long." Nobody wrung the old man's hand. "Form up in your same positions, men. Edmund, drop Elyssa's baggage. Run!"

Jacques and O'Malley sprinted into the jungle. Nobody seized Liana's hand and hurried after, followed by Edmund and the rest of the party. Glancing over his shoulder, Nobody saw the hermit apply an ember to the slow match. A crowd of sailors rounded the corner. The hermit pointed the metal tube towards them, and Stoning heaved upon the bellows—a jet of liquid fire spurted from the siphon and coated the first rank of sailors. He turned his face and ran faster to escape the screams of agony and the horrible stench of roasting flesh.

"Noble, I—can't—do it!" Liana gasped, stumbling against him.

Then I'll have to do it for both of us. "O'Malley, catch!" He tossed his rifle to the Irishman and scooped Liana into his arms. It always looked easier in the picture books. "Edmund, carry Elyssa!"

The faithful lieutenant colonel followed suit, grunting under the strain. "She's heavier than she looks!" he gasped.

"Edmund!"

"Oh, right, er, light as a feather."

Wet drops coursed down Nobody's face and dripped onto his crimson pelisse. *Sweat, or Liana's tears? Probably both.*

They paid no regard to the weeds and high grass that choked the path. A thorn caught on the hem of Liana's dress and rent the light fabric, but he forged ahead. The ground sloped rapidly down, and living rock took the place of grass. *Finally, the bay!* A basin of blue water, scarcely fifty yards wide and as many long, ended the path. Coconuts and palms fringed the bank. Thick ropes were wound round the trunks of two stately banyans, on opposite sides of the bay, and secured to the single mast of a tiny coaster, keeping it floating placidly in the center of the basin. The bay terminated in a narrow passage that snaked towards the sea.

Nobody set Liana down with relief and rubbed his aching arms. The black smoke was clearing from the hillside above them, and the screams had quieted into a distant murmur. He cocked his ear. *Are they coming closer?* Shots sounded distinctly, and a dull crushing sound as if a body of men were smashing through the jungle.

"Men, untie the ropes from the trees and haul her towards the passage." *Hurry, Uncle!*

Four of the men grasped each cable and heaved towards the passage, easily towing the light coaster through the motionless water. Pounding footsteps sounded near at hand. Nobody caught up his rifle and leveled it at the brush. Something was breaking out of the jungle—he fingered the trigger. With a shout, Colonel Hayes and Corporal Stoning burst between two trees and rushed toward him, carrying the barrel of Greek fire between them.

The hermit panted. "To the boat, boy! They're on our heels!" Footsteps crashed close behind.

Without waiting to greet the pursuing sailors, Nobody grabbed Liana's arm and they raced after the two old men to the boat. The rest of the soldiers were on board, pulling the sail loose from its reefs. O'Malley gripped the wheel, using the boat's momentum to guide her through the short passage. Edmund leaped the narrow channel between the shore and her deck, and turned to catch Elyssa and Liana.

A roar burst from the far side of the bay as twenty or thirty sailors poured out of the jungle and caught sight of the departing ship. Desperately, Nobody heaved Elyssa and Liana, one after another, to Edmund. He looked sideways at the sailors. Every loaded gun among the mass was leveled at him. The boy squeezed a shot into them and tensed, waiting for a burst of hot lead to rip into his flesh.

Without warning, a jet of fire hissed over his head into their faces, packing them back into the jungle without a moment's delay. A pile of bodies lay writhing in agony at the waterside.

"Jump!" Edmund cried, stretching his hand over the bulwark. Nobody tossed his rifle and leaped after it—he thudded against the stern, shots of internal fire searing his bones. The woodwork slipped from his grasp, and he felt himself sinking into the cold water below—a hand caught his and tightened, pulling up and away from the beckoning ripples. He felt as if his arm was being pulled out of socket, but another hand grabbed his collar and dragged him, wet and dripping, over the stern.

"No time for a swim right now." Edmund slapped his back. "More pressing matters to attend to."

The men grouped patiently around the stern, waiting for him to scrape himself off the deck and propound a plan of action.

"I am afraid zhat zhis expedition vas very poorly planned," Jacques began. "Ve are overcrowded, on a slow boat vihz only one sail, and, most importantly

332

of all, ve have *no* provisions. I have proved myself capable of foraging upon zhe land, but zhere are not many options vhen on the ocean. Do you have a plan, sir?"

Nobody scratched his head and looked back pensively at the receding passage. "Jacques, the only part of this day that I had planned was the walk from my cottage to the dock. Ever since then I've been dodging surprises right and left. Do you have any recommendations?"

"Vell, sir, I vould advise zhat ve vait until zhe cursed *Hound* comes vihzin range, and zhen spray it vihz Colonel Hayes's discovery. It burns, ve float avay, and land somevhere else. Eh?"

"I wish it could be so." Something in the hermit's voice jolted Nobody, and he glanced quickly at the old man. Colonel Hayes patted his barrel sorrowfully, and shook his head. "There's none left."

"What?" Nobody exclaimed. "None left? Uncle, you've used it all?"

"Yes, my boy. It was a small barrel. Much was needed to burn the wet trees, and to keep the sailors from following. I used the last at the bay, when they would have shot you. Greek fire is no more. It dies with my home, no doubt in cinders already."

"It doesn't die for ever, Colonel Hayes," Liana said softly. "You still have the formula."

"No, I don't. I don't know the proper amounts. I tested constantly, but, I see it was foolish now, I didn't always keep records. I was going to analyze the contents of the barrel and determine the amounts. The barrel's finished. My house is burned. My work is gone." The old man folded his arms.

"You—you used the last of your Greek fire—to save *my* life?"

"My boy, you are more important than Greek fire. You are my only flesh and blood left—you are like a son. Fire burnt my son. I used fire to save my adopted son. Fair." He turned his gaze to the ocean.

Nobody grasped his withered hand silently. It felt more like the old days, before the fire's horror stole the old colonel's mind.

But am I truly saved? He looked at the blank ocean ahead. It was but a matter of time before what was left of *The Hound*'s detachment regained their ship, and the wily old general and his profligate lord set out in pursuit.

Chapter 41

Nobody snapped the spyglass shut. "It's *The Hound*, for sure, with a few merchantmen along for company, probably forced into duty."

He glanced round the narrow deck. The bulwarks were piled with moldy sacks of rotten coconuts from the hold. Small arms fire was his main concern. Bronner was unlikely to fire cannons into a boat that held Liana, but he must know that Nobody would have her and Elyssa in the hold, safe from bullets. In hand-to-hand combat his men were a match for several times their number, but hot lead takes no heed of a man's strength. *How will we board without being mowed down like lambs at the slaughter?* A movement caught his eye, and he found O'Malley measuring his saber against Jacques's. *Powerful lambs.*

"Weather should be clear today, Noble." Edmund stared at the cloud-studded sky and stroked his jaw. "It was a red sky last night. How do you say? Red sky at night, sailor's delight, red sky in morning—"

"Sailor take warning. Yes, Ed, the heavens are clear, but nonetheless it will be a red and bloody day."

O'Malley grinned. "We Irishmen are quite used tae red and bluidy days, Colonel. The bluidier the better, I says. Now the Frinch, on t'other hand, are more ye're fair wayther friends. They look cocky enough in the sun, but oh how their whiskers droop whin the sky starts emptyin' its wash-buckets."

"It is a lie!" Jacques exclaimed hotly.

Perhaps I shouldn't have stationed them next to each other.

"Zhe French are just as goot fighters as any barbarian Irish, you *boeuf.* Better, if you ask me."

"Fer the last time, what does 'boof' mean?" O'Malley shook his fist.

Jacques tilted his nose. "If you do not bohzer to learn zhe only *proper* language on eart, do not expect to have it translated to you."

"I don't care a chipped pence fer ye're *prooper* languages. My language 'as always been sufficient—a swift bloow an' a heavy fall. I'd bet ten pounds as any Irishman could whip two Frogs in a fair fight."

Jacques choked on his pipe. "Two Frenchmen?" he spluttered. "Vhy, one Frenchman could outvit *four* of your blundering Irish, and cook a meal at zhe same time!"

Nobody clapped a hand on each of the disputant's shoulders. "Come now, Jacques. Come, O'Malley. You're both probably exaggerating a bit." He shook his head, wondering whether to laugh or cry at their obstinacy. They watched him sheepishly. "Why don't you two hold a little contest, represent your nations; the man with the most kills wins the day. What do you say?"

The little Frenchman snapped to attention and solemnly bowed. "I vill protect zhe sacred honor of France vihz my blood."

"O'Malley?"

"If Ireland cooms out a loser, sir, it won't be because Patrick O'Malley still has breath in 'is body."

Jacques stroked his beard. "Euh, vould it not be right if zhere vere a small disadvantage given to O'Malley, because of his bulk and height? It vould not be a fair contest, ohzervise."

"Ye see, sir, there he goes alridy, tryin' to make excuses. If anyboody should be giv'n a disadvantage it shood be *him*! I kin only kill 'em one by one, but Jack can take one wi' his sword, and talk the head off of another at the same time."

"No disadvantages." Nobody shielded a smile with his hand. "Marquess of Queensbury rules. Now get down and be quiet!"

The Hound was rapidly cutting them off from the open sea, her superior sail-spread far outmatching the tiny coaster. Flight was no option. Nobody passed the word—no firing until they boarded. No doubt they could pick off a few sailors, but it wasn't worth the risk of exposing themselves.

Edmund crept to his side, a naked blade in his right hand and a primed pistol in his left. He squeezed against the bulwark. "How many sailors do you think Tremont has?"

"He had at least one hundred when he arrived, plus a few in the sick bay. I'd guess that Colonel Hayes decommissioned fifteen or twenty."

"That's eight or ten to our one."

"Basically. We have to finish them quickly, too, before the merchantmen catch up."

Edmund flashed a grin. "No problem. I always work well under pressure."

"Then you should work well. My main concern is the girls—they can't stay here while we all board *The Hound*, but a melee isn't a safe place for two defenseless girls."

"Who said anything about defenseless?" Edmund bristled. "There's eight men and two boys, or ten men, if you like, ready to see them through."

"Yes, ten men who will be rather occupied fighting for their own lives. However, I don't see any options. Get into the hold now, and be ready to lead them on deck when we board. My plan is to cut our way to the quarterdeck and defend that as best we may."

A bullet whined overhead. "Stay under cover!" Nobody shouted. "Let them waste their powder. A few minutes more and we'll give them the cold steel."

Bullets plowed furrows in the deck behind the line of prone men. Splinters scattered in all directions. The main mast began to resemble a smallpox victim, pockmarked and scarred by the flying lead. Nobody wiped his sweaty hands on his tunic and gripped the leather wound round his sword hilt. Every moment brought the ships closer. The shots were dying out, replaced by an angry shouting from the schooner. *Probably waiting to shoot us down as we climb aboard.* He braced himself for the impact. The boats collided with a splintering crash, tilting the deck dangerously to starboard.

"Board!" Nobody shouted.

Each soldier leaped as one man from behind the bulwarks and scrambled up *The Hound*'s side. Instead of the devastating volley he expected, only three muskets blasted. Someone groaned on his right. Old Corporal Stoning stood for a moment upon the schooner's bulwark, clutching his throat, then, with another groan, his knees buckled and he collapsed onto the body of his childhood friend. Colonel Hayes lay motionless in the boat's bottom, blood oozing from his forehead and dyeing his wavy white locks crimson.

For a moment Nobody gazed at the corpses with horror, then, with a hoarse cry, he twirled his sword and dashed into the waiting crowd, slashing right and left. The others charged to his side and formed a wedge with the girls protected inside, relentlessly forcing a path towards the quarterdeck. Cat-eyed Spaniards, swarthy Portuguese, coal-black Negros—the mixed crowd of port-city ruffians that Tremont and Bronner had managed to scrape together fell back before the fierce onslaught, evidently appalled at the fierce execution among their front ranks.

A blur of shapes flashed before the boy's blazing eyes, but he fought the rising rage, forcing himself to keep a steady guard and calculate the risks of each blow. A wild "hooroo" sounded by his side and he vaguely realized that O'Malley had somehow gotten his hands on a boarding-pike, already dripping with blood.

"Three!" the Irishman cried, plunging it into an Italian's chest.

"Four!" Jacques countered, ducking a blow and thrusting upwards into a Greek's exposed stomach.

Nobody saw the quarterdeck looming before them, only a few yards away. A fresh body of sailors charged into the fray and bowled their cowardly comrades out of the way. The impetus of their rush and the crowded deck began to force the wedge inward, crushing the small band against each other. Nobody scanned the deck desperately—in a moment they would be overwhelmed.

"Form round the mast!" he cried, cutting down a sailor and springing to the mizzen-mast.

The soldiers formed a circle with him, able to concentrate on the foes in front without fearing a stab in the back. Liana and Elyssa hugged the foot of the mast. A cutlass nicked Nobody's arm, and he felt the warm blood tricking down his wrist and dripping onto the soaked deck. This was not a time to think about scratches.

Without warning, Edmund sprang into the rigging, climbing hand over hand towards the mizzen-top.

"Edmund!" Nobody leaped after him.

"What are you doing, Noble?"

"What are *you* doing? The enemy's down there, not up here!"

"I'm getting to the quarter-deck."

Nobody stuck his dripping sword into his belt and scrambled higher. "You can't get to the quarter-deck from up here!"

"With a rope I can." Edmund paused at the first yard and uncoiled one of the reefing lines.

"No—no!" Nobody grabbed his leg. "It doesn't work! Just because a romantic landsman wrote about swinging through a ship's rigging doesn't mean that—"

Edmund yanked the rope. "Relax, Noble, I have experience. I have to get to the mainmast and then I'll swing over. Jump on as I swing by."

"Jump on!" Nobody looked down at the flashing blades far below and swallowed against the rising impulse to vomit. "Edmund, you know I can't stand heights."

"Then why did you come up?"

"To stop you from killing yourself!"

Edmund clenched the loose end of the line in his teeth and leaped for a taut rope that led to the mainmast. He gripped the hemp like a monkey, his sword and scabbard slapping against his dangling legs. It was then that Nobody saw them—two sailors perched in the crow's nest, watching the boy cross. Edmund saw them too, but his only options were to drop to his death or continue toward the other mast. One of the sailors leveled a musket at him— Nobody snatched a pistol from his sash and fired. The musket dropped into the crowded mass below, followed by its owner. Nobody dropped his unloaded pistol and fired the other—a miss. Edmund was on his own.

The remaining sailor swung himself out of the wooden perch and slid towards the yard arm. Nobody watched helplessly, his stomach churning with dizziness and anguish for his friend. Without warning, a knife blade sliced the air and stuck quivering in the yardarm, inches from his head. Someone had followed him into the rigging. It was a Negro, his black face gashed by an evil smile, clinging to the ropes three feet below. Wrapping his left arm tightly round the mast, Nobody pulled the sword from his belt and struck out savagely. The ropes to which the Negro clung parted, and, with a horrid scream, he crashed down upon his comrades. The boy turned swiftly towards the mainmast—Edmund stood alone on the yardarm, binding a handkerchief round his bloody arm.

He waved his cap at Nobody and sprang off the spar. Nobody swallowed his fears, grabbed Edmund's waist as he swung past, and held on for dear life. For a moment they swooped down dizzyingly towards the deck, then Edmund let go and they plunged feet first into a band of sailors.

The sky was still swirling before Nobody's eyes when Edmund dispatched the last of the surprised sailors and bent over him.

"Are you there, old chap?"

Nobody scraped himself off the deck. "Wh-where's my sword?" His head ached.

"In your belt."

"Right." He grasped the polished handle and felt the world stop spinning. He glanced round the quarterdeck. A man stood between him and the fight, staring at the sailors' corpses. He held a notebook in his hand.

"Somerset! You, *here!*" Nobody stepped toward the reporter. "I knew you were a coward, but I didn't think you were a traitor!"

"No, sir, I'm not!" Somerset threw his arm up. "You don't understand, sir, please, listen to me!"

"I don't have time." Nobody raised his sword.

"No, sir, please!" He backed down the wooden steps as Nobody advanced. "Why do you think they haven't been shooting their muskets? Why do you think they haven't shot you yet?"

Nobody paused. "Why?"

"Because I emptied their powder barrels last night, sir, in the dark, after I knew you were going to try to escape, and I filled them with sand." He skipped backwards, staying in front of Nobody. "They shot off their available powder at your boat, and didn't find the sand until the powder monkeys brought some up from the hold. Honest, I'm on your side! I came today, hoping that I could help you more in some way."

Nobody stared at him. "You risked your life for me? Why?"

Somerset blushed. "Sir, you think I'm a coward. You saved my life. I wanted to prove that I could be brave. I wanted to help you."

"You're a man, Somerset. A brave man. Thank you." He scooped a sword up from the deck and tossed it to the reporter. "Now, if you want to *be* a man, put away that notebook and use a *man's* tool."

The crowded sailors were so focused on the circle around the mast that they didn't notice the two officers until they were among them. Astonished at this rear attack, men sprang away from the slashing swords and a path opened to Squad One. O'Malley towered high above a pile of bodies, pitching sailors right and left with his boarding pike. Liana stood pressed against the rough mast just behind him, her face white. Dilworth was down, and blood streamed from a nasty gash on the youngest Preston's cheek.

"To the quarterdeck!" Nobody grabbed Liana's hand and led the way. The sailors fell back before his sword, appalled at the carnage among their comrades. O'Malley planted himself at the head of the quarterdeck's single staircase while the others prepared to cut down any who attempted to reach them through the rigging. The sailors grouped together, thirsting for their enemies' blood, but unwilling to lead the assault. At least half of their number lay dead and dying on the bloody deck.

Each party stared silently at the other, strung tight for instant action. Nobody squeezed Liana's hand. "Courage, dear."

Jacques glided to the Irishman's side and whispered something in his ear. O'Malley nodded. Before he knew what they were about, Nobody found himself looking down the barrel of a small carronade, slued round from the stern and pointed at the sailors by O'Malley's brute force. Jacques jerked the lanyard and a blast of grape tore through the remaining sailors, shredding body parts and spraying blood over the deck.

"Make that twinty kills," O'Malley said.

"Vhat? You do not get zhe kills," Jacques said angrily, "*I* get zhe kills!"

"Not a bit o' it! I slued the gun aroond wi' no help o' yereself, Jack Frog!"

"Bah! It vas *my* idea in zhe first place, you vould not have done anyzhing if *I* had not told you."

"Aye, but ye wouldn't have gotten vera far withoot me!"

"Very vell, ve vill split it—ten each."

The remaining sailors cowered behind each other, thoroughly demoralized by this unexpected turn of events. *Now is my time*, Nobody thought.

"Sailors of *The Hound*," he called, "we don't want any more of your blood. It was you who attacked us. Leave now, and we won't kill any more. Your boats are intact. Take your wounded and begone."

They hurriedly availed themselves of this welcome permission, hoisting both boats over the side and lowering them, full of men, into the waves. Nobody scanned the deck; not a man left. Relief flooded every pore of his body. They were alive!

Fire jolted through his right arm and he staggered forward, as if struck. His sword dropped from senseless fingers—his ears rang—his head whirled uncontrollably—his blood squirted onto the deck. He reeled round like a drunken sailor. The cabin door was flung wide open, and Tremont stood in the doorway with a smoking pistol in his hand.

"You thought you'd won!" He pulled another pistol from his belt. "You've bewitched my powder, but I had these left!"

Nobody stared stupidly at the leveled pistol.

A red blur charged towards the villain—Nobody tried to focus on it, but it moved too fast—it struck Tremont down and plunged a sword into his body. His vision cleared, and Edmund lifted the bloody blade and turned toward Bronner. But Bronner was not alone.

The profligate stood with his back to the bulwark, malignant hate showing in every line of his bloated face, with an arm wrapped tightly around Liana's waist, and a dagger to her throat.

"You think you're brave, Nobody. How brave are you now?"

Liana trembled in the villain's grasp, mutely imploring Nobody with her eyes. He ground his teeth. His arm was useless—even if it were not, what could he do while that dagger glinted at her throat, and that horrible visage gleamed triumphantly over her cascading hair.

"What do you ask, Bronner?" he whispered hoarsely, still clutching his torn arm.

"I don't *ask* anything, because I can do as I like. If one of your men takes a step closer, this girl's dress will turn red with her blood. Understand?" He shouted over the ship's side to the boats below, ordering them to come back and take him off. "Now," he resumed, "we'll just sit back and look at each other. You should be happy—you've got your miserable little life, and most of these fools that keep following you all over the face of the earth. And I have the girl. Even, I say."

The darkness was fast engulfing him. Vaguely, as if it were happening in another man's body, he felt the lifeblood dripping down his arm. If he could only get close enough—he opened his eyes.

Bronner was looking down into the boat, gauging his best exit from the deadly ship. *Now!*

He leaped at the villain and grasped the knife with his left hand—Bronner swore a dreadful oath, striving to twist the knife away and plunge it into the boy's chest. Slowly, agonizingly, Nobody's arm gave way. He was strong, but no match, with a weakened left hand, against a full-grown man's right. The blade inched closer. Nobody leaned forward desperately, his cheek squished against Liana's forehead. Bronner grinned.

Suddenly, with a horrid shriek, the nobleman released his grasp and sprang backwards over the bulwark. Nobody looked down vaguely into the swirling water. Sailors from the closest boat reached into the choppy waves and hauled Bronner, limp and bleeding, onto the planks. Trembling, Liana handed him his own dirk, dripping with Bronner's blood, and dropped her head upon his chest to cry away the fear. He wrapped his good arm about her shoulders, and slowly turned to his men.

"Let the villain go. We've shed enough blood today. We're murderers in the eye of the law, now—let's not be murderers in God's eye." He clutched

Liana's shoulder. "Men, our future is unsure. We have resisted the power of the Crown, and even though the Crown's power was being abused, we will still be punished if we are caught. However, there is one thing in my future that is not unsure—I am young still, but at the proper time I promise you that this girl, the love of my heart and saver of my life, will become my wife. Three cheers for the Lady Liana!" He sank to the deck, weakened by the loss of blood, as his loyal men raised three triumphant shouts to the sky.

"Accept my congratulations." Jacques bowed. "You vill be a de *toute beauté* couple."

"An' mine too," O'Malley agreed. "Ye're a splendid man, Colonel, an' ye deserve all the happiness ye can git." He frowned. "By the way," he said, turning to Somerset, "do ye know Frinch?"

Somerset cocked an eyebrow. "To some extent, yes. Why?"

"What does boof mean?"

"*Boeuf*? It means an ox."

"An ox—"

Edmund slapped him on the shoulder. "Leave it be, boys, you know you're both great friends, no need to keep up a show for us. Besides, I've got a little announcement of my own to make." He raised his head proudly, clasping Elyssa's hand. "Boys, when the colonel gets married—well, you're invited to the double wedding!"

And so they sailed into the sunset, a red sunset—a red sky that all on board trusted would bring many more days of sailor's delight to *The Boy Colonel*.

The End